T0357013

FIRECAMP

Praise for Jaycie Morrison

A Perfect Fifth

"Large blocks of internal dialogue create intimacy with all the main characters. The reader may not agree with Constance's meddling or be frustrated with Nelson's cluelessness, but they will certainly understand why everyone does what they do. The author also uses the technique to show intentions and actions that are awfully important to Zara and Jillian but unknown to them. This has the effect of Hitchcock's bomb under the table. The reader knows something bad is coming and can only read on and hope for the best. It's a nail-biting ride, making the romance all the sweeter."—*Lesbian Review*

The Found Jar

"It's a book full of unexpected depth and humanity. I really appreciated how Morrison manages to illustrate that trauma does different things to different people. Both MCs have experienced trauma and loss that has made them who they are, and her characterizations almost depict the two opposites of possible reactions. Having them fall for each other despite the many things they have to work through makes for a really good read. This is Morrison's first foray into contemporary romance, and I hope this continues. I'd definitely recommend giving this book a go as it brings a different approach to romance than I've personally encountered before in the wlw arena, and for that reason alone it's worthwhile giving it a try."—*LGBTQ+ Reader*

"The beach setting and Beck's pure heart help to offset the frustration I felt with Emily and her issues. Beck is an innocent and at times naive young woman who suffered a traumatic brain injury in her teens. Emily writes horror novels and battles nightmares and demons from her past. Beck's kindness and innocence are a balm for Emily's tortured soul. And there are kittens, and they soften some of the harsher scenes. It was interesting seeing the contrast between these two women as their relationship developed. One with a TBI who deals with her disability and tries to face her challenges with a positive attitude versus the other with so much emotional baggage that she can't see past her anger and disgust with herself to allow Beck into her life. Will their friendship develop into the relationship you know they deserve?"
—*LezReviewBooks*

Guarding Hearts

"*Guarding Hearts* was another good installment in the Love & Courage series. My first thought after reading book 2 was that it should be the end of the series, that a third book wasn't really needed. I have to admit I was wrong. I enjoyed this book 3 and felt comfortable reading it. While there are plenty of small plot lines that keep things moving, this really is a character-driven series...Rain and Bett have slowly been making their way up on my list of favorite couples. After all the growth they have had over three books, and Rain being totally crush-on-able, this couple has made their mark on my heart."—*LezReviewBooks*

Heart's Orders

"I am so enamored with this awesome story! While I was reading this book I got so caught up in the struggles the characters faced—I felt as though I was experiencing all of the angst, confusion and elation right along with them. There is one thing that I know for sure; this story is going to stay with me for quite some time. These strong-willed women are truly unforgettable, and they will capture your heart and attention from the first page."— *Lesbian Review*

"Jaycie Morrison has captured the mood of an era really well in these novels, and the determination of the women who have signed up to the WAC to not only do a good job but to forge a place for themselves in the world...The romances are sweet and gentle, the mood is soft focus despite the harsh realities of the time. An excellent follow-up in the Love and Courage Series. I look forward to book three."—*Lesbian Reading Room*

Basic Training of the Heart

"There are some great WWII lesbian romances out there, and you can count *Basic Training of the Heart* among them. It's well worth a read, and I look forward to seeing what's next in this series." —*Lesbian Review–Top 100 Books To Start With*

"My favorite thing about this novel is Morrison's ability to carry the tension throughout the story without letting the story lull. It's paced really well, and left me rooting for the characters without getting impatient for something to happen...If you dig wartime fiction, period pieces, or just a sweet love story that's not too heavy on the sex but still has enough to make it more interesting, give this one a go."—*Kissing Backwards*

By the Author

The Love and Courage Series

Basic Training of the Heart

Hearts Orders

Guarding Hearts

The Found Jar

A Perfect Fifth

On My Way There

Firecamp

Visit us at www.boldstrokesbooks.com

FIRECAMP

by
Jaycie Morrison

2025

FIRECAMP

© 2025 By Jaycie Morrison. All Rights Reserved.

ISBN 13: 978-1-63679-753-3

This Trade Paperback Original Is Published By
Bold Strokes Books, Inc.
P.O. Box 249
Valley Falls, NY 12185

First Edition: April 2025

THIS IS A WORK OF FICTION. NAMES, CHARACTERS, PLACES, AND INCIDENTS ARE THE PRODUCT OF THE AUTHOR'S IMAGINATION OR ARE USED FICTITIOUSLY. ANY RESEMBLANCE TO ACTUAL PERSONS, LIVING OR DEAD, BUSINESS ESTABLISHMENTS, EVENTS, OR LOCALES IS ENTIRELY COINCIDENTAL.

THIS BOOK, OR PARTS THEREOF, MAY NOT BE REPRODUCED IN ANY FORM WITHOUT PERMISSION.

CREDITS

Editor: Barbara Ann Wright
Production Design: Stacia Seaman
Cover Design by Tammy Seidick

Acknowledgments

It's not often that the inspiration for a story drives up your out-of-the-way road and camps in the national forest behind your property, but that was the case with with the wonderful young women of the Southern Conservation Corps saw crew. While this story is not biographical, I've tried to make it as authentic as possible. Aubrey, Annelisa, Sarah, Liz, A.J., and Anna, I hope you are all well and happy.

Additionally, my profound appreciation goes to my personal chainsaw, JL, for help with trimming and shaping this story, and to JR for her sharp, deadline-sensitive eye and bold perusal of synonyms. Kudos to my writing group for always providing entertaining conversations and helpful advice. Y'all are worth getting up for.

I'm also grateful to the team at BSB for all you do for us as writers and readers, and to those who have read and taken the time to review my work—thank you so much!

This book is respectfully dedicated to the women and men of the real Fire Camp, the US Forest Service, and all other groups and individuals who strive to keep our beautiful woodlands safe and healthy. All of us who live, work, or play among these amazing ecosystems owe you our most sincere gratitude.

As always, all my love and devotion to SDL, my muse and guidance in all things romance-related.

PART ONE: TEN YEARS AGO

CHAPTER ONE

When the hum of the highway became a bumpy, crunching dirt road, Nora straightened, rousing herself from pleasant daydreams about what the coming fall would bring. While she'd been imagining her future, the familiar green of her Brighton Valley home had given way to a high desert wilderness; sandy soil grassland presented mixed scrub, including creosote and saltbush, along with yucca and cholla cactus. Here and there, hearty piñon pines and junipers dotted the landscape. The high mountain peaks still held touches of snow, making for a distinct contrast.

Settling back, she closed her eyes again, returning to the dream of reinventing herself by finishing the last two years of her four-year degree with a transfer to Arizona State University. All her life, she'd tried to find a comfortable place in her family, first among her rough-and-tumble older brothers and then as the trendy girl her mother wanted her to be. Her parents had provided a home, food, and clothing, and she'd tried to repay them by being the dutiful daughter they expected. For the most part, anyway. But after this summer, that compliant girl would be gone, and the Nora she'd always wanted to be—truly unfettered and altogether self-reliant—would take her place. She'd planned and strategized for months about how to take a giant step away from her homelife, but all it had taken was goading her father into a simple wager.

"Is that a hitchhiker?" Her younger brother Tyler's adolescent voice cracked in the silence. Their father only grunted as he braked.

Tyler's excited tone piqued Nora's interest, and she squinted into the sunlight. A tall figure stepped out of an ancient car, the kind her older brother Rudy referred to as a land yacht. Though the driver had attempted to angle it off the narrow, two-lane road, her father still needed to swerve slightly to avoid the flared red fender. The person gave a casual wave but didn't approach.

Her father opened his door and stood, the engine still running. "You lost?" he called.

"Not that I know of."

The composed voice was higher pitched, and Nora rubbed at her face, intrigued. *A woman?*

"Breakdown?" her dad pressed.

"Runs like a top." A shrug. "Except when she's out of gas."

"You're not aware there's a gauge for that?"

Nora rolled her eyes. The veiled insult meant the person was definitely female. He'd never say such a thing to another man. She was surprised by the pleasant laugh that answered him.

"Well, she runs good, but a few accessories, including the gas gauge, are a little less dependable."

"How far you going?"

The woman swept an appraising glance over Nora and Tyler, still in the Jeep, before stepping closer. She gestured down the road. "I think it's only a few more miles. It's an outdoor work group thing. Mainly for fire mitigation but also for forest health." She turned and looked out over the scrub oaks and Ponderosa pines now visible from the roadside, drawing Nora's attention to the landscape.

A radiant slant of light caught in the artful curve of a fallen tree made Nora long for her beloved Canon EOS 7D digital SLR camera, but she'd packed it away in her bag since her father would never stop to let her take pictures. Then the woman's words registered. *Outdoor work group? Fire mitigation?* Her interest heightened, and she lowered the window. "Are you going to Firecamp?"

The woman pivoted, leaning to look into the Jeep. "I am." A swish of long dark hair fell forward over her shoulder, pulling the tied red bandana to the side. "It's going to be so great. Are you going too?" Her eyes, almost the exact blue of the Colorado sky, shone as she smiled.

Nora's breath caught. The woman was younger than she'd first thought, closer to her own twenty years, and her enthusiasm seemed entirely genuine. Nora wet her lips and allowed herself to enjoy the pleasant, open expression as the woman waited for her reply.

"Nora." Her father's grating voice ruined the moment as he killed the engine. "Instead of sitting there gawking, why don't you make yourself useful and get the spare gas?"

She gritted her teeth, shoving the door open with enough force that the woman had to jump back. "Oh yeah, I'll be there," she muttered, ignoring the baffled look on the woman's face. Stalking around the rear bumper, she grabbed the five-gallon can that Tyler had barely managed to lift from its mount. His freckled face was flushed with anxiety, and she paused to ruffle his hair. "I got it, kiddo." The last thing she wanted to do was add another father-daughter skirmish to the countless ones Tyler had already witnessed, especially since she was about to leave for three months. From the corner of her eye, she saw the woman watching for a few seconds before she followed their father as he limped purposefully toward her car.

"Name's Jeffrey Palmer. I was a smoke jumper for twelve years," he said, pointing to his leg, "before a fire whirl threw off my landing and put me on disability. But I still do all right." They shook hands.

Nora's familiar anger sparked. *Sure, pretend you care about helping a stranger when all you really want is the opportunity to brag about your so-called heroic exploits.* She knew from experience that anything he did for his family came at a cost. But after this summer, he'd owe her, and she was going to collect.

"Yes, sir." The woman continued the conversation. "I can see you do. But wow. That must have been an exciting life."

She sounded almost awestruck. Nora understood. Her father had seemed godlike to her as a child as she and her older brothers had fought fiercely for his meager consideration and infrequent praise. When Tyler was deemed old enough to begin his indoctrination at her father's hand, Nora had been remitted to her mother's supervision, even though she'd become nearly as proficient as Art and Rudy at handling and repairing the tools of the firefighting trade. Demonstrating strength and toughness had given her a sense of pride, so she'd felt emptied by the rejection, except for a kernel of resentment that had sprouted and grown over the years.

Thankfully, Nora's new duties included babysitting, and Tyler's sweet, loving nature helped offset her bitterness as she struggled with finding her authentic self. Still, Art and Rudy began teasing her about becoming a sissy, and her father never missed a chance to expound on how females were too soft for real work. This from the man who had taught her chainsaw use and maintenance and given her a Pulaski axe for her twelfth birthday. *Irony much?*

Nora watched her father favor the woman with a rare smile. "Well, my oldest boy Arthur commands a hotshot team, and his younger brother, Rudy, joined a helitack crew. So I guess that tells you something."

"And now your daughter's doing her part at Firecamp," the woman said with a glance back. "That's a meaningful contribution as well."

Gratified at having her involvement acknowledged, Nora inclined her head. The woman returned the gesture, but when her father countered with a perfunctory grunt, Nora frowned, not caring if any of them noticed. Her only concern was securing the financial assistance she needed for out-of-state tuition by winning that bet. Successfully completing Firecamp—something her own father didn't think she could do—would get her the funds and a one-way ticket to Arizona, and that was all she wanted from the experience. His much-proclaimed *my word is my bond* mindset meant he wouldn't dare welch on his part of the bargain once she'd fulfilled hers.

Her parents thought college was fine as long as she was also looking for a husband while she was there. They believed she'd need a man to take care of her. But Nora's plans didn't include firefighting, men, or the business marketing degree her parents were anticipating. Her acceptance at ASU's prestigious Herberger Institute School of Art meant she could pursue the calling that stirred her soul. She hoped to have a year before they noticed she'd changed her major to photojournalism. It was all within her grasp, and she'd done everything she could think of to ensure she'd make it through the summer at Firecamp.

Claiming that being around novice chainsaw users made her longer style unsafe, she'd cut her light brown hair daringly short, styling it with enough gel to appease her mother's shock. Along with the camera that had cost her two years' savings, she'd packed the one dress she was willing to wear—at her mother's insistence—but otherwise, her bag was full of the jeans and T-shirts and sweatshirts she'd always preferred but had put aside to make her mother happy. She'd taken weeks to break in her new work boots, and now they fit perfectly.

"Are you gonna stand there like an airhead, Nora, or did you want to put that gas in the tank?"

Embarrassed by her father's derision, she surveyed the driver's side. She couldn't help admiring the vehicle's long lines, though there was no gas cap in sight. She motioned brusquely to Tyler. "Check the other side."

He went and returned, shaking his head.

Her father and the stranded woman were peering under the hood. Nora set the can down none too gently and stalked around the trunk, scanning the passenger's side. Tyler was right. There was no sign of a fuel tank.

Making her way to the front, Nora took a few seconds to appreciate the woman's shapely backside swaying slightly as she pointed out something in the engine. The movement evoked a lovely memory of slow dancing with Addison Bassel at their senior prom, and her stomach clenched as she recalled the rest of their incredible night together. Her father had been displeased to learn she was going to the dance with three other girls. He would have been apoplectic if he'd known they were two couples, but he'd seemed clueless. Even now, she doubted he'd noticed she'd joined the Women's Plus Crew at Firecamp, not that she was looking for any other distractions. It would simply be a nice break from her testosterone-filled home, and not spending the summer dodging advances from male participants or proving she didn't need balls to cut down a tree were definite benefits as well.

Before she could say anything, her father laughed and slapped the woman playfully on the back. Nora tightened her lips in frustration. He hadn't been that affable with her in years. "Excuse me." She made her voice as cool as possible. "But if you want gas in this antique, you'll have to tell me where the tank is hidden."

Her father turned with a scowl as the woman straightened so quickly, she almost hit her head on the hood.

"Oops, sorry. Here, let me—" She reached out as if to take the gas can before noticing Nora wasn't holding it.

"I don't need you to do it," Nora said, hands on her hips. "Just tell me where it goes." She softened as the woman's face fell, and she fidgeted uneasily. "Or show me, maybe?"

"Oh, sure."

They returned to the gas can, and the woman picked it up. Nora stifled her protest. She liked taking charge, and being a champion for someone shy with pretty eyes was surprisingly appealing. But that wasn't why she was here, and it wasn't her car, so she simply kept pace as they walked toward the trunk.

They were about the same height. At least Nora wouldn't be the only tall one at Firecamp. She'd had a growth spurt the summer before high school, and after adding an inch or two prior to graduation, she now stood at just under five-nine. Life with two older brothers had taught her agility and coordination, but she'd quickly tired of fending off questions about playing basketball. Her interests were strictly artistic.

When the woman stopped, their eyes met, and neither moved. Was that a flicker of attraction? Nora reached for the can as the woman lifted it.

"Did you want to—" she began, deliberately letting their fingers touch. The container slipped from the woman's grasp, and Nora caught it before it hit the ground.

"Sorry. I've always been kinda clumsy," the woman said, hiking up the waistband of her jeans as she focused on the ground.

Clumsy? Jumpy seems more like it. But she didn't act that way earlier. "It's fine," Nora said, feeling the need to put her at ease. But why the sudden weirdness? Did that simple touch upset her, or was she interested? Tyler joined them, and Nora's mind returned to the business at hand.

The woman bent and pulled down the license plate, revealing an old screw-off cap. "Ta da," she announced, making Tyler laugh. As Nora began emptying the can, the woman took in a breath. "I can't thank you folks enough for helping me out," she said softly. "My name's Fallon, by the way."

"Fallon? That's a cool name," Tyler said, speaking Nora's thoughts as he often did. He shook her hand. "I'm Tyler."

"Thanks. I like your name, Tyler. And Nora is nice too. The name, I mean." Fallon's cheeks reddened. "And the person, I'm sure."

"Oh, she is. She's the best sister ever."

"I'm your only sister." She nudged his shoulder affectionately.

"Do you have any siblings, Fallon?"

Nora cringed at the personal nature of Tyler's question. He meant well, but he could be relentlessly inquisitive.

Fallon shook her head. "Nope, none."

As Nora was preparing to redirect the conversation, her father yelled, "Don't empty all the gas, Nora. We'll need some to prime the carburetor."

Deliberately waiting a few beats, she finally pulled the can away from the tank and handed it to Tyler. "You heard His Majesty. Get this to him before it's off with our heads."

Tyler giggled before making his way to the front of the car.

Fallon shuffled her feet, tugging at her threadbare T-shirt. "Listen, I'm sorry if I've caused a problem. I was really anxious about getting to Firecamp on time, and I thought I could make it with the gas I had."

Her gaze still on Tyler, Nora shook her head. "It's nothing you've done. You know that old saying about oil and water? That's my father and me. Both our lives will be better when we're as far apart as possible. Or farther."

"I've read that it can be hard for parents to adjust when their children reach adulthood. Maybe it's as tough for grown children to understand their parents as people." Fallon swallowed before continuing. "But family is something to cherish."

Nora shot her a glare. "Cherish? Not likely. Our relationship consists of equal parts antagonism and argument."

"Is that really true? Your father is—" Fallon broke off at the cough of an engine. A belch of blue smoke rose into the air.

"Looks like you'll be on your way." Nora heard the sharpness in her tone, and at Fallon's rueful expression, she forced a smile, adding, "I'll see you there, okay?"

Fallon nodded, then made her way to where Nora's father stood with his arms crossed, a smug look on his face. She reached into her pocket, pulling out a few bills and some coins, her manner relaxing after he waved away the offering.

Tyler hopped around them, his face glowing. Nora caught only the last of his joyful boast about how he'd started the car all by himself as she returned to her seat in the Jeep. She watched as her father gestured toward her, and Fallon refocused in her direction. She couldn't hear but could easily predict what her father was saying: *Nora and I have a wager that she won't make the full hitch at Firecamp. You make sure she calls us when she's ready to quit, okay?*

She found herself hoping that Fallon would believe she would win the bet. It would be nice to have someone other than Tyler on her side. When Fallon looked back at her father and nodded, Nora turned away, the familiar combination of hurt and anger rising inside. It didn't matter what some stranger thought. After finishing Firecamp, she'd collect her tuition and be Arizona-bound. It wasn't like this Fallon person had anything she needed or wanted. And she certainly wasn't going to confide in someone who fawned over her father as if he was the second coming, even if she was struggling at Firecamp. She knew better than to let anyone get that close.

❖

When Fallon's 1987 Cadillac had sputtered and coughed to a stop only a few miles from Firecamp, she'd been prepared to walk the rest of the way. She'd let her cell service go when money had run short, and hitchhiking had always seemed risky, though she had nothing but sympathy for those who did, especially women.

On her trek across Colorado, she'd picked up two other women who'd needed a lift before that last kindness had almost cost her everything she'd planned and worked for. Fallon's heart had shattered after she'd opened the coffee can where she'd kept her savings and found it empty. Evie had left her with nothing but a wave—and a new conviction that she needed to be less trusting of strangers—after she'd hopped into the cab of an eighteen-wheeler at the truck stop where they'd grabbed a sandwich.

So she'd been wary when the Jeep had pulled in alongside her car. Managing a cautious greeting when a man had appeared from the driver's side, she'd maintained her distance until she'd seen he was traveling with a boy and a young woman. Thankfully, Mr. Palmer had been pleasant and generous. She hoped it was a sign of things to come.

Back on the road now, she watched carefully until she spotted the small wooden Firecamp sign referred to in the directions she'd received. She took a shaky breath as she braked, relieved at reaching the end of her long trip. Those who talked about the journey being more important than the destination hadn't lived her life. She pulled herself together, slowing as she approached, eager for her first glimpse of the camp.

Numerous log buildings were nestled in a large clearing. People milled around them, some in groups, others carrying various tools or containers and striding purposefully across the grounds. A few heads turned at the sight of her car, which made her smile.

When the Palmers parked near her, Fallon's nerves settled further. At least she'd already met one person, though she was still having trouble reconciling the generosity of her rescuer with the mercurial behavior of his daughter. Mr. Palmer had given her close to five gallons of gas and declined her pitiful offer of payment, while Nora had an appealing self-assurance when she wasn't acting like her dad was a candidate for Worst Father Ever. Whatever the cause of her hard-hearted tone when referencing him, Nora at least stood up for herself. Fallon had never been good at that.

And while she had no business offering advice about a father-daughter relationship—her own being so far back in her childhood she barely remembered it—Fallon had learned to deal with men like Jeffrey Palmer from all the years she'd hung around diners while her mother waited tables. Most of them were decent, hardworking types who responded best to kindness mingled with a healthy dose of respect. With that in mind, Fallon ran over to thank Mr. Palmer again.

He lifted a scarred hand from the steering wheel in casual acknowledgment of her gratitude, but a smile softened his weathered face. Tyler called good-bye from the passenger's side, his open expression and friendly grin making her think he was perhaps less jaded than his sister. Fallon peeked into the back seat, hoping Nora might walk over with her, but when she didn't even look up from her phone or make a move to get out, Fallon took the hint. Apparently, she wasn't going to get another glimpse of those rich brown eyes and full lips right now, but that wasn't what she was here for anyway.

Trying to contain the excitement and nervousness bubbling inside her, she headed in the direction of the women who were gathered outside the biggest building. Being an outsider had defined most of her life experience, but as she tugged at the pants that had gotten too big for her since she'd had to cut back to one meal a day and pulled at the frayed hem of her T-shirt to straighten it, she let herself hope that things would be different this time.

As she approached, a compact woman with short, dark, curly hair stepped forward and motioned to her. "Hi, I'm Jade. If you're here for the Women's Plus Crew, I'll be your group leader."

Jade's voice was cordial and confident. Fallon's anxiety eased as they shook hands. She didn't think of herself as shy, but limited interaction with her peers had made her feel awkward around them. And despite the hits her heart and finances had suffered, her first instinct was still to assume the best of others.

Relieved that Jade seemed genuine, she turned to meet the rest of the group. Hannah, a blonde from California, had a funny nervous giggle, and Kennedy, a black woman from Cleveland, spoke with a slight lisp. They were joined by a younger Latina from Texas who was introduced as Delores.

"Obviously, you'll be in charge of trimming the high branches," Delores said, looking up at her.

Fallon's cheeks and ears burned. Her height, combined with years of a substandard diet of gas station junk and fried diner food, had made her self-conscious about her body. Having almost no opportunity to exercise properly, she felt lumpy and graceless. She forced a grin. "I'm happy to help out wherever I can."

"You're each going to learn everything about being both sawyers and swampers," Jade said. "But Fallon, I think you have some paperwork to finish up in Mae's office."

Fallon nodded, knowing from her last phone conversation with the supervisor of the camp that since she hadn't given a permanent address, there were a few details to be filled in on her application.

"Who's Mae?" Kennedy asked.

"MaryAnn Elkhart," Jade said. "She coordinates base camp here. We all call her Mae. You'll meet her before long."

Before heading into the building, Fallon glanced at the Palmers' Jeep, seeing Nora gathering her gear. Clearly, Fallon had overstepped a boundary earlier when she'd shared her thoughts on the importance of family—something Nora evidently didn't agree with—but Nora's obvious affection for Tyler had emboldened her. She hoped Nora would take a moment to say good-bye to them. Three months wasn't forever, but it was a long time to be apart from those she loved. Nora probably wouldn't admit she cared about them, but people didn't always appreciate what they had until it was gone.

Fallon peeked into the first room as she passed. When Ranger Reva looked up from a large desk near the window and nodded, Fallon couldn't hide her smile. Reva Upshaw was the reason she was excited to be at Firecamp, eagerly anticipating what it could offer. They'd met at the diner in Yuma, a small city on the eastern plains of Colorado, where Fallon had continued to work even after her whole life had been turned inside out.

She and her mother had been forced to stop there after the steering coupler on their previously reliable Geo Prizm had gone out and the local mechanic had informed Fallon's mother that parts for that model were hard to find and would also cost way more than the change jingling in her purse. So they'd fallen into a new kind of routine: working and waiting. Fallon's mother had waited tables for two shifts at Yuma's Sunshine Diner most days while Fallon, seventeen by then, had bused tables and washed dishes or did odd jobs in town once her schoolwork was done. Her mother had signed her up for online homeschooling not long after their odyssey had begun, and she had been close to completing her high school degree.

She'd liked Mr. Jamar, the big black man who was the cook. He'd made her mother laugh and sometimes gave Fallon suggestions about someone in town who might be willing to pay for a few hours' work. Making money of her own felt good, but some of the groups who came to the diner made her gut twist with longing. Observing a world so different from her own was like reading a utopian story. The idea of living in one place and caring about people who cared about her seemed like the most implausible fantasy.

Three years later, Ranger Reva had been in the diner, traveling with several of her colleagues. Fallon had been mindlessly going through her shifts, still unable to figure out what she wanted to do with herself. Certain there was more to life than what she had in Yuma but with no sense of other options or guidance on how to change, she'd simply been putting one foot in front of the other during the days and crying herself to sleep most nights. She'd overheard the rangers—all dressed in khaki shirts and green pants—talking excitedly about their next assignments. It had seemed like forever since Fallon had noticed such enthusiasm, and the mention of something new had caught her attention. She'd lingered nearby, and when the woman had smiled at her, Fallon had felt like smiling back for the first time in months.

Seeing they were ready to pay, she'd worked up the nerve to ask, "Is it true, what you were saying about the mountains?"

The ranger had taken out her phone and shown Fallon some pictures. "These are from the San Isabel National Forest where I'll be working." She'd swiped through photo after photo of striking landscapes. "It's one of eleven national forests in Colorado and contains the Sawatch Range, the Collegiate Peaks, and Sangre de Cristo Range. It has well over a million acres, spread out over parts of eleven counties in central Colorado." Flushing slightly, she'd added, "I guess you can tell I'm pretty excited about getting to work there."

Fallon knew something about the geography of the West. Her homeschool classmates had frequently asked if she skied, and she'd explained numerous times that she wasn't in that part of the state. But she'd had no idea it could be so beautiful. The thought of starting over in such a different world had made her heart lift. "Would there be work for me there?" she'd asked.

The woman had stood, looking up at her. "Did you want to wait tables?"

Fallon had shaken her head. "I want a different life. Something useful. Something better."

Taking a business card out of her pocket, the ranger had written something on the back before handing it to Fallon.

"Reva Upshaw, USFS." Fallon had read aloud.

"Let's go, Ranger Reva," one of the men had called. "We've got a long drive ahead of us."

"That's my personal cell number on the back," Reva had said before turning to go. "Call me if you're coming that way, and we can talk about opportunities."

After six months of planning and saving, Fallon was on the road, but it was almost a year later before she'd made the call. Travel was more expensive than ever, and many people seemed apprehensive about strangers, but this was the life she'd always known, stopping along the way, working at whatever she could find when her funds got low. It was hard to save, though. In most of the bigger towns, people were holding signs asking for help, and Fallon found herself dipping into her cash every time. Then, in the last month of her journey, she'd picked up Evie, who had traveled with her for almost three weeks, sharing her bed and board. Fallon had thought there might be something more between them, but then Evie had found Fallon's cash reserves, and well, that had been that.

During their last phone conversation, Ranger Reva had told her when she needed to report for this year's Firecamp program, stressing that late arrivals would not be admitted. Fallon had calculated that stopping to work again meant she wouldn't make it on time. With a rising sense of panic, she'd counted what remained in her wallet, putting everything but a few ones and some change into the Caddy's gas tank. Her last meal had been a bag of convenience store popcorn and a container of yogurt. Yesterday. Exhausting her fuel when she was almost there had made her insides seize up, desperation and determination warring with self-recrimination. As she'd drifted to the side of the road, she'd resolved it was time to keep her guard up, to not be so gullible. If she made it to Firecamp, she'd change her stripes, get tougher.

Her mother had sometimes talked about them turning over a new leaf, and Fallon was determined now was that time for her. She wasn't always going to be the one giving. Not without getting something back. Mr. Palmer had shown up and helped her out, and that was a start. So no more wishing. She had to make a life for herself rather than simply hoping for possibilities to come to her.

She'd felt a little dejected when Nora hadn't walked over with her to meet the crew, but there were other women here. This was a new place to belong, with possibilities for real friends, and Nora didn't have to be one of them. Nora didn't owe her anything. In fact, the opposite was true. Fallon understood her not wanting to hang around with someone who'd mooched a few gallons of gas and tried to meddle in her family business. Maybe if they'd had more time, they could have become friends, but Fallon wasn't sure she had much to offer someone like her. Nora's dark eyes shone with confidence, and Fallon couldn't help but notice her solid build. She didn't look like she'd have trouble managing any of the activities that Fallon anticipated, even using a chainsaw.

I'll be all right too. Things are going to change out here, and definitely for the better.

CHAPTER TWO

As they'd approached Firecamp, Nora's thoughts had lingered on Fallon. It was odd how her clothes didn't seem to fit quite right, like they'd been bought for someone else. She wasn't drop-dead gorgeous, but she had beautiful eyes and a nice smile. But when Fallon had looked into the back seat, Nora had pretended to be consumed by her phone for a reason. She didn't want to walk into camp and have people assume they were buddies. Nora intended to move on from here with no additional encumbrances, so she'd start Firecamp in the same way she would finish it: alone. Besides, Fallon's moments of bashfulness and uncertainty seemed like the behavior of someone immature, and there was no chance of them being BFFs anyway, given Fallon's remarks about family being something to cherish. Nora adored Tyler, but she could take or leave the rest of them. And why shouldn't she? Her older brothers were already out on their own, and she'd certainly be disappointing her parents when she didn't present a husband.

Nora watched Fallon head toward the small group of women standing near the largest of the wooden buildings. Her pace was uneven, like she wanted to run but was holding herself back. Someone with that kind of energy could be really fun in bed. Nora gave a short cough, squelching the unexpected thought as quickly as it appeared. Fallon might be moving the way she did because she'd been driving for a while—before running out of gas—and the relief of having reached her destination hadn't sunk in yet.

"Now, that's someone you could learn something from while you're here." Her father's voice boomed in the confines of the Jeep. "That young woman understands respect and gratitude."

Accustomed to his verbal jabs, Nora didn't answer. She climbed out of the back seat and stretched, surprised to see Fallon stopping short of the group. In spite of her eagerness, she now seemed hesitant, almost wary, until another woman stepped forward, her expression and manner welcoming. When Fallon smiled and shook her hand, Nora found herself hoping Firecamp would be everything Fallon wanted it to be. But when Fallon glanced back at the Jeep, Nora hurriedly shifted her attention to collecting her gear. *Why should I care what kind of camp she has?* She wasn't taking on a broke, wide-eyed underdog as a project.

Gathering her rolling duffel and backpack, Nora stole another look at the group. Fallon had disappeared. Unexpectedly, Nora felt a familiar edginess creep over her. She knew what it was to be the odd one out, and not only in her family. During her junior year in high school, a girl named Darcy Ellerbee had moved to town and changed the dynamics of their high school class, including Nora's standing with friends she'd had for years.

On Darcy's first day, Nora had made some teasing remark about her drawl, unaware she was making an enemy for life. Darcy had joined every club, charmed her way into various groups, and won over anyone who mattered, including all the popular kids and many of the teachers. She'd begun spreading rumors about Nora every chance she got, and by the time Nora started hearing passing comments in the hall and catching odd looks in class, the damage was done.

She'd never imagined that her classmates, many of whom she'd known since first grade, would be so quick to listen to some new kid. Soon, her usual seat at lunch was unavailable, and the people she'd sat with before school had gone somewhere else. The desolation of being cast aside had strengthened her defensive walls, and she'd learned to keep her head high and her heart protected.

Eventually, she'd made her way into Addison's artsy group, aligning with the quirky clique who didn't care what anyone else thought. They were the first people other than Tyler to compliment her photographs, and they'd commiserated with her when she'd lost three of her favorite images while trying to transfer them to the school's computer. The lessons about being selective and safeguarding what she most treasured had become second nature.

She gave her head a quick shake, bringing herself out of the past. Whether she got along with the others here or not, this was the last step before she could learn her craft while finishing college, and create the life she wanted. And nothing that happened in the next three months would interfere with that. *Get in, get out, get on with your life.*

Her father gave her only a brusque nod as a good-bye—thank God—but she held Tyler tightly for an extra moment. "Hang in there, bro. Try to enjoy your summer."

He shuddered. "It won't be the same with you gone."

Nora fought back tears. Without her at home to speak up for him, they both knew their father would work on making her baby brother into his version of what a man should be. She'd talked to Tyler about when to just go along and when he should stand his ground, but it was one thing to discuss it in the abstract and something completely different to live it across a whole summer. Their father would be relentless in his ridicule if he saw Tyler crying now, so for his sake, Nora ripped off the proverbial Band-Aid. She gave him a hard squeeze and kept her voice light. "You'll be fine. And I'll see you soon."

She hoisted her backpack and started toward the group just as two more young women got out of a small sedan across the dusty parking area. When they met at the back of the car, the driver looked around the rocky and rugged terrain and the log buildings that comprised Firecamp headquarters and rolled her eyes. The other leaned into her and whispered something that made the first girl laugh as she shook her head.

Here was the flip side of the coin. Contrasting with Fallon's enthusiasm and the goodwill of those who had greeted her, these two were probably more like Nora, here to do their time and move on. Angling by them, trying to avoid eye contact so she could avoid conversation, she could just make out the words "the stuff" and "cool, or we'll get busted" as the driver heaved a large suitcase out of the trunk.

Nora must have gotten too close because the passenger fixed reddened eyes on her as she walked by. She jerked her thumb in the group's direction. "You going over there?" Her tone suggested that Nora's reply held very little interest for her. Both girls moved closer to the large bag as they assessed her.

Nora considered repeating her father's commentary about how government programs didn't need a warrant to do searches if contraband was suspected. But she wasn't the Firecamp police, nor was she a narc. She'd gotten high a few times at parties with Addison. It was all right, but she didn't like the idea of not being in control, especially around strangers. Shrugging, she said, "Yeah. I just got here."

As if on cue to ruin Nora's anonymous entrance, someone called her name. She winced but turned. Fallon and the woman who'd greeted her were waving at them.

The girls looked at each other and burst into laughter. "But someone knows you...Nora," the first one said, swaying slightly.

Nora eyed them, feeling no need to explain herself. "You know, the sooner we get started, the sooner we can get out of here. I don't know about you, but that's my plan."

The two girls blinked. Too harsh? "That and maybe a little relaxation along the way," she added in a softer tone, nodding at the suitcase.

"Now you're talking," they both said at once.

Nora managed a wry smile while hoping they were too high to remember what she'd said. In any case, once camp got underway, they'd all be too busy for any prohibited partying.

"I'm Gwen," the driver said, and the passenger introduced herself as Tina. "We're down for anything as long as it doesn't involve hard work or staying sober." They laughed as if hearing the funniest joke ever told.

Was it a joke? Nora bit her cheek to keep from telling them they'd certainly come to the wrong place. Did they not read the online information before they'd signed up? Had they ever handled a chainsaw before? Both women were heavily made-up and wore activewear sets. Nora couldn't envision either of them spending three weeks out of each of the next three months roughing it in the great outdoors. Sleeping in tents, cooking, and doing personal business outside, all while doing an incredibly demanding and dangerous job didn't seem like these girls' jam. Fallon might not have been any better prepared, with her baggy jeans and ratty T-shirt, but at least she was eager.

Not my circus, not my monkeys, as her brother Art always said. With a shrug, she hoisted her backpack and began walking toward the group, intending to distance herself from these stoned amateurs.

"Hey, wait up," one of them called after her.

She winced as they caught up. So much for her plan to go it alone. Momentarily, she regretted not following Fallon. Then again, hanging out with these two might help maintain her goal of detachment and disinterest, unlike associating with Fallon, who seemed already in with the rest of the group.

The woman who'd been waving introduced herself as Jade, their group leader. She gave Gwen and Tina a long look but said nothing about their apparent condition. After everyone exchanged names, she announced, "Welcome to the Women's Plus Firecamp Crew. We'll be working hard, but we'll be working together. Follow me, and we'll ditch your gear for now and get to know each other a little better."

Gwen and Tina elbowed each other. Nora had watched enough reruns of *Beavis and Butt-Head* with her brothers to recognize an infantile reaction to perceived innuendo, but she ignored it.

Jade directed them to a building at the edge of the forest. "This will be your group accommodation while we're in camp. Put your gear on a cot, and we'll head back to the main building."

Nora looked inside. It was one big room with a woodstove in the center and a single opening toward the back. Bare cots were spaced along the walls and in the middle.

"Excuse me," Nora said, "but I thought we were going to be in individual tents."

Jade laughed. "Oh, we will. And this will seem like the height of luxury then. But we've got training and team building to do first. We'll be here for a few more days."

Nora suppressed a sigh and nodded, tossing her duffel onto the first cot on the east wall. Gwen and Tina followed, choosing the next spaces along the same wall. Fallon hadn't moved, seeming confounded by all the choices. Nora started to gesture to the cot across from her, but Jade put her hand on Fallon's arm.

"I'm here in the middle," she said quietly, setting a small backpack on the bed in front of her. "Wanna be there?" She pointed to the next one down.

"Uh, sure. Yeah. Thanks." Fallon pulled in a small wheeled suitcase.

Hannah, Kennedy, and Delores claimed the west wall.

"The bathroom has two of everything," Jade said, moving to the doorway. "Sinks, toilets, and shower stalls. Make use of it now if you need to. Meet back at the main building when you hear the triangle, and we'll go over the schedule for the next couple of days."

"Will one of those little silver things ring loud enough for us to hear?" Hannah asked.

"Oh, you'll hear it, don't worry." Jade strode across the floor to the exit. "Think cowboy chuckwagon triangle, not elementary school rhythm band. And that will always be our notice to gather."

Twenty minutes later, the clear, resonating tone was as distinct as Jade promised, and soon, they were into one of Nora's least favorite activities: an ice-breaking exercise. She understood the getting-to-know-you rationale. Whether the questions were serious or funny, each person's answers revealed something about them. It'd help them bond and work together through the weeks ahead, but she still didn't like the open-ended, intrusive nature of the topics. Worse, she hated appearing hard-hearted and callous like her father, so she joined in with as much enthusiasm as she could muster, while mentally repeating, "Cash, college, career."

"Do you fold your pizza?" was Jade's first question.

"Is that a thing?" Fallon asked.

"Oh yeah," Kennedy said. "New York and Chicago style, for sure."

No one else ate their pizza folded. When Jade asked, "What's your go-to karaoke anthem?" Gwen and Tina were all in.

"'Only Girl in the World,'" they squealed together. They were off on the chorus until Hannah covered her ears.

"'Need You Now,'" Hannah said for her song.

Delores quickly chimed in with "Love Story," by Taylor Swift.

Nora hid a smile at the memory of singing Tegan and Sara's "Boyfriend" with Addison, but she told the group her song was "Born This Way." Kennedy made the monster hand, and they all laughed.

When everyone looked to Fallon, she shrugged. "I've never done karaoke."

"What?" Kennedy said, the pitch of her voice rising. "We'll have to fix that, first chance we get."

"For sure," Hannah added with emphasis.

Jade looked over her list of prompts. "How about this, Fallon? Does your car have a name? What is it?"

Fallon admitted to calling her car Big Red. Gwen had no name for hers, and the rest didn't have their own, although Delores said her mother called theirs a POS. As the group giggled, Nora suspected that Jade had chosen that question to keep Fallon from feeling left out. Maybe she'd even made it up. It was a nice gesture, not that it mattered.

"Delores, you first this time," Jade said. "Would you go in the mothership with aliens if they landed on Earth tomorrow?"

"Oh, hell no. I was born in Texas, but way too many people have called me an alien, usually with *illegal* in front of it. I don't need any more of that."

Hannah said yes, while Fallon appeared to give the matter serious thought before agreeing to go. No one else was interested.

"Gwen, what is an easy item on your bucket list that you haven't done yet?" Jade asked.

Gwen licked her lips. "There's not much I haven't done."

Tina clapped. "Me neither."

"I'd like a dog," Fallon volunteered. "I've never had one, and I think it would be great to have a friend like that."

The group made sympathetic sounds, and Delores showed her a picture of her dog, a medium-sized mixed mutt named Georgie. Hannah wanted to see the Country Music Hall of Fame in Nashville, and Kennedy wanted to learn to play pickleball. Nora said she couldn't think of anything offhand and kept her dream of seeing one of her photographs in a national publication, or at least somewhere besides the school website, to herself. She wasn't exactly shy about her work, but she would have to feel a lot more comfortable before sharing something so personal and important to her.

"Okay, last one for now," Jade announced. "What person from history would you add to Mount Rushmore?"

Kennedy asked if it had to be a president. When Jade said no, she suggested Martin Luther King Jr. Delores nodded her agreement.

"Reagan," Gwen said.

Tina chimed in with "Lincoln."

"I think he's already on there," Fallon said gently.

"Well, who would you pick?" Tina sounded like she would make any answer into an argument.

"No one." Fallon's tone was composed. "I think it should be left as it is. But I'd sure like to see it someday. That and the Crazy Horse Memorial."

Nora looked between the two. "I agree," she said in hopes of circumventing any confrontation. She didn't think Fallon was up to dueling with Tina and Gwen. And those two obviously came as a package deal.

"Okay. Let's talk schedules," Jade said, unfolding a paper from her pocket. She clearly wanted to change the subject as well.

Fallon shuffled her feet, and Nora got the sense she was forcing herself to speak. "But we didn't get your answers, Jade. Aren't we supposed to know you too?"

Jade hesitated, and a smile stretched across her full lips. "You're right, Fallon." She took a breath. "I have eaten folded pizza, and my karaoke song depends on my mood." At the sounds of protest, Jade held up her hands. "'Unstoppable,' when I'm single. 'A Thousand Years' if I'm in love."

A whoop rose from the group.

"Which one would it be now?" Hannah asked coyly.

Jade shook her head. "We don't know each other that well. Yet." Amid the laughter, she went on to list her car—an aging Toyota Corona she called the Green M&M—and her bucket list item—taking a painting class. "For Mount Rushmore, I'd like to see a woman. Maybe Sandra Day O'Connor or Hillary Clinton?"

Nora nodded in approval as the group clapped. "I'd definitely want to see that."

"Me too," Fallon said, meeting Nora's eyes.

That smile. Something in Nora's gut gave a pleasant tug. *Oh no. Not going there.* She turned back toward Jade. "So what about the schedule?"

"Let's start with getting the most important part of your gear," Jade said. "Your chainsaw."

Nora had wanted to bring her own, but the instructions were clear. Everyone could use only Firecamp equipment. It made sense. That way, the camp only needed to stock parts—chains, housing, bar nuts, and so on—for one make and model.

Relieved the touchy-feely stuff was over, Nora followed as they walked toward what Jade called the equipment hut. It was actually one of the largest structures in the compound, which made sense, assuming all the gear was in one location. Before entering, Nora took a deep breath of the clean, cool air, knowing that once the saws started up, the tang of gas and oil would dominate nature. She'd always associated that smell with sweating and laboring with her father and brothers, but the feeling of accomplishment and the confidence she'd developed made that memory more pleasant. And now one more summer's worth of hard work would earn her the future she wanted.

Inside, Jade indicated a wide counter where a row of identical chainsaws waited. The crew lined up two deep. A graying older man as big as a standing bear stood facing them. Despite his menacing size, he sported a friendly grin and a playful gleam in his eye. "Welcome, Women's Plus Crew. In addition to your cutting equipment, we'll be fitting you with your PPE. Can anyone tell me what that means?"

Nora answered automatically. "Personal protective equipment."

He focused on her. "Very good. My name's Hal. What's yours?"

"Nora Palmer."

"Okay, Nora Palmer. You get to go first if you can name any three pieces of basic PPE."

Nora tilted her head as if thinking, though this was no challenge for her. "Ear and eye protection, hard hat, high visibility vest, and Kevlar chaps and gloves."

He bowed to her as Gwen said, "Damn, girl."

"Step right up, Nora Palmer, and be served."

Scattered applause broke out as Nora examined the saws. None looked "out of the box" new, but that was fine. She wanted one that was broken in, and they all seemed in good condition. She carefully touched a couple of the chains, finding them sharp as expected.

She laid her hand on the one in front of her, and Hal said, "Excellent choice." He eyed her in a strictly professional way. "You're a tall one."

"She's not alone," Jade said, pulling Fallon to the front.

"Twin peaks, huh?" Hal mused. He turned to a stack of items behind him, coming back with two sets of chaps. "You two try these on while I work with some of the others."

Nora stepped to the side, Fallon following her tentatively. "What are these?" she whispered, holding the garment at arm's length.

"Chaps. Probably men's sizes." Nora held them up at her waist. "But I think they'll be okay." Fallon hadn't moved. "Try them on," Nora ordered.

"I don't...I haven't ever..."

Nora wasn't surprised that Fallon had no experience with PPE. She'd noticed her looking at the chainsaws with near panic. She tried to soften her tone. "They go over your legs. Mainly for protection but also to help keep your pants clean. Just do what I'm doing." She fastened the belt at her waist, watching Fallon as she did. "Good. Maybe that will help keep those jeans up." Nora had meant it as a tease, but Fallon blushed and looked down.

"Yeah. I guess I've lost some weight recently. But I couldn't shop for anything new because..." She looked away, and Nora recalled the few dollars Fallon had offered her father.

"I'm just kidding. You're doing fine." Nora finished putting on her chaps, pointing to herself again. "Now, wrap the straps around your legs like this."

Fallon nodded. "I see." They seemed to fit her well. "But what about..." She indicated the unprotected space on the insides of her thighs.

"If your saw gets up there, your life won't be worth living anyway." Nora hated hearing her father's words come out of her mouth, but they were apt in this case.

Fallon stared at her for a few seconds and then began laughing with a deep, unaffected resonance that made Nora join in. "I suppose you're right," she said when they'd caught their breath. "I haven't laughed like that in a long time." She gave herself a little shake. "It sure does make me feel a little less anxious."

"Good." Nora heard herself sounding more encouraging than she intended, but Fallon smiled, and she couldn't be sorry. *Enough of that.* She looked back toward Hal. "We're done."

He looked over. "Those fit okay?"

"Do you have any extra Velcro?" Nora asked, moving away abruptly. "I'd like these legs a little tighter."

"I think we can fix you up," he said. "Come get the rest of your equipment."

The shadows were lengthening by the time the Women's Plus Crew was completely outfitted. Everyone moved a little awkwardly in their new gear. Kennedy's hat seemed ready to fall off, and Delores was trying to fix Hannah's eye protection, which was slightly askew on her face. Gwen and Tina were complaining about everything from the weight of the saw to the bright color of their vests when a forest ranger stepped from the main building. She approached, and something in her manner as she appraised them made everyone quiet down and stand a little straighter.

"Good afternoon," she said, and everyone answered in unison. "I'm Reva Upshaw, Forest Service liaison to the Southern Conservation Corps Firecamp program. I want to welcome you all and commend you for being part of the Women's Plus Crew. Your work this summer will add to the outstanding reputation established by previous crews, who have shown to the SCC what women are capable of. I'm confident that after this summer, the rest of the world will know it too."

Fallon started to applaud, but Upshaw held up her hand. "I also want you all to know that you are contributing to something incredibly important. You'll be making neighborhoods and towns safer, and by helping to prevent large-scale forest fires, you'll be keeping tons of carbon from being released into the atmosphere that would contribute to climate change. So thank you for stepping in and making a meaningful contribution to our state and our planet."

Upshaw moved around the group, making encouraging comments

as she shook everyone's hand. Nora thought she saw her give Fallon a wink, but it happened so fast, she wasn't sure. When Upshaw took her leave after giving the group another wave, Hannah cleared her throat. "Wow. She's something."

Fallon nodded, giving a little sigh. "Yeah. She's the reason I'm here."

At that, the warmth that Upshaw's words had given Nora suddenly cooled.

CHAPTER THREE

Fallon couldn't take her eyes off Nora. The confident, comfortable way she wore her PPE added to her presence. She held the chainsaw with such ease that it looked like an extension of her body rather than the fearsome cutting device that could take off a human limb just as easily as one from a tree. Even though only Fallon knew that Nora came from a family of firefighters, Jade clearly recognized that Nora knew what she was doing and promptly appointed her as a co-trainer. Fallon wanted to be in Nora's group, but Nora sidled up to Gwen and Tina, and the three of them immediately started giggling at some private joke. There were still things about people—especially women—that puzzled her, but she always knew when she wasn't welcome.

Kennedy had gone back to the equipment hut to get a loose piece of ear protection fixed, so Fallon teamed with Hannah and Delores, both of whom seemed equally uneasy with their new equipment. While Jade talked to Nora, Fallon said the reassuring words she'd hoped someone would say to her. "Don't worry. Jade will teach us everything we need to know, and we'll be sawing away in no time."

"You really think so?" Hannah's eyes darted around the rest of the group.

"Uh-huh," Fallon said, grimacing at the lack of confidence she heard in her own voice. How would she ever become a group leader if she couldn't do better than that? Squaring her shoulders, she added, "You heard what Ranger Reva said. This Women's Plus Crew is going to be the best ever." Putting her hand on Hannah's arm, she added, "And that's us."

Hannah smiled up at her. "Yeah, okay." She hefted the chainsaw. "I'm ready."

Delores stepped in beside her. "Me too. Let's fly, Falcon."

❖

"What difference does it make if I call it the housing or the faceplate?" Tina whined. "They're pretty much the same thing, right?"

Fallon could hear the complaint in Tina's voice from across the yard where the two groups were getting their separate instruction. She thought Nora might be gritting her teeth when she answered, "No, they're not. Look—"

Fallon presumed this wasn't Tina's first lesson. After a few practices, Fallon and Hannah and Delores were able to identify the parts of their saws to Jade's satisfaction, but from Nora's tone and Gwen's sigh of frustration, Jade seemed to recognize that she needed to step in. Addressing her group, she said, "Why don't you three take a break and report back in fifteen? Hopefully, we'll be able to start our saws then."

As they walked toward their cabin, Gwen's voice rose. "See the bar nuts. See the faceplate. Nuts. Face. Think of Danny's nuts in your face. That's how you can remember it."

Hannah and Delores burst out laughing. "Well, that's an image we'll all be stuck with for a while," Hannah said.

"Yeah, I guess she'll be calling her chainsaw Danny," Delores added.

The sound of footsteps behind them saved Fallon from having to respond. "Are you guys finished already?" Nora asked.

"Yeah." Hannah nodded. "And we didn't even have Danny to help us."

"Oh God." Nora's cheeks pinked as she gave a short laugh. "My brothers would never let me hear the end of it if I told them that."

As the talk turned to siblings and extended families, Fallon focused on the trees and the rise of the land nearby. She felt surprisingly at home for being in such a new and different place. A chipmunk darted through the low brush, stopping to watch her briefly before disappearing. She smiled, heartened by a surge of certainty. This must be it. Her new place. Her new job. Her new chance.

"Ooh, look at that grin. Fallon must have someone in mind." Hannah and Delores were looking at her expectantly.

"I'm sorry. What?"

"Delores was asking if you have a boyfriend," Hannah explained.

"I, uh, no."

Nora was looking at her intently. "Or maybe a girlfriend?"

"Not that either." Fallon hesitated. She'd never talked to anyone about her sexuality, and she'd often wondered how her mother would've reacted if they'd had the chance to discuss it. These women seemed genuinely interested and nonjudgmental. "Or not now. I was with someone on my way here, but she ran off after stealing most of my money." Had Nora told anyone about rescuing her? Fallon didn't think so but risked a quick glance. "I almost didn't make it here."

Hannah touched her hand, drawing her attention away from Nora's quick nod. "I'm sorry that happened to you. I guess you can never tell about people."

"Bad behavior is about who somebody is, not who they want to be with," Delores said. "It doesn't matter if you're gay, straight, or bi like me. Stealing's wrong, no matter what."

Nora looked like she was about to say something, but the triangle sounded. "Five minutes to dinner, ladies," Jade's voice called. After a spontaneous race to the bathroom, which Hannah won, the group met up with Gwen and Tina in the dining area. The room was surprisingly crowded, almost entirely with men who sat in groups at long, picnic-style tables.

"About time we saw some dating material," Gwen murmured, and Tina hummed her agreement. Fallon watched them both eyeing the room as if lining up their next conquests. She was too hungry to wait, so she stepped around them, falling in behind Jade and the rest of the group.

"Enjoy this luxury too," Jade remarked, leading them down the cafeteria line. "You'll be eating your own cooking for the next three weeks."

"Not my cooking," Gwen said as she joined the line. "Unless you want to spend the day puking. Even my drunk-ass mother wouldn't eat it."

"Sounds like a candidate for full-time KP," a voice behind them said.

Jade looked around. "Hi, Mae. Join us and meet the newest Women's Plus Crew."

"It would be my pleasure."

After they settled around an empty table, introductions were made. Jade looked like she could be Mae's daughter, as they shared the same compact build and dark hair and eyes. The friendly, comfortable way they had between them made Fallon's heart ache with missing her mother, and she dabbed at her eyes with her napkin.

"You okay?" Kennedy asked as she slid in beside her.

"Yeah." Fallon tried to clear the lump in her throat. "Sawdust, I think."

"Plenty of that here, for sure," Kennedy agreed. "Who are all those guys?"

Mae gestured with her head. "That's the Veterans Crew. First-timers like you but all from various branches of the service." Hannah turned to look, and several of the men nodded cordially. She blushed and went back to her food. "Most of the others are here with tree trimming businesses that are getting their B or C Feller certification."

"They all look like A-plus fellas to me," Gwen purred.

"A Feller is someone professionally trained to cut—or fell—trees. It's not a gender reference," Mae said. Fallon supposed Mae had explained that numerous times. "For example, Jade's B Feller certification means she can supervise your operations on Forest Service land."

As Mae continued, Kennedy leaned closer to Fallon. "Listen, we barely know each other, but I have a favor to ask."

Fallon tried to cover her surprise. "Sure. What do you need?"

"Don't ever stick me with those two again." Kennedy inclined her head toward Gwen and Tina. "They couldn't be less interested in what we're doing here, plus they're rude and nasty and just…uncool." Fallon gave a quick nod, and Kennedy continued, "I really don't understand why Nora wants to hang out with them. She seems nice enough, but my dad always said you're judged by the company you keep, so…"

"If we get paired up again, I'd be glad to work with you," Fallon said, not wanting to talk about Nora. "But you should know, I have no experience with chainsaws, and I'm kinda worried about that."

"Don't be." Kennedy grinned, touching Fallon's arm. "I can help you some. My dad used to work at a nursery. The plant kind, not the baby kind. Whenever a big storm hit, he'd get a bunch of guys and they'd go through neighborhoods, offering their services to people with fallen trees or broken-off limbs. I'd ride with him, and when I was old enough, I'd help cut the small stuff so we could chip it or carry it off in the truck. I've never cut down a whole tree, but I'm ready to learn."

"Is that what you want to do after Firecamp?" Fallon asked, leaning closer. Conversation around them had grown louder, and she had to practically read Kennedy's lips to understand her.

"Yeah. I want to become a certified arborist. I figured this would look good on my résumé. What about you?"

"Uh, I'm not sure yet." Fallon looked away, anxiety rippling through her. She didn't want to jinx her plans by discussing them. *Don't wish for it. Make it happen.*

"No worries," Kennedy said, giving Fallon's arm a squeeze before moving her hand. "You've got all summer to figure it out."

❖

Getting ready for bed with seven other people was a new experience. Fallon and Nora had ended up together on the bathroom schedule and were brushing their teeth at the sinks, having already changed into sleepwear. "So this is what it's like when you have a big family, huh?" Kinda lame, but Fallon wanted to make conversation. Nora hadn't said two words to her since their PPE fitting.

"If you're that kind of unlucky, yeah." Apparently, Nora was in her snarky mood.

"Gwen and Tina seem like fun." Fallon tried again.

Nora eyed her. "Not your kind of fun, Fallon. Stick with your buddy Kennedy. She's more your speed."

Fallon frowned. "What?" Then she remembered the conversation at dinner, heads close and Kennedy touching her arm. Nora almost sounded jealous. But that was preposterous. "Oh yeah, we were talking because her father taught her about using a chainsaw, and—"

"I don't care who you talk to or what you talk about, Fallon." Nora's voice was hard. "My plans don't include socializing or making friends. I'm here for the summer, and then I'm gone." She rinsed and spit with what seemed like more force than necessary before leaving without another word.

Dumbstruck, Fallon stared after her. She waited a few moments before making her way toward her bed, but she needn't have worried. Nora looked like a mummy, completely covered up and facing the wall. Fallon stifled a sigh, settling in, grateful to feel the warmth of the stove at her feet. The evening was cool, the kind of night where she'd often worn socks to bed in the cheap motels they'd stayed in over the years. Tonight, she was cozy and comfortable without them. Yawning, she replayed the conversation with Nora, trying to figure out if she'd said or done something wrong or if Nora just didn't like her. She was asleep before an answer came.

❖

After breakfast, Jade gathered the group for chainsaw practice. "There are situations in which everyone can do their own thing. Starting your saw is *not* one of them. We're going to do this the same way—the right way—every time. Can anyone tell me why?"

Several sets of eyes turned in Nora's direction, but she was steadfastly looking at the ground.

"Somebody want to take a guess? Come on," Jade said. "I won't make you run laps or do push-ups if you get it wrong."

Fallon knew she should speak up. She needed to learn to take risks, to be bolder, if she was going to be a leader like Jade. "Because if we all do it the right way, no one gets hurt?"

"That's a good point but not quite what I was looking for." There was another beat of silence.

"Because if we do it the same way every time and there's a malfunction, we know it's with the equipment and not operator error." Nora sounded tired and a little annoyed.

"Right. And that can save us a lot of hassle. Especially if we're in the field. So here we go." Jade put her chainsaw on the ground. "Follow me exactly." She talked through the hot or cold position for the master switch, engaging the chain brake, and squeezing the throttle trigger.

Fallon followed as if dealing with a nuclear bomb, with equal parts trepidation and respect.

"Anchor the machine with your toes below the trigger and pull until you get resistance."

Heart pounding, Fallon reminded herself that she trusted Jade. Her calm, clear directions made everything sound simple. When the saws roared to life, everyone cheered.

"Squeeze the trigger once to bring the engine speed to idle," Jade called.

"Woo-hoo." Tina lifted her saw and gunned it like a race car engine. A thin stream of smoke poured from the housing.

Jade made a "cut" gesture, but Nora, who was closer, yelled, "No, Tina. Stop," motioning to put the saw down. Tina frowned but obeyed, and Jade signaled everyone else to turn their saws off. For a few seconds, the silence seemed louder than the roar of the machines had been.

Jade took a breath. "Tina, please come with me. The rest of you take a break."

The group looked around at each other. "I could use a refill," Fallon said, holding up her water bottle. "Can I get anybody anything?"

"I'll go with you," Delores said. Kennedy and Hannah handed over their reusable bottles. Nora was talking to Gwen and didn't look around.

When they were almost to the dining area, Delores said, "Wow. That scared the shit out of me."

"Me too," Fallon agreed. "I'm nervous enough about these chainsaws without some crazy woman waving one around like Leatherface's disorderly sister."

Delores laughed as they began filling the bottles. "What do you think is going to happen to her? Will she get kicked out?"

"I don't think so. But she might have to do push-ups or run laps."

"Or do KP," they said together.

When they returned, Jade was in front of the group with Tina beside her. There was only one saw between them. Fallon and Delores handed out the water as Jade cleared her throat. "Tina has something she'd like to say to all of you."

"I'm sincerely sorry I acted recklessly." Tina's voice was whispery soft. "I got carried away, but I understand I could've seriously hurt someone, and I apologize to each of you." She glanced at Jade as if confirming she was finished. Jade murmured something, and Tina said, "Oh yeah. Because of my irresponsible behavior, I've lost my chainsaw privileges for the first week. I'll be a swamper when we go to the field."

Hannah raised her hand. "What's a swamper again?"

"Swampers pull the cut limbs away from the tree trunks and pile them at a designated location," Jade said. "Usually, we trade off this duty throughout the day, but not in Tina's case. For now."

Fallon didn't think being a swamper sounded so bad, but Nora's expression suggested otherwise. Or maybe Nora was irritated that her new friend was being punished.

"Let's get to work," Jade said. Two hours later, everyone had successfully started and shut down their saws multiple times, and they'd all cut a medium-size limb apart, learning about pinching or binding the chain and various kinds of cuts in the process. They'd also practiced maintenance, cleaning out the sawdust and other gunk, sharpening the chain, and refilling the fuel and bar oil. Tina followed Jade like a shadow, listening attentively and watching everything that each person did. When Jade announced their lunch break, Tina looked at her hopefully, and Jade gave a slight nod. Tina skipped over to Gwen and Nora. Fallon had been the last one to finish maintenance duties, and she was brushing the grit from her chaps and wiping her hands as Tina reached her friends.

"My punishment is over. For now, at least." Tina confirmed that Jade and the others were already heading toward the dining room, neglecting to look back to where Fallon stood. "God, I'm desperate for a smoke. Let's stop by the cabin before lunch."

"Sure thing, sweetie," Gwen said. "I know that was pure torture, and you deserve a reward."

"I'll pass, thanks." Nora was watching Jade too.

"Well, come be our lookout," Gwen said, taking Nora's arm. Fallon observed Nora tense at the touch. "We don't need any other fuckups today."

Fallon sneezed. She'd been trying to hold it in, but it exploded out of her like a gunshot. Gwen, Tina, and Nora turned at once, and Gwen groaned. "Oh, great. The Firecamp Five-O."

"I'm not," Fallon said, trying to stay calm. "And I don't want to be. I only want to get my lunch. Excuse me."

She tried to brush past, but Gwen stepped into her path, her expression menacing. "If you narc on us, I guarantee they'll find some on you too. I'm really good at hiding shit, and I'll plant something harder than weed on you. You'll do time, and it won't be a picnic like this."

"So you promise not to say anything, right?" Nora asked, moving alongside Gwen. "Because what Gwen says is true. You or anyone else in the crew could get kicked out too."

Was that a warning or a threat? And was Nora really siding with these two? "Yes, I swear." Fallon hid her disillusionment. "You don't have to worry about me."

"Okay, good." Nora jerked her head toward the mess hall, and Fallon understood she should go. She didn't run, though she wanted to. She definitely didn't look back. Inside, she saw Kennedy waving. Fallon was always hungry, but right now, she wasn't sure if she could eat. Realizing it would look suspicious if she didn't get any food, she took her usual portions.

"Where you been? I couldn't convince this band of heathens to wait for you." Kennedy scooted over to make room on the bench.

Fallon worked to keep her voice neutral. "No worries. I wanted to clean up first. Didn't want to come to the table dirty."

"See? Raised right." Delores gestured toward Fallon. "That's what I was talking about."

Fallon lifted her tea glass, hoping anyone who noticed her hand shaking would write it off as the residual effects of using the chainsaw. Conversation swirled around her, and she managed a few bites of food. When she thought about the afternoon ahead, she realized her anxiety about handling potentially dangerous equipment was practically gone. It didn't help to know she had something else to worry about, and it hurt that she couldn't tell what part Nora played in those worries.

CHAPTER FOUR

Nora was hangry. Hungry because she'd missed lunch, and angry because it was her own fault for associating with Gwen and Tina. Her plan had been to keep to herself at Firecamp, but after watching Fallon buddy up to the rest of the crew, Gwen and Tina's sarcasm and indifference seemed like the right kind of part-time company. She'd always thought of casual dope use as a victimless crime, until Gwen had started threatening Fallon.

Was Gwen telling the truth about having stuff other than weed? Hearing that Fallon had run out of gas due to being ripped off by some random woman and not because of her own carelessness reinforced Nora's impression of her as inexperienced and naïve about the ways of the world. She probably should have stood up for Fallon, but her aloof behavior was intended to make it clear that she wasn't signing on to be her protector. Still, she couldn't stand by and let Gwen take charge through intimidation.

After keeping watch outside the cabin for ten minutes while Gwen and Tina vaped, Nora looked in to see them finishing off a bag of Doritos, something that could have taken the edge off her appetite if they'd bothered to share. Fallon would have shared, a little voice inside her head suggested. *That's not the point. Get in. Get out. Get on with your life.*

❖

The cry of triumph as the tree fell made Nora smile. But when Fallon split her two-handed high fives between Jade and Kennedy, and then Hannah and Delores before stopping and turning away from her,

Nora's enjoyment faded. Clearly, Fallon considered her "unfriended." Nora had worried as Fallon leaned into her cut with that long, elegant mane, but she'd done well. And none of that mattered, even when Gwen and Tina taunted Nora about being teacher's pet. She was the best sawyer in the crew, and that was more important to her than who she was or wasn't friends with. She'd be done with this place soon enough, and her real life would begin.

"Okay, crew." Jade's voice broke into her thoughts. "Do a quick cleanup and meet here in thirty minutes. I have a surprise for you."

Nora found herself sharing the restroom with Fallon again, but Fallon seemed to have no interest in conversation as they washed up. Unaccountably, Nora felt obliged to try. "Hey, don't worry about Gwen. She's just—"

"I don't care what you do or who you hang out with, Nora," Fallon said, throwing Nora's words from last night back at her. "My plans may include socializing or making friends, but not with people like—" She cut herself off. "I'm here for the summer, and longer, I hope." She faced Nora. "So you go your way, and I'll go mine, okay?"

Nora was too stunned to reply. Where had this tough-talking woman come from? Fallon was gone before she could even blink.

As they gathered around the parked cars, Fallon stood next to Ranger Upshaw, grinning as she chatted with Kennedy. "Now that everyone has successfully completed chainsaw training, we have a special treat for you," Upshaw said, nodding to Jade.

"We're going into town to get ice cream," Jade announced. Hannah and Delores began murmuring excitedly. The day had been unseasonably warm, and Nora thought ice cream sounded good, but Gwen called, "How 'bout margaritas instead?" and Tina raised her fist in salute.

Jade just shook her head. "Fallon and Ranger Reva will each drive. But we need to be back in two hours. We break camp early tomorrow, and there'll be lots of prep. Get it?"

"Got it," the group called.

"Good. Now let's get going."

Hannah, Delores, and Kennedy rushed to Fallon's car, leaving Nora, Gwen, and Tina to ride with Ranger Upshaw in her Ford Lariat. Nora anticipated a lecture on their lack of enthusiasm, but Upshaw fiddled with the radio as soon as they were underway. "There are two oldies stations in this valley," she said. "One only does pre-2000s, but the other is pretty good." Turning up the volume, she began to hum along to the tune that came on. The song was almost to the chorus before Nora recognized it. "Complicated" by Avril Lavigne.

Her brother Rudy had called her in to watch Lavigne's video on MTV one day. "I'm going to marry that girl someday." Rudy had said that about every singer or actress that he found intriguing, but in this case, Nora could see the attraction quite clearly. She hadn't really listened to the words at the time but had begged Rudy to loan her a tie so she could imitate Avril's look.

Gwen's reminiscence sounded entirely different. "This is exactly what my sister taught me about life," she yelled from the back seat before bellowing out the words.

The lesson fit what little Nora knew about Gwen, someone whose life seemed full of falls, breaks, and taking. By the next chorus, they'd all joined in, laughing at each other's rock star moves in the confines of the truck's crew cab. When the song was over, Gwen leaned out her window and howled like a coyote.

"What do you think that song was about?" Upshaw asked Nora when a commercial came on.

Feeling like she'd been called on to explain a poem back in English class, Nora stuttered. "Uh. I…not being fake, I guess."

"I think so too. Like, not pretending to be something you aren't just to impress others." Reva spoke softly, cutting her a quick glance before turning onto a paved road. Nora sighed and looked out the window. Lecture delivered, however subtle.

The small town of Cascada was nestled about twenty miles below base camp. After they parked at the Swift River Ice Cream Shop, Gwen and Tina occupied themselves with primping as Nora casually scanned for Fallon's car.

Upshaw apparently noticed. "Fallon told us about running out of gas and how your father saved her," she said, opening her door. "He must be a really great guy, and from what Jade says, he's certainly taught you a lot. Anyway, I gave Fallon the staff credit card to fill up her tank since she's driving for the crew tonight. She'll be here in a minute." Upshaw squinted into the back seat, adding, "Don't waste time, girls. We need to head out before long. And along with the best ice cream in town, this place has nice souvenirs if you're interested." She disappeared into the shop.

Nora clenched her fists. Of course Fallon had painted her father as her savior, the lone hero. She lurched from the truck, slamming the door hard enough that Gwen and Tina stared after her as she threw herself onto one of the benches outside the shop door.

Gwen came over and patted Nora's arm. "That's bullshit," she said. "I asked for an advance, and they flat said no."

"Yeah," Tina said. "How come Fallon gets special treatment?"

There was no way Nora was going to tell them what had actually upset her, so she kept quiet. Right then, the classic red Cadillac pulled in next to Upshaw's pickup, the radio blaring another oldie, "Livin' La Vida Loca." Hannah hopped out of the passenger's side, still singing along. Fallon cut the engine but let the song continue to serenade the parking lot. Delores got out of the back and opened the driver's door, laughing as she pulled Fallon out, taking her hands and dancing with her. Nora tried not to stare at the way Fallon moved and how her face lit up when she smiled.

"I guess having Mae's credit card makes everyone else happy," Tina said.

The song ended, and Jade began herding them inside. "I have an idea," Nora said, working to unclench her jaw.

❖

Upshaw's pickup arrived at Firecamp, and Mae watched them all pile out before looking down the road. "Where's Fallon?"

"She told us to go on, so we all rode together." Delores worked her fingers through her hair, pulling out a few pine needles she'd gotten from riding in the truck bed. She turned to Kennedy. "Maybe she wanted to buy something more personal at the shop? It was really sweet of her to treat us all."

Kennedy nodded. "And it fits that she didn't say anything about it ahead of time."

Nora hid her smirk. Fallon wouldn't have said anything because she didn't know she was buying until after the fact. Then Upshaw walked over to Mae, handing her the credit card. "I'm sure she'll be right behind us. She should have a full tank of gas. Check the charge when you have a minute, and we'll know how much to deduct from her first paycheck."

Oh no. Nora swallowed before biting at her thumbnail. If Upshaw had already taken the card back, that meant Fallon couldn't use it to pay for the ice cream. Gwen evidently reached the same conclusion and started to laugh.

"What?" Tina asked, always a little slow. Gwen whispered in her ear, and Tina giggled. "No way!"

"Shut up," Nora said, running a hand through her hair. She recalled the paltry bills that Fallon had offered her father. Without that card, she could be charged with theft and an arrest on her record would… "Shit." Nora groaned. Once Fallon realized what was happening, why hadn't she told someone, stopped them from leaving? Nora turned abruptly to Jade, who'd walked up behind her.

"What's going on, Nora? What are your buddies laughing at?"

"I think…" Nora took a breath. "I think there may be a problem."

On the way back to town, Nora truly wished Upshaw would yell at her or at least give her a real lecture. The falling darkness made her feel worse. "It was supposed to be a joke," she offered. "My brothers and I pulled this kind of stunt all the time."

"So you said." Reva's voice was low and solemn. "We'll see how funny Fallon thinks it is."

Earlier, Nora had only needed a few words of explanation before Gwen and Tina were nodding in agreement. Tina went to distract Fallon by asking about her car while Gwen had passed the word to everyone that ice cream was Fallon's treat, admonishing them not to say anything, as Fallon wanted it to be a surprise. Nora had spoken to the lady behind the counter, telling her that the tall woman with long hair at the end of the line would be paying for everyone. When Fallon had come in, Tina had sidetracked her by pointing out various items in the shop. Everyone else had left with their ice cream before Fallon got to order, and after several more minutes, she'd appeared in the doorway, murmuring something to Delores. Upshaw was outside as well, checking her phone. "We need to go," she'd called.

As Nora had watched, Delores relayed the message, and Upshaw had started getting out of the truck. Fallon had waved from the doorway. "Please take everyone with you. I should be there before too long," she'd called.

"What is she doing?" Upshaw had asked.

"She said something about getting a different kind of surprise," Delores had said, hopping into the truck bed along with the others.

Now Nora cringed as the lights of the ice cream shop came into view. The red Cadillac was still parked outside, and Fallon's tall form could clearly be seen moving along an aisle of the shop. The owners were sitting on the bench outside holding hands.

"Hi, folks," Reva said as she approached. "We seem to be missing a crew member. She was last seen enjoying some ice cream, so we thought we'd check at the scene of the crime."

"Crime is right," the man said, standing as he gestured at Reva's uniform. "We've always welcomed your crews here because they've never shoplifted or tried to rip us off. Until now. Apparently, someone thought it'd be funny to stick that young lady with the bill for your entire group, and she barely has enough cash to pay for a single scoop."

"I apologize, sir. There was a misunderstanding about her having the staff credit card and—"

"It's my fault." Nora stepped forward. "I meant it as a joke, but—"

"A joke?"

Nora tried not to squirm under his glare.

"Well, I guess she didn't get the memo. She's been here since you all left, trying to work off what we're owed. She's washed the serving dishes and utensils, tidied our inventory, and now she's sweeping the floor. I'd hire her full-time in a minute, but she said she's hoping for something else."

Reva offered him the credit card. "Yes, sir. Well, I'd like to pay off whatever's left on our debt."

He waved dismissively. "The missus and I have had a real nice time sitting out here, enjoying the evening. Without lifting a finger, we're ready to open tomorrow, so I think we're even."

Nora wondered what it would take to even things between her and Fallon. But at Upshaw's gesture, she forced herself into the shop.

Fallon watched as she came down the aisle. "It was you?" Accusation and sadness mingled in her tone.

Nora opened her hands before clenching them again. "I'm really, really sorry. I honestly thought you still had the credit card. I knew everyone would pay you back once you told them what happened." She tried not to notice how tired Fallon looked as she swept the debris into a dustpan and emptied it into the trash.

"Am I paid up now?"

Nora gestured to the couple. "I think so. They seem happy to have had the evening off."

"That's not enough. I don't like owing anyone anything." Fallon stepped closer. "In fact, I was going to give you money for the gas your father gave me once I got my first paycheck. But now I think I should send it to him directly. I'm not at all sure you're trustworthy."

Nora looked away, surprised by how much that assessment hurt. Her gut tightened with the need to change Fallon's opinion. "That's not true. And I'll prove it to you, starting by working with you on your cutting technique." Fallon started to speak, but Nora pressed on. "You're doing okay, but I can make you better. Faster. Save you wear and tear on your body. Deal?"

Fallon shuffled her feet. Nora could practically hear the wheels turning in her head. "What if your buddies get suspicious of you spending extra time with me? I'm not going to let them get anyone else in trouble." Straightening, she stepped forward. "I mean it, Nora. I'll protect this program, even if I end up ratting on you in the process."

Nora shrugged, not wanting to admit she'd been so focused on making things right with Fallon that she'd forgotten about Gwen and Tina. "I'll tell them it's part of my punishment for pulling this prank on you."

"Are we all good here?" Upshaw asked from the doorway. Nora froze. How much had she heard?

Fallon bit her lip before nodding. "All good."

"Nora?" Upshaw said. "Understand that regardless of any agreement you and Fallon have come to, you'll have additional consequences for this stunt."

"Yes, ma'am."

❖

"Giving lessons to that buzzkill and KP for the whole first week? That's total bullshit." It was almost dark, but Gwen had declared she was dying for a real cigarette, so they'd walked far enough away from camp that the smoke wouldn't be detected. She'd dragged Nora along, claiming she'd get lost otherwise.

Nora didn't like it that Gwen still referred to Fallon as a threat, but it'd be a mistake to protest too much. "Well, it's like what Tina got, just in a different area. The thing with Fallon is for team building. You know, to make sure we can work together."

"Still." Gwen lit another cigarette off the one she'd finished, dropping the first one on the ground and kicking it aside. Nora picked up the butt and fieldstripped it before putting the filter in her pocket. "Oh my God. Are you turning into Smokey the Bear?"

"No, I'm turning into 'I'm tired of having my ass in a jam, and setting the forest on fire would be way more trouble than any of us could handle.'" Nora was about done with Gwen and her attitude. At least tomorrow, they'd be in their own tents, and she could get some space. Then a thought struck her. *Surely, they won't want me in with them.* Panic struck. She needed someone else to at least pretend they wanted to bunk with her. *Someone like Fallon?* "Get in. Get out. Get on with your life," Nora told herself again.

The atmosphere in the cabin was decidedly frosty as the crew readied for bed, though not in terms of actual temperature. After bumping Nora's arm, causing her to drop her shampoo and brush, Kennedy mumbled something that might or might not have been "Sorry." Fallon took her turn in the restroom with Hannah, and Delores showed up to be with Nora.

After what felt like two solid minutes of Delores's glowering expression, Nora finally snapped. "What? If you've got something to say to me, say it."

Delores rinsed the soap off before toweling her face. "I hadn't pegged you for a loser, but now I'm thinking I might be wrong."

"Fuck you. You don't know anything about me."

Delores put her hands on her hips. "And why is that? Maybe because you've been too busy with your bad girl buddies to bother becoming a part of this crew. And, hey, if that's what you want to do with your summer, go ahead. We'd be better if you joined us—really *joined* us—but we'll be fine without you." Nora sniffed, watching the last of Delores's soapy water go down the drain. "But I promise you this, if you or your delinquent friends mess with Fallon again, you'll be more than sorry."

Gwen and Tina were due in next, so Nora couldn't linger. Was Delores aware of their illegal activities, or was she merely using an expression? Nora knew from her father that some minimum-security prisons had programs to train smoke jumpers, and her debate team had argued the viability of good works programs for minor criminals. Could Gwen and Tina have been given the option to avoid prison time by attending Firecamp? She had no intention of asking, but it didn't seem impossible, given their disregard for rules and animosity toward authority. But their crime couldn't have been anything more than a misdemeanor, like some lesser drug possession, right? Hearing footsteps outside, Nora quickly gathered her things.

"What's up?" Gwen asked. "Did your previous bathroom buddy kick you to the curb?"

Nora shrugged. "Who cares? We're out of here tomorrow anyway."

"Yeah, about that," Tina said, her voice a bit squeaky. "Gwen and I would like to share a tent. Just the two of us. That okay with you?"

Relief rushed through Nora like a soothing breeze, but she remained composed. "Oh, sure. No problem." If she'd been alone, she might've skipped out of the restroom in celebration. This was her chance to peel off their unpleasant company and revert to the Nora she'd planned to be. Alone, self-sufficient, and drama free.

❖

Due to their late night at the ice cream shop, Nora and Fallon had to pick up their field gear from the equipment hut the next morning.

Hal smiled as they entered. "Ah, my twin towers." At Nora's grimace, he sobered. "Too soon?"

"She doesn't want to be lumped in with me," Fallon said.

"Rugged individualist, huh?" Hal put his chin in his hand and regarded her.

"Don't presume to speak for me," Nora said to Fallon, but there was no bite in her tone. After Tina's announcement, she'd had a restful night's sleep, and it felt like today was her first real day at Firecamp.

"Will that be two single tents or one double?" Hal asked, looking back and forth between them.

"Singles," they said together, and Hal laughed.

"Okay, got that message loud and clear. Who's the adventurous type, and who's more traditional?"

"That depends on what we're talking about," Nora replied, and Fallon nodded.

"Tents," Hal said, and Nora responded, "Traditional."

"What's adventurous about a tent?" Fallon looked to Nora, who shrugged.

"I'm glad you asked," he said. "And I think this one is going to be right up your alley." He pulled out a large, deep green roll. "It's a new style. Could almost be a two-person size, and here's why. The entrance has a vestibule that's tall enough for even you to stand up in. Lots of room for gear too. Then you pass through another flap into the sleeping area, with a traditional low ceiling to keep the body heat in. A little more storage in there but not much. What do you think?"

"I think it sounds great," Fallon agreed. "I'll take it."

"Attagirl."

Nora suppressed a smile at Fallon's expression as Hal loaded them down with sleeping bags, thermal ground pads, toolbelts, shirts with the SCC logo, and heavy jackets. She looked like a kid at Christmas.

When he offered her a new pair of boots and thick socks, she sat on the equipment hut floor to try them on.

"Perfect," she declared. "You're really good at this, Hal."

"Yeah, well…" He trailed off but seemed pleased. "You're gonna wear out those jeans pretty quick. Got another pair?"

"Nothing that fits. I've lost some weight lately."

"If you'll let me measure you, I'll have the right size in tough khakis waiting when you come in for break."

Fallon's eyes misted. "You'd do that for me?"

"Honey, we take care of our sawyers here." Hal touched her arm. "Hell, I'd even do it for Miss Traditional over there."

Fallon smiled weakly, her emotion evident. "Could I…could I get another bandana for my hair?"

Hal returned with a pack of three. "You be careful with that mop around those saws."

"I will. Thank you so much."

When they left the equipment hut fifteen minutes later, Hal had added a quilted flannel shirt and a thick hoodie to Fallon's stack, and Nora caught herself smiling at seeing her so happy. Hardening her tone, she said, "Remember, this is a government program, and your tax dollars support it. It's like you had a savings account, and now you're withdrawing some in the form of goods."

Fallon's smile faded. "Maybe so. But I still appreciate it. Sometimes you don't get anything back for what you've given."

CHAPTER FIVE

Only Fallon's concern about getting lost if Ranger Reva got too far ahead kept her from stopping to admire the view at each turn along the winding dirt road. The trees were much taller here, the ground covered with pine needles and scattered cones, the air cooler. Occasional rocky outcroppings showed an incredible variety of geology that she couldn't begin to identify but still found exciting to look at. The snowcapped mountains looked even more magnificent than they had in Ranger Reva's photos.

When they began passing through a remote residential area, a twinge of apprehension tempered her exhilaration. How would she perform on their first job? Jade had explained they'd start by cutting trees that were growing too close to the narrow roads in the community before thinning forty yards into the forest along the perimeter of the development to accommodate firefighting equipment. A few folks who were out walking or working on their property waved as they passed, and Fallon waved back.

"You're such a nerd," Gwen said from beside her. Tina laughed from the back. Fallon glanced in the rearview mirror. Delores and Kennedy were both asleep.

Jade had assigned seating for the ride, probably to encourage new friendships, but Fallon already knew friendship wasn't going to happen with her and Gwen. Or Tina. She bit back the retort that came to her mind: *I'd rather be a nerd than a bitch.* Instead, she asked, "Why are you here if you hate everything about it?"

Gwen pulled her sunglasses down and looked over them. "Some of you volunteered. Some of us got drafted."

"What does that mean?"

Gwen sighed as she turned to the window, keeping her voice low.

"Never mind. But remember our deal. Tents are even easier to hide shit in."

Fallon gritted her teeth. Everything about Firecamp was great, except for Gwen's threat. She'd spent some of last night trying to think of a solution that wouldn't risk any of the others, but drugs could already have been planted in someone's gear for all she knew. Maybe she could find time to talk to Jade about wanting to be a crew leader and present the situation as a hypothetical. Like, "What would you do if..."

After another twenty minutes, Reva's brake lights came on. The road ended in a wide turnaround at the edge of a dense forest. Fallon waited to pull in until Reva had maneuvered the truck and cargo trailer to make unloading easier. Everyone climbed out, and Reva directed them to begin with kitchen equipment. No sooner had they started than Gwen announced she needed to go to the bathroom. "Me too," Tina chimed in.

Reva gestured toward the forest. "There it is. Don't get lost."

Working alongside Delores and Kennedy, Fallon carried coolers and cookstoves and boxes of pans and utensils to an area where Jade was standing. Pulling out a tarp, Jade indicated three trees that made an almost perfect triangle. "This will give us shelter when we cook and eat and keep things covered at night."

Fallon was tying one corner of the tarp high on a trunk when she felt the other side lift.

"I see you got tall duty," Nora said. "Can't let you have all the glory."

Fallon grinned. "I don't mind sharing with you." A light blush showed on Nora's cheeks, and Fallon realized her comment might be misinterpreted. Time for a subject change. "How was your ride over?"

"Fine." Nora secured the last side of the tarp. "Ranger Upshaw is quite impressive. I can see why you like her."

"She is, and I do," Fallon remarked. "She told me about this program and encouraged me to come. But I don't *like her*, like her, you know?"

Nora didn't react. "See you later," she said, walking over to where Reva was sorting out the rest of the gear. Fallon could have kicked herself. They'd had a nice moment in the equipment hut, but Nora repeatedly made it clear she didn't care about anyone else. Fallon needed to keep that foremost in her mind.

Kennedy and Delores brought in another load, and Kennedy pulled on Fallon's arm. "We want to talk to you." Delores nodded.

Hannah was helping Jade arrange the kitchen supplies while Nora and Reva organized the tents and bags. "Let's go get another load," Fallon said.

At the truck, Delores looked around, checking that the forest was clear before speaking. "I heard part of what Gwen said."

Fallon stiffened. "Oh, that. Uh, I…" She couldn't think of what to say that wasn't a lie.

"When she talked about hiding shit, she didn't mean bathroom shit, did she?" Kennedy asked.

Picking up another container from the cargo trailer, Fallon shook her head. "I can't talk about it now. Please. It's…we could all get in trouble."

Delores and Kennedy exchanged glances. "Uh-huh, yeah," said Kennedy, lifting a box. "But we'll get back to this later, understand?"

Fallon swallowed. "Okay."

When the unloading and sorting was finished, Ranger Reva called everyone together. Looking over the group, she said, "Where are those two nitwits who went to the bathroom forty-five minutes ago?"

The whole crew formed a search line, walking into the forest as they called out, staying within sight of each other. They'd walked only a few dozen yards when Fallon heard a sharp whistle. She angled in that direction and came upon Nora glaring at Gwen and Tina, who were perched on the side of a large boulder.

"What the actual fuck?" Nora was saying in a stage whisper.

"We got up and couldn't get down," Tina explained. Gwen giggled. Even from where she was, Fallon could tell they were high.

"You guys better unfuck yourselves real quick, or your asses are going to be kicked out." Nora didn't sound the least bit amused.

"Yeah, shit," Gwen said. "Well, at least help me."

"No," Fallon said, walking toward them. "Jump."

Gwen rolled her eyes. "You've got to be kidding."

"Best case, you'll hurt yourself and have an excuse for not making it to camp."

"Ooh," Tina said. "That's smart." Standing, she launched herself off the rock, lighting on her feet in catlike perfection. "Stuck the landing," she announced, arms above her head.

"Well, hell." Gwen stood but lost her balance almost immediately and slid down the rock on her backside. Her screams alarmed the rest of the crew, and by the time they arrived, Gwen was sobbing, propped between Nora and Tina as they tried to help her walk.

Fallon made it a point not to look at Delores or Kennedy as Tina said, "Gwen got hurt, and we made a wrong turn. Then we heard you calling and saw that we'd nearly made it back to camp. I'm sorry if we worried you," she added, looking at Ranger Reva.

Reva studied them critically before stepping forward and hoisting Gwen over her shoulders. "This is something you all need to learn, but not tonight," she said, oblivious to Gwen's cries. "It's called the dead man's carry. Jade, you're our first aid expert, so you follow me. The rest of you, get your tents up before the sun goes down."

❖

From her campsite, Fallon watched Nora pitching her tent under a huge Douglas fir. "There sure are a lot of dead branches in that tree, Nora."

Nora gave her a look. "I know what I'm doing. Don't worry about me."

Fallon sighed. Of course Nora would take her concern the wrong way. At least she was happy with her site. Situated in front of a good-sized rock that offered shelter from the wind, it only needed a little grooming to be level. But after unrolling her new tent, she realized she should have asked Hal for instructions. It was hard to know which end was up. She set the stakes aside and tried holding the poles with one hand while raising the tent with the other, but the canvas was too heavy. Not knowing how the whole thing should look when it was assembled made it difficult to determine where to start. After a while, she gave up and wandered over to where Jade was chopping something in their group kitchen, having already finished with her tent.

Hannah, Delores, and Kennedy all had single tents too. Gwen and Tina were sharing, and their setup resembled a high-tech pup tent that looked big enough for four. They were farthest from the rest of the group. Appropriate, given all the trouble they'd already caused. What would it would take for Jade to get involved in disciplining them?

"Can I help you with something?" she asked Jade.

Jade smiled at her. "That would be great, thanks. Did you get your tent finished?"

"Not yet. I, uh, I haven't quite figured out how it goes."

"Hey, I can help you." Kennedy poked her head out from the bright orange dome she'd set up close to the kitchen.

"Thanks. But finish what you need to do. I'm in no hurry." Fallon stretched her arms over her head, breathing in deeply. The smell of pine and clean mountain air was invigorating.

"I'm through." Hannah appeared from behind her. Her mustard-colored tent had a slightly more elongated shape. "And you won't believe how quickly it gets dark once the sun goes behind that mountain." She gestured up the hill. "Let's take a look."

The three of them walked past Delores, who was setting poles on an extra flap in front of her tent, giving it a covered porch entry. "That's really cool," Fallon said.

"Thanks. Where's everyone going?" Delores asked.

"Falcon needs some help with her nest," Hannah said, giving Fallon a wink.

They all laughed, but it seemed congenial, not like mean, derisive teasing, so she grinned at them. Nora was wiping dirt from her hands as they passed. She eyed the group and looked up the hill where Fallon's tent was unrolled. "Having trouble with your adventurous model?"

Fallon shrugged, and Kennedy waved Nora off. "Thanks for offering, but we got this."

Nora gave a huff and went into her tent.

By the time Fallon's tent was up and had been appropriately admired, it was nearly dark. She found her flashlight, and the group headed back to the kitchen. If she'd been alone, Fallon would have checked on Nora but was pleasantly surprised to find her standing by Jade and stirring one of two bubbling pots on a propane cooktop.

"That smells wonderful," Hannah said.

"Good. It's a thick stew with chicken, and we have a vegetarian version also," Jade said. "And Nora has been an excellent sous chef."

"All right, Nora," Delores said, and the group applauded. Fallon appreciated the way everyone was so supportive. Well, almost everyone.

"Let's eat." Jade indicated the other folding table where bowls, utensils, and foil-wrapped bread waited.

The line formed quickly, and Nora ladled out generous portions. Fallon positioned herself at the end. "How's Gwen?" she asked as she was served.

"Just scratches, a few pretty deep, though. She and Tina are probably sleeping it off."

Fallon was pleased when Nora filled her own bowl and followed her to the circle where the crew sat. "This is delicious," she told Nora. Looking into the darkness where Tina and Gwen's tent was located, she asked, "Should we take a bowl to them?"

Nora sighed. "That would be a nice thing to do, but I've had enough of their scene for today. I'll save some in case they wake up before we finish here. If not, they can have it in the morning." Fallon made a face at the thought of stew for breakfast, and Nora laughed. "Hey, if you're hungry, you're hungry. Besides, you know the two choices in Firecamp dining?"

"Take it or leave it?" Fallon asked.

"Exactly."

There'd been a sign with a similar sentiment in the Sunshine Diner. The memory still stung, but the pain of it seemed less sharp in this new place surrounded by prospective friends.

Once they finished eating, Jade said, "After all the excitement earlier, we didn't have time to talk about schedules for our various tasks, but we can do that tomorrow. Right now, we need to clean up and get some sleep. But first, we have a tradition in the Women's Plus Crew. Each evening, we'll go around and tell something we did well and something we want to improve on."

"I need to improve on managing that tent by myself," Fallon said.

"No," Hannah and Delores protested together.

"We're here to help each other," Kennedy added. "And I'm learning that's something I like doing."

"Maybe that's what you're doing well," Fallon suggested, pleased by Kennedy's smile in response.

Nora stood, announcing, "If I'm going to do something well, I'll need to start my KP now."

"Wait a second, Nora," Jade said. "I want to keep this conversation on track, so let me answer too. I think I did well on arranging the kitchen, but I need to improve on letting newbies wander off into the forest by themselves." She rubbed her forehead, looking toward Gwen and Tina's tent. "They could have been really hurt or worse."

Nora walked to Jade, putting a hand on her shoulder. "No. Those two are grown women, and they have to take responsibility for their actions."

Nobody spoke as the words settled. Then Hannah, Delores, and Kennedy began making sounds of agreement, and Jade smiled. A weight lifted from Fallon's chest. Maybe Nora's defense of Jade meant she was moving away from Gwen and Tina's influence.

❖

Fallon had volunteered to cook breakfast the next morning, and she admitted that part of the reason was hoping that Nora would be her sous chef. Instead, she found Gwen going through the kitchen supplies, half of which she'd put on the ground.

Fallon cleared her throat, and Gwen jumped. "Is there something in particular you're looking for?"

"Anything resembling some goddamn coffee would be great." Gwen still managed to sound like the injured party, though she seemed to be moving without any ill effects from her adventure. She was wearing a tracksuit and filthy tennis shoes, but her hair was brushed and her face was clean.

Fallon handed her the can of coffee and pointed at the large, old-style percolator that Gwen had discarded. "I'm sure most of us would like some, so make a whole pot." After lighting the cookstove, she turned her back, finding eggs and bacon in the cooler.

Fully expecting Gwen to ask for help, she was gratified to see her measuring scoops into the basket. Apparently, Gwen had experience with older devices. When she asked about the water, Fallon simply pointed to the Igloo. Once the coffee was on, Fallon asked, "Are you hungry?"

"Starving."

Fallon dug into the second cooler, finding the bowl of leftover stew from last night. "If you can't wait for breakfast, there's this."

Gwen took a small bite, and her lips twisted. "Where's a microwave when you need one?"

"Miles and miles from here, I'm afraid."

Gwen ate some more, watching as Fallon put bacon on a griddle. "You make me nervous."

Fallon turned to look at her. "What do you mean?"

"Everyone wants something. With most people, it's pretty easy to tell what it is. People like you who act nice are just better at hiding your agenda."

"I don't have an agenda."

Gwen smirked, wiping her mouth as she finished the stew. "You sure? I think you want Nora to stop hanging with us and be your friend, right? You want to protect your little Firecamp crew. Oh, and you've clearly got a thing for Ranger Reva, but I can't quite tell if it's a gay crush or hero worship."

"That's not...I don't—" Fallon sputtered.

"You'd better turn that bacon before it burns." Nora's voice came from behind her, and Fallon flinched. How much had she heard? Nora pointed at Gwen's bowl. "There's another one of those for Tina. Maybe you should get her up. We've got to do actual work today."

"Speaking of agendas, here's another mystery." Gwen jerked her thumb in Nora's direction. "She says she wants to party but never does. Pretends she wants to go it alone but joins in on every Kumbaya moment. And why didn't I see you checking out any of those hunks in the dining area?" She took a step closer. "Who are you crushing on, Nora?"

"God, shut up, Gwen." Fallon turned the bacon and reduced the heat before taking the bowl from her. "Get some coffee or go get stoned or whatever it takes to make you a decent human being." When Gwen turned away laughing, Fallon added, "And don't be late for breakfast. We're not keeping back food for you anymore."

"No one died and made you Firecamp queen, did they?" Gwen called back as she walked toward her tent.

Fallon turned to Nora, who was busy scrambling eggs in a bowl. There were a dozen things she wanted to say, but Nora had the closed-off expression that Fallon was learning to recognize. "Am I still getting my chainsaw lesson today?" She hoped her voice carried the casual tone she was going for.

Nora didn't look up, but she stopped scrambling. "Sure, if you want."

Fallon flipped the bacon again. It was ready, and so was she. "Yeah, I do."

❖

Fallon gripped the chainsaw as Nora stood close, her hand wrapped around Fallon's. Between the heat of Nora's body and the press of her touch—even through their thick gloves—Fallon had to concentrate twice as hard.

"Thumb under the bar and fingers against it," Nora said.

"Right. Okay."

Nora released her grasp, adding, "You don't need heavy pressure, just steady. You work the saw, don't let it work you." She shifted, and for a quick second, her breasts slid across Fallon's back. It was all she could do not to close her eyes at the thrill of it. "Keep your balance, but let your weight help move the blade."

"Uh-huh."

Fallon hoped she wouldn't be asked to repeat any of this because she wasn't thinking about her saw. Or anything that wasn't the excitement of Nora's nearness. Then Nora eased away, gesturing at the chain. "If your blade pinches, what's the first thing you do?"

Fallon tried to recall the instructions in Jade's friendly voice, which was less distracting than Nora's sultry alto. "Turn the saw off."

"Yes. Very good." Nora came around to face her. "Now tell me one thing to do to avoid getting injured by kickback?"

"Uh…" Fallon told herself to focus on anything except those deep brown eyes, but it was futile.

Nora lightly thumped her on the arm with her fist. "Come on. This is important. A lot of injuries happen due to kickback."

Fallon liked this Nora. Serious but not angry. Offering instruction, not criticism. She'd found Nora attractive from their first meeting, but she'd been too nervous about making it to Firecamp to think beyond that. She detested how Gwen and Tina had pulled Nora into their web, but given the conversation before breakfast, maybe their bonds weren't as tight as Fallon had thought. She smiled, and Nora tilted her head. "Why are you smiling? Did you think of the answer?"

Fallon shook her head, her gaze never leaving Nora's. "No. Something else. I was thinking about you."

Nora's brow furrowed, and her lips parted slightly. Fallon followed the movement of her mouth. They both stilled. Fallon had never been with someone her height, and she was enjoying looking directly into Nora's eyes until Nora's expression hardened, and she took a step back.

"Oh no. Uh-uh." Nora turned and walked toward the camp. Fallon didn't bother to call after her.

CHAPTER SIX

Nora was pissed, mostly at herself. Why had she played with Fallon, behaving more physically than normal? She'd seen the way Fallon looked at her at times, with what was almost certainly a spark of interest. And once she'd confirmed that Fallon was gay, she'd let her mind go there on occasion. But she had no interest in pursuing anyone, even for a fling, which was why it was better for her to be around unquestionably heterosexual Gwen and Tina. *Get in. Get out. Get on with your life.*

The triangle sounded, and Nora swore. Time to go to work. She sincerely hoped she wouldn't be paired with Fallon today.

Relieved when Hannah called "Over here, partner," Nora went to stand beside her while she finished putting on her PPE. Fallon was doing the same next to Tina. Nora assumed Jade had given out posts, and they'd rotate teams in the same way they'd been assigned their chores in camp. This part of the sawing job would be easier since the local fire department had consulted with the community in marking trees that needed to be felled. The teams spread out to their positions along either side of the road, and Jade called "Firing up" as her saw roared to life. Soon, the air was filled with buzzing and the sappy smell of cut pine.

It might have been only an hour when Jade walked by, making sure each team stopped for a water and snack break. Nora and Hannah had already traded off sawing and swamping once, and they'd made decent progress in their section. "How's Fallon doing handling all the sawing?" Hannah asked Jade.

"She's holding up okay, but I'm going to trade out with Tina so Fallon can swamp for a while. Unless one of you would like to volunteer to switch?"

Nora made a point of not looking where Fallon and Tina were working. "I'll trade. Fallon can come work with you, okay, Hannah?"

"Sure."

Nora ate a protein bar and drank some water, feeling the beginnings of sore muscles as she watched Jade walk down the road to tell Fallon about the change. As Nora arrived at their worksite, Tina practically fell on her.

"Thank God. Tell me you'll have mercy. Fallon was working like someone possessed." She pointed at the slash pile that the community would later turn into chip mulch. Nora estimated that Fallon's work was almost double hers and Hannah's. And Fallon had been the only one sawing. Nora was no stranger to rejection-fueled energy but couldn't help worrying for Fallon who, as far as she knew, had no previous experience with this kind of physical labor. Tina pointed at the adjacent property. "Fallon went there. Through the woods. Maybe she had to pee or something."

Or maybe she wanted to avoid seeing me. Nora sighed. "Okay. Let's hit it."

It was dusk when Jade came to collect them. "Good work for the first day. Kennedy's already started on dinner, so let's all get ready to eat and then we can talk about how things went."

Washing up was everyone's first priority. Sawing and swamping were both hard, dirty work, as sawdust and pine needles combined with layers of sweat. Fallon wasn't at the cleanup station, and it wasn't her turn to help with cooking, but Nora couldn't tell if she'd gone to her tent. As the crew gathered for their meal, she overheard Kennedy talking to Delores. "Fallon came by and got one of those electrolyte drinks and two more protein bars. She said she wasn't coming to dinner."

Nora stepped in like she was part of the conversation. "That's not good. I'm sure she's tired, but she needs to eat to reenergize her body. Otherwise, she won't be worth shit tomorrow."

"That's so sympathetic of you, Nora." Kennedy put her hands on her hips. "Tina said Fallon was working like she had something to prove. I don't suppose you know why."

Nora held herself still. "All I know is, this work we're doing can drain you to the point that you'd rather sleep than eat. But that's dangerous. Ask Jade."

"You think you know everything. Go ask her yourself."

Delores cleared her throat. "Come on, you two. This pissing contest isn't solving anything." Kennedy turned to the Dutch oven and stirred the contents. Delores tried again. "That smells really good, Kenn. When will it be ready?"

"We can eat it now, but it can cook for a few more minutes until everyone"—she gave Nora a sideways look—"or whoever wants to eat is ready."

That did it. Nora strode to the table of plates and utensils. Returning to Kennedy, she held out a dish. "I'm ready now."

Kennedy sighed and dished out a portion.

"Looks great," Nora said, grabbing a napkin and walking out of the kitchen area.

"Hey," Kennedy yelled, but Nora kept going. When she reached Fallon's tent, she called out, "Fallon? It's Nora. I've got food here, and I want you to eat it before you sleep."

There was no answer, so she tried again. "Fallon. Wake up. You can eat in there, but you need nourishment." She pulled the zipper on the big flap.

Faintly, she heard, "Go away."

"I will, I promise. But let me leave you this food. Kennedy made it, and it looks delicious."

Stepping into the vestibule, Nora was impressed by the height. It would be nice to change standing up. Fallon's boots lay on one side, her new flannel shirt on the other. Nora knelt at the smaller entrance to the sleeping area. "I want to hand this to you and watch you take a bite. Then I'll leave."

After several long seconds, she heard the inside zipper. Fallon's upper half appeared in the opening, her hair loose over her shoulders, framing her full breasts beneath the thin undershirt she wore. Nora swallowed. "Here." She held out the plate.

Fallon's hand shook as she leaned over to take a bite.

"Did you refill your water? You'll need to hydrate as much as you can."

Fallon nodded as she swallowed. "This is good. Thanks."

"I'm glad. And listen, I'm sorry about…about earlier."

Fallon coughed and turned away, grabbing her water bottle. After she drank, she said, "I should be the one apologizing. You've made it clear what you want and what you don't. Just know that you have other options here beside Gwen and Tina if you want friends. Other options besides me, even."

She ate quickly while Nora tried to work down the lump in her throat. Why did Fallon have to be so damned nice? "Okay, well, you need to take it a little easier tomorrow," she said as Fallon finished eating. "Tina said you were working really hard."

"Tina wouldn't recognize hard work if she went out on a date with it," Fallon said dryly. Nora couldn't help laughing. Fallon handed her the plate. "Thank you for this. You were right. I feel better already."

Nora let her fingers touch Fallon's before she said, "Good. I'm glad." She wasn't going to think about why she did that or how nice it felt.

❖

The days blurred into a routine as they worked their way down the roadside. Nora appreciated Jade's leadership, how she ensured the chores and assignments were balanced between firm and fair while accounting for individual talents and concerns. An exception seemed to be that Fallon and Gwen never worked together. Was that at Fallon's request? Jade also guided Nora and Kennedy through their differences, and they'd reached concessions on both sides. It didn't come out in their talk, but Nora suspected that Kennedy had a crush on Fallon, and her animosity was at least partly due to worrying about competition. Nora had mixed feelings about being considered part of a contest she hadn't entered. But at least she and Fallon had reached a kind of truce as well.

When Nora lay in her cozy tent, listening to the early sounds of nature stirring before the rest of the camp began to revive, she found her mind at peace for the first time in a long time. The discontent that had been her frequent companion at home had been replaced by a sense of purpose and a feeling of accomplishment, an unexpected benefit of her determination to win this bet. She didn't foresee years of exchanging Christmas cards with the crew, but at least the atmosphere was generally one of camaraderie and encouragement. Under different circumstances, she'd be carrying her camera everywhere, utilizing the wonderful morning light for her photography, but that wasn't her job here. Besides, people acted differently toward someone taking pictures.

After dressing, Nora followed sounds and smells to the kitchen. Since Fallon seemed to be an early riser as well and was able to cook a group breakfast as if she'd been doing it her whole life, Jade had offered her the job in exchange for being excused from other tasks. Nora had finished her disciplinary KP, but she regularly joined Fallon to mix ingredients or flip pancakes. It amazed her how adept Fallon was at cooking for eight people, how she broke eggs with one hand and could fry bacon in one pan and vegetarian sausage in the other and never burn anything.

"How did you learn to cook this way?" Nora asked as Fallon browned slices of toast on a square skillet.

Fallon hesitated. "A genuinely nice man taught me," she said, her voice quiet. "In my previous life."

Nora would have laughed, but Fallon seemed serious. "So you've been reincarnated?"

"Oh. No. Well, I don't know about that, but I meant in my life before being here at Firecamp."

Nora would have pursued it, but Kennedy came shuffling into the kitchen area, followed by Jade, and the morning meal was underway. Except for Hannah, who sometimes talked to herself if no one else would join in, Fallon's breakfasts were generally a quiet, though welcome, start to the day. The rest of their meals became somewhat routine as well. Tina proved to be proficient at helping to pack lunches, even remembering who was vegetarian. Since Gwen flatly refused anything to do with cooking, she was generally called upon to do cleanup. Dinner duties were rotated through the rest of the crew, and they held their nightly "What did I do well, and what can I do better?" conversation as the meal cooked.

The first week, everyone headed to their tents as soon as dinner and cleanup were done. Between getting up with the sun and spending all day sawing and swamping, no one had the energy for extended evenings. Into the second week, Nora was still following the pattern of her early bedtime when she heard extended conversation from the kitchen area.

"We should have special sawyer names," Hannah said.

"Yeah, like Speedy or Killer," Kennedy agreed.

Nora slowed as she recognized Fallon's laugh. "Those are a little extreme, don't you think? Shouldn't nicknames fit our personalities or our looks or something more specific?"

"Easy for you to say, Falcon," Delores teased. "You've already got your sawyer name."

Nora kept walking, recalling that she'd heard some of the group using "Falcon" before. She actually liked it and wondered if Fallon did.

The days grew longer and dinners became livelier as the crew got accustomed to laboring for hours in their gritty clothes. Delores had a lovely voice, and when she sang a familiar song, those who could carry a tune would join her, sometimes creating unexpected harmonies. Kennedy seemed to have an endless supply of jokes, most of which were R-rated but not nasty. Sometimes Nora stayed up and chatted, but she had a sense that the conversation was a bit more stilted when she was there. She attributed the discomfort to her association with Gwen and Tina, even though the two of them consistently retreated to their tent as soon as cleanup was finished. Nora couldn't tell if no one else noticed or if they simply didn't care. What struck her as most peculiar was that Fallon never took part whenever the talk turned more personal. No one tried to draw her out during these discussions, and Nora wondered about the cause of Fallon's silence, especially knowing her belief about the importance of family.

They'd just finished breakfast on Sunday of the second week when Jade stood to announce that it would be a cleanup day.

"I do cleanup every day," Gwen whined.

"So you're not interested in going into Kamberto for a visit to the community showers, followed by the laundromat?" Jade asked.

Whoops and cheers greeted the offer. "My jeans are about to stand up by themselves," Delores said, and Hannah added, "I was thinking of shaving my head rather than going through another day with it dirty like this."

Jade nodded. "Okay. Twenty minutes to gather laundry and shower supplies. Reva's on her way. She's going to meet with the community managers and the fire marshal to evaluate our work thus far, so we'll all ride together in the truck."

There were four shower stalls in town, and the crew voted Jade should go first. She opted to include Nora, Tina, and Gwen in the first round. Nora grimaced as she slipped on the only clean thing she had to wear after showering, her dress. Gwen and Tina were in dresses as well, and their heels gave the appearance of two friends going clubbing, while Nora wore Chucks with her more conservatively tailored outfit.

She saw Fallon examining her with wide eyes. Taking a step closer, Fallon lowered her voice. "Would it be inappropriate to say you look exceptionally nice?"

Nora's face flushed. "My mother insisted that I bring this outfit. I'm sure this wasn't how she imagined me wearing it, but it's the least dirty thing I have."

"It looks exactly the right amount of dirty to me." Fallon grinned, and Nora wondered if her sudden self-consciousness was obvious.

While the second group finished their showers, Nora sorted her laundry. Gwen was on her phone conferring with Tina about some destination, and Jade was going over the grocery list. When Kennedy appeared, followed by Hannah, they were both wearing what looked like pajama bottoms and oversized, long-sleeved T-shirts.

Nora started to tease them about coordinating their outfits when Fallon emerged. Her long hair was down, still damp, and she wore a tight, hooded, tunic-style coverup over board shorts. She was obviously braless. Nora suspected they all were and probably commando too, but she was having a hard time not staring at Fallon's breasts, which were even more exquisite than she remembered. *Shit, I need to get laid.*

The crew settled in at the laundromat, and Jade left to get gas and stock up on groceries after Delores promised to look after her clothes. Fallon threw her garments into a washer, revealing a stack of books in her basket.

"I brought these in case anyone wanted to do something besides sit," she said.

"The way we've been working, sitting sounds pretty good to me," Kennedy said as she looked into the basket. "But judging the books by their covers, I'd say you're into sci-fi."

"Yeah, I…" Fallon hesitated. "I used to like the escape."

"Used to?" Nora asked. "And now?"

Fallon smiled shyly. "I like my reality a lot better now."

"Aw." Hannah gave her a side-arm hug. "We like you too, Falcon." She pulled out a book with a spaceship on it. "But if you're actually offering, I'll take one."

"Good choice, Gabby."

"Why do I get the feeling that sitting around a laundromat reading is not something new for you, Falcon?" Delores asked.

Fallon held up her hands. "Guilty as charged." She leaned over, pulling out a book with a view of an intricate galaxy. "But this is the story for a secret romantic like you, Lolo."

Gwen turned from the washer she was loading. "What's with these names? Are you all into secret identities or something?"

No one responded, busying themselves with putting their clothes into the machines. Apparently, the conversation Nora had heard earlier had progressed to the creation of actual nicknames. Nora privately thought the affectionate terms were cute, though she couldn't help wondering if they had one for her. She looked into the basket, seeing only one book remaining. Feeling an odd resentment that Delores had nabbed the secretly romantic book, Nora started to turn away until

Fallon said, "That is one of my long-time favorites. I've bought three different copies over the years because I keep giving it away."

"Maybe you wouldn't be broke if you weren't such a soft touch," Gwen jeered.

Everyone had probably seen Fallon speaking to Reva when they arrived, obviously getting another advance on her paycheck in order to make use of the shower and laundry facilities. But leave it to Gwen to be rude enough to mention it. Nora had the sudden impulse to slap the smug expression off her face.

But Fallon cocked her head as if thinking. "You know, I came to Firecamp thinking I would change. That I'd get tougher, meaner, more self-serving. You've helped me realize that's not who or what I want to be. So thanks."

Kennedy and Delores edged closer, clearly concerned about the growing tension in the room. Nora stepped into the space between Fallon and Gwen. "*Seafire*, huh?" she read, picking up the novel and observing the water-themed cover. "You're a long way from the ocean, you know."

Fallon's mouth opened slightly. "Yeah, I—" She turned to the washer, which had just started, clearing her throat. "I know."

Nora wondered at the change in Fallon's tone, but before she could think of what to say, Gwen announced, "The only thing I want to read is the label on a bottle of beer." She grabbed Tina's hand. "Let's go for a walk and see what we can find." Pausing at the door, she looked to Nora. "You coming?" When Nora shook her head, Gwen said, "Then move our stuff to the dryer after it's done." Without waiting for an answer, she pulled Tina out the door.

Fallon watched them until they disappeared. Standing abruptly, she pulled out her phone. "Shit. Kenn, lend me your phone, will you? I forgot to charge mine at the showers."

Nora looked up from the book Fallon had given her. "Mine's at about seventy percent if you want—"

"Here." Kennedy was already handing Fallon hers. She moved closer, whispering in Fallon's ear.

"Thanks." Fallon tried the passcode, then gave a thumbs-up. She didn't look at Nora. "This might be my chance to level the playing field." Fallon was out the door without another word, walking cautiously in the direction Gwen and Tina had gone.

Hannah looked around. "Where's she going?"

Delores cut her eyes at Nora before answering. "We think Gwen and Tina were blackmailing Fallon about something, don't we, Kenn?" As Kennedy nodded, Delores lowered her voice. "She wouldn't tell us, but Kenn said it had something to do with drugs."

"Fallon's doing drugs?" Hannah asked incredulously.

"No," Nora said. She hated the idea that someone might mistake Fallon's intentions. "She overheard Gwen and Tina talking about their stash. Gwen threatened to plant something on the rest of you if Fallon told."

"That's some real nice friends you've got," Kennedy said.

"We're not friends. They're just who I was hanging around with. But not lately, if you hadn't noticed."

At Kennedy's derisive grunt, Hannah said, "But why did she want your phone?"

"Fallon told us after dinner last night. She partnered with Jade yesterday, and they worked out a plan. She's going to try catching them doing something against camp rules and take some photos for proof," Delores said.

Nora thought about the unsophisticated woman who had run out of gas on her way to her dream opportunity because of her willingness to help someone else. "I don't think Fallon should try that on her own. Gwen especially isn't someone to mess with. I'm going with her."

"Why you?" Kennedy asked. "I could go with her."

"Because Gwen and Tina trust me...sort of." Nora hated to admit it, but it was true. "If there's trouble, I might be able to smooth things over."

After glancing briefly at the others, Kennedy nodded, and Nora hurried to catch sight of Fallon. About three blocks down the main street, she saw her leaning against the side of a brick building, her face expressionless as she watched Nora approach. The sign out front featured a drunken-looking bird holding a large bottle and the words *The Green Parrot Lounge*.

"Are you joining them?" Fallon inclined her head in the direction of the bar.

Nora leaned against the bricks next to her. "No, I'm here as an impartial witness."

The corner of Fallon's mouth quirked. "To what?"

"To whatever it is that you're doing here."

Fallon's eyes met hers. "What do you think I'm doing?"

Nora took a breath. "Exactly what you told me you'd do. You're trying to protect the program and the people in it."

Fallon nodded. "And you're okay with that? At the cost of—"

She was interrupted by the creak of the bar door opening. Giggling and footsteps came in their direction. Before Nora knew what was happening, Fallon had pulled up her hood, and turning her back to the street, she took Nora in her arms and pressed her against the building, drawing Nora's face into her neck. Nora was overwhelmed by the woodsy scents of pine and dirt clinging to Fallon's clothes and the distant remnants of chainsaw oil and sweat on her skin. She couldn't move. Or was it that she didn't want to?

"Ooh, romance." Tina's giggly voice filtered through Nora's turmoil. "Look, Gwen."

"Who cares?" Gwen sounded tipsy enough not to realize what was going on. "The pot shop is this way. Come on."

The footsteps faded. Nora wondered if Fallon's arms had always been so strong or if it was a result of the last two weeks of work. More slowly than she would have thought possible, Fallon's grasp loosened, and she turned toward the street.

"They're gone." Fallon's voice was rough. She took a step back. "That was terribly abrupt, and I apologize. I didn't want us to be seen, you understand?"

"Sure." Nora cleared her throat. "Let's go."

Fallon put a hand on her arm. "Slowly. They're a little unsteady, but they'll still notice us if we get too close."

"Right." Nora stopped. "I'll follow your lead."

Fallon grinned. "Well, that'll be a first."

"The second, if we count what just happened," Nora countered, conscious that Fallon was also very cute when she blushed.

Forty-five minutes later, they came through the door of the laundromat, and Fallon walked directly to Kennedy. "Thanks, dude. I think we got it."

"Your phone's charged now. I can AirDrop the photos over if you want."

"That would be perfect."

By the time Gwen and Tina came stumbling in, everyone else's clothes were folded and ready. Gwen looked around, her eyes bleary. "Where's our stuff?"

"In the dryers," Hannah gestured. "Nora moved it over like you asked."

Gwen put her hands on her hips, glaring at the crew. Her gaze landed on Kennedy. "I can't believe y'all are so stupid that you didn't think to take them out and fold them when they were done."

Kennedy stepped into Gwen's face. "Do I look stupid to you?"

Gwen seemed to realize she'd gone too far. "No, um, you look like someone who already finished their clothes and had time to relax."

"Damn right," Kennedy said.

"Kenn, would you mind taking everyone outside?" Fallon said.

Fallon moved toward Tina, thumbing through her phone as the rest of the crew gathered out on the sidewalk. Gwen grabbed Nora's arm as she passed. "What the fuck is going on?"

"How should I know?" Nora replied, displaying the cover of *Seafire*. "I've been sitting here reading my book." She joined the group outside, studiously watching for Jade in the pickup that pulled up soon after.

Fallon emerged from the laundromat, followed by a very subdued Gwen and Tina.

"Clothes inside. Bodies outside," Jade called cheerfully. "Except you two glamour girls can sit up with me," she added, indicating Gwen and Tina. "That okay with you, Nora?"

"Just fine."

As they arranged themselves among the groceries in the truck bed, Nora suspected that the lightness she felt had to do with more than being clean.

CHAPTER SEVEN

Fallon turned over again, frustrated that sleep wouldn't come. Initially, she'd attributed her restlessness to lack of physical activity. Compared to most days at Firecamp, today had been practically sedentary. But her mind kept sending reminders of the feel of Nora's body against hers. The fresh scent of her shampoo, combined with the smooth material of the dress that clung to her in all the right places, had embedded themselves in Fallon's memory and were playing on a loop in her thoughts. She'd admitted to herself on more than one occasion that she found Nora alluring, but before, it had always been abstract, like appreciating a beautiful painting she could never afford. Having held her took that appeal to a whole other level of physical awareness.

She played through it again, her surprise at having Nora join her and how Nora's casual lean against the wall next to her had set Fallon's heart rate soaring. So much so that when the creak of the bar door and the tipsy giggling had announced it was Gwen and Tina, pulling Nora to her had seemed like the most natural thing she'd ever done. Afterward, and despite her immediate apology, she'd half expected Nora to slap her or cuss her out. But in rerunning the incident now, she could feel Nora's momentary surrender.

That astonishing feeling was keeping her awake. Nora giving in to her. Wanting her?

Fallon sighed and shifted, agitated. It was one thing to have plans or even dreams, but such yearning was useless. She'd heard Nora talking one night after dinner about her intention to finish college in Arizona. She envisioned it as mostly desert, although she knew there were higher elevation areas in that state too. But why anyone would go there when they could stay in a beautiful location like this, Fallon couldn't imagine. It didn't matter what she thought, though. After all, she'd never included someone like Nora in her own prospects, mostly because she'd been by herself way longer than she'd ever been with someone else.

She tried to think about the future, as she'd always done when the present seemed unmanageable. After dinner, Jade had told them their work on the road had been exemplary, and they'd begin the next phase of their task tomorrow. It would be different, she warned them, sawing in the forest. The trees would be closer together, and unlike their last cut, where the road was their escape route, each step would have to be carefully planned. They'd be working farther apart to minimize any possible accidents, but that meant it would be harder to get help if someone got into trouble. "You'll be counting on your partner more than ever, so I'm not going to assign teams for this week. Since you know each other pretty well by now, you can pick who you want to work with. And I'd be happy to work with any one of you. Talk it over and let me know in the morning."

After Jade had said good night, Gwen and Tina went to their tent without comment. Shortly after, Nora had excused herself and walked toward her tent. The rest of them sat quietly. Everyone knew Gwen and Tina would partner up. Next to Jade, Nora was the most experienced and should have been working with the person who needed the most help. But Fallon hadn't been able to stop thinking of sitting next to Nora in the truck bed, of Nora's thigh against hers, of Nora's hands as she'd tried to keep her dress from blowing, and how Fallon had wanted those hands to be hers and for the hemline to be going up, not down.

"I'll partner with any of you," Kennedy had offered, but she was looking at Fallon when she spoke.

"Same," Delores had said.

Hannah had nodded, and Fallon had said, "Me too," though she'd very much wanted to team with Nora, just to spend time together talking about their next cut and watching the way Nora's arms flexed as she worked the chainsaw.

Now she wasn't sure it was a good idea. Maybe it was best to keep admiring her from afar, as they said in books.

She hadn't gotten much sleep, but Fallon couldn't lie there anymore. She'd started breakfast when she heard someone come up behind her. "So who are you going to work with, Falcon?"

Nora's voice was softer than usual and husky from sleep, but what struck Fallon was that Nora had never called her by her sawyer name before. Frozen in place, Fallon couldn't bring herself to turn. She wondered if Nora could hear her breathing. A sound in the woods drew her attention, and Jade appeared in front of her. Fallon knew her face was flushed with emotion, but apparently, all Jade saw was uncertainty.

"Fallon's working with me for today. I need to show her some things about leading a group that's doing wildland cutting. Who are you working with, Nora?"

After the slightest pause, Nora said, "I'm not sure. Hannah and I have always gotten along, so maybe her?"

"Great. Let's see what the rest of the crew has decided after we have breakfast."

❖

Walking through the forest, Fallon felt her equilibrium returning. Following as Jade led the crew, she watched how different areas were assigned and helped mark which trees to cut by spraying a dot of bright blue paint at eye level on each trunk. This was what she had come here for, she reminded herself. Not to lose herself over someone who had other plans.

It took the better part of the morning, but Fallon began to distinguish the different tree species and find the sick or crooked or what Jade referred to as "worst offenders," small trees that had sprung up too close to established ones. She explained how those types would never get much bigger but would steal much-needed nutrients from their older neighbors.

Nora and Hannah were assigned to the area closest to camp. Jade had consulted with Nora after breakfast, and they'd sketched out who should be where, settling on Nora at one end and Jade on the other. "What about Gwen and Tina?" Jade had asked.

"Put them next to you. They should be as far from camp as possible," Nora had said. Jade had simply nodded.

Watching as they talked, Fallon concluded she'd made entirely too much of what had happened yesterday. Her emotions had carried her into some place that didn't actually exist, like escaping into science fiction novels. The most important thing was Nora's willingness to reduce the possibility of Gwen making good on her threat. That explained everything else. And as for this morning, Nora regularly helped with breakfast, and her question was just a question. Using her sawyer name was a way to tease, to say everything was okay between them, no matter how sexy it had sounded.

After the other teams were set, the buzzing of chainsaws and cracking of splitting timber filled the air. As she and Jade set out their supplies, watching with amusement as Gwen and Tina argued over who would do what, Fallon appreciated being able to focus on the job.

Jade stopped before firing up her saw, surprising Fallon when she asked, "Is everything okay between you and Nora?"

"Uh-huh, sure," Fallon said quickly. "She actually helped me with something yesterday, so…yeah."

"Good. Her skills are a real asset."

Tina's voice carried over to them. "It is *so* my turn."

Jade shook her head. "I'd really like to see those two make it through the program, but I have my doubts. What do you think?"

Fallon stopped herself from mentioning Gwen's threats. "I want to see everyone make it. But do you think they have enough motivation?"

Jade shrugged. "They need to work on their commitment to the team. It's too soon to tell, but I've seen Firecamp make a real difference in people's lives. Still, old habits can be hard to break."

"Do you think I'll succeed in this program? I mean, can I become a leader like you?"

Jade turned to face her. "I'm sure you can make it through Firecamp. But don't try to be a leader like me. Be a leader like you." She spread her hands. "You have a good way with people, and your confidence will come in time. If you practice taking charge, you'll find it feels more natural. I know you can do it, but I'll try to help you get there quicker."

Fallon nodded, tightened the bandana on her hair, and they went to work.

❖

Nora didn't appear to help with breakfast the next morning. When she joined the rest of the crew to eat, she looked tired. Fallon stood behind her as they scraped their dishes into the trash. "You doing okay?"

"I'm fine." Nora's voice had a snappish tone.

"I missed you this morning. As my assistant, I mean."

Nora didn't turn. Her voice was low, but Fallon heard every word. "Yeah, but you're not missing me on your team, are you? I'm sure you and Jade are getting along just fine."

"She's helping me—" Fallon had to stop as Kennedy came up beside them.

"Are you the new teacher's pet, Falcon?"

Nora moved away without another word. Jade's words about taking charge echoed in Fallon's head. It was time. She punched Kennedy lightly on the shoulder. "You know how you asked me what I wanted to do after Firecamp? Well, I think I've figured it out. I don't want Firecamp to end. I want to be Jade someday. That's why she's working with me. So I can learn at least some of what she knows."

"Very cool, dude." Kennedy punched her back. "You'd be a great Jade."

Fallon made a point of not trying to see where Nora had gone. It didn't matter. She had a job to do.

Her day got better when Jade had her assign the areas for the crew and only made one correction about the alignment. Fallon worked with each team to decide which trees to cut, and Jade marked them without comment.

"You did good," Jade told her before they started work.

"Thank you for the opportunity. I know I have a lot to learn, but…"

"You'll get there. Don't worry."

At their lunch break, Jade had Fallon walk through the other teams' areas and assess their progress. Fallon reported that, as usual, Gwen and Tina were behind, but everyone else was doing well. "That's good to hear. Let's finish limbing this one, and you can start felling that worst offender right there."

Jade was repositioning the running saw with one hand, her other holding the limb. Fallon bit back a warning. The crew had been trained to always turn off the saw first, but maybe someone with more experience could do it this way. While trying to steady herself, Jade unintentionally pressed the trigger, and the saw bucked, coming down on her arm. In two steps, Fallon was beside her. She expanded the rip in Jade's sleeve to reveal a nasty, jagged gash on her forearm, blood bubbling from just above her glove.

"Shit," Jade said through gritted teeth.

Fallon pulled the bandana from her hair and wrapped it around the wound. "I'll get our equipment. Can you walk to camp?"

"I'll be okay. Let's keep working." Jade wiped her eyes. "Damn, that stings."

"No, we're not going to keep working. I'm driving you to base camp, and they can decide if you need stitches."

"Fallon…" Jade sounded exasperated, but Fallon wasn't having it.

"That's what you'd do if it was me, so no argument. Get going. I'll be right behind you."

"Someone else has to be in charge if we're both gone," Jade insisted. "Nora is the obvious choice." She pulled a radio off her belt. "Give her this so she can communicate with base camp."

Fallon stopped briefly to inform each team what had happened. When she got to Nora, she signaled to her and Hannah to cut their saws. "Jade's hurt. It's not life-threatening, but she may need stitches. I'm taking her to base camp. I've told all the others that you'll be in charge, Nora. Keep them working, but take it easy on them tonight. I probably won't be back until well after dinner." She handed her the radio. "Use this if you need to contact base camp."

Nora took a step toward her, shock evident on her face. "Okay, I—yeah, okay."

Fallon nodded, moving in the direction of the camp.

"Tell Jade…" Nora began, and Fallon turned, walking backward. "Tell her we're all thinking of her and not to worry. We've got this. And you—"

Fallon stopped.

"Be careful driving back here. Lots of wildlife and stuff in the mountains at night, you know?"

"I will. Thanks."

Jade held pressure on her arm as she leaned her head back and closed her eyes. It was still light, so Fallon drove as quickly as she dared. Apparently, Nora had thought to inform base camp of their arrival because Reva and Hal were both waiting when she pulled in. Reva took Jade to medical, and Hal escorted Fallon to the dining hall. He sat with her while she ate, and Fallon updated him on the crew's progress. Reva joined them just as Fallon finished.

"How is she?" Fallon tried to keep the apprehension out of her voice.

"Pissed," Reva said, and Hal laughed.

Fallon gestured impatiently. "Did she need stitches?"

"Yeah, five." Reva patted her arm. "You did the right thing bringing her in. It took a while to clean out the wound. Lots of grit, sawdust, wood pieces, even fabric from her shirt."

Fallon felt her stomach lurch. She took a deep breath. "But she'll be able to come back, right?"

"Oh, sure. Tomorrow. The doc wants to look at her first thing in the morning." Reva held out her radio. "Call your crew and let them know what's going on. Then we'll find you a place to crash for the night."

Hal patted her shoulder as he went by. "Stop by the equipment hut before you leave. I've got those new pants for you."

"Thanks." Fallon stepped outside the dining room, ready for some fresh air. "Nora?" she called into the radio. "Nora, this is Fallon. Over?" She felt silly, but wasn't that what you were supposed to say?

"Fallon. We're all here. How's Jade?"

Nora didn't say *over*. "Five stitches, but Reva says we can come back tomorrow after the doctor looks at her in the morning."

"So not tonight?"

"No. Sorry."

"It's probably best. Tell Jade everyone says hi. We'll see you both tomorrow."

"Okay. Tell everyone good night for me."

Nora must have held up the radio because a chorus of voices yelled out. She heard "good night" and "sleep tight" and "see you tomorrow."

Fallon wanted to ask Nora how the rest of the day went. She wanted to tell her how strange it felt being away from…everyone. But she simply said, "Roger. Over and out." She found Reva in her office. "Would it be unfair for me to have a shower before bed?"

Reva grinned. "I think the rest of your cot mates would appreciate it."

❖

Fallon joined Jade in staring at the sky. Jade had been banned from sawing for the rest of the week, and Hannah had insisted on covering the bandage on Jade's arm with plastic wrap to keep it cleaner. Fallon worked with Gwen and Tina to get them caught up or by herself with Jade looking on. They had two days to finish the forest cutting, and making their goal was questionable.

"I don't like the look of those clouds." Jade pointed at the dark billows boiling up behind Brownly Mountain. "Weather forecasts for this range are notoriously unreliable, but thunderstorms were predicted for the area. Let's shut it down for today and get everyone fed and in their tents as soon as we can."

Nodding, Fallon jogged off, spreading the word to the different teams scattered through the forest. The air quieted, and as the group cleaned up, the rapidly cooling wind sent everyone back to their tents for an extra layer. Hannah had planned a more elaborate, stroganoff-style dinner but agreed to offer burgers as a quicker alternative. Dinner was a more subdued affair than usual as the intensifying wind made everyone focus on eating.

"Make sure your tents are staked down tight, and check the trench around them, digging them out again if necessary," Jade told the group.

"Why can't we go sit in the car until this blows over?" Gwen was trying for her usual, indifferent tone, but Fallon thought she detected a bit of panic.

"The storm might last for a few hours, and it's not practical for eight people to try to sleep in one vehicle," Jade said. "We'll be fine in the shelters we have. I just want to make sure everyone is prepared."

Gwen fussed so much about having to clean up with a storm coming that Delores offered to help. As they secured the kitchen supplies, Fallon went over to help Tina tighten the rain fly on the big tent she and Gwen shared. Another gust of wind brought the first few drops of rain, and after a boom of thunder echoed around them, Jade yelled, "Everybody inside!"

Fallon was only marginally damp by the time she made it into her cozy tent. She'd strung a makeshift clothesline across one side of the vestibule, and after draping her hoodie over it, she finished undressing and crawled through to what she mentally thought of as her bedroom. She was safely snug in her sleeping bag by the time the hard rain hit and flashes of lightning illuminated the deep green of her tent.

She'd been dozing for a time, relaxed by the feeling of being toasty and dry, when a loud crack nearby was followed by a scream. She hurriedly stepped into her pants and threw on her hoodie, not bothering to put on socks before pushing her feet into her boots. Shrugging into her rain jacket, she unzipped the vestibule, shining her flashlight into the darkness. Rain was still falling but lighter now. Another light came from the kitchen area, and she started in that direction, but Jade came toward her as someone from down the hill called again for help.

"It's Nora," Fallon said, and they both ran. Through the drizzle, they could see a large dead branch had blown onto Nora's tent, ripping through the material.

"Nora," Jade called. "Are you hurt?" Fallon's heart pounded as she waited for Nora's reply.

"I don't think so, but I can't move." Nora's voice was shakier than

Fallon had ever heard it, but simply knowing she could answer was relief enough. "There's something on top of me. Something besides all this rain."

"Okay. Hang tight. We'll have you out of there in just a minute." Jade gestured to Fallon, and they each grabbed an end of the log. Maybe it was adrenaline or that deadwood was lighter, but Fallon felt like she could have lifted five times that much to free Nora.

Once the limb was moved, and Nora's torso became visible, Jade said, "Stay with her. I'm going to get a couple of the others in case we need help."

Fallon knelt, laying a hand on Nora's arm. "Hey, it's Fallon. Wiggle your fingers and toes and see if you can move a little."

"Yeah. I think I'm all right." Nora sat up slowly. Suddenly, her face changed. "Oh God. My camera." She began looking around frantically.

"Don't move too fast. You might have an injury that—"

"Please, help me. I don't care about anything else in here, but I've got to find…" Nora trailed off, feeling along the sides of her sleeping bag. "It was down by my feet. In a black case."

Fallon crawled forward, shining her light into the rip in the fabric. Between the rain and the water sluicing off what remained of the tent, she hoped the camera case was waterproof. When her hand brushed against something hard, she grabbed it. Nora was struggling out of her soggy sleeping bag, her quick, shallow breathing growing increasingly unsteady.

"Here." Fallon held it out. "Here. Is this it?"

Nora's fingers closed around hers, slipping onto the object. "Yes. Oh, thank you. Shine your light on it, please."

Fallon did as she was asked, ignoring the chill penetrating her rain jacket. The tremor in her hand made the beam unsteady, but Nora was absorbed in her examination. Fallon caught sight of Nora's firm breasts, hard nipples showing through her soaked sleepshirt. She looked away as voices began coming nearer.

Nora sighed. "I think it's okay. This is a hard-shell, waterproof case, and I don't think it got damaged."

"Good. Let's see if we can get you both out of here."

Once they stood clear of the tent, Fallon took off her raincoat and put it over Nora's shoulders. "Are you always so chivalrous?" Nora asked, slipping her arms into the sleeves. Her whole body was starting to shake with the cold.

Fallon shrugged. "It's a habit I can't seem to break. Even when it works against me."

Hannah's voice reached them first as several lights bobbed toward them through the rain. "Oh my God. Where's Nora? Is she all right?"

"I'm okay," Nora called back.

Delores gave a cry as her flashlight illuminated first Nora and then her tent. "Oh, Nora. Your clothes and everything."

"They'll dry," Jade said. "The main thing is that Nora's okay."

"For sure," Kennedy agreed.

Another flash of lightning made everyone flinch. "Gwen and Tina have enough room to put you up for one night," Jade said, motioning at the large pup tent on the other side of the kitchen. "Do you need to get anything else first?"

Nora shook her head, and the crew headed toward Gwen and Tina's site.

"Hey!" Jade called loudly. "Gwen. Tina. Wake up." When there was no response, Jade thumped her fist on the rain fly. Big drops flew everywhere as she called, "Wake up. We've got a problem."

Shuffling noises came from inside, and Gwen's voice murmured something indistinct. Then, Tina asked, "What?"

"Nora needs to crash with you, just for tonight."

As the shuffling continued, Nora turned to Fallon, putting the camera case in her hands. "Would you keep this for me? Please?"

Her voice quavered seemingly from the cold, but Fallon understood what she meant. Gwen and Tina couldn't be trusted around something so important. "Of course."

The tent zipper moved, and Tina's head poked out. "What's going on?"

Jade explained what had happened. "Nora needs to stay with you for the rest of the night. We can get her new equipment from base camp tomorrow."

Gwen's voice came from inside. "We don't have enough room."

"What do you mean? You have the biggest tent here," Kennedy said. Jade shook her head as she put her hand on Kenn's arm.

"Well, our stuff is everywhere, and there's no place for her," Gwen insisted, her voice muffled.

"Sorry, Nora." Tina's head disappeared, and the flap zipped shut.

Nora took a step back, looking away from the group. "It's fine. I'll sleep in Fallon's car."

"No." When Nora looked at her with a frown, Fallon added, "You won't be able to dry off or get warm in there. It might be kinda close, but we'll fit in my tent."

"Listen, Nora. I can stay with Fallon," Kennedy offered. "Just give me a second to grab my stuff, and you can sleep in mine."

The rain picked up, and Jade directed the group to the kitchen area, the steady barrage of water on the tarp making conversation harder. "It's your call, Nora. Whatever makes you most comfortable. But you need to decide before we're all soaked."

Nora wrapped her arms around herself before turning to Fallon. "You sure you don't mind? I'm getting really cold, and I want to get out of this weather."

"It's fine," Fallon said, resisting the urge to smile. "And thanks for the offer, Kenn."

"We'll sleep in an extra hour in the morning," Jade said. "Everyone get dry and warm as fast as you can."

Delores murmured, "Nice try, homie," as she and Kennedy walked toward their tents.

"Let me know if you need anything," Hannah said, giving Nora's arm a squeeze.

Everyone dispersed, and Fallon and Nora quickly shook off as best they could before stepping into the vestibule. "Stand here," Fallon said, ducking into the bedroom. After locating a fairly fresh towel and some long underwear, she returned, handing them to Nora. "Lucky for you, I've still got one clean pair."

"I can't take your last thermal layer," Nora protested through chattering teeth.

"You can, and you will. We're returning to base camp in two days," Fallon said. "Major laundry facilities there." She stepped out of her wet boots, putting them on the far side of the vestibule. "Dry off as best you can before you put them on. Then put the towel on the floor so you don't get dirty crawling through. I'll finish changing inside."

Before Nora could protest further, Fallon unzipped her pants and hung them on the line. "Put whatever you want on there too. Just make sure nothing drips into our boots."

She'd completely forgotten that she wasn't wearing any underwear, but the sudden draft from below, combined with the stunned look on Nora's face, brought her instant recall. "Oh my God...I...I was in a hurry when I heard you scream." Was it possible to literally die of embarrassment?

A wry grin replaced Nora's shocked expression. "Chivalrous to a fault yet again." She extended the towel, and Fallon grabbed it, covering herself. Backing into the Velcro flap of the bedroom, she tossed it back out once she was all the way inside.

"See you in there." Nora's voice shook with laughter. Or maybe it was the cold. Fallon was so flushed, she actually felt warmer.

CHAPTER EIGHT

So much for Nora's anxiety about some sophisticated seduction technique that had made her hesitate about staying with Fallon. Nora hadn't had a woman flash her like that since…well, ever. Thinking of Fallon's horrified expression, she would have laughed again, but she was too fucking cold. Dropping her wet sleepwear into a pile, she toweled off as quickly as her shaking hands would allow before pulling on Fallon's thermals, grateful they were her size. Her feet were freezing, but she wasn't about to ask Fallon for anything else.

Crawling through into the lower section of the tent, she could barely make out Fallon's shape. It looked like she was also wearing thermals as she shined her flashlight onto a stack of clothing. Her hair was down and falling loose.

"Ah!" Fallon turned. "Here." She held out a pair of thick socks. "They don't fit with my boots, so I haven't worn them."

"Bless you," Nora said, eagerly putting them on. She was still trembling, but at least she was dry now.

"Roll that way a little, and I can finish setting up the bed. Uh, sleeping area."

Nora chewed her lip to keep from smiling and moved against the flap, her eyes gradually adjusting to the small beam from the flashlight. Fallon had unzipped her sleeping bag to make a sort of mattress pad, the waterproofed exterior positioned to protect them from the damp that was bound to seep through the thick flooring of the tent. Watching her spreading a sheet and blanket, Nora asked, "Where did you get those?"

"They were in my car. I've had them in here for a while. Just haven't needed them."

Fallon was vague about her past, as usual, but this wasn't the time to pursue it.

There was a zipping sound, and Fallon said, "Luckily, I got this new down bag when I took Jade to base camp, but it's not waterproof." She arranged it over the top of the blanket like a comforter. "There."

"Nice," Nora said, having arrived at the point of being more interested in getting warm than she was worried about being close.

"Get in." Fallon handed her a pillow.

Nora slid under the layers, sighing with relief as her head sank into something soft. "I think you already put a pillow here for me."

"Uh-huh." Fallon's body eased in beside her. "Turn on your side away from me, and put that on your chest."

"Okay." Nora moved as Fallon directed. "But why?"

"Because I'm going to snug up behind and put my arms around you to heat you up. With the pillow, it won't feel so...personal."

"Intimate?" Nora asked.

"Yeah, that," Fallon agreed, doing exactly as she'd described. The length of her body melded against Nora's backside. Nora tried and failed to suppress a moan, but accompanied by her tremors, it sounded almost like pain. "Too much?" Fallon asked.

"No, I...no, it's fine."

"Okay if I hold you now?"

Nora nodded, feeling herself tense. Another shudder went through her, and then Fallon's arms encircled her. She lay stiff, expecting the anger she always felt when situations had gotten out of her control or at least the indifference of being next to a woman she barely knew. Distant thunder rumbled down the valley.

"Seeing that big branch on top of your tent really scared me," Fallon said, her voice close and low. "I'm so glad you weren't hurt."

Nora relaxed somewhat. "Is this your way of saying I told you so?"

Fallon chuckled, her chest vibrating against Nora's back. "Maybe I should, but somehow, I don't think it would help." She shifted momentarily, causing air to rush in between them. "Oh, and your camera's here by your head."

Nora heard the thunking sound as Fallon patted the case, but she risked pulling her arm out of the warmth they were creating to feel it for herself. "It's still okay?"

"I put it in here right away, and as far as I know, it's fine. Isn't it digital? No film to get ruined?"

Nora nodded, grateful they weren't facing each other as unexpected tears appeared. "You must think I'm the worst person in the world. I haven't even said thank you."

Fallon's arms tightened slightly. "You don't have to thank me, Nora. We may have different objectives, but we're part of a team. You'd do the same for me."

"You don't know that."

"I think I do. Now, let's get some sleep. Jade's only giving us one extra hour, and we used half of that getting in here."

Nora closed her eyes. She was safe, and her body had stopped shaking, but her mind was worried about what might happen in the night. Would she forget herself and touch Fallon inappropriately? What would she do if Fallon touched her?

"I can feel you thinking, Nora. It'll be okay. It's one night, then we'll figure something else out for you."

Nora took a deep breath. As she let the air out of her lungs, profound fatigue rushed in.

Sometime later, an ache on her side woke her. She needed to move. "Fallon?"

"Hmm?"

"My hip is sore where the branch landed. I need to turn over."

"'Kay." Fallon cleared her throat. Nora could feel her stretching her legs, trying to wake up. "Yeah." She rolled away, and Nora followed, careful not to lose the heat between them.

"Here's the pillow." Nora laid it across Fallon's body. After Fallon pulled it to her chest, Nora said, "Is it all right if I—"

Before she could finish, Fallon had taken her arm and pulled it around her. "More sleep," she said, her voice dreamy.

Nora forced down a laugh. She'd imagined an early riser like Fallon must be a light sleeper, but apparently, that was not the case. In less than a minute, Fallon's breathing was deep and steady. Shifting her arm away, Nora adjusted the pillow under her head and made sure the blanket was tucked in around her back. Then she was almost getting hot, so she wiggled down and took off the thick socks. Rolling them together, she tossed them into the pile at the edge of the tent. Fallon never stirred, and Nora smiled, trying to remember what Fallon had called it when she moved to heat them up. *Not spoon. Snug.* She wasn't cold anymore, but lying that way was so comfortable that she snugged closer, slipping her arm around Fallon. Fallon made a soft hum of approval.

Nora didn't remember falling asleep again, but she and Fallon both woke as voices from outside called "When is breakfast, Delores?" and "How late did you say we were going to sleep, Jade?" and "Hey, Hannah, is everyone else awake?" Bright light filtered through the green fabric of the tent.

Fallon raised onto her elbows. "Shit. What time is it?"

Nora yawned. "Late is my guess, based on that heckling out there." Copying Fallon's posture, she yelled, "Shut up, you heathens. Have pity on someone who practically froze to death last night."

The giggling increased. Jade's voice called, "Glad you're alive, Nora, but could I speak to Fallon, please?"

Fallon threw off their coverings, stripping off her thermal bottoms as she reached for her jeans. Nora was amused to see she was wearing briefs underneath those, apparently making up for last night's indiscretion. "I'm sorry, Jade. I'll be out and have breakfast going right away."

"That's fine, Fallon. As long as you're both all right."

When Nora emerged, dressed entirely in Fallon's clothes, including some clean pants that Fallon had insisted on loaning her, hints of coffee and bacon floated on the breeze. She stretched, amazed at how good she felt. Yeah, there had to be a bruise on her hip, but the air had that wonderfully clean, after-the-rain scent, and hearing Hannah's laughter always made her happy. She started to call to Fallon and tell her not to hurry, but the flap unzipped, and Fallon stepped out wearing jeans and a sweatshirt that badly needed another trip to the laundry. "You told me you had something to wear," Nora accused.

"I do have something to wear. And this is it." Fallon sniffed the air. "Are they cooking already?"

"I'd say so. You'd think they like you or something."

Fallon smiled, and something inside Nora expanded as if she'd been released from a too small container. Disregarding all the other things her mind unexpectedly suggested, she rested a hand on Fallon's arm. "I do want to thank you for taking me in last night. Besides being chivalrous, you're generous to a fault. But I truly appreciate being the beneficiary of that."

Fallon's expression changed from amusement to something deeper as their eyes met. Her mouth opened slightly as if she was about to say something. When the triangle rang, she sighed instead.

Nora realized her hand was still on Fallon's arm, so she gave it a quick squeeze before letting go. "I'm starving, and without coffee, it could get ugly."

"You? Ugly? Never."

Nora gave her a little shove. "Go on, Falcon. Let's fly to breakfast."

Jade grinned as they approached, and Hannah elbowed Delores. Kennedy busied herself with stirring the eggs. "Welcome, sleeping beauties," Delores said, pointing behind them. "Your dwarfs have been busy."

They turned to see Nora's clothes hanging from a rope stretched between three trees close to the front of their camp. Nora gaped, somewhere between embarrassed and humbled. At a subtle nudge from Fallon, she said, "Wow. Thanks so much, you guys."

"Your tent is definitely toast," Jade said. "But it seems silly to drive all the way back to base camp to get you a new one for one night." She tilted her head in the direction of Gwen and Tina's tent. "Once the Kardashians get out here, we can talk about how they might make room for you tonight." Jade paused, gesturing between them. "Unless…"

Fallon shrugged, her words sounding carefully casual. "I'm fine either way, Nora. It's totally up to you."

Nora couldn't bring herself to meet Fallon's eyes, but she tried to match her tone. "Well, if you're sure. I'd rather not move again for just one night."

Jade seemed pleased. "Good. That's settled."

Kennedy rang the triangle again, calling, "Everything's ready. Come eat."

During breakfast, Jade said, "Since we're breaking camp tomorrow, I'm going to spend the day packing as much of the kitchen as I can. Hannah's volunteered to help me, and Delores wants to team with Kennedy, so are you two okay to work together?"

"Sure," Nora said. Fallon nodded.

Addressing the whole group, Jade added, "Let's get as close as we can to finishing this section, but don't push yourselves too hard. I don't want anyone hurt on the last day."

As they began eating, Gwen and Tina appeared. While Tina filled her plate, Gwen motioned Nora aside. In a near whisper, she said, "Listen, I'm sorry about last night, but you know how it is."

"I'm not sure I do." Nora wasn't going to pretend it was acceptable to refuse someone in need. Especially after Fallon's example.

Gwen seemed confused but lowered her voice even further. "Our shit, you know. It would have been in plain sight. Plus, Tina's such a slob. Her clothes and stuff were everywhere." When Nora didn't respond, Gwen took her arm. "But listen, we're going to make it up to

you. We want you to hang out with us in Denver during our week off."
With a squeeze she added, "Nonstop partying without having to look
over your shoulder, right? And we know a guy we want to hook you up
with. Super hot and a good dancer too."

Nora hadn't given any thought to what she'd do during her time
off, other than not going home. No one else had mentioned their plans,
making her wonder if she'd gotten left out of other options. "I'll think
about it," she said to Gwen, who seemed satisfied.

Fallon was quiet as they walked toward their assigned area. "What
are you going to do next week?" Nora asked, genuinely curious but also
trying to get back to casual conversation.

"Oh, I'll be staying at base camp doing some training. What about
you?"

"I'm not sure." Nora could feel her indecision. "Gwen invited me
to join them in Denver, so maybe that."

Fallon tilted her head curiously. "Why don't you go home?"

"Why don't you?" she countered.

"Because I'm getting trained to be a crew leader." Fallon's tone
was a cross between patient and strained. "I told you, this is what I want
to do and where I want to do it. What about you?"

"It would be tough on Tyler to have me home for a week when
I'll just have to leave again. Not to mention all the interrogation and
harassment from my father. It's not worth it."

Fallon didn't respond for a few minutes. They reached the part
of the forest where they'd be cutting and found a spot to put their
equipment. Nora was priming her saw when Fallon said, "You didn't
ask for my opinion, but I'm going to give it to you anyway. I think
going anywhere or doing anything with those two would be foolish at
best and possibly unsafe. You'd be better off making peace with your
family."

Putting her saw down, Nora faced Fallon. "You talked to me
before about how wonderful family is, but you never say anything
about yours. Why is that?"

Fallon sniffed once, adjusting the bandana that held back her hair.
"Maybe I do have an idealized version of what family is. But if that's
true, it's probably because I don't have one. I'm an only child. My
father was killed in a hit-and-run accident when I was young, and my
mother died a couple of years ago."

Nora covered her mouth, wordless.

Fallon turned away and began priming her saw. "About a year after that, the man who was looking after me had a stroke, and he wasn't ever the same again. Eventually, his sister came and got him and took him to live with her somewhere in California. I got by, you know, but I feel those losses every day. I guess that's why I don't talk about it."

Nora laid a hand on her back. "I'm really sorry, Fallon. For what you went through and for being such a bitch."

Fallon didn't turn, brushing sawdust from her blade. "And I apologize for pushing you about your family. I guess we should get busy, don't you think?"

Nora recognized classic avoidance behavior, something she'd mastered years ago. "Sure."

Later, when Jade came by, reminding them to take a break, they sat on a fallen log, eating their protein bars and drinking water, catching their breath. Fallon caught her eye. Cocking her head, she asked, "Why don't you stay around camp next week and help with some of the incoming sawyers?"

"Generous and persistent. What a combo."

"I was simply offering you an option."

"I thought you might be looking for a tentmate for the week," she teased, amused when Fallon's color rose.

"Why don't you ever use your camera here at camp?" Fallon asked, the unexpected change of subject throwing Nora off-balance. "Most people like to have their picture taken."

"Should I assume your use of 'most people' means not you?"

Fallon sighed. "Yeah, I never look right. Too serious, I guess."

Nudging her, Nora said, "I bet I could make you smile." An even deeper color crept up Fallon's neck, making Nora grin. She liked playing with her this way. Fallon felt safe but somehow intriguing at the same time.

"Is that why you're going to school in Arizona? To make people smile?"

"I'm going to major in photojournalism with a prestigious program. Photography is something that lights me up inside. I've loved it ever since my brother Art gave me his old cell phone before he went off to hotshot training." She could clearly remember the wonder and the intensity of those first months. "Every day was new when I was experimenting with light and shape and learning about composition in pictures. Going to the grocery store or on my usual route to school, things like that rusted car on blocks I'd seen a hundred times would look different, extraordinary, highlighted with uncommon shading or color. I learned that by crouching or bending or lying prone, I could capture a sense of motion. It changed the way I saw the world."

"Then why are you at Firecamp this summer? Why aren't you out taking pictures?"

Knowing that Fallon had a positive impression of her father, she phrased her answer carefully. "My father doesn't think I can make a living at photography. He thinks it's unladylike to make all those contortions while carrying around a bag of equipment. But at the same time, he sees firefighting as strictly man's work. So we made a bet. I finish the whole summer at Firecamp, and he'll pay the last two years of my college tuition."

"Wow," Fallon said. "I can't believe he would take that bet knowing how good you are with the chainsaw."

She swallowed another harsh response. "That's just it, Fallon. He doesn't know me. Not anymore. I was his little buddy once, and I gave my older brothers a run for their money, trying to get a smile or a pat on the head. And then one day, with no explanation, he handed me off to my mother like I'd unexpectedly become worthless. I'll never understand it."

"And you can't forgive him, either."

"Could you?"

"I don't know, Nora. I haven't lived your life. But flavoring all your memories with resentment might only serve to make your future bitter."

Nora stood, her irritation flaring. "Well, if Firecamp doesn't work out for you, maybe you can go to work writing fortune cookies."

"Ouch."

Ignoring Fallon's comment, Nora fired up her saw. They worked until lunch when Kennedy came by, making her mood worse.

"Hey, you two. I think someone else got my sandwich. Would you mind checking?"

"Sure." Fallon went to their lunch bag, examining one of the meals. "Yep. Veggie special right here. Sorry, dude. I didn't even think to look."

"No worries. Just wanted to catch it before I had to go over to camp and get another one." Kenn handed over the sandwich she'd brought. "Here's yours." She cut her eyes at Nora. "Or whoever's."

Fallon looked at Nora. "I think we're about ready for lunch, aren't we?" When she didn't respond, Fallon checked the other sandwich before turning back to Kennedy. "These both look fine. Why don't you sit and eat with us before you head back? There's a log over there with your name on it."

"Thanks. I am really hungry." Kenn sat, and Fallon handed her a water bottle.

Nora tried to hide her annoyance. It wasn't that she didn't like Kennedy. Not exactly. She was attractive, with a pleasant face, her close-cropped hair and slight swagger giving off a small butch vibe. But Nora didn't appreciate the way Kennedy always seemed to be looking for ways to be around Fallon. And if she was honest, she didn't like the way Fallon seemed to enjoy Kennedy's company.

"I'm going to visit a friendly tree," she said, using their code for peeing in the forest. "I'll be right back." Fallon waved, her mouth full. Kennedy ignored her.

Relieving herself alone in the quiet of the forest, she recognized the need for an attitude adjustment. Again. It shouldn't matter to her what Fallon did or didn't do. It was true that events had conspired to derail her plan of going it alone at Firecamp. Initially, hanging out with Gwen and Tina had served to keep her less connected to the rest of the crew, but since they'd been camping, she'd let herself be drawn into more group interactions. And Fallon's kindness after the incident with her tent might have been why she was feeling unusually possessive. That needed to stop.

Having cleared her thoughts, she returned to the area where they'd been cutting, almost stumbling at the sight of Fallon and Kennedy sitting close on the same log, facing each other and holding hands. Her suspicion must have shown on her face because Kenn stood and stretched.

"Guess I'd better get back to work." She looked at Fallon. "Thanks. For everything."

"Anytime." Fallon began tidying their lunch remains as Nora's temper simmered.

"See ya, Nora," Kennedy called over her shoulder.

She managed a wave before turning back to Fallon. "What was that all about?"

"Oh, some personal stuff Kenn wanted to talk about. You'll hear more about it tonight." Fallon started her saw before Nora could say another word which, she decided, was probably just as well.

That night, when Kennedy stood and cleared her throat after dinner, Nora watched with interest. "I know this is our last night before break, but I wanted to add something to our usual conversation." Kenn shuffled her feet. "I've been thinking about this for a while, and I'd like to start using different pronouns."

Gwen looked up from her plate. "Oh no. Not some they-them bullshit."

Fallon rose and walked over to where Gwen sat. Even while towering over her, Fallon kept her voice calm. "Everyone is allowed their own opinion. But here, we also respect what someone is saying enough to not be rude. Can you handle that?"

Gwen tossed her head as if to say she didn't care either way, but she returned to eating without further comment.

Fallon turned back to Kenn. "Go ahead," and Hannah gestured encouragingly.

Kennedy took a couple of deep breaths. "In the book that Fallon loaned me, there was a character I totally identified with. They didn't say they were non-binary, but when we first talked about the story, Fallon used that term. I called one of the toll-free support groups last night and…yeah. It fits me like nothing else ever has." She kept her eyes down. "So I do want to start going by 'they' and 'them.'"

Delores got up and hugged Kenn, murmuring, "I know that took a lot of courage on your part. And if you'll be patient with us if we screw up, we're all in." She turned to look at the rest of the crew. "Right?"

Nora clapped along with them, a little ashamed for her resentment toward Kennedy. Gwen made a face as she passed on her way to her tent. Tina smiled, as usual, and Nora nodded at them both. Fallon's assessment of them as being dangerous to hang out with was undoubtedly a bit extreme. Denver was a big city, and Nora could find her own entertainment away from them if necessary. It seemed like every time she tried to reset her distance from the group, she got pulled in by some emotional scene, like with Kenn. She needed to return to the detachment she'd had at the start of Firecamp.

"Big day tomorrow, crew. I'll finish up here." Jade's voice broke through her musings.

Everyone took the hint, gathering last-minute items and calling good night as they headed to their tents. Nora had suppressed the fluttery feelings that had materialized throughout the day at the thought of sleeping with Fallon again, but they reemerged full force as they made their way over. "You go ahead in," she told Fallon. "Get things how you want them. I'll make sure Jade doesn't need any help."

She had every intention of doing that, but Fallon stopped her. "Look up."

Nora did, gasping as her vision swam at the incredible array of stars. She hadn't thought about the lack of light pollution in their forest habitat.

They stood silently, awestruck by the vastness. "I'm going to start learning the constellations next week," Fallon said, her voice low. "Reva said she'd work with me. Do you know any?"

"Some," Nora admitted, fighting against the memory of sitting on her father's lap as a toddler, trying hard to envision the images he'd named as he pointed. "That's the Big Dipper. If you make an imaginary line from the last two stars in the cup, it'll lead you to Polaris, the North Star. It's the first star in the handle of the Little Dipper." She indicated the path, and Fallon stepped closer, trying to follow. "Do you see it?"

"I'm not sure." Fallon sounded doubtful.

"If you're going to learn constellations, this is the place to start." She drew the imaginary line again. "You know why Polaris is so important, right?"

"It can be used for navigation because it never changes location." Fallon sighed. "That's what I want. Something steady I can count on. A North Star life."

Nora looked over, realizing how close they were. An almost magnetic pull lured her gaze to Fallon's lips. What would it be like to kiss her? Would they start out soft and sweet and work their way to deep and passionate? She spoke before thinking better of it, shifting to meet Fallon's eyes. "Some*thing* steady? Not someone?"

Those beautiful eyes were liquid. "It's easier to trust a place. Even the stars that move are more reliable than most people." Fallon took in a shaky breath as she looked toward the kitchen. Nora saw the light was out there as well. Jade was finished. Everyone else had gone to bed. Stepping nearer her tent, Fallon asked, "Maybe you could show me again tomorrow night?"

Nora wasn't sure if she was being invited or rejected. "I might not be here tomorrow night."

"But the stars will be." Fallon gave a humorless chuckle. "Thanks for making my point."

She wasn't nearly as cold as she had been last night, but Nora waited until she was borderline uncomfortable to make her way into the vestibule. She found the thermal underwear from last night hanging on the line and changed quickly. "Knock, knock."

"Come on in."

Nora crawled forward, fastening the Velcro flap before sliding in beside Fallon.

"Do you need to warm up like last night?"

"I think I'll be okay if you'll let me use those socks again."

Fallon lay on her back. "They're under your pillow."

Nora slipped on the cozy wool before lying beside her, unable to avoid having their shoulders touch. "Thanks again for—"

"Don't mention it," Fallon cut her off, turning away. "Sleep well."

Nora didn't think she would, until she woke up curled around Fallon's body with her head on Fallon's shoulder. The sky was getting lighter, and a few sounds were coming from the camp. She pulled away, putting her hand where her head had been and giving a careful shake. "Fallon. It's morning."

Fallon mumbled something unintelligible and stretched like a long, lazy cat.

Then Jade's voice carried into the tent. "Where's my cook?"

Fallon was up and into the vestibule, dressing almost before Nora could blink. By the time she gathered her things, Fallon was frying bacon, and she could hear teasing remarks about them oversleeping again. Ranger Upshaw stood in the center of the breakfast activity, and when she looked around the camp, Nora could see that everyone else had broken down their tents, and most of the gear was stacked in the trailer.

"Nora," Jade called. "Come take over breakfast so Fallon can pack."

Everyone was too excited about their week off to be upset about the slightly burned toast and undercooked bacon, and within a half hour, all traces of their temporary home were gone. Nora chose to ride with Upshaw, needing to think about how she'd awakened that morning but not wanting to be anywhere near Fallon while she did. What would it be like between them if she did stay around and help with the incoming sawyers? Teaming up to school the noobs might be enjoyable, but while Firecamp wasn't technically firefighting, it was firefighting adjacent, putting her right back into the life she wanted to escape. She closed her eyes against the vision of her father snapping commands at her and at the memory of his contempt when he deemed her efforts inadequate. But Fallon wasn't like that, and neither was Firecamp. What did she want?

The parking area at base camp held several extra vehicles, and

Nora heard Hannah's laugh as she ran to the family car. Delores's mother was talking excitedly in Spanish as she hugged her daughter. Upshaw had reminded them of their last duty—unloading the gear—which was done more quickly than seemed humanly possible. They were also to take anything that needed repair to the equipment hut. Nora got the ribbing she'd expected from Hal when she delivered her ruined tent, but he let her off fairly easy, assuming she was ready to head out. As she left the hut, Kennedy was throwing their arms around Fallon's neck. Fallon bent slightly, and they touched foreheads. Then Kennedy lifted their face and touched their lips to Fallon's. Struck by a sharp, unexpected pain, Nora turned away, seeing Tina and Gwen hurriedly putting their things into Gwen's car.

"You coming or what?" Gwen yelled.

Suddenly, this was the last place she wanted to be. "Yeah, I am."

CHAPTER NINE

Fallon closed the manual she'd been studying and stretched. In the three days since the Women's Plus Crew had left, she'd discovered there was still plenty going on at base camp with other teams and staff and equipment. A Firecamp leader had plenty to learn besides how to handle a chainsaw, but for now, her head was full, and she was ready to do something active. Or at least have lunch.

As Fallon neared Reva's open office door, the phone rang. After her usual greeting, Reva's next words were "Nora? Slow down. Where are you?"

Her urgency might have been enough to make Fallon hesitate, but hearing Nora's name made her stop in her tracks.

"I see…uh-huh…and they're both in jail? But you're secure at the moment?" After a pause, Reva said, "Okay, good. I'll be on my way as soon as I can get Jade to cover for me here. Stay where you are or text me if you move." She rattled off her number, then said it again more slowly. "Yes. You did the right thing to call. Good. See you soon."

Fallon counted to five before resuming her casual stroll past the doorway. When Reva called her name, she turned, doing her best to act clueless. "Yes, ma'am?"

Reva had her cell to her ear as she spoke. "I need you to find Jade for me. I think she must be having lunch. She's not answering."

"Is anything wrong?"

"Just hurry. Please."

The politeness sounded like an afterthought, so Fallon knew she had gotten all she was going to get. "Yes, ma'am."

Racing to the dining hall, Fallon found Jade laughing at a table with Mae. She tried not to sound flustered. "Ranger Reva needs to see you immediately. It sounded urgent."

Jade took a quick swallow of water, looking wistfully at her untouched plate while Mae said, "Go. I'll bus your tray."

As they ran toward the office, Jade pulled her phone out of her pocket. "Shit. Three missed calls. Do you know what this is about?"

Fallon didn't want to lie, but she didn't want to admit to eavesdropping. "I'm not sure, but I think I heard her giving out her cell number to someone."

"Sounds serious. Reva rarely does that."

She'd given it to Fallon to invite her to Firecamp, but this was as different as it could be. Once they'd reached the office, Fallon followed Jade in, trying to act like she belonged.

It didn't work. "Thank you, Fallon. Please close the door on your way out."

Knowing Reva's office window was almost always open, Fallon sprinted to the outside wall. She heard the words "incident around a drug deal" and "Nora managed to stay out of" before a group walked by, and the sound of their conversation drowned out Reva's voice. After they passed, Fallon stretched to hear better as Reva said, "pretty shaken up, but at least she didn't get busted, unlike Gwen and Tina."

"So what happens now?" Jade's voice sounded unsteady.

"Gwen and Tina will probably have to do time. This program was their chance to avoid incarceration, and obviously, they've blown that. Their future is out of our hands." Paper shuffled, and a chair scraped. "As for Nora—" The jingle of keys muffled the next few words. Fallon strained to hear, but all she caught was "when I get back."

She stayed pressed against the wall until the sound of Reva's engine faded. When Fallon returned to the office, Jade's grim expression made her heart race. "Please tell me what's going on. I know it has to do with Nora, and she's in some kind of trouble. I promise Reva will never know you told me. Please?"

Jade shook her head. Fallon opened her mouth to protest, but Jade stopped her with a hand. "I'm not the one to talk to about it. You'll need to take it up with Reva. Or Nora."

Fallon hung her head. She shouldn't have asked. From her studies of the manual, she'd learned Jade could get in real trouble for sharing anything about an ongoing incident.

Jade cleared her throat. "I didn't actually get to eat lunch. Do you think you could grab me a sandwich? Tell Mae it's for me and that I'm covering for Reva this afternoon."

Fallon hoped the walk would help settle her nerves, but Mae took one look at her and asked what was going on. Fallon only meant to say "Nora's in trouble," but the rest spilled out of her.

Mae sighed. "We've had similar trouble with a couple of the male crews before. I guess it's the women's turn."

"Does it matter that Nora wasn't arrested?"

"I'm sure Reva will get the whole story out of her during the drive. And she has the final say. This is a Forest Service program, so she's the boss."

Fallon fought not to clench her fists. "But how will our crew function if we're three people down?"

Mae blew out a breath. "I don't know. Your sawyers may be absorbed into another team."

"But this was the year for the Women's Plus Crew to show our stuff to the world. And Nora's our best, besides Jade."

Patting her arm, Mae said, "I know, honey. All I can tell you is if you're going to be her advocate, you'll need to state your case right away. Once Reva makes up her mind about something, she doesn't usually change it." She gave Fallon a hard look. "And don't go putting your own future here on the line. Especially if there's no chance of saving Nora."

After delivering Jade's lunch, Fallon returned to the desk she'd been using and began making a pros and cons list, grounds for Nora to be kicked out of Firecamp and reasons for her to stay. This had always been her way of dealing with something she wasn't sure she could control. Otherwise, the swirl of emotions—from anger to fear to a deeper distress about the future—would be overwhelming. After an hour, the list was somewhat weighted against Nora, but Fallon knew she had one big leverage point. The trick would be using it at the right moment.

Too restless to sit any longer, she went outside. Almost everyone else was at dinner, so she found a quiet spot and took deep breaths while she surveyed Brownly Mountain. The rugged peak, its avalanche chutes green with small shrubs, still had a few patches of snow. Paltry human struggles seemed inconsequential in the presence of such timeless beauty, and she felt her tension ease. The sunset had faded to deep purple by the time she heard the rumble of Reva's truck.

Moving quickly, she positioned herself outside the office to wait. Her hope that Nora had been able to explain herself faded at Reva's grim expression as she entered the building. When Fallon looked past her to see Nora, she gasped. A bruise colored her right cheek, and dried blood crusted her split lip. Fallon wanted to comfort her, but she knew this wasn't the time. "Hey," she said quietly.

"Hey, Fallon." Nora's eyes filled with tears, but her voice was steady.

Jade moved into the hallway to stand beside Fallon, nodding at Nora as she passed.

"This young lady and I need to finish our conversation," Reva said, guiding Nora into her office. "So if you two don't mind..." She started to close the door.

Fallon steeled herself, stopping Reva's motion by stepping into the small room. "As someone who's worked on the Women's Plus Crew with Nora, I'd like to stay. I have information to offer on her behalf."

"This isn't a trial, Fallon."

"Isn't it?" Ignoring her frown, Fallon pushed on. "I mean, what happens now will determine Nora's future here, so you're like the judge and jury. But her actions took place during the break week. She wasn't on the grounds or doing anything related to Firecamp work. She wasn't identifiable as a member of the Women's Plus Crew. Shouldn't that be considered before a decision is made?"

"Fallon, don't." Nora's voice was low, as if she was speaking only to her. "I screwed up. I already admitted I shouldn't have put myself in that position."

"Nora is unquestionably the best sawyer on the crew." Fallon and Nora both turned at Jade's comment from the doorway. "And she's been willing to work with others to improve the overall production of our group. She's never caused any trouble and has pitched in when asked, even volunteering for extra duties at times."

Ranger Reva sighed. "I'm sure she's an absolute saint in camp. But there was the incident at the ice cream shop, and now this. The reputation of our program in the local community and across the state needs to be upheld."

Nora stared at the floor as Reva reached into her desk and pulled out an official-looking form. Fallon looked to Jade, who only shrugged. It was time to play her final card.

"Speaking of our program's reputation, have you been able to generate any widespread publicity for the Women's Plus Crew?"

Reva stopped writing and let out a short breath. "Fallon, let me deal with one thing at a time, okay?"

"No, this is related." Fallon gave Nora a quick glance before pressing on. "Did you know Nora is practically a professional photographer? She's been admitted to a prestigious photojournalism school in Arizona. If you don't want her on the crew, couldn't she stay on as our official publicist? Assign her to get pictures of us doing our jobs and put it together into some kind of video for the website or to send to the TV stations or something?"

Reva turned. "Is that true? You're a photographer?" Nora seemed reluctant, but she nodded. "And you have your camera here with you?"

"In my bag." Nora pointed to the duffel she'd left outside the door.

"Bring it in, please." Reva seemed to go through everything else in the bag before placing the camera on her desk. "Why haven't you been using this all along?"

"I didn't want to be a distraction. Someone holding a running chainsaw doesn't need to be thinking about posing for candid shots. And I didn't have permission to take publicity photos. Those require people to sign a waiver."

"She has a point," Jade said. "But if she's staying, I need her sawing. We're already down two people."

Reva carefully repacked Nora's bag before tapping her pen on the desk, her expression detached. "Fallon, Nora, step outside for a moment and let me confer with my crew chief."

In the hallway, Nora slumped against the wall. "Why did you tell them that?" She didn't sound angry, just defeated. "You don't even know if I'm any good."

"I'm betting you're one of those people who's good at whatever you do," Fallon said. "But mainly, it seemed like the best way to keep you from getting kicked out. You want to win that bet, don't you?"

Nora buried her face in her hands, but her voice was full of fury. "Oh God, Fallon. I can't believe I was so stupid." She shook her head, almost violently. "Stupid, stupid, stupid!"

"Hey," Fallon tried to sound reassuring. "Everyone makes mistakes."

"No, I'm an idiot. I didn't really want to go with them in the first place."

Fallon stepped closer, putting her hand lightly on Nora's back. "Why did you?"

Nora ran her hands through her hair. Then she sighed, looking away. "I couldn't…something made me want to get away for a while."

"What?"

"I can't explain it right now."

"But you want to stay at Firecamp, don't you?"

"That's up to Ranger Upshaw." Nora shrugged, still staring down the hallway.

"That's it?" Fallon tried not to sound as frustrated as she felt. "You won't even try to make your case?"

"Look, it never mattered what I wanted at home, why should this be any different?" Nora snapped, turning back to her. "My father decreed I couldn't hang out with him anymore. My mother concluded I needed to look more girly. The kids at school decided they didn't want to be friends anymore. I had to trick my folks into giving me a chance at what I most wanted, to become a photographer, but now I've screwed that up, so I might as well give—"

Nora stopped abruptly as the door opened. Jade motioned them inside. The form was still on the desk, but Fallon didn't think anything more had been written on it. "Are you really as good a sawyer as Jade seems to think you are?" Reva asked.

Nora inclined her head. "Yes, but I believe it's mostly because I have more experience than the rest of the crew. I'm sure they'll be right with me by the end of the summer."

Reva grunted and turned to Fallon. "And you sincerely believe there won't be another serious infraction like the two we've already had?"

"Without those negative influences, yes." Reva tapped her pen again for what felt like an hour. Fallon worked not to hold her breath.

"Here's what's going to happen," Reva said finally, shifting her gaze between them. "Jade, since you have super sawyer here, I'm not going to reduce the assignment for your crew this hitch. You'll be expected to do the work of eight, even with six, and you'll be evaluated at regular intervals. Understood?"

Jade paled slightly but agreed.

"And Fallon, I'll be holding you responsible for everything outside of work hours. If there's the slightest whiff of a problem anywhere, anytime, she's gone, and you'll be back on a crew next year. Any kind of leadership position will have to wait."

"That's not fair," Nora blurted.

"Nora—"

"No, Fallon. She can't hold you responsible for my behavior."

Reva's stare was glacial. "That's where you're wrong, Ms. Palmer.

And if you're going to disregard the exceptional support you're being offered, then you can leave now." She picked up her pen and examined the form. Nora fidgeted. Fallon shifted enough to brush Nora's shoulder with her own. "What's it going to be?" Reva demanded, looking up. "I've already spent way too much time on this."

"Okay. I mean, yes, I'd like another chance." Nora's voice was almost a whisper. "Please."

"And you completely understand the consequences of any other trouble? Not only for yourself?"

Nora nodded, looking at Jade and returning the light pressure against Fallon's arm. "Thank you both. I promise, there won't be any more problems."

"Good. There's one other condition."

Nora stiffened.

"You will be taking promotional pictures for us in whatever time you can spare. It will be up to you to get releases from your crew and anyone else you photograph. It will also be your responsibility to put together some kind of video or presentation, the details of which I'll give you before your next break. Do we have an agreement?"

Fallon looked at Nora with apprehension but saw her lips curve slightly. "Yes, ma'am."

"Good. I expect to be impressed. Don't disappoint me, any of you."

"Yes, ma'am," they said in chorus. Fallon tried not to smile as Nora picked up her bag.

As they started out the door, Reva added, "Jade, take her over to medical and get that lip looked at. Wake someone if you have to. Ms. Palmer needs to be one hundred percent in two days."

Fallon hung around outside medical, keeping to the shadows in case Nora didn't want anything more to do with her this evening. Jade had called good night moments before, and when Nora exited the building, her head turning, Fallon's heart skipped, hoping she was the one Nora was looking for. "How'd it go?" she asked, trying to sound casual as she walked toward her.

Nora shrugged. "It was fine."

"Do you need to talk about how that happened?"

"Not even a little bit." Nora eyed her. "Do you try to save everyone, or should I feel special?"

"Can I say both?"

Nora laughed, then grimaced, putting her hand to her mouth. "The doctor said I should put something cold on this. Will you take me to get some ice cream?"

"Sure." Fallon realized she sounded much too eager, so she added a frown. "But who's paying?"

The couple at the Swift River Ice Cream shop obviously remembered them, as they had the same question. Nora handed over a twenty-dollar bill and told them to keep the change, ordering a hot fudge sundae and gesturing to Fallon, who couldn't resist ordering a banana split. They sat on the bench outside to eat.

"Didn't you have dinner?" Nora asked as Fallon consumed nearly half her dish in less than a minute.

"No. I was working on something. What about you?"

Nora gave a grim chuckle. "No, I was explaining my stupidity to Ranger Upshaw."

With a grunt, Fallon went back to her ice cream. Nora had almost finished when Fallon said, "You know you don't have to explain yourself to me. But if you ever want to talk about it…"

"Yeah. Thanks. I'll let you know."

Fallon took their empty dishes inside, taking a little while to chat with the owners. Nora seemed lost in thought when she returned. She cleared her throat. "Are you ready to head back to the barracks?"

"Oh." Nora startled slightly. "I hadn't thought about my return to communal living."

"The rest of the crew comes in tomorrow, so it'll just be us tonight."

"Well, I suppose that will be okay." Nora stood, giving herself a quick shake. "Especially since we've already slept together."

Fallon hoped it was dark enough to hide her blush.

The moaning woke her when it was still dark. While working at the diner, she'd trained herself to wake at first light, though her internal alarm had failed on those nights that Nora had shared her tent. Shaking off sleep, she questioned whether the sounds were in a dream or coming from something outside, but then she remembered Nora was back. At a whimper, followed by some mumbled words, Fallon was up.

"Hey." She bent and hesitantly touched Nora's arm.

"Get off," Nora shouted, flailing wildly.

"Shh. It's okay. You're safe." Fallon caught one of Nora's arms right before it hit her in the chest.

"No." Nora sat up abruptly, still struggling. She blinked, obviously trying to bring Fallon into focus. "What…what are you doing?"

"You were having a nightmare."

Nora took a few deep breaths. "Oh, okay. Yeah. Sorry." She regarded Fallon. "I can't believe you woke up. You sleep like the dead."

Fallon straightened, letting go of Nora's arm. "I do not." She hadn't meant to sound so offended, but at Nora's amused snort, she decided not to protest again. "Though if you're okay, I'm going back to bed."

"Since I'm awake, I'm going to make use of our modern toilet."

Fallon turned on her side, trying not to let her mind start up. She heard the flush, followed by water in the sink. After a rustling sound she couldn't identify, a cool hand touched her face. Her eyes snapped open. Nora was holding something out to her. "Here's your book. I finished it in Denver."

Fallon tucked *Seafire* under her pillow, thrilled that Nora had returned it. Everyone else on the crew had returned theirs as well. "Did you like it?"

"Very much. And I have some extra insight into Fallon Monroe now, knowing it was your favorite."

"Well, that was during my impressionable youth."

Nora lowered herself to the edge of Fallon's cot. "I don't know why I'm bad about saying thank you."

Fallon took Nora's hand in hers. "Maybe you're not used to someone who cares about you without any expectations."

Nora's breath caught, and she slowly pulled her hand away. "Other than the pressure to not ruin your plans for the rest of your life, that is."

Fallon raised onto her elbows. "Yes, Jade and I are both taking a chance on you, but the idea was to keep you from ruining your goals too."

"I screwed up so much, maybe my goals deserve to be ruined."

Making a sound of protest, Fallon tried to rise, but Nora held her shoulders down as she stood. "Go back to sleep, Falcon."

But she didn't. Fallon lay awake, wondering what it was she found attractive about thorny women who were broken, who were dispassionate and emotionally unavailable. Somehow, her willingness to help people in need had turned into believing she could fix people who were damaged. Or maybe she was the one who was defective, with her wishes and her gullible nature. She hadn't cried since Mr. Jamar's sister had taken him away, but she felt very close to tears now. She turned onto her other side, reminding herself that tomorrow, the rest of the crew would be back. Kennedy had been so sweet when they'd said good-bye. Why couldn't she fall for someone like that? She hoped the rest of the team wouldn't be mad about their workload. Hopefully, not having to deal with Gwen and Tina's ill-tempered slacking would make up for it. And she needed to thank Jade for supporting her and Nora.

Her and Nora. Would there ever be such a thing?

❖

The light woke Fallon from a decidedly inappropriate dream. She went to shower, needing to wash away her imagination and reset her mind on business. By the time she was done, Nora was gone. She hurried to the dining hall. Nora knew how important this place was to her. Surely, she wouldn't do anything to jeopardize her position. When she stepped inside and Nora looked up, smiled, and waved from their usual table, a feeling of absolute certainty swept over her. Everything—whatever that turned out to mean—was going to be fine.

After the rest of the crew returned, and hugs and excited shrieks had been exchanged, Fallon turned to Nora. "Is this what a family reunion feels like?"

"This is much better," Nora replied. "No weird uncles."

Jade laughed. "I heard that. And you're right." They'd gathered in the barracks, Gwen and Tina's cots conspicuously empty. "Okay, I want to talk about the project for our next hitch. We'll be about twenty miles from the previous development, with only a forest road in and out and no civilization nearby. We're going to create a fuel break by clear-cutting a twenty-five-foot-wide space in the San Isabel National Forest. That might sound easier since we won't have to decide which trees to cut, but in some ways it'll be harder because we'll have to haul all those logs out, and you know they'll be heavy."

Nods and mutters of agreement met this remark. "We'll have a little help in the form of an ATV and trailer that we'll use to move the cut trees to the road," Jade resumed. "A local Boy Scout troop will assist us at that point. They'll load and remove the wood to split and sell."

Fallon raised her hand. "When do we get trained on the ATV? I've never driven one, but they sure look like fun."

Everyone laughed. "We'll bring it out later today, and you can all get some time on it," Jade said. "But there's one more thing we need to discuss first." She seemed more solemn, and the crew quieted quickly. "You may have noticed that we're missing a couple of people. That will be permanent. Unfortunately, the expectations for our workload will be the same."

Delores shifted on her cot before asking, "So the six of us will still have to do the same amount of work?"

"The six of us usually did most of it anyway," Kennedy remarked, and Hannah nodded.

"Tina did good with packing lunches, though," Fallon said.

A few sounds of agreement followed before Nora spoke. "And I need to let you know that I've been asked to take publicity photos for the Women's Plus Crew." She took her camera out of its case and held it up. "If anyone objects to having their picture taken, please tell me now. Otherwise, I'll need each of you to sign a release." With her other hand, she held up the forms Upshaw had printed. Without being asked, Fallon took them and began passing them out, including the three pens other staff members had loaned her.

"Wow," Delores said. "This is exciting."

"You'll only get my good side, right?" Hannah asked.

"You don't have to worry," Nora assured her. "None of you has a bad side."

While Hannah and Delores giggled, Kennedy studied the form. "Why did you decide to do this?"

"Actually, Ranger Reva asked her to," Fallon said.

"After you suggested it," Nora said, giving Fallon a smile as she took the paperwork back.

"Well, I…" Fallon's cheeks colored. Kennedy gave a little cough.

"Sometimes we'll use posed shots, and other times, I might sneak up on you." Nora addressed the group again. "I think Ranger Upshaw wants to show both the hard work and the fun side of what we're doing here. But I promise, I'll make you all look good, and I want to show how great this program is."

It was quiet while the crew signed their names and handed the releases back to Nora. Then Jade said, "Okay, let's go get our gear. Obviously, Nora will want a new tent, but if anyone else wants a change, now is the time."

"I'm keeping mine, so nobody get any ideas," Fallon said.

"Race you," Hannah called, and everyone scrambled out.

ATV training proved to be the highlight of her day. Fallon had seen dozens of similar machines on the backs of trucks and in trailers on the highways she'd traveled with her mother and always thought they looked exciting. But being on one was incredible. The throttle, the brakes, the steering, everything was easy, and the power she felt while roaring through base camp was exhilarating.

When Jade finally flagged her down, she hopped off reluctantly. "All right now, Fallon," Jade said in her most adult voice. "You have to let the other kids take a turn."

"Aw, Mom," Fallon protested, grinning. She stood by Nora, watching as she took photos of each rider. "Will you use all of those?"

"No, only one or two of the best ones. Including you, of course."

"Oh no, please," Fallon said, suddenly self-conscious.

"Don't worry. You weren't serious," Nora gave a half laugh. "Far from it, in fact."

Next, each crew member took turns with the trailer attached and practiced finding a path through the forest. It was fun too, but in a different way. She watched as Nora snapped pictures of the different buildings, of the group at dinner, and one of Delores at the sink, toothbrush in hand, sticking out her tongue with her mouth full of foam.

"What makes a good photograph?" Fallon asked.

"Oh, part of it is technical things, like lighting and composition, color and tonal range. But mainly, it's how the picture makes you feel." Nora turned the camera, showing Fallon the screen, an image of the equipment hut with the last of the day's sunlight shining on the roof. "This isn't a great photo, but it gives you some sense of what I mean."

Fallon studied the familiar sight that seemed much more dramatic in Nora's picture. "Wow. I'd hang this on my wall."

"You don't have a wall," Nora teased, taking the camera back.

"Don't be so sure." Fallon nudged her shoulder. She liked how things were between her and Nora now. It seemed like they were truly becoming friends, and even if that was all they ever were, it would be enough.

CHAPTER TEN

That evening, Nora stood at the sink after Fallon had finished her shower and was apparently still dressing.

Kennedy's voice carried into the bathroom. "I'm just saying, it's interesting that Gwen and Tina are gone, but Nora's still here. Weren't they all in Denver together? Seems like whatever they did to get kicked out, she would have been there too."

"I'm suspicious that she's suddenly so friendly," Delores remarked. "The whole first hitch, she mostly buddied around with Gwen and Tina, who only cared about themselves, and all of a sudden, it's all about making us and the program look good."

"Didn't you see that bruise and the cut on her lip?" Hannah asked. "Maybe she got in over her head and paid the price for it. Let's give her a chance."

Fallon stepped out from behind the shower curtain wearing the pajamas Hal had ordered for her. The top was plain, but the bottoms had cartoon dogs all over them. Her smile faded quickly, and Nora realized her expression must be giving her away. "What's the matter?" Fallon asked.

"Nothing." Nora turned on the water and began brushing her teeth.

Fallon squeezed her elbow as she walked by. "Be yourself and give them time. They'll come around."

So she'd heard them too. If it had been anyone but Fallon, Nora would make some dismissive response, but she held back. The crew had reasons to question the difference in her behavior, she supposed. At least they didn't know the whole story. Then again, neither did Fallon, but she'd been willing to stick up for Nora anyway. Maybe the rest of them would do the same. Eventually.

❖

Setup for the new camp seemed to go more quickly than last time, although Fallon sheepishly accepted help pitching her tent again. She'd indicated a nice spot for Nora's tent close by, and Nora had made a show of scanning the nearby trees for any threatening dead branches, which had made the whole crew laugh. It seemed like everything was lighter and easier without Gwen and Tina. And once she had her camera in hand again, she felt the special energy that photography always gave her. Even routine scenery appeared illuminated through her lens. After getting a few good shots of making camp, she pressed the shutter button repeatedly as the crew began marking the fuel break area. Intermittently, she pointed out different flowers and shrubs to whoever was nearby.

"I didn't take you for a gardener," Delores said.

"Oh, I'm not. My little brother is into plants, and I guess I picked up some stuff from him."

Within the area to be cut was a majestic Douglas fir so large Fallon couldn't get her arms around half of it. "Couldn't we spare this beauty?" she asked, still hugging the trunk. "It must be over a hundred years old."

Jade shook her head. "We can't leave anything standing in a clear-cut."

Fallon's dejected expression made Nora's heart hurt. "What about shifting the boundary far enough to let big beauty live?" she asked.

Jade eyed the other edge of the zone. "That could work. Hannah, would you run about thirty feet that way and see if there's any obstruction or other reason why we can't modify our position?"

"Good thinking," Kenn acknowledged. Nora nodded gratefully.

After a few minutes, Hannah's voice carried over to them. "Looks okay from here."

"Obviously, we won't have to designate the boundary on this side," Jade said.

"Big Beauty, our landmark," Delores said, and everyone clapped. Fallon's smile made Nora feel like she'd done something right for the first time in days.

By late afternoon, they were back in camp for a final equipment check. No one wanted to get out to the clear-cut area and find they'd forgotten something since it was almost a mile away. They still had an hour before sunset, and Nora hid her amusement as Fallon eyed the ATV hopefully.

Jade shook her head. "Sorry, Falcon, but we're going to have to be stingy with gas to make it through the week." Fallon sighed. "How about if you take the first load to the road tomorrow?"

"Deal."

Jade made dinner, and it was nice to have a relaxed meal while they were still clean. They chatted past dark about their week off. Delores had flown to Texas to meet her new niece, and Hannah had taken her parents to Estes Park. Kennedy had spent a few days volunteering at an LGBTQ+ community center in Colorado Springs. "And doing some clubbing," they added to enthusiastic cheers. Nora felt herself getting increasingly anxious, knowing someone might ask her, and she couldn't give them an honest answer.

Standing before anyone could question her, she said, "I need to find a friendly tree. Fallon, can I borrow your flashlight?"

"I'm about ready to turn in." Fallon rose and stretched. "I'll go with you."

Everyone else groaned, but Jade got to her feet as well. "Back in the saddle tomorrow, crew. Let's be ready to hit it."

As Nora and Fallon walked toward their tents, Fallon touched her arm. "Did you really want to go?"

"Yeah, I think I will." She didn't actually need to but couldn't bring herself to admit it. "You didn't have to come with me, you know. You could have stayed with the gang."

"They'll catch on and stop asking. Soon, if not already." Fallon handed her the flashlight. "Keep it till tomorrow. I'll be fine by moonlight."

❖

Nora's long-sleeved T-shirts had ensured no one had seen the bruises on her arm, the ones in the shape of a big man's handprint, although they throbbed when she lay down. But turning on her other side made her lip ache. It wasn't terribly painful, but the awareness of it made her hurt inside. Sleeping on her back wasn't particularly comfortable, but it was better than the memory of panic, of the sheer terror unlike anything she'd ever experienced. She'd never expected for this camp to become her safe place or that the supportive companionship of one particular woman would make her feel like sleep was possible.

"Fallon." The word left her lips on a cry as she sat up, instantly awake as her head brushed the top of the small tent. As her breathing gradually returned to normal, Nora recalled the dream, a patchwork of those dreadful moments in Denver when she'd thought her life was over. Parts of the nightmare were frighteningly close to reality, but Fallon hadn't been with her there. Fallon had been here, like she was now, in her own bed. And her tent wasn't far away.

Distractedly, Nora slipped on her mocs and unzipped her tent flap. She stood at the tall vestibule entrance to Fallon's tent for a full minute, trying to rationalize what she wanted and what to say to get it.

"Fallon," she whispered as loudly as she dared. "Fallon, it's Nora. Can I…I need to talk to you." After a few seconds, she heard Fallon's muffled voice. "It's Nora," she repeated. "Could you please let me in?"

At the sound of a zipper, she almost wanted to cry. Fallon, silhouetted in the opening, peered out at her. "Nora? What's wrong?"

"Nothing. Yeah. I just…uh, could I…" She couldn't finish her thought. But when Fallon held out a hand, the intensity of Nora's need overwhelmed her. Something inside was about to give way, and she was desperate to be steadied, to be strengthened.

Fallon studied her for a few seconds. "Stay here. I'll be right back, okay?" Without waiting for a reply, she ducked into the sleeping area.

"I know it's late, and I woke you. I'm sorry. I think it's being in this new place or how it's nice to see everyone again but also kinda weird or maybe because I keep—" Nora's words started out in a rush, but she abruptly ran out of clarification. She stood, waiting for Fallon to insist on some excuse, but instead, there was only movement. Then the flap opened again, and Fallon said, "Okay." It was not a question but an answer.

Nora ducked inside, barely able to hide her relief as her eyes adjusted to the darkness. "You kept both sleeping bags."

Fallon pulled back the top covering. "Blankets and pillows too."

"Why?"

Fallon didn't answer as they settled on their sides. For some reason, lying in the warmth of the padded sleeping bag didn't make Nora's arm ache. She positioned the extra pillow, and when Fallon reached across her, snugging close, the tension that had gripped her from the moment she'd gotten into Gwen's car eased for the first time since her return to camp. "A girl can hope," Fallon whispered, the slightest tease in her tone.

Later, Nora told herself, pushing away the wave of relief. She could cry later when she was alone. Now she wanted to rest, to sleep and not dream. She tried to form the words "Thank you," but she was already drifting, not away, but toward the certainty of strength.

Sometime in the night, they'd turned the other way, but Nora didn't remember waking to do so. Now dim light was filtering in, and Fallon stirred. "I've got to cook." Her voice was so soothing, Nora wanted to keep sleeping. "Stay awhile if you want." Fallon moved through the flap, and Nora heard her dressing.

Shit. She'd intended to leave before daylight. How galling to be doing the walk of shame when nothing sexual had even happened. Maybe if she stood outside the tent, she could act like they'd met up this morning. She crawled into the vestibule just as Fallon pulled a long-sleeved T-shirt over her head. She hadn't thought about it until now, how different Addison's body had been. Addison was a wisp, almost delicate in size and shape. None of those words described Fallon, but when Nora compared her impression at their first meeting to now, she saw someone who seemed to be a little more confident, if not more comfortable, in her skin.

Nora decided she didn't care what anyone thought as Fallon turned to her and smiled. "See you out there."

❖

Creating a fuel break was every bit as hard as Jade had said it would be. It didn't help that over the last couple of days, the temperature had risen by fifteen degrees, and there was no cloud cover. They took more frequent breaks, always in the shade of Big Beauty, and Jade made sure everyone carried extra water. The area was too dense for them to be in teams, so they staggered their positions, orchestrating a ballet of felling and limbing and swamping, giving Nora little time to take photos.

Fallon's joy in riding the ATV might have been the only thing guaranteed to make everyone smile, though she took turns without being prompted. Nora felt an odd sense of pride that Fallon's sawing technique had improved. She'd gotten stronger and more self-assured. Everyone had, but Fallon's improvement was significant. Nora began to think there was a chance they'd make their quota, but they were all paying for it with long days under less-than-ideal conditions, plastered in the dirt and grit that seemed to coat every pore and crevasse.

Everyone was bone weary, spending the first part of their evenings trying to clean up and passing less time socializing after dinner. Nora fell asleep as soon as her head hit the pillow, which was probably why she hadn't had more nightmares. She sometimes thought about visiting Fallon's tent anyway, simply for the comfort of her company. Despite Nora's plan to go it alone, she couldn't deny that Fallon had gotten her through times when she might not have finished Firecamp.

Did that mean they were friends? Fallon seemed to think so, and Nora supposed it wouldn't be the worst thing, though nothing more could come of it. She did find herself waiting for Fallon at meals and routinely sitting next to her when they'd gather for a meeting.

On Thursday afternoon, Jade announced that one of the families in the neighborhood where they'd worked before had offered the use of their shower, and they'd have the rest of the day off. The best the exhausted crew could manage was a ragged cheer. The downstairs bathroom of the modest mountain home had been designed for guests. It was accessible through a private entrance, and the shower and toilet were separated by a pocket door from the back-to-back sinks. Drawing lots, they worked out a system where someone would be in each area, either getting clean or drying hair and doing other personal maintenance, while everyone else waited on camp chairs. When the family's new dog squeezed out the front door, frantic to pay them a visit, Fallon skipped her shower twice to play with the exuberant puppy. They ran, they chased, and they wrestled. Nora, waiting for her turn, couldn't keep from smiling at the two of them when Fallon finally sat with her eyes closed, her back to a tree, the puppy sleeping on her lap. They'd tired each other out.

"Cute, huh?" Kennedy said from beside her.

"Yeah." Nora tried not to act like she'd been watching.

"The puppy too." It was an old bit but still made Nora laugh. "It's cool to see someone coming into their own."

Nora turned. "That's your experience too, isn't it?"

"Yeah. I think it's the confidence of doing the work, combined with Jade's leadership and everyone else's support." They paused. "What about you? Are you getting what you wanted out of this summer?"

It was such a simple question, but Nora struggled with her reply. "I don't think I had any expectations, so...sure."

Kenn turned to face her. "Maybe you're missing out on what you could have."

Hannah called that Nora was next, and she walked briskly away from Kenn and everything they'd implied, feeling a blush rising. Yes, Fallon had been thoughtful and sensitive to her, and her antics with the puppy were endearing, but what mattered most was the plan for her future. *Get in. Get out. Get on with your life.* Kennedy's unsubtle hint wouldn't change that.

Her phone was completely dead, so she plugged it in while washing her hair. She'd scarcely turned off the dryer when it rang, startling her into answering without looking. "Nora?" a familiar voice said. "Nora, this is Tina. You've got to help us."

Nora jumped when a knock came on the door between her and the shower. "You about through in there?" Jade asked.

"Uh, yeah, just a second," Nora answered. Into the phone, she whispered, "Call me back in five," before hanging up. Raising her voice, she said, "Okay, all done," and Jade came through, still in her towel.

Grinning at Nora's surprise, she said, "Not trying to dazzle you. I wanted a couple more minutes of feeling totally clean."

"I get that," Nora said. "But I think Fallon will be coming in next." "Fine."

Nora left, opening the door to the outside as Fallon walked up. "You look nice. And clean," Fallon said. "I probably smell like a dog."

"There's worse things to smell like, I think," Nora said.

"Let's not make a list," Fallon teased.

Nora pointed toward the bathroom. "Jade's in there."

"I bet she smells good."

Nora raised her eyebrows. "Oh, you think so, do you?" Her ringing cell phone interrupted any response Fallon might have had. She tried to keep her expression calm. "Sorry, I need to get this."

"Is everything okay?" Fallon asked.

"Yeah, I'm sure it's Tyler telling me how much he misses me." Nora walked away, blowing out a breath. Why had she lied?

"Tell him hi for me," Fallon called after her.

❖

At the sensation of her head snapping back, Nora jerked awake. It was like those dreams of falling, but echoing in her mind was the sound of a slap. His ring had cut her. She must have blocked that out until now. Rolling her lips, she thought her mouth felt almost normal. She touched the bruise on her cheek. It hardly hurt at all. The thought transposed into the idea of brushing her fingers across Fallon's cheek. It would be soft and warm.

No, she told herself, I'm not being fair. She'd avoided Fallon all evening because she didn't want to dig herself any deeper into the lie about Tina's phone call. She replayed the conversation over in her mind, as she had dozens of times already:

"Bryson and Gwen are still in jail, but my folks paid my fine."

"Did you get caught with drugs too, Tina?" Nora asked.

"No, but I had rolling papers on me and trace amounts of coke in my bag. That fine was five hundred dollars."

"Where are you now?"

"I'm still at my parents' house. They're really pissed." That explained why she'd been whispering the whole time. *"Gwen was busted before, but she didn't have much on her then. That's why we were at Firecamp. Her other lawyer got us community restitution. But now..."*

She trailed off, and the silence dragged until Nora said, *"Were you getting over two ounces of pot? Is that why..."*

"No, there was other stuff too. We like blow, and they were going to sell some MDMA."

Nora grimaced. *"I don't know how I can help. I don't know a lawyer or anything like that."*

"But don't you have money? You could help with her bail maybe? It's, like, fifteen hundred dollars."

Nora scoffed. *"No one here has that kind of money, Tina. We wouldn't be spending our summer working our asses off if we had fifteen hundred dollars sitting around."*

Tina sighed. *"Gwen said to tell you that someone could get hurt if you don't help her."*

A chill ran through her. *"What does that mean?"*

"I guess she might already have planted something on someone." Her tone bordered on sad, and Nora had to work at not letting Tina hear her agitation.

"You guess, or you know?"

"It was when we were packing to go to Denver. She talked about having insurance. That's what I thought she meant, but I didn't ask."

Nora would go to Jade. Explain she'd heard Gwen talk about insurance and hadn't realized what she meant until their drug bust. But then Jade would get everyone together, and Fallon would figure out Nora had lied about the call. *"Did Gwen say who...who her insurance was?"*

"No. It could have been anyone, but most likely Jade or Fallon. She doesn't like either of them."

"Look, I'll ask around. See if anyone wants to chip in. But I expect you to find out who she set up before I give you anything. Understand?"

"Okay, yeah. I'll call you again in a couple of days."

Nora wouldn't ask the crew for money, and she wouldn't wait a couple of days to talk to Jade either. Though the night was still warm, she put on her sweatpants and hoodie, wishing they could shield her like armor. Retrieving her borrowed flashlight, she started to cross the campsite. Looking over at Fallon's tent, it occurred to her that if she could find the dope, she wouldn't have to involve anyone else. Without bothering to call out, she unzipped the flap and stepped into the vestibule.

Fallon made a noise that sounded like "Huh?"

"It's Nora. I'm coming in."

"Wait—" Fallon said, but Nora was already crawling into the sleeping area. There was a shuffle and a flash of something white. A leg?

Nora stopped short. She couldn't see much, but Fallon's voice sounded strained. And what was that shuffling noise? Was she hiding something? *Or someone?* "Oh, excuse me." This time, she didn't try to conceal her agitation. "I didn't think to ask if you were alone." *The flash of skin was too light to be Kenn. Maybe Delores?*

"What?" Fallon coughed. "Of course I'm alone." She sank under the covers, squirming a bit.

"Then why are you acting so weird?" Nora demanded.

"Because I'm naked." Exasperation colored Fallon's reply.

"Oh." After a pause, Nora said, "Should I wait…uh, out in the…" She couldn't think beyond the unexpected relief. And an image of Fallon's body under the sheet.

"Yes, please."

Nora crawled back out and sat. A giggle rose in her throat, and she tried to stifle it, but the absurdity of the moment expanded. Had Fallon been sleeping with someone else? No, she was sleeping in the nude because it was warm. Her shyness contrasted with Gwen's threat was almost farcical. And Fallon probably wouldn't appreciate being reminded that Nora had already been exposed to her lower half. When the word "exposed" entered her mind, she couldn't contain herself. She covered her mouth, but a snort escaped, and then she was laughing out loud.

"It's not funny, Nora."

Oh, but it was, and Fallon's awkward modesty made it even more so. She rolled onto her side, holding herself, feeling nearly hysterical. Fallon's head and T-shirt-covered shoulders appeared through the flap. With great dignity, she asked, "Was there something you wanted?"

"Oh. Yes." Nora sobered as she remembered the purpose of her visit. "Yes, there is. I need to talk to you."

"Go ahead." Her tone cool, Fallon propped her elbow on the floor, putting her chin in her hand.

Why is she being super sensitive? "I'm sorry I laughed. I think the heat must have made me kinda punch drunk or something."

Fallon eyed the sweats she was wearing but only said, "Is this going to take long? I'm really tired."

Is that all? Is she really just tired? "No, I…it's about…" Now the lie of the phone call would come out, not to mention that Gwen might have made good on her threat to put Fallon in danger. And what was Nora thinking? That she could search the tent with Fallon in it? "I'm sorry. I guess it can wait till morning." She stood and began working the long zipper. "I'll talk to you tomorrow."

Fallon sighed. "Fine."

"Fine," Nora echoed, stumbling back to her tent. She was tired too, damn it. And now she was worried about more than goddamn Gwen.

After breakfast the next morning, she asked Jade for a few minutes to talk privately, so the others were sent on ahead. "What is it?"

Nora had just begun fumbling her way through her account of the situation when Jade stopped her. "Fallon told us about Gwen and her threats as soon as everyone else left on break. Hal did a thorough search of all the equipment, and we sent out emails warning the crew about a tick infestation and advising them to search their belongings thoroughly. Knowing this group, I'm confident that if anyone found anything, they disposed of it."

Nora blinked. "Oh." Jade waited. "I didn't get that email."

"No, and neither did Gwen or Tina. The plan was to search each of you upon your return to base camp."

Nora was struck by the memory of Reva going through her duffel during the conversation about her camera. "I see," she said slowly. "And Fallon was in on this?"

"She didn't have any choice. But I can tell you that she was convinced you weren't involved in carrying or using drugs. As was I." Nora's throat tightened. "But I would recommend you block any further calls from Tina or Gwen." At Nora's nod, Jade asked, "Is that what was wrong with Fallon? Was she worried about this?"

"No, I...I was going to tell her, but I didn't. What do you mean what was wrong?"

"She wasn't her usual self. Kinda down, you know?"

At the rumble of the ATV in the distance, Nora pointed. "I'll get my stuff and meet you up there, okay?"

"Sure."

Nora hurried as much as she could while wearing her PPE and carrying her chainsaw. At the road where the Boy Scouts were to pick up their firewood, Kennedy was stacking logs. They looked at Nora without smiling. "What's up?"

She'd been expecting Fallon but nodded cordially. "I was wondering if I could catch a ride with you?" She moved to help Kenn unload the trailer.

"Aren't you working with Jade today?"

"Yeah. I'm going to meet her there. I need to tell Fallon something first."

Kenn sighed, crossing their arms tightly. "Maybe that's not a good idea right now."

Nora wanted to tell Kennedy to butt out, but their expression made her rethink her next words. "Oh? Why not?"

"I don't know if you'll want to hear it."

"Try me."

Kenn shook their head. "Okay. It's this. You talk to Fallon when you feel like it and ignore her when you don't. Like, you're nice to her if you want something, but that's not what a friend does. It makes you a user, in my opinion. The rest of us, we've taken the time to know her better. We know what her life was like before Firecamp and how she felt about herself then and how she feels now. She knows us too because we've shared things, each of us. If one of us is upset about something, we talk to each other, and it helps. Right now, Fallon is upset because of you."

Nora tried not to react. As much as she hated to admit it, maybe Kennedy had a point. "Then I should apologize, right?"

"And what are you apologizing for, exactly?" Kenn scrutinized her.

A flip answer like "Everything" wouldn't do. She thought about last night and how unexpectedly hurt Fallon had seemed. Admitting she had been the cause meant she should find a way to fix it. "I guess I should ask her."

"Bingo." Kenn started the ATV. Looking back at Nora, they said, "Well, get on. We haven't got all day."

CHAPTER ELEVEN

Fallon wasn't feeling particularly sociable, so she excused herself after dinner and went to her tent to read. Not long after, when Nora called her name, she wasn't surprised. Nora had tried to catch her eye several times during the day, but Fallon had turned away each time, keeping busy with work. Nora's gleeful laughter at her nudity last night still rang in her ears, and while she'd been able to rationalize away some of the hurt, she wasn't quite sure how to find her way back to their friendship.

After the last time the crew had gotten showers, Fallon had actually studied herself in the mirror—something she normally avoided—and had felt a small jolt of pride. She wasn't ever going to be thin like Hannah, but they'd talked about it once, and Hannah had said body image standards were arbitrary, and the ideal was to be happy with the shape you had.

Fallon had flexed her arms, seeing an outline of muscles. Doing odd jobs, busing tables, even learning short-order cooking from Mr. Jamar, all of it had been hard work, but her body hadn't reflected it. Maybe it had to do with eating better too. Either way, she'd been desperate to leave that chunky, self-conscious kid behind, but when Nora had laughed at seeing her naked, she knew it hadn't happened. She thought she understood the reason. Nora's body had probably always been as gorgeous as it was now, and she might never have had a moment of self-doubt. Fallon couldn't pretend she didn't fantasize about being with Nora, getting her hands on that amazing body and being begged for more. But after the fantasy was over, she could admit that was all it would ever be.

Nora called again. Fallon closed her book, reminding herself that she had the responsibility of making sure Nora didn't get into trouble.

She'd just fake her way through whatever conversation Nora wanted to have and then get ready for bed.

"Yeah?" she called.

"Fallon, I'd like to show you something, if I may." Nora sounded oddly formal.

"Come on in." At the sound of the vestibule zipper, she turned off the battery-powered lantern she'd been using. She heard rustling, then nothing else.

"Could you bring that light in here, please?"

Fallon flipped the switch and pushed the lantern through the flap. The illumination was dim but adequate to make her way into the vestibule and establish where Nora was standing. Once clear, she stood, taking an extra breath as her eyes traveled toward Nora's face. Was she wearing a towel? Uh, only a towel? She wet her suddenly dry lips. "Did something happen to your clothes?"

"No." Nora stood waiting. Barefoot. Smelling like some incredibly delicious spicy candy. One hand was by her side holding something, the other resting casually on the place where the towel was tucked in over her breasts. Fallon was sure there was another question she should ask, but she couldn't find it. Finally, Nora took a breath. "After last night, it occurred to me that we're not even. I mean, I've had the opportunity to see more of you than you have of me, so I thought I'd remedy that."

Fallon stared, dumbfounded.

Nora added, "If you'd be interested."

"Interested?" Fallon cleared her throat. She needed to stop sounding absurdly inane. Forcing herself to look at the floor, she said, "Nora, we don't need to be even. This isn't a game."

Nora grinned. "But it could be." Holding her hand out, she displayed a deck of cards. "Have you ever played strip poker?"

"I've never played any kind of poker."

"I didn't think so. That's why I'm giving you an advantage." She indicated the towel. "See? Keeping it even." She used both hands to loosely shuffle the cards.

"Wait. I don't…I can't…" Fallon stopped, needing to consider her words carefully. "This isn't what I—" She looked away again.

Filling in when her stuttering diminished, Nora fanned out the deck facedown. "I'll make it easy on you. Pick one card. Go on."

Not knowing what else to do, Fallon sighed and chose. Nora pulled one as well, and they turned them over together. Fallon had the nine of diamonds, Nora the jack of clubs. "Am I supposed to take something off now?"

"No, that was practice." She gave the cards a quick shuffle. "Again."

This time, her three of clubs lost to Nora's six of spades, then a seven lost to a ten. "Oh, for fuck's sake," Nora muttered.

Fallon had to smile. "I'll admit to enjoying your frustration, but I need to ask, what are you trying to accomplish?"

"Either find an excuse to flash you or at least make you laugh."

"Why?"

"Because I think you misunderstood something last night, and I wanted a chance to explain. Once we're even, I thought you might be more willing to listen."

Fallon crossed her arms. "I don't understand this fixation you have about being even. From what I can tell, most relationships ebb and flow."

"Well then, I feel like I've been stuck in an ebb. You didn't hesitate to let me crash with you when my tent got trashed, and you put yourself on the line for me with Reva. Then, after I had that nightmare, you…" She broke off. "Let's just say, you're a nice person, and I haven't been." Fallon started to say something, but Nora pressed on. "But you need to know that I started laughing because…well, for a minute, I thought you were with someone, and that made me momentarily irrational. When you told me you were acting peculiar because you were naked, it struck me as funny because you were being so damn cute about it, but it was also, like, relief too." She took a step closer. "Then it got more absurd because I was super stressed about having heard from Tina, and I was in an absolute panic about what Gwen might do to someone, probably you or Jade. I just…you need to know that my hysteria wasn't about you being naked. Not at all."

Fallon studied her. "For real?" Nora nodded vigorously. After a few long seconds, Fallon said, "You thought me being naked was cute?"

"I thought the way you were acting all shy and modest was cute. After all, I've already seen your, uh, lower extremity."

"That was an accident."

Nora grinned, saying nothing.

Fallon cleared her throat. "Okay."

"Okay?"

"Yeah, okay. You can take the towel off now." The expression on Nora's face showed even more shock than she'd expected, and she burst out laughing.

Nora stared at her until she'd collected herself. "So you've had your laugh at me now."

"I couldn't resist." Fallon was still chuckling.

"But I suppose you can resist this." Nora turned away, unzipping the flap before slowly lowering the towel, revealing her muscled back and for half a second, her shapely ass. She quickly refastened the towel around her and stepped out into the night without turning. "Sleep well, Falcon."

If she'd been a dog, she would have panted. Maybe she would anyway. Resist? Not in her dreams, she wouldn't.

❖

Fallon looked up as Nora stepped into the kitchen area. "I hope you slept better than I did," she whispered, winking as she scrambled the eggs. To her amazement, Nora blushed.

"I honestly don't know what came over me," she whispered back. After a quick glance to confirm that no one else was up yet, she moved closer. "I've never done anything like that before in my life."

"Hmm." Fallon rubbed her chin. "In that case, I'm going to suggest we're still not even, and you should bring your cards over tonight."

Nora swiped at her arm. "You wish."

"I sure do." She hadn't meant to sound so earnest. Nora broke off her questioning gaze at the sound of someone coming for breakfast.

But after that, it felt like there was something different between them. Nora photographed everyone, but Fallon began to catch the lens pointed at her more often. Sometimes she made a face, just to ensure the picture wouldn't be used. Still, Nora sat by her, though they didn't talk more than usual, and almost every time Fallon felled a tree, she'd catch a glimpse of Nora grinning at her proudly. They often worked near each other, and once, when Fallon saw Nora put her hand on her back to stretch, it brought a very vivid memory of the way she'd looked without that towel. Fallon knew her attraction to Nora was deepening into something more, but she told herself repeatedly that there was no future for them. Acknowledging that reality didn't help much.

By the second Sunday day off, the crew was nearly on schedule. Ranger Reva had visited and seemed duly impressed with their progress.

They'd had their showers the night before, and everyone was looking forward to sleeping in and enjoying a well-deserved day off. Fallon was awake but not dressed when she heard voices outside her tent.

"Fallon." It was Jade's voice, and her tone was urgent. "Hannah's been stung by something, and I think she's having an allergic reaction. She's getting hives and maybe a fever. I need you to take her to the clinic in town."

"On it." Fallon threw on something that wasn't too dirty and hurried to her car. Hannah seemed dizzy as Kennedy and Delores helped her into the back seat. Nora held the door, watching with a concerned expression.

"I'll stay here with the rest of the crew," Jade said, digging into her medical kit. "But here's the credit card, and take this EpiPen in case she gets worse."

"I've never used one of these," Fallon said, hoping her voice didn't indicate her rising panic. "And how will I give it to her if I'm driving?"

"I'll go with you," Nora said. "But I can't stand the idea of needles. If she gets worse, I'll drive, and you'll have to administer it."

Fallon agreed, the thought of Nora's presence easing some of her worry. "Let's go."

Nora sat with Hannah's head on her lap, talking to her softly. They were almost to the main road when Nora said, "She's starting to have trouble breathing, and her pulse is getting faster. I think you need to give her the injection."

After stopping, Fallon took the EpiPen, reading over the instructions. "Okay. Hold her leg still."

"I feel kinda sick," Hannah wheezed.

Nora turned her head away as Fallon used the device. "You drive," Fallon said. Her hands were trembling, the aftereffects of sticking a needle in someone, she supposed. "I'll stay back here with her. Be careful, but hurry."

Fallon tried to block out the last time she'd rushed someone to a clinic and what that outcome had been, trying to convince herself of the many ways this situation was different. Hannah was young and healthy. They had given her medication right away, something that should have been helping already. Fallon didn't think she could bring herself to accompany Hannah into the examining room, but Nora could.

Hannah groaned, and Nora asked, "How is she?"

Fallon looked out the window, seeing they were approaching the town. "I think she's breathing better, but her heartbeat is still fast." When Nora squealed the tires around a sharp corner, she added, "Please get us there without getting pulled over."

"Sorry. This car has more power than I'm used to." Nora pulled into the space nearest the entrance and threw the car into park. They helped Hannah inside, and as soon as they explained what had happened, a wheelchair was brought out and Hannah was taken back to an examining room.

"Go with her." Fallon gave Nora a little push. "Every patient needs an advocate."

Nora gave her an odd look but did as she suggested. Fallon went to the bathroom before telling the receptionist she'd wait outside. She supposed every medical facility smelled and sounded the same, but she couldn't bear it. She paced, ignoring the bench near the door. Later, she watched a woman bring in a young girl who was holding her abdomen. She was clearly flushed with fever. Fallon closed her eyes and tried to steady her breathing. Such indicators could be anything from appendicitis to food poisoning, which was the problem. It had to be hard for medical personnel to get an accurate diagnosis with such general symptoms. She resumed her pacing.

Finally, a nurse came out and asked, "Are you here with Hannah?"

"Yes, is she all right?"

"She's doing much better, but we'd like to keep her for a few more hours, just to be sure."

Fallon sat on the bench, putting her head in her hands as she exhaled with relief. The nurse gave her a little pat before handing her two twenty-dollar bills. "Your other friend said to tell you to please find something for breakfast."

Fallon looked up, and the nurse pointed down the street. "There's a place right there that does great coffee and baked goods."

The parking lot was much more crowded after Fallon returned fifteen minutes later carrying a cardboard container of four coffees and eight assorted pastries. Nora smiled at her from the bench. "Why aren't you with Hannah?" Fallon asked, hearing herself sound more cross than she'd intended.

Nora's pleased expression fell. "The nurse said Hannah's fine." Fallon must have looked doubtful because Nora struck a dramatic pose, throwing her arm up to her forehead. "I want nothing more than to watch her sleep for three more hours, but I must have sustenance first."

"Okay." Fallon put the food and drinks on the bench before

handing Nora her change. "I'm sorry you had to pay. I'll reimburse you when—"

Nora stopped her with a hand on her arm, shaking her head. "I'm still trying to make us even for that ice cream stunt."

Fallon grinned as she took a deep drink of coffee. "I liked your other approach better." Nora smirked and drank without comment. As she selected a lemon Danish, Fallon noticed the crowded waiting area. "What's going on in there?"

"Apparently, a propane barbecue grill exploded at a family reunion," Nora reported, patting the bench after she scooted over to make room. "Amazingly, no one was killed, but there are a few burns and maybe a broken arm, along with lots of scrapes and bruises."

"Wow."

"Yeah. Anyway, I told the receptionist to come get us when we can take Hannah home."

"Home, huh?" Fallon smiled for what might have been the first time since Jade had awakened her that morning. "You better be careful, or someone might get the idea you actually like this gig."

Nora punched her arm but not hard. "I do like your car, by the way."

"Yeah? Well, don't get any ideas. Big Red and I have been through a lot together, and she has sentimental value for me. Plus, she's a workhorse. I can't imagine ever parting with her."

"Then you better get your gas gauge fixed," Nora teased.

They had finished most of the pastries and coffee when an ambulance without lights or siren pulled up out front. Fallon stood, shifting her attention to the people inside the clinic. The nurse moved the family group off to one side as the EMTs entered. Soon after, they guided the mother and feverish girl inside the vehicle. Lights and sirens came on as they drove off.

Fallon trembled, turning away. When Nora asked what was wrong, she said, "Ask the nurse if we can take Hannah now. We can watch her sleep just as well at camp." Nora hesitated, and Fallon looked at her, eyes full of tears. "Please, Nora."

Fallon had the car waiting at the door when Nora brought out a groggy Hannah. Fallon jumped out, helping them both into the back seat before quickly driving away.

"You should try to avoid getting a ticket too, you know," Nora suggested.

Fallon couldn't bring herself to say how critical it was, her nearly uncontrollable need to get away from sickness, from the medical facility, from the echoes of loss in her head.

"Fallon?" Nora asked, as if making sure she'd heard.

Nodding, she slowed to a few miles over the speed limit. Nora was talking to Hannah, but Fallon couldn't focus on the words. As she turned off onto the dirt road, she did hear Hannah say, "Much better, thank you."

Her heart rate slowed gradually. There wasn't another sound for the rest of the drive, but Fallon didn't care. She knew what she knew. They didn't. After they arrived back at camp, everyone rushed to see Hannah, hugging and fussing over her. Fallon went to her tent, stripping off her clothes and putting on her pajamas. Curling up on top of her bed, she closed her eyes, a wave of anguish washing over her.

She'd been so excited the day her mother had accompanied her to the high school to register her for the SAT. After looking at the booklet, she'd been confident about the reading section, but geometry was a puzzle. The more she'd read over the sample questions, the more confused she'd gotten, and there hadn't been anyone to ask.

When Fallon had confessed her opinion that the test would be a total waste of time, her mother had taken her back to the high school to find out about tutoring, and they'd learned it started in two days.

Fallon had barely waited until they were out of the office to hug her mother. "You're the best mom ever."

Her mom had scoffed. "We both know that's not true." But she'd hugged Fallon back.

At the diner that evening, there'd been much commotion and banging of pots in the kitchen, while Roxie had been scrubbing the front counter like she was mad at it. In addition to explaining that the boss was coming the next day, Mr. Jamar had added that Fallon shouldn't come around until Mr. Hickson was gone, since she wasn't officially an employee.

Fallon had spent the day studying, and when her mother had finally come home, she'd headed straight for the shower. Afterward, she'd described sweeping out the long-neglected storage shed in the back after Mr. Hickson had gone out there first. She'd laughed at the idea that "Those vermin that had set up house in there probably scared him more than he did them."

Two weeks later, Mr. Hickson was long gone, but her mom had seemed more tired and achy than usual. She'd begun popping aspirin, hoping it would help the pains and a headache she hadn't been able to shake. When she'd started having chills and diarrhea, Fallon had taken her to the local clinic. The overworked staff had been treating cases of flu for months and offered a rapid influenza diagnostic test, though the nurse had said it could show negative even if her mom actually had the flu.

"We don't need to spend money on something that doesn't work," her mother had insisted.

"Rest, fluids, Tylenol or Advil." The nurse had called on her way out the door. "Come back if you start having chest pain or trouble breathing."

Fallon took in a shaky breath as she turned over, trying not to relive the way it had all ended. If she started crying, she might never stop. Keeping the memory dammed up was the only way to keep from coming apart. Sounds of lively conversation drifted over; the crew was at dinner, celebrating Hannah's recovery. Good. That would keep everyone occupied, and she could have this time to regain her stability. *I'll check with Hannah tomorrow*, she decided. *Or someone will call if there's any problem.*

Normally, she would read to take her mind off the real world, but if she turned on her light, someone might see, and she'd have to talk to them. She knew Nora had noticed her odd behavior on the drive back, but it didn't matter now. Tomorrow. She would be fine by then.

She tried to empty her mind, but now that thoughts of Nora had made their way in, they grabbed center stage. Nora in her PPE, chips flying all around her as she sawed through a trunk as if it was made of butter. Nora cooking, her face glowing from the camp stove. And Nora slowly lowering the towel, revealing her—

At the sound of the vestibule zipper, she started to sit up, then decided to feign sleep. Turning away from the entrance, she pulled the sheet and light blanket around her and closed her eyes. Hearing the sound of the flap being pushed aside and put back into place, she steadied her breathing and tried to relax. After some rustling, she felt someone slide in beside her. She'd known from the first sound that it was Nora, but at the nearness of her body, the urge to cry threatened to overpower her again.

"I know you're awake," Nora whispered. "But you don't have to say anything. I just want to be here for you. Okay?"

Fallon gave the slightest nod, but somehow, that opened the floodgates, and she began to sob.

"Oh, baby." Nora snugged against her, tightening her arms. "Go ahead, get it out of your system." Turning her head into the pillow, Fallon tried to muffle her cries and blot her tears. They stayed like that until Fallon was completely spent and too hoarse to speak. Nora tugged her gently. "Turn this way."

Fallon did, finding herself facing Nora, who had rolled onto her back.

"Right here." Nora patted her shoulder, and Fallon slipped under her arm, sighing deeply. She grasped Nora's waist as if they might be torn apart at any moment. "It's all right," Nora told her. "I'm not going anywhere."

Fallon relaxed her hold and slept.

When she awoke, it was totally dark. Nora's steady breathing, a sound she'd relished on other occasions, sounded closer than usual. They were facing each other, Nora's head half buried in Fallon's chest, held in place by her close embrace. Fallon's mouth was terribly dry and her eyes felt raw, but she feared any movement would wake Nora. Clearing her throat or rubbing her face would have the same effect, though, so very slowly, she removed one arm from around Nora and tried to reach for her water bottle. Nora's breathing changed, and she stirred, making a little sound in her throat.

"I'm sorry," Fallon whispered. "I didn't mean to wake you, but I need a drink."

"Me too," Nora said, lifting her face as she spoke. Their lips were mere inches apart.

"You were really sweet to stay with me," Fallon murmured, still fumbling for her water.

Nora's body shifted against hers, sending arousal skimming down to her toes. "You know I'm not that sweet. Maybe I have ulterior motives."

"Here." She handed the reusable bottle to Nora, who took a deep swallow while Fallon rubbed her eyes with her free hand.

Just as she stopped, Nora pushed her onto her back, hovering over her. "Allow me." Grinning, she aimed the opening at Fallon's mouth. Fallon felt powerless and galvanized at the same time. She parted her lips and received a delicate stream of water that she swallowed eagerly, trusting Nora's intention and her ability. It was the most sensual thing she'd ever experienced. "Enough?" Nora asked, pulling back.

Fallon couldn't answer. Nora had quenched one thirst, but a different kind raged through her. Nora smiled as if she knew exactly what effect she'd had and leaned away to put the bottle down. *To hell with restraint and resistance.* While Nora was off-balance, Fallon copied her earlier move, pushing Nora onto her back. "I'm going to kiss you now," she announced, not stopping to figure out where this confidence had come from. "If you don't want that, you need to leave."

Nora's body tightened beneath her, but she was still smiling. "How am I supposed to go with you half on top of me?"

"You're not."

CHAPTER TWELVE

The weight of Fallon's warm body above her and the commanding intensity in her voice made Nora wet. She'd always been the one to make the first move, and she never would have expected Fallon to be so bold, though she was more than willing to be kissed, especially by this appealing woman she couldn't seem to stay away from.

She lifted her chin slightly, giving Fallon easier access to her mouth. She'd honestly intended only comfort when she'd made her way into Fallon's tent tonight, and her heart had ached at Fallon's tears. The visit to the clinic had obviously triggered something, but Nora had no interest in being a sympathy kiss.

Fallon's lips were exactly as she'd imagined them: careful but passionately demanding. Nora responded eagerly, pushing her hands into Fallon's hair, holding her in place. Fallon groaned, and Nora's nipples tightened in response. Why had she not recognized how much she wanted this? She'd convinced herself that her feelings were incidental, what she might have for any teammate. But Fallon was the one she'd gone to every time she was in need, frightened, or lonely.

Momentarily overcome, she broke the kiss and put her head against Fallon's chest.

"Nora? I didn't mean to upset you."

The concern in Fallon's voice was sincere, so Nora kissed Fallon's neck. "You didn't. Not at all. I feel like I might be the one taking advantage. You were emotional earlier, and maybe that's why—"

"No," Fallon said firmly. "Earlier, I was grieving because I was remembering what happened to my mom. I've learned to suppress those sad times, maybe because it's more painful to relive them when I'm alone. But having you near made it safe to let go. I think that's why

I stopped holding back on what I feel for you. Kissing you is something I've wanted to do for weeks now. What I kept hoping you might want too."

"I did. And I do." Nora kissed her gently on the mouth. "But will you tell me what happened to your mom?"

Fallon sighed and rolled onto her back. Nora followed, resting her head on Fallon's chest, listening to her strong, steady heart. "My mom died in a clinic very much like the one we went to today. She was only forty years old."

Both of Nora's parents were older than that, and strained though their relationship might be, she'd never thought of what it might be like to lose them both. No wonder Fallon placed such importance on family, on having someone she could count on. "What happened?" she asked softly.

"It was nobody's fault," Fallon said, "though it took me a long time to truly accept that. She was misdiagnosed and never treated for the virus that killed her." Her voice trembled. "She was suffering, and nothing I tried helped. It was awful."

Nora stroked Fallon's cheek before tucking a long strand of hair behind her ear. "I can't imagine how hard that must have been."

"Harder than anything before or since."

They lay quietly for a time. "What did she die of?" Nora whispered.

"Hantavirus. We went to the clinic twice, but they thought it was the flu. The symptoms are similar, especially at first. Neither of us knew to tell them how a few weeks before, she'd cleaned out a storage area that had been home to a nest of rodents. It wasn't until they did an autopsy that they found out what it was."

Nora shuddered. Her father had been the one to warn her and her brothers of the danger of mouse nests or droppings that could gather around firewood or in dark, musty places such as seldom-used cabins or storerooms. He'd stressed that early treatment was essential.

"I'm so sorry." Nora hated the inadequacy of those words, but she had to say something.

"Me too." Fallon swallowed. "I think she would have liked you."

Oh God. Now Nora was going to cry. That was the last thing Fallon needed. The night had already been a roller coaster of emotions. "Maybe…" She cleared her throat. "Maybe we should get some sleep."

"Only if you promise to come back tomorrow night. I'd like to pick up where we left off."

"I think that could be arranged." Nora turned on her side, smiling when Fallon snugged against her.

The next morning, a comforting aroma coaxed Nora into consciousness. *Coffee?* Definitely. She blinked into awareness that she was alone in Fallon's tent. The bedding was cool in the space where Fallon had been. How had she slept through Fallon getting up? Stretching, she remembered the kisses they'd shared last night. Sweet and sexy as it had been, the bright light of day made her wonder if it'd been a good idea. Would Fallon have expectations about what came next? Was she the type to create an instant future together? Fallon was a good person, but Nora had plans. She'd gotten in, and now she was closer to getting out of Firecamp, and the rest of her life was waiting.

Nora moved into the vestibule, dressing in yesterday's clothes. Not that it mattered. The crew had stopped paying any attention to what anyone wore weeks ago. Circling past her own tent to grab her camera, she made her way to the kitchen area. Hannah stood next to Fallon, holding her hand and swinging it slowly. Nora took the photo even as her chest tensed, but she calmed herself when Hannah shouted her name and ran over, enfolding her in a warm hug.

"My other hero! You saved my life too," she said, squeezing a little tighter. "How can I ever repay you?"

Nora squeezed back before stepping away slightly. "Don't be silly. There's no repayment necessary. You would have done the same for me."

"Did you two practice this?" Nora frowned as Jade joined them, pointing at Fallon. "That's exactly what she said." Nora couldn't think of an explanation, but Jade didn't seem to notice. "At least we don't have to take turns watching this one sleep anymore." She poked Hannah playfully in the stomach. "She snores something fierce."

"Hey, I was drugged," Hannah protested as they made their way to rejoin the group.

Nora couldn't resist a glance at Fallon, despite her plan to avoid anything obvious. Fallon grinned and gave her a quick wink. Great, now she was blushing. Thankfully, everyone else was still focused on Hannah.

Breakfast became a contest of who could come up with the silliest bee jokes. Nora couldn't help rolling her eyes when Fallon started them off with an old one. "Why do bees hum?"

Kennedy elbowed her. "Because they don't know the words."

"A man went to buy some bees," Jade said. "He paid for a dozen but got an extra one. That was the free-bee."

Everyone groaned. Hannah begged for mercy, but Delores said, "I saw a bee who was having a bad hair day. It was a frizz-bee."

They must have sat around last night thinking of words with the "bee" sound, Nora decided. Thinking quickly, she asked, "What do you call a bee who is under a spell?"

"Bee-witched." Hannah clapped. "I loved watching reruns of that show with my dad."

"Hannah got it. Game over," Jade said, standing. "Last week. Big push. Everyone ready?"

"We are bee-side ourselves with eagerness," Fallon said, dodging as Jade swatted at her.

As she worked, Nora kept one eye on the marker at the end of their clear-cut. It was getting closer, and Kenn and Delores were now at the head of their crew. Hannah was given ATV duty for the day, though someone always went with her to help unload. When it was Nora's turn, Hannah smiled at her while they stacked the logs.

"Is there something going on between you and Falcon?"

Taken by surprise, Nora took a moment to respond. She finally managed, "Not really." At Hannah's doubtful expression, she added, "I mean, I'm going off to college after I'm done here, and Fallon wants to stay and work for Firecamp. There's no future, so no point in someone getting hurt."

Hannah frowned but didn't say anything more until they were back at the clear-cut and Nora was getting off the ATV. "My folks once went to a seminar by this guy named Jim Rand. Apparently, he was an especially good motivational speaker, you know?" Nora nodded. "One thing I remember my dad telling me from that talk was 'Happiness is not something you postpone for the future. It is something you design for the present.' Maybe you should design your present happiness and let the future take care of itself."

"Is that what you do?" Nora asked. Once, she would have said this with all the cynicism she could muster. Now she genuinely wanted to know.

"If I had someone who looked at me like Fallon looks at you? For sure I would. For now, my present includes gratitude for my life and for my new friends. I plan to enjoy both for as long as I have them."

Nora smiled thoughtfully, giving Hannah a quick wave as Jade and Delores began loading the next pile of logs. If Fallon was okay with focusing on the present happiness, maybe they could share it.

Early that evening, she was waiting her turn at the wash bucket when Jade ran up, holding out the radio. "You have a message from base."

Ranger Upshaw's familiar voice crackled through the small speaker. "Your brother has been in an accident. If you can get to base tonight, we can call your family for details."

"Which brother?" Nora asked, though there was no good answer.

After a pause, Upshaw came back on. "Tyler."

As Nora took in a breath, a warm hand caressed her shoulder. Fallon seemed to have a sixth sense about where and when Nora needed her. Had anyone else's presence given her such immediate comfort? "Tell her you'll be there. You can take my car," Fallon said from beside her.

Five minutes later, they were at Big Red's door. Nora had packed a small bag of essentials, and Fallon handed her the keys. "I'd go with you, but I can't leave Jade any more shorthanded than we'll be without you."

"I know. I promise I'll be very careful with your car."

"Be sure to fill the tank every chance you get." Fallon smiled before pulling Nora close. "Be careful with yourself. Tell Tyler I'm thinking of him."

"I'm sorry we won't be able to pick up where we left off," Nora whispered.

"I've been waiting since the first day I saw you. I can wait a little longer."

Meeting Fallon's gaze, Nora found herself overflowing with hundreds of things to say, passionate things, funny things, sentimental things. She opened her mouth, but nothing came out. Instead, she pulled her camera out of her overnight bag. She always had it with her, but now she handed it to Fallon. "Hang on to this for me."

Fallon's eyes widened, and she touched Nora's cheek. "We'll both be here when you get back." She took a step away, clutching the camera to her chest.

Nora nodded, appreciating that Fallon understood how much the Canon meant to her. She waved to the rest of the crew and got in the car. As she drove, she remembered Hannah's comment about gratitude. Right now, she was grateful it was light later and that summer meant she didn't have to worry about driving in snow. Mostly, she hoped she could be grateful that Tyler would be all right.

Ranger Upshaw raised an eyebrow when she pulled up. "I see you were able to talk Fallon into using her car."

"Yes, she was very gracious about it, but you know Jade needed her to stay at camp." Upshaw gave her a look, and she added, "Fallon met Tyler when we found her on the road to Firecamp. They hit it off quite well, so I'm sure she's concerned about him too."

Upshaw nodded. "Come on." She left Nora in the office. After long minutes of waiting and lots of static, she was connected to her mother's cell phone. The voice that answered was weak and nervous.

"Mom? It's Nora. What's wrong with Tyler?"

"Nora? Oh, thank God. I don't understand exactly what happened, but the doctors say your brother has a broken arm and a concussion. He's already been given a mild sedative, but he keeps fighting them and insisting he has to talk to you first. We've already been here for at least three hours, and if you can't convince him to let the doctors set his arm, they'll have to put him under, and that won't help the concussion."

Nora knew she should sympathize, agree with her mother about how terrible the situation was, but she simply didn't have the stamina for it. "Put him on."

After some shuffling, she could hear her brother crying in the background. Her mother must have covered the phone because she couldn't make out anything that was being said, but after another long minute, Tyler breathed, "H...hello? N...Nora? Is it really you?"

"Hi, buddy. Yeah, it's really me. Mom said you broke your arm." Tyler started crying again. "Hey, hey now. Talk to me, Ty. Let's figure the angles out together, the way we do for my pictures."

"It hurts real bad, but I'm afraid they'll make it hurt worse."

"But what if they don't? What if setting it makes it feel better? Besides, you'll probably get a cast, and everyone can sign it or draw something on it." Nora thought she'd made a good point, but Tyler started crying again. "What's the matter?"

"I've been doing a lot of drawing this summer, but now I won't be able to," he blubbered.

"Maybe you won't, but maybe you will. It depends on where the break is. They might be able to leave your fingers out of the cast."

He quieted. "You think so?"

"Yeah. That's something you can ask the doctor."

"I don't think he likes me," he whispered. "He always looks mad the way Daddy does."

"Maybe he's worried that you don't like him since you won't let him help you."

Tyler breathed quietly. "If I let him fix me, will you come home and sign my cast?"

"I'll sign it as soon as I can, but till then, you'll need to draw a big square and write 'Reserved for Nora' outside it."

"Okay—" He started to say something else, and then he was crying again. "No! No, I'm not finished."

After more muffled sounds, her father came on. "Nora, you need to come on home now. I'll be there in the morning to pick you up."

Nora knew better than to simply refuse. "What about the nearly six weeks I still have in my hitch here?"

"Well." He hedged, clearing his throat as if he'd forgotten. "That's too bad, but you can try again next year. We'll let our wager stand until then. But your mother and your brother need you."

Nora felt her temper rising. "You're perfectly capable of helping my mother and my brother. I'm going to finish my hitch this summer, not next year. That was our deal."

"Nora…" His voice had that warning, practically threatening tone that had made her give in so often before.

Not this time. "I'm not leaving until I'm done. In case you don't remember when that is, I'm sure Mom has the date circled on the calendar. Don't bother coming before then because I won't be here." She started to end the call but added, "Tell Tyler that Fallon said hi. She wants to sign his cast too."

"Who? What the hell are you talking about?"

"Tell him what I said. I'll see you in six weeks." She disconnected, lowering herself on shaking legs into the chair behind the desk. She worked to control her breathing, stunned that she'd stood up to him at last. A discreet knock sounded after a few minutes, and she stood.

"All done?" Upshaw asked, sounding surprisingly gentle.

"Yeah." Nora looked at the wall clock. "I guess it's too late to drive back."

"I'd say so. Why don't you get cleaned up, and we'll find you a cot."

"That sounds great. Thank you."

They started out into the cool evening. "Jade tells me your crew has been doing quite well," Upshaw said conversationally. "Is this situation with your family anything we need to worry about?"

Nora understood the question. Would this phone call mean she might get herself into trouble again? "I promise you, as long as I can be back with my crew tomorrow morning, there won't be anything else to worry about." *Except possibly a very angry ex-smoke jumper showing up.*

"I think I'll come with you," Upshaw mused, studying her. "Things are pretty calm here, and Hal can cover for me until the end of the week. I could do with some field work."

Nora would have paid to see her father trying to take on Hal, but getting back to Fallon was even more appealing.

They left at first light and made it to camp as the crew was finishing breakfast. After Fallon hugged her in the same friendly way as everyone else, Nora assumed it was the presence of Reva Upshaw that inhibited their greeting. "How did it go?" Fallon asked.

Nora sighed. "My mother was a wreck, as usual. I think Tyler will be okay, though he was crying when I talked to him." Fallon touched her heart in sympathy, but Nora shook her head. "It's just a broken arm and a concussion."

"Just?"

"Well, he's fourteen now. And intellectually, he's super smart, but emotionally, he's still immature sometimes. I got him to calm down by promising to come sign his cast. I didn't say exactly when, though." She crossed her arms. "I'm sure those tears are why my father wanted me to come home."

"He did?"

"Yeah. He informed me that he was coming to get me and said we could wait a year before settling our bet. I told him not to bother because I wouldn't be there."

"How did he take it?"

"Not very well, I imagine. But I hung up on him, so I can't really say." Nora couldn't tell if Fallon was shocked by her behavior or relieved that she wasn't leaving. Leaning in, she whispered, "At least we can pick up where we left off."

Fallon took a step back. "I don't know, Nora. With Ranger Reva here, maybe we—"

Jade called from the kitchen, asking if Fallon could make an extra breakfast for the new arrivals. Nora tried to hide her dismay. Her return wasn't going at all the way she'd imagined.

Jade, on the other hand, was ecstatic, declaring, "We'll finish that clear-cut now for sure," drawing a pleased expression from the normally stoic Ranger Upshaw.

Once they got to work, Nora saw that Upshaw indeed had serious cutting skills. The whole crew picked up the pace as sawdust flew, and the sound of tree trunks cracking as they fell was almost constant. By evening, everyone was even more exhausted, but their progress was evident. As they ate dinner, enjoying Hannah's long-promised stroganoff, Ranger Upshaw told stories of the best and worst of Firecamps past.

"Where do we rank?" Kennedy asked, leaning forward.

"Oh, absolutely among the best." Upshaw winked at them. "Maybe even number one."

Everyone cheered. When Delores got the group singing during cleanup, Nora put her hand on Fallon's knee. "Can you at least walk me to the bathroom?"

Before she got a reply, Upshaw called, "Fallon? Could I speak with you please?"

"Sorry," Fallon said before hurrying away, but Nora wasn't sure she was. What was different? Yes, the arrival of the almighty Ranger Upshaw, but there seemed to be something else.

She had all night alone to think about it. While tossing and turning, she'd almost decided to forget about anything more with Fallon, though kissing her was the nicest thing that had happened in a long time. The answer came to her early the next morning as she replayed the conversation they'd had when she'd returned to camp. Everything she'd said about her family had sounded cold and hard. Her mother was a mess. Tyler was too emotional for his age, and she didn't want him to need her. And she'd practically gloated about hanging up on her father. Fallon was sweet and kind and eager to care for those she considered family, while Nora had shown herself to be none of those things. Maybe she never would be.

"Nora," Fallon stage-whispered outside her tent. "Nora, are you up?"

She rolled toward the opening, answering quietly, "Yeah, I'm awake."

"I don't think we can both fit in there. Could you come out? I have something to tell you."

Nora missed Fallon's vestibule as she struggled into her clothes.

The moment she stepped outside, Fallon hugged her like she'd been gone for months. "I missed you."

It felt so good that Nora forgot she was a terrible person, letting herself relax into Fallon's body. "I missed you too. But what's going on? You said you had something to tell me."

"Yeah, I do. Last night, Ranger Reva told me I'd passed the first segment of the Firecamp leadership program." Fallon looked into her eyes, her face practically glowing with pride.

"That's great. I'm happy for you." She was, even though the news was clearing Fallon's path to somewhere Nora wouldn't be.

"And another reason why it's great is it means I don't have to hang around at our upcoming break and take the test again. So, uh, if you want to go home and check on Tyler, I could go with you. And I have my own reasons for making sure you get back here okay." Nora took a step away. Fallon's face fell.

Nora tried to smile and touched her arm. "That's very nice of you, but—" *Think about it, Nora. Think instead of reacting.* "Let me think about it, okay?"

"Of course. If I may offer some additional incentive?" Fallon cocked her head and raised her eyebrows, obviously waiting for permission. Why did she have to be so charming on top of the kind and sweet stuff? Nora gestured for her to continue. "After two short days with your family, we could spend the rest of our week at my place." She took Nora's hands, gently rubbing her thumbs across them. "I'd really like to show it to you."

"You…you have a place? Like, a house or an apartment or something?" This was unexpected news. "Where?"

"Kinda like that, yeah. And I'm not going to tell you where it is. You'll simply have to come see it." Fallon bounced a little and grinned, obviously pleased with herself. "Although I have to warn you, there's only one bed."

Nora liked the sound of that. Her body heated the way it did since she'd first thought about Fallon as something more than a fellow sawyer. "Why can't we skip the family visit and just go there?"

Fallon inhaled slowly. "We could. But I think it would be more enjoyable if we didn't have that niggling worry in the back of our minds."

Nora pulled her hands away and crossed her arms. "Who is 'we' in this narrative? You and the mouse in your pocket?"

"You know it's you and me, Nora. You've been worrying about Tyler, though you'd deny it. And I don't know him well, but he seems like a great kid, so I'd like to say hello. We don't even have to stay at your house. Isn't there a hotel in your town?"

"There are three, actually. A ritzy one, a decent one, and a no-tell motel that no one will admit to setting foot in, though they always seem to have cars parked there." Nora couldn't believe she was talking about this like it was some kind of possibility.

"I vote for the decent one," Fallon said. "And we can go dutch. I'll finally get to keep most of my paycheck this time. What do you think?"

Jade called from across the camp, "Stove's ready, Fallon."

"Saved by the bell." Nora was both relieved at not having to make a decision and amused by the irritated glare Fallon sent in Jade's direction. She started for the kitchen, giving a little squeak when Fallon acted like she might pinch her arm as she went by. Since when did she squeak?

"I didn't hear any bell," Fallon growled. "And I can't guarantee you'll be safe once I get you to my place."

Nora quickened her pace, trying not to giggle. Giggle?

All through breakfast, she thought about Fallon's offer. It was true that her parents had always been on their best behavior on the rare occasions she'd had someone over. And she *was* worried about Tyler. She would call Rudy and Art as soon as she got her phone charged. Someone needed to tell her what had happened to Tyler's arm and how he'd gotten a concussion, and she wanted the details before she got there. Two days would be a short visit compared to the time they'd have afterward.

Watching Fallon as she chatted with Jade, Nora tried to imagine what her place would be like. Appealing and genial like she was? Fallon threw back her head and laughed at something Jade said, and Nora imagined running her tongue along the column of her neck, finishing with a long, deep kiss. No, not finishing. She wanted more than that, and Fallon's place could be the ideal location. Remembering what Hannah had said about designing her present, Nora decided that present happiness would be enough. For now.

❖

Having thought better of a surprise visit, Nora had called her parents once they'd reached Brighton Valley in the early evening. Her mother had insisted they wait to come by until the next morning, so they'd gone on the not-so-thrilling tour of her hometown. Naturally, Fallon had acted delighted. When they'd gone to dinner at one of the nicer restaurants, they'd run into Addison, who had the nerve to flirt shamelessly with Fallon, even commenting on how much she preferred longer hair. By the time they got to their room at the Best Western, Nora was too stressed to think clearly. Drained by apprehension and the smothering feeling of being back home, she was desperate for her own space. After asking Fallon to sleep in the other queen bed, she'd realized her mistake halfway through the night and had crawled in next to the most caring person she knew, who'd welcomed her the way she always did.

Not wanting Fallon to be disillusioned, exactly, Nora did want her to see the Palmer family's true colors. But of course, the visit went wonderfully. Her mother was agreeable and friendly, more gracious than she'd ever seen her. And once her father remembered who Fallon was, he was on his best behavior.

"The way he carried on, anyone would have thought you were war buddies," Nora muttered as Fallon drove them away.

"But Tyler cried when he saw you," Fallon reminded her.

"Tyler cries at *Finding Nemo*, and he's seen it at least twenty times," Nora answered. "But he let you sign his cast first."

"That's because your mom wouldn't let me in the kitchen, so you had to help."

"As usual." Nora slumped against the comfortable seat.

"But she gave you those beautiful brown eyes. And your smile looks just like hers. You're a good three inches taller, though. I guess you must've gotten that from your dad."

Nora rolled her eyes. "You and your fairy-tale image of a family. For me, it's the same, dull routine and tedious talk. I don't know why I expect anything to be different."

"Probably because you've changed, and you expect them to change along with you. Unfortunately, it doesn't automatically happen that way."

Nora shrugged, setting her mouth in a firm line. Was she upset because they seemed to be doing all right without her? Or because Fallon was apparently her father's new favorite? He'd almost talked her into staying another day, saying he wanted to take her fishing. Obviously, he'd forgotten that his only daughter was the one who'd loved fishing with him.

After Fallon had cautioned her that they probably wouldn't have cell coverage once they got to her place, Nora had tried again to reach Art before they left town but had hung up rather than leaving another message. She'd had a brief conversation with Rudy from the home phone earlier. He didn't know exactly what had caused Tyler's injury, only that he'd been out with their father when it had happened. No surprise there. Her mother had been oblivious, and there had never been a time to talk to Tyler alone. She'd made sure he knew to leave a message on her cell phone, promising she'd get back to him ASAP, but he'd seemed oddly disinterested. At least Rudy had felt guilty enough that he promised to take some time off next week to come help out, the most positive outcome of her visit.

After a quick stop for groceries, they got on the road. Nora rested her head on the plush seat, feeling her tension subside as Fallon pointed out signs and wildlife and made vague references to other travel experiences. "You're so solid, so steady," Nora said, speaking aloud without really thinking about it. "Nothing seems to affect you. How do you do that?"

"First, you affect me, so that part isn't true."

Nora leaned over and kissed her cheek. "Thank you."

"For what?"

"For being steady and solid and nice to my family."

Fallon was quiet for a few minutes. "Seeing where you came from, what your life was like, was fascinating because it's very different from how I grew up. My life was constant change, continuous motion. Everything was in flux. I learned to hold myself still because I needed a fixed point, like your North Star."

"It's not mine, you know." Nora yawned. She hadn't slept well, even when she'd started out the second night in bed with Fallon. The hum of the highway made her eyes feel heavy, and just before she dropped off, she heard Fallon say something about being hers, but she couldn't quite make sense of it.

CHAPTER THIRTEEN

Fallon was relieved when Nora woke cheerful and chatty from her nap.

"Where are we going?" Nora asked for the third time.

"I'm still not telling," she answered, reaching for Nora's hand. "But if you don't like it, we can go right back to your parents' house." At Nora's groan, she offered, "Or show up early back at Firecamp."

"This is supposed to be a break, if you'll recall," Nora said pointedly, but she was smiling as she pulled Fallon's hand onto her thigh. "It's pretty here. But you're kinda far away from everything."

"I know. I really lucked into this deal."

"How long have you had this...cabin?" Nora's obvious fishing expedition made Fallon smile.

"We're almost there." She squeezed Nora's fingers before letting go. The road was getting rougher, and mist spotted the windshield. She needed to concentrate on steering around the potholes and washboards. "Then I'll tell you everything."

The drizzle had become a light rain when she turned at the sign for Arrowhead State Recreation Area. "Oh, you're by a park?" Nora said. "That's cool."

A few miles later, Fallon pulled up to the barred entrance. Putting on the brake, she grabbed a jacket. "Slide over and drive through after I unlock the gate." Opening her door, she stepped out into the rain.

Nora glanced at the Closed sign. "Is this legal?" she asked, giving Fallon the side eye as she moved behind the wheel.

"As far as I know, yes."

"You're hedging."

Fallon grinned, and after securing the entrance, she settled into the passenger's seat. Pointing down the narrow road to where her trailer was parked in the space marked Campground Host, she said, "We're here."

"Wait, you live in a state park?"

"Not exactly. The campground is closed for repairs, but Ranger Reva helped me get permission to set up here while I'm at Firecamp. That trailer is my home. I call her Silver Bird."

Nora blinked. "Wow. I didn't see this coming."

"Let's go inside, and I'll give you the tour. Then you can bring in the groceries and your bag, and I'll put stuff away." Before Nora could protest, Fallon added. "And I'll loan you my raincoat so you don't melt. If stuff isn't organized, a trailer can get junky real fast."

"A place for everything and everything in its place?" Nora asked, clearly amused.

"You'll see." Fallon opened the door, relieved the tiny opening she'd left in the roof vent had kept the inside air fresh. As she narrated, she tried to see her home through Nora's eyes. The coolness of the classic silver airplane-style interior was offset by a warm wood floor and royal blue pillows on the light gray, L-shaped couch at the entrance. "There's storage under the sofa. That's where I usually keep my winter things."

The patchwork of rugs was a close match to the quilt on her bed.

Nora looked as Fallon pointed at the dinette.

"Perfect for two. I'm glad we didn't invite anyone else."

Nora had already stepped toward the kitchen, obviously intrigued, so Fallon pointed out the various appliances, along with the bathroom sink and separate toilet and shower room. "Airstream trailers have a good reputation, don't they?" Nora asked, turning to face her.

Fallon nodded, the nervousness she'd felt about bringing Nora to her home falling away at her approval. "They're made to hold up. Could you tell this one is seven years old?"

"I can tell you've taken care of it." She pointed at the bathroom. "May I test out your facilities?"

"Uh, yeah, if you can wait just a sec. I have to turn the water on outside."

"Can I go too?" Nora asked. "I'd like to see your setup."

Fallon knew she was grinning like an idiot, but she couldn't help it. "Sure."

Nora stopped her at the door. Stepping into Fallon's body, she put her arms around her neck. "Your home is wonderful. I'm very glad you brought me here."

Fallon hugged her close because she didn't want Nora to see her fighting back happy tears.

They finished the leftovers that Nora's mother had insisted they take as the rain continued to fall, making the trailer feel extra cozy. Wiping her mouth, Nora said, "All right. Now tell me how this came to be your home."

Fallon went cold. She'd never told anyone the story. But something made her want to share whatever Nora wanted to know. She cleared her throat. "Well, I told you how Mom and I were always traveling, looking for evidence in my dad's death. And you know how my mom died." Nora nodded. "We'd been staying in a very sketchy motel, and as soon as the owner heard she was gone, he offered me a free week if I'd have sex with him."

Nora's eyes widened. "What a scumbag. I'm sorry that happened to you."

The sympathy in Nora's tone heartened her. "I was really hurting and sad, and then I got scared, knowing I couldn't stay there but not sure of anyplace else I could afford. I thought about taking off, but where could I go with no options and less than a hundred dollars? Plus, why would I leave the only people I had left in the world?"

Nora stood, holding out her hand. "I want to be closer while you tell me the rest of this. Could we go sit on the couch?"

Nora sat with her back against the short side cushion, pulling Fallon against her. Fallon sighed and rested her head on Nora's chest, stretching out her legs.

After a minute, she began again. "The person I was closest to was the cook at the diner, Mr. Jamar. He'd cried at my mom's funeral and told me to let him know if I needed anything. So I came in to work early after I got that 'offer' and asked if he knew of a place I could rent. He put up the 'Back in 30 Minutes' sign and took me over to the trailer park where he stayed. He knew the manager, and before those minutes were up, we'd negotiated a rate I could afford for a trailer, smaller than this one, in exchange for me taking care of the grounds three days a week." She took a shaky breath, anxious at the memory. "Then Mr. Jamar followed me to the motel and stood in the doorway while I packed. He said the owner walked past once or twice, but that bastard never said another word to me."

Nora's arms tightened around her. "Is Mr. Jamar the one who had a stroke?"

Fallon craned her neck to look up at her. "You remember that?"

Nora ran her fingers through Fallon's hair. "I think I remember everything you've ever said to me."

Fallon sat up, twisting until they were face-to-face, and cupped Nora's cheek, kissing her gently. "I want to tell you the rest, but it's really hard. I think I'm done for tonight. Could I show you the bedroom instead?"

❖

Fallon stretched, her arm hitting empty space where Nora had been. Smiling, she knew she'd never forget the image of Nora under her, arching and coming as she dug her nails into Fallon's back. Or maybe it would be the way Nora touched her so tenderly, stroking until Fallon thought she would come undone.

They'd slept for a time until she'd awakened to Nora murmuring "You're so beautiful" as she'd kissed her way down Fallon's body. Tears had threatened again until Nora's lips had reached her clit, and then she was transported.

Once she'd recovered, she'd flipped Nora onto her back and told her, "I know who's beautiful here, and it's you. In fact, you are exquisite." Running her tongue along the inside of Nora's muscled thigh, she'd added, "And delicious."

Afterward, lying with Nora sleeping in her arms, Fallon accepted that what was between them, said and unsaid, was the most meaningful experience she'd ever had.

When the smell of bacon began to permeate the trailer, Fallon jumped up, calling, "You have to turn on the hood vent or—"

A piercing whistle sounded, and Fallon rushed past Nora to the stovetop. "This," she said, flipping the switch before grabbing a towel and fanning the smoke detector until the sound stopped.

"Sorry," Nora said, looking down. "I wanted to bring you breakfast in bed."

Fallon didn't think about the fact that she was nude. What she noticed was Nora wearing a T-shirt and nothing else. "You know what I'd really like in bed? You."

Two hours later, after turning the vent fan off, Fallon put the burned, greasy bacon in the trash and made coffee. She added cream to Nora's and carried it into the bedroom. Nora stirred in the tangled sheets, and when she looked up and smiled, Fallon thought her heart would burst.

"Hi," she managed to croak as she held out the coffee mug.

"Hi yourself, Falcon."

They didn't leave the trailer until almost two, having finally eaten and showered. The air, washed by the rain, was breathtakingly brisk, accompanied by the familiar smell of pine and wet duff. As they walked hand in hand around the deserted park, Nora pointed out a few late summer flowers: asters, sedum, and phlox. Fallon led them off the road onto a small trail that wound into the forest. "I sure am happy we don't have to cut any of these trees," she said.

"I know, but this forest could use some fire mitigation, don't you think?"

Fallon nodded somewhat reluctantly. "I suppose we'll never stop looking at woodland that way." She paused before adding, "Or I won't. Maybe in Arizona, you—"

Nora stopped her with a finger on her lips. "Not now, okay? Later, we can talk about that. Let's keep this time for us, here, now."

Fallon kissed Nora's fingers, then her hand, and stole little bites along her arm, making her squirm. "Anything you say, Rah-Rah."

Nora's eyes narrowed. "What did you call me?"

Fallon laughed, taking a step back. "I didn't make it up. Delores did. Once you started taking photos and joining in with the rest of the crew, they called you Rah-Rah."

"Not to my face," Nora protested.

"No, because you're kinda scary sometimes. Especially when you're wielding a chainsaw."

The sun was nearly down when they made their way to the campground loop, coming upon three deer grazing along the roadside. "I think that one's pregnant," Nora whispered, pointing at a doe.

"Do you think you'll ever want kids?" Fallon asked as the deer moved on.

Nora shook her head. "I'm not particularly maternal."

"What if you were with someone who wanted them?" Fallon persisted.

"Would that someone be you?" Nora asked, sounding coy.

"Oh no. I can't see myself bringing a child into this world. How could I explain the frightening and cruel things that happen?"

They walked quietly toward Silver Bird. "Would you be able to finish telling me how you got this trailer now?" Nora asked after they got inside.

Fallon looked over from the stove where she'd begun making

chicken strips and steaming broccoli for dinner. Nora looked adorable with a blanket from the couch wrapped around her shoulders. Fallon gestured with her spatula. "This was Mr. Jamar's. He lived in it at the same trailer park. When his sister came to get him, she was worried about what to do with it. He told her he was going to sell it to me, and he did, along with Big Red. For a dollar."

Nora laughed and clapped. "Perfect."

"I told myself I'd make enough money to get to California and pay him what they were really worth, but before that happened, his sister called and said that Mr. Jamar had died." At the sting of tears, Fallon excused herself and went to the bathroom. Sometimes, it seemed like all her stories had sad endings. Hard as she tried, she couldn't shake the worry that the same would be true of her and Nora.

That night, they made love slowly, exploring each other carefully, as if wanting to avoid old injuries.

Fallon knew from her visit with the Palmers that fishing ranked far above firefighting for Nora. So while Nora slept the next morning, she dressed and went outside to find Mr. Jamar's poles and tackle box in an outside compartment. Making her way farther along the forest trail, she found the stream that Ranger Reva had told her about, exploring until she found a wide, deep pond.

Outside the trailer, Nora waited, coffee mug in hand. "Where the hell were you?"

Fallon realized she would have felt the same if she'd awakened to find Nora gone. "I'm sorry. I should have left you a note. I went to find a fishing hole."

Nora blinked. "Why?"

"Because I know you like it, and I've never fished, so maybe you could teach me?"

Nora turned without another word and went inside. After a few seconds, Fallon followed. She watched as Nora paced in the small space and muttered to herself. Fallon sat on the couch, bracing for the explosion she suspected was coming.

Finally, Nora stopped and stood in front of her, hands on her hips. "Goddamn it, I was worried. Then I got mad. I was going to tell you to take me back to camp because I can't stand feeling like this."

Fallon kept her voice quiet. "Like what?"

"Like I care. Like I need to make sure you're all right. We're supposed to be having fun, having a nice time together. Not this..."

She gestured haphazardly between them. After a minute, she gave up, repeating, "Not this."

Certain she was on dangerous ground, Fallon said, "Would fishing help?"

Nora jumped on her, and they wrestled until Fallon let Nora pin her.

"I give," Fallon said. The idea that Nora cared, that something mutual was growing between them, made her heart surge.

Nora, still breathing heavily, leaned down and kissed her. "Next time, leave a note."

They each caught a decent-size trout, and even though Fallon had to look away as Nora was cleaning and gutting them, they made for a wonderful dinner.

Chilly, gusty winds cut their last day's walk short. Curled up together on the couch, they discovered a mutual love of NPR and a disparity of opinion about country music, and agreed to disagree during a discussion on the use of social media. When there was a lull, Fallon mustered the courage to ask what she'd been wanting to know ever since Nora had gone to Denver. "Will you tell me what happened with Gwen and Tina?" When Nora looked down, Fallon added, "I hope you know you can trust me."

Nora said nothing for a time. "I do trust you," she said finally. "And I'm sure a shrink would say I need to talk about it." Fallon nodded.

Nora took a deep breath. "Gwen and Tina had been talking practically nonstop about this guy, Bryson. They said he was fun and a great dancer. We met up in a bar in a seedy part of town, the kind of place where women know to keep an eye on their drinks. I declined repeated offers to dance, mostly from him, but also from some other guys. Bryson kept looking at his watch, and when he stood, suggesting we go for a walk, I told him I was worried about the neighborhood. He laughed and said the neighborhood should be worried about him. But I was more than ready to leave, and when Gwen and Tina came outside with us, I felt a little better."

She sighed, shaking her head. "We started down an alley that I assumed would connect to the next street over, but instead, it dead-ended into an area with overflowing dumpsters and recycle bins. It smelled disgusting. A car was idling there, and Bryson told me to stay put while Gwen and Tina went around to the passenger window. They were all chatting and laughing, so I took a few casual steps back down the alley, deliberately not paying attention to what they were doing, trying to act like I was keeping watch instead.

"Someone in the car must have told Bryson I was walking away because I heard heavy footsteps coming up fast behind me. He caught me by the arm and swung me back to face him, saying, 'Where the hell do you think you're going? Goddamn it, bitch, I told you to wait for me.' That's when I knew it was going to be bad."

Fallon sat close, trying to offer comfort without interfering. Fighting the urge to hold her, she settled for a gentle squeeze of Nora's hand from time to time. She was pretty sure Nora needed to tell the story even more than she needed to hear it.

"He was holding on so tightly, I got a bruise from his fingers digging into my arm. But I still tried to jerk away, and that's when he slapped me and cut my lip." Nora took a shuddering breath. "So I did what Rudy had taught me. I brought my knee up as hard as I could into the bastard's groin. As soon as he hit the ground, I ran. I—I was desperate, but I knew I couldn't be reckless. I had to watch my footing in the alley to avoid falling while I looked for the sign of the bar we'd come out of." Her breathing was shallow, as if she was rushing away from the scene, even now. "I could hear him cursing behind me, calling for Gwen, and there was no doubt in my mind that I was running for my life. He might not literally have killed me, but the life I had and the life I wanted would both be over if he caught me. I ran up the steps of the Lariat Bar and Grill right as a car screeched around the corner. I prayed it was the police and not another drug dealer."

Nora paused, and Fallon's pulse began to slow. "God, Nora. I hate it that you went through that alone. I feel like I should have been there."

Nora shook her head. "It's funny you say that because when I heard the bar door open and someone joined me on the steps, I imagined it was you. But it was just someone attracted by the high-speed passing of a second car and the sounds of people arguing from somewhere in the dark."

She didn't cry then, but that night in bed, Nora woke Fallon, weeping. "I thought my life was over, but you saved me. I didn't want to feel this way about you, and now I can't stop. Please, don't let me go."

She'd never seen Nora so vulnerable, and it split Fallon's heart wide open. "As much as I crave your body," she told her, holding tightly, "I crave this more. This connection with you. This being together. I have to believe that we'll make it work somehow. I don't want to imagine anything else."

They slept in as late as possible the next morning, throwing their things into the car at the last minute. Fallon finished her leaving checklist, and as she was locking the door, Nora laid her hands on Fallon's shoulders. "This time, I'm going to say it properly. Thank you for bringing me here. I'll never forget it."

The drive home was quiet. As much as Fallon wanted to know what Nora was thinking, she was too apprehensive to ask. When she caught Nora looking at her, she smiled hopefully. "Are you feeling all right about going back to work?" Apparently, Nora knew what she was really saying.

"They're going to know about us," Nora said. "Hannah already suspects."

"Jade too."

"As long as you don't grab my ass in front of them, we'll be okay."

"Damn," Fallon said. "I guess you can't squeeze my boobs, either."

Nora cast a longing look at Fallon's chest before meeting her eyes again. "I still want to sleep with you, though. We can share a tent, right?"

Fallon hoped Nora couldn't read her relief. "Hal will probably give us some shit, but yeah. I don't see why not."

"And what about Ranger Reva?" Nora asked demurely.

"I'm sure all will be well when I give her my report about what a good girl you've been."

Nora laughed and swiped at her arm. "Are you ever going to let me drive this car again?"

"How about after we stop for gas?" Fallon offered. "You can make our grand entrance." She'd almost offered to give Nora the car if she promised to come back after college. Almost.

Fallon was embarrassed that they were the last two returning to base, but the crew greeted them warmly, and Ranger Reva offered only a slightly raised eyebrow. Nora went first to Hannah, hugging her and saying something Fallon couldn't hear. Hannah gave a little hop, clapping, and by dinner, there were lots of knowing smiles.

Even Hal had apparently gotten the word, as he referenced Fallon's "adventurous model tent" with a nod to Nora. "Finally caught on to what's worth having, huh?" he asked. When Fallon risked a look, Nora winked in return. It was great to be back.

Jade briefed them on their last hitch, calling it the easiest work yet. Only forty-five minutes from base was a well-known ski slope that the forest service had been working from the top of the tree line. The Women's Plus Crew was assigned to thin what Jade referred to as "dog hair pines," a dense stand of lodgepoles about halfway down the mountain. Because the trees were too close together, they hadn't grown very big around, so cutting would be easy. The SCC would transport the logs for use in construction of new buildings in other camps or to sell for pulpwood. "The good news is, we'll be staying at base, which means nighttime bathroom facilities and availability of washers and dryers and sleeping indoors on cots. Adding nearly two hours of driving to every day is the bad news."

Reva stepped in to add that due to the additional mileage, they wouldn't be using Fallon's car. Instead, two vans would haul people and equipment.

The weather cooperated beautifully for the first week, the skies sunny with hints of fall in the air. Sleeping in the same room with Nora but not being in the same bed was torturous. On their day off, Nora demanded the key to Big Red, driving them to a "clothing optional" hot springs. Self-conscious in just a towel, Fallon stayed as close as possible behind Nora until they were in the water.

The soak was heavenly. "Almost as relaxing as sex," Fallon whispered, pleased when Nora brushed a hand along the inside of her thigh.

"Let's do a comparison later," Nora whispered.

Luckily, Big Red's back seat was roomy and warm. "Back when we were traveling around, I'd sometimes find used jigsaw puzzles in the thrift stores," Fallon told her as they snuggled close. "If we had a little extra money, Mom would buy one for me, but I learned pretty quickly that they always had missing pieces. I used to feel kinda like that, but I don't when I'm with you." She kissed Nora gently. "I'm whole."

Nora sighed. "As a kid, I was never enough. Competing with my older brothers, I was always too slow or weak or inept in some way. And my father made sure I knew it. Ever since I realized that I'd never measure up, I've felt such hostility, resenting the unfairness." When she moved on top, Fallon closed her eyes at the sweet heat that spread between them. "I've let a lot of that go here at Firecamp. And with you, I feel like I am enough."

"Nora," Fallon's voice was almost a groan, "you're more than enough. You're everything."

❖

The second week began with three solid days of heavy thunderstorms. Rain was one thing, but they weren't allowed to work if there was lightning. After spending the morning cleaning and sharpening their cutting equipment and making sure everyone's tools were organized, Fallon, Kennedy, and Hannah volunteered to help Hal in the equipment hut. Nora wandered in and out, snapping random photos there and in the dining hall where Delores and Jade were watching the Olympics.

At breakfast on the second day, with thunderstorms still forecast, Ranger Reva announced that this was now their day off, and they'd probably have to work all weekend.

Fallon turned to Nora. "Let's go somewhere and talk."

"Just talk?"

The way Nora was smiling made Fallon want to put her against the wall and kiss her senseless. Among other things.

Nora's eyes shifted past her, and Fallon heard Reva's voice behind her. "Nora, would you mind taking a look at some printed photos we have from other crews? I don't know if or how you could use them, but…"

Nora stepped away, her attention now focused on Ranger Reva. "Do you have a scanner?"

"I'm not sure. I had older equipment moved to storage because we weren't using it. Maybe you could look and see if…" Reva seemed to notice Fallon, and she blushed slightly. "I'm sorry. Did you two have other plans?"

Nora touched Fallon's arm. "This will only take an hour or two at most. Meet me for lunch, and we'll go from there, okay?"

Unable to form a reasonable protest, Fallon nodded.

Nora wasn't at lunch. Fallon went back to their sleeping quarters, but Nora wasn't there, either. Fallon decided to partake of her usual escape—reading—before realizing she hadn't brought any new books during the break, a lapse that was so unlike her, she was shaken. Had she been utterly consumed with Nora to the point that she'd let an important piece of herself go? Was that a sign of love or of an unhealthy obsession? In this place where she'd been secure, she felt unexpectedly vulnerable.

Kennedy came out of the bathroom. "What's up?" they asked.

"Do you think there's a bookstore in town?" Fallon asked, relieved to see a friend.

"Decent-size place, I bet there probably is," Kennedy remarked. "Mae might know for sure."

Fallon felt lost in time, almost immobile. She'd based her day on Nora being available, but Nora had apparently forgotten about her. Or maybe as soon as she went to town, Nora would get finished and come looking for her. When she looked searchingly around the room, Kenn put a hand on her shoulder. "Want company?"

Fallon could use a sounding board. "Yeah."

"Wanna stop by the ranger's office first?"

The question led her to a stunning realization. Was this what life with Nora would be like if Fallon changed her plans and followed her to Arizona? Nora would be in college, pursuing her passion, and Fallon would be…what? Waiting?

"No. Let's go."

❖

Fallon had no memory of being "poured into bed," as Kenn later put it, but she could detect a stack of books beside her on the cot. As she pieced together the previous afternoon, she established that they'd apparently found the bookstore, followed by a bar and then a liquor store. Sitting up, she was grateful she didn't have to work since the thunder outside matched what was happening in her head. Nora's face swam into focus, and Fallon smiled. Nora didn't.

"Seems like you and Kennedy had a lot more fun than I did."

Dismayed by the cool tone, Fallon felt the need to defend herself. "You weren't at lunch." She looked around. They were alone. "I can't wait and wait without knowing—"

"You knew I was working with Ranger Reva."

"I knew you said an hour or two." When Nora had the grace to look a little uncomfortable, Fallon added, "I wanted to spend some time together." She didn't say what was on her heart. *We don't have much of it left.*

Nora looked down. "I know. But this is something I have to do." Her tone brightened. "And Reva's got these great old photos. We found a scanner, which probably came over on the *Mayflower*, but we couldn't get it to work. I've got to figure out how to get these photos into the video without a scanner."

For all her apprehension about their future, Fallon had to smile. Nora was never more appealing than when her intensity was on display. "Why don't you take pictures of the pictures?" she suggested. "Then you'll have them digitally on your camera."

Nora stared at her, lips parted. "Oh my God. Why didn't I think of that? I was just so obsessed with getting the scanner to work…" She hugged Fallon tightly. "You are a frigging genius."

Not really, Fallon thought. *I've just lost you for another day.*

"Come get me after lunch," Nora said as she started for the door. When Fallon didn't answer, she said, "Promise?"

Was she promising or asking Fallon to promise? Did it matter? "Sure."

Instead, there was a surprise birthday party for Mae that lasted all afternoon and featured terrible singing and gag gifts. Nora came in late and was stuck standing in the back. Fallon couldn't even get close to her. Half the time, Fallon was angry, and the other half, she was sad. She couldn't tell if Nora was either, and of course, they still hadn't had "the talk" about their future.

Jade seemed to feel guilty after the "easiest work yet" she'd promised them turned into ten straight days of muddy, slippery sawing. She took Fallon aside and asked her to think of ways to cheer up the crew. It wasn't until later that Fallon figured out Jade was trying to cheer *her* up. It seemed that everyone but Nora was finding ways to make their remaining time special, with a quick touch or an extra smile. But when she joined the group at dinner or got into her cot, conversations about the end of the summer and talk of returning to their regular lives seemed to stop. Nora, on the other hand, was so distracted with taking photos that Jade had to remind her that her primary job was sawing, and the pictures were to be shot on her own time.

Then, on Wednesday of the last week, Ranger Reva pulled Nora off the crew to work full-time on her presentation. After joining them for dinner, Nora described excitedly how they had watched video examples from other groups and discussed at length what kind of shots to use and what kinds of information to include. Everyone nodded politely, but Fallon noticed they all glanced at her as Nora talked. Finally, Delores pulled Fallon aside.

"I don't know what's going on with you two, but we can all see you're miserable, and Nora's burying herself in work so she won't have to deal with it."

Fallon hadn't thought of that, but it made sense. Rather than letting herself think or talk or feel, Nora was exhausting herself with this video. "What should I do?"

"Do something nice. Remind her of why she 'likes' you." Delores made air quotes. "She's every bit as raw as you are, so be gentle. But tell her what you want, what you need."

When Nora didn't appear in the dining room Thursday night, Fallon made her move. Carrying a plate to the office, she approached quietly, finding Nora hunched over Ranger Reva's computer. Tiny blue images moved in a stream across the monitor.

"I'm backing up photos from my camera into separate folders to be used in the video and for the individual files," Nora said without turning. "And I'm not hungry."

"Individual files?"

Nora sat back and stretched. "I'll tell you, but you must swear not to tell anyone." Fallon nodded. "Besides this project for Ranger Reva, I'm making each member of the crew a personalized file that they can keep as a memento of Firecamp."

More work to make sure she doesn't have a moment for us. Fallon cleared her throat. "I know that's important, but I also know you need fuel like I did after that first day of sawing when you brought dinner to my tent."

The stream stopped. Nora breathed out and smiled. "You're right." She rubbed Fallon's leg. "Just like I was then."

"I couldn't agree more." Fallon leaned down to kiss her head. "And following your example, I'm going to wait until you take two bites before I leave you to it."

Once Nora got to her third bite, Fallon started for the door. "Thank you, Falcon," Nora said through a mouthful.

On her cot that night, Fallon considered how obvious it was that Nora was stressed about getting everything finished on time and to her own exacting standards. If Fallon got to stay on here, she could build her reputation over the years. This project was Nora's way to leave something of herself for Firecamp crews to come. What she didn't understand was how Nora could give up so easily on what they had together. Their phenomenal physical compatibility had surprised her; the deeper, more intimate emotional connection touched Fallon in a place that no one else had ever been. Did Nora not feel the same?

Even though Nora worked late and started early, at least Fallon got to hear her voice and see her around camp. She now knew that watching Nora leave for college was going to be the hardest thing she'd ever done. Her mother's passing had hurt her to the core, but there was nothing she could have done differently. She couldn't stop thinking that she had a chance to change the outcome with Nora, if they could just figure out how to meet halfway.

With no idea of where that middle ground could be, Fallon did the only thing that seemed to make headway between them: She brought dinner again. This time, Nora let out an exasperated breath as Fallon stepped into the room. "Upshaw wants three minutes. I could easily do fifteen. It's gonna be hard to make these cuts."

Fallon leaned in, handing her a plate. "Can I help?"

"No," Nora said quickly, turning off the monitor. "This part of the project really is top secret."

"You know it won't hurt my feelings if you leave me out entirely."

"As if. Your pictures are some of the best ones." Nora smiled and touched her face before turning back to the keyboard. "I promise to eat, but you have to go."

In a testament to how strongly the crew had bonded, no one left Saturday afternoon, even though their summer duties were officially over. They were all staying for the Sunday morning video premiere, and anticipation was high.

Fallon dropped by late Saturday afternoon, surprised when Nora wasn't in the office. Her camera sat on the desk, disconnected from the computer. Fallon carefully moved it away from the edge. The monitor showed dozens of folders, each marked with names of their crew members. Fallon looked away, listening. There wasn't a sound in the building. Tempted, she moved the mouse over the folder with her name. A square highlighted around it. She noted the other items on the desktop, including the video folder. Looking at that would ruin Nora's top secret surprise, but the folder with Fallon's name should only have her photos, and she already knew about that part of Nora's work. *What could it hurt?*

She double-clicked, and the folder opened, showing a list of file names. Fallon clicked on the first one. A new program opened, filling the screen with her photo. She was riding the ATV with a wild, silly expression, looking absurdly juvenile. Embarrassed, she closed the image, accidentally closing the program in the process. Moving the mouse over the folder again, she hesitated for a second before clicking on the second image. Again, the program opened, revealing a close-up of her making a face—head tilted, tongue out, eyes crossed—while holding her chainsaw. She remembered Nora snapping her photo during their work on the fuel break, but she didn't realize it was such a closeup. Why would Nora keep a picture of her looking so foolish? Clicking the next one revealed a photo from that rainy day when Fallon had helped organize the tools. Her eyelids were half-closed, and she held a screwdriver in her teeth like a rose. She looked idiotic. Despondent, she was about to close the image when she noticed an option offering "Slide Show."

Fallon took her hand off the mouse. She should probably stop. But after having seen three examples of herself looking laughable and unattractive, she was desperate to find a decent depiction. Surely, these first ones were rejects Nora had kept as a joke, not that they were funny in that way. The appalling thought that one or all had made it into the video made Fallon touch the mouse again. At the beginning of this project, Nora had promised that she'd make them look good. Did that mean everyone but her? She went back to the folder and clicked on the next file, barely stifling a gasp at the image of herself sleeping naked in the trailer. Fallon closed her eyes, shocked that Nora would be so intrusive. Worse, all her old insecurities were reawakened at seeing her body fully revealed. She was awkward and gawky, with a thick and shapeless build, and Nora had her on full display. As of that moment, her concern was no longer about infringing on Nora's work. It was about safeguarding herself.

She was about to click on "Slide Show" when she heard the door to the building open. Closing the program, she dragged the folder with her name on it to the recycle bin and hit empty. Footsteps came down the hall. Fallon stood, moving away from the desk.

"Hey. I thought you'd be with..." Nora trailed off, and Fallon knew her face showed only resentment instead of her usual delight at Nora's presence. "What's going on?"

Fallon stepped toward her, her insides growing rigid. "I trusted you. I thought you cared for me."

"What do you mean? I do care for you."

"Not according to the pictures I saw. You think making me look stupid or taking an invasive photo of me in a compromising position is caring?"

"Wait. You've been looking at my project?" Nora's voice rose in the way it did when she was affronted. She pushed past to the computer, her eyes roving over the screen. "What did you do?"

Fallon drew herself up, facing Nora at the side of the desk. "I protected myself since you obviously weren't going to."

Nora clicked on the recycle bin. "You destroyed my work? You had no right—"

"And what right did you have to embarrass me with humiliating photos? Or worse, vulgar ones?" Fallon could tell Nora wasn't listening. Instead, she was opening various folders and closing them again.

When she finally turned to Fallon, her face was hard. "Did you think you could keep me here by making me fail? Was that your plan? You're so desperate to have me stay with you that you'll wipe out all the time and effort I put into this? Are you thinking Ranger Reva will tell my father I failed if I don't have this work finished?"

Fallon's mouth dropped open. Nora was accusing *her* of having an ulterior motive? She couldn't remember ever being this angry. "Oh, I don't know. Were those uncomplimentary pictures of me meant to make me look unsuitable for a leadership position, so I'd have no choice but to tag along with you like some sad puppy you could abandon the first chance you got? You know, the way you do with everyone you profess to love, like Tyler?" Somewhere in the back of her mind, Fallon knew they were both going too far. The viciousness they were spewing had nothing to do with Nora's project. It was because the summer was over, and there was no path for them to go forward together.

Nora apparently hadn't reached the same conclusion as she picked up her camera. "What a shame your fabulous homeschool education didn't include anything about graphic arts. All the photos you hate so much are still here. It won't take me more than a couple of hours to make that folder again." She wiggled the camera tauntingly. "And the ones I wanted are already in the video too. That means all your sneaky espionage did was to show me who you really are. A big chickenshit, with no chance of ever being anything but that."

Fallon's rage returned. She grabbed for the camera as Nora tried to yank it away. Their hands collided, and the camera fell to the floor with a sickening crash. The unmistakable sounds of splintering plastic and shattering glass made them both freeze. Fallon's anger died even more quickly than it had flamed, and she forced herself to meet Nora's agonized expression.

"Oh God. Nora, I never meant to…" She couldn't finish, knowing she'd ruined anything she might want. For herself or for Nora. "Please forgive me." She rushed from the room and outside into the place she'd hoped would be her forever home.

An impossible dream had been destroyed along with that camera, and she couldn't envision any way to repair either of them. How could she stay in the place that held memories of Nora at every turn? Even if they had to part, she'd hoped that there might be a promise for some future together, but now there would only be pain. And how could she face everyone at Firecamp once they'd seen those pictures in Nora's video? *Just leave. Go back to the life you know.* She texted a quick message to Ranger Reva on her way to her car. Big Red started up on the first try, and Fallon knew she'd been right all along about being able to count on things more than people, including herself.

PART TWO: NOW

CHAPTER FOURTEEN

The faint buzz against Nora's fingers intensified until the vibration pushed up her arm to her shoulder. Gas and oil fumes from the chainsaw were gradually joined by the sweet scent of pine as the pile of sawdust grew beside her boots. A cracking sound warned her that the tree was almost ready to fall. She stepped away to assess the final cut angle but caught her heel on a stump. Flailing against the falling sensation, she bit back a cry of terror at the vision of a running chainsaw flying toward her face.

Strong arms caught her. "You're okay, I've got you." Fallon's voice was steady in her ear.

Nora jerked awake. Her breathing calmed, but not her heartbeat. She blinked furiously against the shaft of sunlight that always found its way through the edge of the window shade, aware that the air cooling the sweat on her neck was a product of a very busy air-conditioning unit and not a mountain breeze. She was in Arizona, not Colorado, and Fallon's arms weren't anywhere near her.

It had been nearly ten years since that summer in the mountains. She rarely thought of it anymore, not deliberately, but her dreams still seemed to take her there at the least provocation. She'd been stupid then, and so stubborn. Maybe everyone was at twenty, but she'd done a better job of it than most. And as a result, she'd lost something she hadn't been able to replace.

She'd fallen asleep with the phone in her hand—again—and the buzzing of the alarm had obviously kindled her recurring dream. Hitting snooze out of habit, she sat up and rubbed her eyes, trying to push the remnants of that time out of her mind. After attending the ASU for its photojournalism program, staying in Arizona had helped her escape the memories of Colorado's woodland environment, and she'd forced herself through that painful separation by doing the same thing that had caused it: living solely for her work. At college, where there was no Fallon to bring her into community life, she'd lived as she'd intended to at Firecamp, as a loner. But even with her outsider status, she'd become known as a remarkable talent with a flair for dramatic, narrative photographs.

Upon landing her dream job as a photojournalist with the *Arizona Daily Star* immediately after college, she'd been almost as ecstatic about not having to job hunt—something only marginally better than a first date, in her opinion, and the move from Tempe to Tucson was easy. The downside was not having time for a return visit to Colorado. But who knew if she'd have found any of her old crew still at Firecamp, especially Fallon, who might have returned to the nomadic existence she'd lived before arriving at Firecamp. Fallon had always claimed she wanted a stable life with a family of choice, but when it had come down to it, she'd run. Not that Nora could blame her. She'd replayed those last moments in Ranger Upshaw's office enough times to see how the disaster had unfolded over that final week from both their points of view.

It was hard to believe she'd been with the paper for seven years, refining her style and making her mark on the local beat as she befriended reporters and photographed everything from parades to crime scenes to ribbon-cutting politicians. In the face of stunning changes to journalism in general and photography in particular, she'd expanded her skill set to include independent photo editing and retouching, especially relishing any film work those 35mm stalwarts would offer, along with dabbling in simple web design. Though her pictures were often picked up by other papers, both regional and statewide, she'd steadfastly avoided wedding photography or anything similarly personal until Collin Becker, the man who'd hired her and supervised the first six years of her career, had died suddenly of a brain aneurysm. Yielding to repeated requests from her colleagues and one emotional phone call from Collin's widow, Nora had reluctantly agreed to make a video for his memorial service. The process had brought her close to tears, partly for the man who'd guided her into the world of print and online media, but also because of the memories it had evoked of the last video she'd put together.

After his funeral and the four-hour gathering at the *Star* employees' favorite bar, her last bit of good sense had her taking an Uber to her town house. Safe at home, right on the edge between maudlin drunk and self-pitying frustration, she'd decided to view her only other previous video. After finding the website for the Southern Conservation Corps Firecamp Program, she'd been dimly impressed with the slightly amateurish introduction she'd created, convinced she'd make it through the whole thing until Fallon's face came on the screen.

She still remembered exactly when she'd taken the shot. Fallon had been focused on something just beyond her, but as her gaze had shifted and she'd seen Nora, she'd smiled. It was the look she'd given Nora during the days they'd spent together in Fallon's Silver Bird trailer, the expression that said she saw Nora fully and completely and welcomed her to do the same.

No one else would know that look, but she had. And she still did. *Oh God.* Nora's heart had seized, and she'd turned off her computer and fallen into bed, clenching her jaw so tight, she'd awakened with a massive headache, though she'd pretended it was the whiskey she'd had at Collin's commemoration.

Her alarm went off again, and before she could get any deeper into melancholy memories, she texted Tyler. *Up yet?*

Her bedroom door opened a crack, and her brother's pleasant tenor voice answered, "Depends. Are you decent?"

"*Decent* depends on whether you've done battle with Decker the Dripper yet," Nora replied.

"Oh no. You're the one who can slay that demon. I only stand and wait."

Her ancient coffee machine was becoming increasingly temperamental. She kept babying it because it made an excellent brew, but it seemed to know if Nora turned her back for even a second, and the results would be half an inch of light brown liquid in the pot while the rest of the steaming coffee and wet grounds were deposited all over the kitchen floor. Not in the mood for the Dripper's tricks today, she'd stand over it and fix travel mugs for her and Tyler once she dressed.

After pulling on worn, faded jeans and a T-shirt, she ran a brush through her hair. She'd let it grow for almost a year before deciding on the shoulder-length style she currently wore. It gave her a softer look, another thing that was different from what she'd imagined about her life. "You all packed?"

Tyler nodded. "What is it, eleven hours?"

"Probably more like twelve if we stop as often as we want. But we'll take turns driving." She hadn't realized how lonely she'd been until he'd moved in with her five years ago after spending the obligatory freshman year in a dorm at the University of Arizona. He'd graduated high school a year early and did the same with both his BS and master's degrees in plant science as they'd weathered the pandemic together. As one of the youngest former students to be offered a position in the university's research department, he was making his mark with specialties in plant genetics and medicinal plants. She was incredibly proud of him.

It'd be Tyler's first trip home since he started college. Nora hadn't returned since leaving for photojournalism school. But it was their father's sixtieth birthday, which meant a command appearance for all Palmers, no exceptions. "I tried to talk Mom into letting us stay in a hotel, but apparently, we're all going to be in our old rooms to further the appearance of a normal family."

"Further proof that appearances can be deceiving," Tyler remarked, making Nora laugh.

It was after ten p.m. when they arrived, but her father was up drinking with Art and Rudy. "Ah, our prodigal siblings return." Nora recognized Art's teasing tone.

Rudy rose and hugged them both. "Welcome home."

When Nora turned to her father, she was shocked at his appearance. His once ruddy face was haggard, and his thick hair was almost completely white with a few streaks of dark gray.

"Hi, Dad," Tyler said.

Their father mumbled something unintelligible by way of reply.

"Is he okay?" Nora whispered to Rudy.

"Old and drunk," Rudy whispered back. "Not a good combination, but he wouldn't go to bed until you guys got here."

"Grab that pill bottle." Art pointed to the table. "He'll need one first thing in the morning."

"Diovan?" Nora asked, reading the label.

"Blood pressure med," Art said, standing. "Listen, we'll get him to the door of his room, but Tyler, you and Nora will have to help him into bed. Mom's too embarrassed to have her 'big boys' in the bedroom."

Nora moved as quietly as possible, trying not to wake her mother. Her father weighed much less than she'd imagined, and Nora steered the three of them to the bedside. After she'd gotten her father seated, he looked up at her. "Where's your friend?"

His voice was unexpectedly clear, but Nora wasn't sure he knew what he was saying. "What friend?"

"Tall like you. Ran outta gas. Came here that other time."

Tyler cleared his throat and busied himself getting their father's shoes off. He'd learned very soon after moving in with her not to ask questions about Firecamp and especially Fallon.

"She's not coming this time," Nora muttered. "Lie down, Dad."

"Working, is she?"

"Nora? Is Tyler with you?" Remarkably, her mother's voice saved her from further explanation. Nora looked across the bed. In the light that spilled in from the hallway, she saw that time had taken a similar toll on her mother. Her eyes looked sunken and her lined cheeks were hollow. Her hair appeared to have thinned from the fullness Nora remembered.

"Yes, Mother. We're both here now."

"Well, go to bed. It's late."

They mumbled their good nights and left the dark room.

The next day was a strange combination of uncomfortable and nostalgic. Nora texted Tyler as usual, and they met in the kitchen where a strange woman was drinking coffee.

"Who are you?" Tyler blurted.

Before the woman could answer, their mother joined them. "Tyler, this is your cousin, Anita. You were a baby the last time she visited. Nora, I think you were five then, do you remember?" When Nora shook her head, her mother said, "Well, anyway, she's here to help me with your father."

Anita looked to be ten or fifteen years younger than their mother, with dark lustrous hair and only a few wrinkles, compared to their mother's simple gray hairstyle and deeply lined face. Nora's curiosity was piqued by the way her mother looked perkier and sounded much less anxious than usual. Hoping to spend a little more time with Anita, Nora offered to lend a hand with the cooking, causing Tyler to give her a disbelieving look.

"No, this is your vacation," Anita said, speaking with a hint of a Spanish accent. "You'll want to spend time with your family."

After their father was up and in his chair, they passed the afternoon talking about her older brothers' latest experiences on the fire line. During a pause, Nora began telling everyone how well Tyler was doing.

"Where's your friend?"

Her father's interruption annoyed her, but more than that, it worried her that he'd already asked. At least this time, she knew who he meant. "We lost touch a few years ago," she said tightly.

"Shame. She was good people."

Rudy looked at her with a quizzical expression, but once their father turned aside, she simply rolled her eyes. "I'm going for a walk. Anyone want to come?"

Tyler jumped up. Art and Rudy declined. Nora got her camera, and they followed the familiar path into the woods beyond the Palmer property. Neither spoke until they got to the old stump where they'd always sat to talk. It was almost entirely decayed, leaving only a few chunks of rotting wood.

Nora stared at it. "I'm sorry," she said.

Tyler gave a half-smile. "I was about to say that to you."

She took a deep breath. "God, I'd forgotten how the air here smells like trees."

"Nothing like our dry desert, right? Do you miss it?"

Do I? Nora wondered, offering a vague tilt of her head in reply. Despite making her pensive now, a Colorado forest still felt like home in a way Tucson never had. When they were almost back, she took a quick shot of Tyler walking toward their family farmhouse, both bathed in the golden light of sunset. It was her only photo of the day, and one of the best she'd taken in weeks.

"I'm going to get some group shots before we go home," she said, thinking how neither of them had any such photographs in their town house.

Tyler grinned. "I think that's a great idea."

❖

Everyone was nicely dressed, and the men had shaved. To her surprise, they posed perfectly, smiling enough to make it believable. The image was boring by Nora's standards, but it was exactly the family photo they'd all appreciate. She wouldn't wait for a holiday or someone's birthday; she'd get prints made and send each person their own framed copy when she got back to Tucson.

She'd also gotten candid shots the night before when they'd sung "Happy Birthday" as her father's candlelit cake was carried out. The images of Art wolfing down a huge slice, of her mother kissing her father's head, and Rudy with his arms around both their parents could be sent to the updated email addresses they'd exchanged.

After hauling her gear to the car, along with her suitcase, Nora snapped one more picture as their mother hugged Tyler. It was inelegant but better than the brief shoulder pat she'd gotten. Their father was standing with Art and Rudy, gesturing in a jerky fashion, when both brothers suddenly reached for their phones and stepped away to read a text. They exchanged glances and a few brief words before running into the house. Nora rushed after them.

"What's up?" she asked Rudy, who was throwing clothes into his bag.

"A neighborhood burn has broken containment near Kamberto. Art and I are both on standby. We've got to get back."

Nora blinked, recalling the pleasant mountain town where the Firecamp crew had taken showers and done laundry all those years ago. Outside the bar was where Fallon had...

Before she could finish that thought, her phone rang. Recognizing the readout, she answered.

"Are you still in Colorado?" Abel Griffin, her new boss, barked. He wasn't actually "new" anymore, but it still felt like it. "At some family thing, right?"

"Yes," Nora confirmed. "And a controlled burn has broken containment in a neighborhood a few hundred miles from here."

"How do you already know that? It just came over the wire."

There was no wire anymore, but everyone still used that terminology, even when referring to digital updates. It hurt to think how Collin would have remembered about Art and Rudy. He'd taken the time to know his people, and he'd genuinely cared about their lives. She'd learned far more than the ins and outs of photojournalism from him. He'd been the one who'd helped her let go of some residual anger from her early years, teaching her that when she risked caring about her subject, she got better photos.

"My brothers are both firefighters. They got an alert."

"Huh, okay. Well, can you get over there today? The locals are busy evacuating, and someone is already covering that. We need a good angle of action that we can sell there and maybe nationally. Not the same smoke and flame and exhausted firefighters. Something new."

Nora opened her mouth and closed it again. Abel was a schmuck, but that didn't mean she would pass on shooting the story. "Yeah. Give me a few hours, and I'll get back to you with something."

"Make it good."

Fortunately, he hung up before she could say "Oh, are you sure you don't want something shitty?"

Tyler stood near the car. "Are you going to the fire too?"

"I need to, yeah. Do you mind staying here a few more days? I'll come get you as soon as—"

"No way." He broke in. "I'm coming with you. I can get releases signed or take notes on whatever you want the story to be. Or I can help with your gear, your lenses and stuff. But I'm coming."

Nora gave it about two seconds' thought before nodding. "Let's go."

It felt weird driving the same route she'd taken with Tyler and her father all those years ago. But this time, she wasn't distracted by the scenery or daydreams about her future. She did think about Firecamp, though, and speculating if a Women's Plus Crew might be involved in mitigation for the Kamberto blaze. If so, could she shoot that story? She lost count of how many times she'd forced her thoughts from wondering if Fallon might still be there, anticipating disappointment if she wasn't and apprehension if she was. Either way, she'd have to face those feelings.

After parking, she took a moment to look over the base. It seemed basically the same, although there were two new buildings in the latter stages of construction. Nora handed Tyler her bag, keeping her camera around her neck. As they crossed the grounds, activity intensified. Several men wearing full wildland firefighting gear ran past them and jumped into a van that kicked up dust as it pulled away. Numerous personnel were gathering and distributing equipment while shouts and occasional curses filled the air. Approaching the building where Ranger Upshaw's office had been, she and Tyler slowed at the sound of yelling that exploded through the open door.

"Maris had strict instructions to tell those fatheads not to burn. The forecast was for increasing wind—"

"Yes, sir." Another voice, quieter but no less certain. "Maris knew that, and I'm sure she made your instructions clear."

At the elation of a memory, Nora's breath caught. *Fallon.*

"Apparently, not goddamn clear enough. Now it's our fucking problem. Get your crew assembled and report here in thirty minutes. We'll go over the map then."

A door slammed inside, and a blond woman Nora hadn't seen before came around the far side of the building where she'd apparently been listening. She hurried to the front screen and intercepted Fallon as she exited. Seeing Fallon, Nora's heartbeat quickened, but she bit back the greeting that had risen to her lips as the blonde stepped into Fallon's open arms.

"God, I'm sorry. I'm so sorry. I told them, I swear I did." The blonde's voice broke, and she melted into sobs. "I told them," she repeated. Fallon held her quietly.

Years of sharpening her instincts for a good photo op overtook every other emotion, and Nora stepped to the side. Framing the pair in profile, she took three quick shots. Both women turned in her direction at the sound of the shutter clicking, and the crying blonde stepped away, scrubbing at her face. Fallon focused on Nora, emotions ranging from resentment to shock to hurt flashing in those unforgettable sky-blue eyes.

"Hello, Falcon," Nora said softly.

"Nor—" Fallon's voice cracked on her name. Composure returning quickly, her tone flattened, and she gave a curt nod. "Nora." Her hair was as short as Nora's had once been, and she ran one hand through it in a gesture that Nora guessed implied uncertainty. "I'd ask what you're doing here, but it's pretty obvious it's the same old shit."

The words, even more than the tone, pierced her, and Nora took a step back. Fallon turned to the blonde. "Maris, please make sure everyone is geared up, and tell them I'll be there in a few."

As the blonde moved away, after cutting her eyes at Nora in passing, Tyler shuffled forward, waving in his boyish way. "Hi, Fallon. Remember me?"

Fallon blinked, and the tightness in her face softened. "Oh my God. Tyler, is that you?"

"Yeah. I'm all healed up from the last time you saw me."

"Healed up and grown up, I'd say." Fallon came down the steps, her gaze fixed on him. They met and hugged quickly. "Listen, I don't mean to be rude, but this isn't a good occasion for a visit." She gave Nora a quick glance. "I'm sure you're aware there's a fire nearby, and we're going to be involved in making a break somewhere close to town. So if you'll excuse me—"

"We're going with you," Tyler said, excitement in his tone. "Nora's going to take pictures of your crew, and I'll be helping with... whatever."

"I don't think that will be possible. We'll be on an active, potentially dangerous perimeter. It's not a place for tourists."

Nora stiffened. She held back the retort that came to mind regarding her past chainsaw skills. Instead, she said, "That will be up to the ranger, won't it?"

Fallon's expression darkened, but she made no comment. As if summoned, a uniformed man stepped through the door and onto the porch. He looked to be about five inches shorter than Fallon and moved with the puffed-up manner of some men who were insecure about their height.

Nora took advantage of the moment. Favoring him with her most professional smile, she nodded cordially. "Hi, I'm Nora Palmer, press photographer for the *Arizona Star*. My managing editor thinks the work by your Women's Plus Crew will make a great story, so my assistant and I would like permission to ride along." The ranger stared at her, cocking his head as if she was speaking a different language. "I'm sure the SCC would be pleased to have your team presented in a favorable light, which I assure you will be my intention."

Fallon snorted, and the ranger's eyes narrowed. "You have a problem with this, Monroe?"

Nora couldn't remember ever hearing anyone address Fallon by her last name. Obviously, the leadership style here had changed, but Fallon had evidently become accustomed to it, as she answered coolly. "I do, sir. It's extremely unwise to have civilians in an unstable situation such as what we have right now. Perhaps tomorrow?"

"This goddamn—" The ranger broke off for a second, scanning Nora's body before starting again. "This godforsaken fire better be out by tomorrow." Fallon shook her head at the idea, but he wasn't watching her. "But it would probably be best if you rode with me, Miss…"

Nora pretended she didn't realize he'd already forgotten her name. "Normally, I'd love to take you up on that, Mister…" From the corner of her eye, she could see Fallon hiding a grin as she turned the tables on him.

The ranger descended the steps with his hand out, obviously intending a congenial greeting, but faltered. Short man syndrome? Nora speculated as he played off the outstretched hand by adjusting his hat. "Ranger Nick Richards," he said, throwing back his shoulders.

"Ranger Richards, for authenticity, it's best if I ride with the crew. We don't want anything to look faked. That's the worst thing we could do." When his brow furrowed, she added, "I'm sure you understand, given all your dealings with the media."

"Yes, of course. But there could be circumstances—not likely, mind you—but we would need to be prepared on the odd chance that your safety could be an issue." He stroked his chin as if grooming an invisible beard. "Monroe, issue our visitor a radio so she can contact me in case of an emergency." Nora kept her smile in place as his gaze lingered on her breasts. "Rest assured, I'll drop everything and come to your rescue. All you have to do is call."

"I'm deeply grateful for your cooperation, Ranger Richards."

"It's my pleasure, Miss…"

"Palmer." Fallon spat her name into his pause. Nora couldn't tell if she was disgusted by the ranger or upset that she and Tyler would be coming along with the crew.

"Right," Richards said slowly. He glared at Fallon. "Keep in mind, you'll be responsible for Miss Palmer's well-being while she's with your crew. And you'd better have them over here geared up and ready in"—he looked at his watch—"fifteen minutes, or I'll find someone who can."

Nora watched as he made his way carefully up the stairs before slamming the door. When she looked back, Fallon had her face to the sky, mumbling words that sounded something like "Not again!"

The ranger's directive wasn't at all what she'd anticipated, and Nora would've apologized to Fallon if she thought it would do any good. Instead, as Fallon turned her back, Nora wondered what to do about the swell of emotion at seeing her again. And at seeing her walk away.

CHAPTER FIFTEEN

Fallon strode toward the barracks, her mind going in five directions at once. First, hoping her crew was ready and that Maris had pulled herself together enough that Fallon could count on her. Second, that Nora fucking Palmer would decide that being back at Firecamp was too much déjà vu and elect to get her story elsewhere. Third, if she did come, maybe Tyler would prove to be such a liability that Nora would see her misjudgment in bringing him, and they'd both leave. Fourth, asking for the millionth time why Reva Upshaw had to fall in love and go off to have a family, which had brought Ranger Dick into her life. And fifth, hoping against hope that the advance teams had somehow gotten the fire under control, and the first three contemplations wouldn't be factors. A strong gust of wind assured her that last one wasn't the case, which meant all of the rest were still in play.

Shit. At the door of the crew quarters, she looked back. Nora followed, lagging several feet behind, her focus on the ground. Tyler stood outside the office building as if he wasn't sure any of this was happening. *I know the feeling, pal.*

Fallon opened the door, relieved to see her crew was ready. "Great job, everyone. Five minutes. Take one last bathroom break and check your pack load. That novel you think you're going to read is going to feel like a twenty-pound brick when you're hauling it up Porter's Peak." She smiled briefly, remembering her own experience. It had been two books, actually. "This is not a drill, but I know you're ready." She nodded at Maris. "You okay?"

"I'm steady, Falcon."

"Stick by me. You may have some babysitting duties on this hitch."

Maris rolled her eyes but gave a quick two-fingered salute. "Whatever you need."

Fallon surveyed her team once more, pleased at their focus, though she'd expected no less. She needed to reengage as the crew coordinator and let the distraction of her history with Nora go. *Just think of it as having inconvenient visitors.* Right. Gathering herself, she turned sharply, fixing her mind on simply dealing with a news photographer and her assistant, when she collided with something. No, someone. The unexpected impact threw the other off-balance, and Fallon automatically reached out to stabilize the floundering body. Of course it was Nora. No one else would have stood so close behind her. And just that quickly, touching Nora again made her double-crossing body come alive in ways it hadn't for almost ten years. But in her mind, the sound of breaking plastic and shattering glass brought her back to their last moments together, and she recoiled.

"Damn. Is your camera all right?" Fallon asked before she could think better of it.

"I'm sorry. I was—" Nora spoke at the same time. She grabbed the sling strap, ensuring the camera still lay firmly against her body. "Yes, it's fine, thanks. I've learned not to wave it around when I'm not using it."

For several uncomfortable seconds, they simply looked at each other. Nora's mouth opened, but before she could speak, the triangle sounded from across the way, and the room behind them filled with sound and movement. Fallon's mind cleared. "We're heading out soon. Grab whatever you and Tyler need and toss it into the van."

Fallon started away, the clicks from Nora's camera echoing in her ears. A few of the young women made pleased sounds, and some would certainly pose for pictures. The faint smell of smoke, like from a distant campfire, reminded her that none of that mattered. In a few hours, the air would be as thick as the breath of hell, and they would be working like fiends to keep its hungry mouth from swallowing any more of the forest or the nearby town. She'd only done mitigation for an active fire once before, but that memory was enough to make her veer in the direction of the equipment hut. Given Nora's previous skill with a saw, she and Tyler might be pressed into service in ways none of them had planned.

❖

Fallon frowned. "Is there anything current from the weather service about the wind? Speed? Possible direction change?"

Ranger Dick scowled, obviously wanting to end the briefing, so he'd probably punish her for asking such obvious questions by giving her crew an undesirable assignment. At this point, anything near the fire would be hot, smoky work, but she needed these vital pieces of information. He shuffled the papers he carried, handing one to her. "You can disseminate the details to the other crew chiefs, Monroe. That is your job, after all."

In a way, he was right, though he'd made up the position of crew coordinator to give himself less to do. Reading over the data, she sighed. The report was two hours old, but she got on the radio anyway, stressing the volatile situation and advising everyone to ask for updates as needed. Might as well keep Ranger Dick awake.

While her crew settled in the van, Fallon checked the map again. The fire burned in a section not yet worked by the SCC, and her crew had been given the task of creating a break by clearing either side of the road approaching the town of Kamberto. It was a better assignment than she'd expected, undoubtedly because of Nora's schmoozing of Ranger Dick.

During her past years at camp, Fallon had continued the work that Ranger Reva had started, making sure that any grants or community projects accepted by the SCC fit into a strategic plan. When given the chance, she'd made sure to assign each crew to areas that would make the best use of their time and skills. Last year, there had been a terrible fire almost four hundred and fifty miles south and west of them that had burned over 125,000 acres and caused fourteen fatalities. In the aftermath, several branches of the SCC had come together at a meeting in Denver, and Fallon was called upon to present her model that other AmeriCorps divisions then adopted as a blueprint.

Proud as Fallon was of their work, she'd been even happier to return to the base. The city was loud, crowded, and much too bright, but it had been even more uncomfortable being in the same room as Vivian Adams, an administrator for AmeriCorps who'd visited one of her worksites six months before the pandemic. Vivian had asked Fallon to dinner after viewing the project, and they'd hit it off relatively well, but nothing more had come of it. After COVID shut everything down, Fallon had volunteered to remain at the base alone, freeing everyone else to return to their loved ones.

She'd kept busy during the days, maintaining the equipment and monitoring any fire activity, but the nights were long. Vivian's call had come just after the first round of vaccinations, when Fallon's isolation had become nearly intolerable. After several nights of phone conversations—and a week of quarantine for Vivian—she'd come for an in-person visit. Soon, she was staying the night a couple of times a month. It was a satisfying arrangement, as far as it went, but they'd agreed to go their separate ways once things opened up again. Fallon was still comparing every woman to Nora, which made disappointment inevitable. Vivian had continued to call every few months, and repeatedly declining her company was becoming increasingly awkward.

Now, finding herself unexpectedly in Nora's presence again only served as a painful reminder that all those old feelings were still simmering just below the surface of her consciousness. For years, she'd pushed down the hurt and the overwhelming sense of loss, and after a few false starts, she'd made the life she wanted. But the longing was still there, and now that she'd had a moment to catch her breath and acknowledge Nora's presence—again—the yearning to go back and find a way to mend what had torn them apart was just as strong as it had been ten years ago. The passage of time hadn't lessened Nora's desirability; rather, it had transformed her youthful appeal and girlish swagger into a striking, confident woman. Fallon had accepted Nora as a vision in her dreams, but she'd never expected to confront those feelings while looking into her eyes. She could only hope that once Nora left again, she could go back to a reasonable level of denial.

After checking that everyone was accounted for, Fallon concentrated on what was to come as she drove them toward their work zone. Tyler and Nora's presence made it more crowded in the van than usual, but Tyler sat on the floor grinning while Nora squeezed onto a seat where she chatted with the rest of the crew. Fallon had to admit that the two of them seemed to put everyone else at ease since they probably thought Ranger Dick wouldn't allow the media to join them if there was real danger. That was the case in theory, but given the windy conditions and the abundance of fuel in the area, anything could happen.

Once they were on the highway and the road noise increased, Maris leaned over to her. "Who is that photographer? Is she someone you know?"

Fallon struggled with her answer. "I used to know her. We didn't part as friends, but that was years ago." She could feel Maris's curious gaze.

"Why not? Everyone likes you."

Fallon gave a dry chuckle. "We both know that's not true."

"Well, all of us do."

Laughter rose from the rear of the van. Fallon heard Nora's camera clicking again. "Let's drop it, okay? Right now, we both need to have our heads in the game." Despite her words, Fallon's mind wandered to the past.

After the promising relationship with Nora had shattered before her eyes, Fallon had texted Reva on her way out of Firecamp. Along with authorization to give Nora her paycheck to replace the broken camera, Fallon had stated that she was taking a short break and left it at that. Being back in her trailer alone would have added to the hurt, so she'd headed south. At one time, she had been able to drive for hours, lulled into lassitude by the familiar sound and sights of travel. Now she couldn't seem to go an hour without being inundated by thoughts, feelings, or tears. By dusk, she'd been exhausted and emotionally drained and almost to the border of New Mexico. Leaving Colorado had seemed like a line she shouldn't cross, and when it struck her that she was doing exactly what her mother had done for all those years—running from her pain—she'd found a clean motel in the small town of Mason's Bluff and stopped.

There, she'd written dozens of letters to Nora, ultimately tearing up each one. A day later, she'd bought a six-pack of beer and drunk the whole thing before stumbling to the bathroom and puking for what felt like hours. Walking the streets of the small town, she'd seen three Help Wanted signs, but the ads for waitstaff, stocking, or clerical jobs held no appeal. More certain than ever that Firecamp was the place for her, she'd sought a way to be there without being crushed by sadness and shame.

Calling Reva to confirm she'd be allowed to come back, she'd learned that a crew leader from Oregon had transferred to her base and would be next in line for the job Fallon had wanted. In truth, she'd been relieved. The way things had ended with Nora had made her realize that she wasn't just young, she was immature, and she needed to learn to deal with her own issues before she could lead a team.

After her next year at Firecamp—and one messy, ill-advised relationship with another crew member—she'd begun seeing a counselor once or twice a week. Reva had made her therapy a mandatory condition for any potential promotion, and in retrospect, Fallon was glad.

Dr. Ann Carver had been kind but firm in her insistence that Fallon develop a realistic view of herself. "Most of us go through a gawky period in our adolescence. Your body has moved on, but your mind hasn't." When Fallon admitted that she'd never watched Nora's video, no matter how many recruits claimed it had inspired them, Ann had encouraged her to do so. "That reaction to Nora's photos was based on how you saw yourself, not on what she saw in you. Maybe you need to figure out which was accurate."

Fallon had dodged the issue of Nora's video by asking, "Then how can I avoid making the same mistakes in my next relationship?"

Ann had answered with a question of her own. "Why didn't you tell Nora that you wanted to talk about a future together?" Fallon had shrugged. She'd done a lot of that during their first sessions, but Ann wouldn't let her off the hook. "Because you're so nice, you wanted to put her needs first?"

"Well, she was busy. Besides, I shouldn't have had to say. She knew."

"Did you tell her that you loved her?" It was a simple question, but Fallon's mouth had gone dry. "People can't read your mind," Ann had said gently, "no matter how many hints you give. There's no magic in getting what you want. You're the one responsible for your needs, no one else. Wishing or hoping that someone will meet your expectations is not only futile, it's incredibly frustrating, for everyone."

Fallon had looked at her clenched hands. She already knew about not wishing, but Ann was right about how frustrating those last days had been. "The way to finding real love is to believe you're worthy of it," Ann had said, her voice soft with compassion. "Daring to want something special in life is no reason for guilt or shame. The right person won't judge you or be annoyed when you ask for what you deserve. Otherwise, you're just settling, and those unfulfilled desires can fester inside, creating persistent depression or igniting in rage."

It hadn't been rage, but Fallon knew she'd expressed her feelings quite clearly when she'd looked up at the sound of a camera shutter only to see Nora Palmer photographing her and Maris in what could be considered a compromising position. She should have simply reminded Nora that Maris hadn't signed a release and asked her to delete the shots. But after she'd accused Nora of the "same old shit," she'd seen the split-second of hurt on her face before Nora had taken a step back. Both reactions were unusual for the woman she remembered.

"We're at mile marker 162," Maris said quietly.

"What?" Fallon pulled off, and Maris handed her the map. They were in the middle of the area assigned to them, but based on the prevailing winds and the current position of the fire, work done here would have little to no effect. Clearly, Ranger Dick planned to ensure the safety of Nora and Tyler, even at the risk of the lives and property of the people of Kamberto. And if things went to shit, he'd probably find a way to make her take the fall for it. She turned to the crew. "Everybody stretch your legs. Get some water and find a friendly tree if you need to."

The van door opened, and Fallon could hear her people moving around outside. She turned to Maris. "We've been given incorrect coordinates. But if we contact Ranger Dick…"

She trailed off, and Maris filled in the rest. "He'll either put someone else in charge and we'll stay right here, or he'll pull those media people out and send us into the hot zone."

Nora appeared between them from the rear of the van. "What do you mean 'incorrect coordinates'?"

Maris looked away, and Fallon leaned back in her seat, staring out the windshield. "This isn't part of your story, Ms. Palmer. Why don't you take a break with the rest of the crew?"

"Why are you so certain I'm not on your side? I don't have to document anything, but if you'll explain what's going on, I could still help." Something in Nora's tone made Fallon turn to look at her. "I made a mistake once before," Nora whispered, though Maris had to have heard. "And I can't ever make things even, but I'd still like the chance to do something right this time."

She was always about making things even. But it was impossible to look away from the earnestness in Nora's deep brown eyes. After a long pause, Fallon said, "Maris, could you please check the pressure in the two rear tires? We might need more air with the extra load we're carrying."

"Falcon, no. I—"

Fallon held up her hand. "You've got a solid career ahead of you, which means you need to have plausible deniability about my decisions. And I'm counting on you to take the lead with the crew if anything happens to me. Step outside."

Maris got out without another word. Fallon shifted in her seat to face Nora again. "You probably heard enough to know what's going on. Apparently, our ranger wants to make sure you and Tyler are safe because he's sent us so far out of the way, we're basically doing yard work."

Nora nodded. "I didn't ask for his protection, you know."

"I do know that."

"Then take us where we need to go. And if I need to make it part of my story, there are many ways I can spin this depending on what kind of ball your ranger wants to play. Coordinates typo or computer error? Weather forecast inaccuracy or misprint on the map? I'll cover his ass with glory any way I need to as long as it keeps you in the clear."

Fallon chewed her lip. "I, uh, I didn't mean to be so harsh earlier. But you don't owe me anything, you know?"

"I do, but that's a conversation for another time. Don't we have a fire to get to, Falcon?"

Opening her door, Fallon yelled, "Everybody in. We're moving in two minutes."

At their new location, Fallon and Maris calculated the best place to create the firebreak. Mileage-wise, it wasn't much farther, but they positioned themselves almost opposite of where they'd been sent in terms of the road to town and the fire itself. Within the hour, they'd started work, and as bad as the wind was for fighting the fire, everyone was grateful that it helped blow at least some of the smoke past them. For a time, Fallon kept an eye on Nora as she snapped photos from various angles, but watching her move and seeing her concentration as she worked was rekindling feelings from their time together ten years ago. Fallon forced herself to look away, turning her attention to the job at hand.

After an hour or so, Nora and Tyler joined her at one of the large water jugs as she soaked a bandana before returning it to one of her newest crew members. Nora's camera clicked again as Fallon said, "You're doing great, Caden. Hang in there."

After Caden left, Fallon scanned her crew as they worked, pretending not to listen as Nora spoke to Tyler. "My editor told me to get some good stuff, and I'm super impressed with the speed and competence of these sawyers," she told him. "I should have all the shots I need for today, but I'm sure you can catch anything more that comes up. Just be careful."

The seriousness in her tone made Fallon turn, and she watched in surprise as Nora handed Tyler her camera. "It's on autofocus. Leave it that way. If something happens, try to get as many different angles as you can, but stay clear of falling trees."

"Check," he said. "But what are you going to do?"

"Help." Nora looked to Fallon, touching her arm briefly. "I know you didn't leave base without loading PPE and an extra saw for me. I'm ready."

Fallon pushed down her own bandana and grinned. "I thought you'd never ask. Follow me."

The chainsaw was the same brand they'd used at Firecamp all those years ago but a different model. Undoubtedly, Nora could have figured everything out on her own, but Fallon took an extra minute to point out the master switch and the priming bulb.

"When is the heavy equipment coming?" Nora asked, adjusting her hard hat.

Fallon wasn't surprised by the question. Nora would know they couldn't take the time to haul out the downed trees that would serve as fuel if they left them on the ground. For mitigation during an actual fire, the forest service dispatched a picker that would load the cut sections onto a logging truck.

"Tomorrow." Fallon pressed her lips together. "After we disclose our actual location."

"Think they'll send an ATV for you?"

Fallon shook her head and chuckled, her anxiety lifting marginally. "I doubt it."

Nora nudged her with her shoulder. "It'll be okay. Let's worry about the fire for now. Where do you want me, chief?"

Fallon directed her to the far line nearest the forest, presuming she still had the skill to direct her falls. Watching Nora walk away, Fallon couldn't help but admire the familiar swagger that Nora had when she carried a saw. Fallon had never known another woman who projected that kind of confidence while backing it up with action.

Maris's voice came from behind her. "That photographer is a sawyer too?"

Fallon had been caught staring, so no point in pretending otherwise. "Yeah. One of the best I've ever seen."

After taking a long drink, Maris poured some water on her head before replacing her hard hat. "You two had a thing or something, didn't you?"

"Or something." The answer sounded distant to her own ears. She took a shallow breath before turning to face Maris, a future crew chief herself. "You up for taking point with me? We can let everyone else do some limbing."

"Fly on, Falcon," Maris said.

The crew didn't quit until almost full dark. The wind had died down, the smoke hung heavy in the air. Tyler had proven to be a useful gofer, bringing gas or water and sharpening chains as needed, and he was now setting out the packed dinners on a folding table, having already prepared two large buckets for washing up.

"Good work." Fallon patted his shoulder. "We might have to keep you."

He blushed. "Thanks, but I already have a job."

"Tell me about it while you help me grab our goodies out of the van."

His enthusiasm was apparent, and Fallon was impressed with the obvious value of the work he described. Knowing that he and Nora had always been close, she was especially glad to learn they shared a townhome.

"I'm sorry we don't have something more fitting for a scientist of your caliber to do." She handed him a cooler, grabbing a second one herself. "But I can guarantee you'll be quite popular when you show up with this."

"These ladies seem very nice, but I prefer male company," he said.

"Ah, well, it's not my place to give you specifics, but we have some diversity. Just for conversation, mind you. We don't have time for…distractions."

He nodded, clearly intrigued. After they rejoined the group, Fallon handed him a meal and got one for herself. Nora sat on a stump, stretching her back with her eyes closed. Resisting the thought that she was even more remarkable than she'd been ten years ago, Fallon turned away, making the circle of her crew with the cooler in hand. Each person dug in and pulled out one of a variety of beers. They teased and heckled each other, some trading, some refusing to do so. When she came to Shandra, Fallon stopped and produced a bottle from behind her back, a nonalcoholic Heineken. Nora pulled out one of the two remaining Colorado Native brews, an IPA, and Fallon held out the last one, a pilsner, to Tyler.

He shook his head. "Thanks, but I never cared for the taste of beer. You go ahead."

"How about a soda?" Fallon asked, opening the other cooler and pulling out a Coke.

"Now you're talking."

By the time Fallon sat to eat, almost everyone else had finished and was enjoying their beer.

"So, Nora," Brooke called. "Where'd you learn to handle a saw like that?"

"At Firecamp, of course," Nora answered, and the crew cheered.

"Sorry, but I have to call BS on that," Fallon said. "She came to camp with those skills and was nice enough to help the rest of us who didn't even know which end was sharp."

Everyone laughed. "And now you take pictures of fabulous sawyers?" Caden asked.

"Sawyer, swampers, beauty queens—oh, same thing, excuse me."

A few laughed, but Brooke said, "Fuck that. I'm a hell of a sawyer, but I ain't no beauty queen."

Fallon stood. "All right, drink up and hit the sack. I'm calling for heavies tomorrow, and we want to give them plenty to do." As the crew dispersed, Fallon turned back, "I only brought one tent for you and Tyler. I hope that's okay."

Nora looked out at the assortment of shelters, watching as the sawyer's lights began to glow inside them. "Are you still in your adventurous model?"

Fallon sniffed. "No, I…it would have been too big for this operation."

"Sure was nice to change standing up, though."

The wistfulness in her voice made Fallon's throat tighten. "Listen, if you're not comfortable sharing with Tyler, I can sleep with Maris—I mean, you know, share the tent with her—and you can have mine."

Nora laughed. "When Kennedy made that same kind of suggestion, I didn't want you to take them up on it. Why would you offer it to me now?"

Was Nora flirting? Fallon cleared her throat. "Well, let me know what you decide. I need to know where you'll be, since I'm sure Ranger Dick will want a full report."

"I don't care what Ranger Dick wants. What do you want?"

"A decent night's sleep would be a good start." At Nora's frown, Fallon shook her head. "Okay, Nora. You tell me. What do you want?" She hadn't meant to leave Nora such an easy opening, but she couldn't take it back now.

Nora moved closer. Fallon had learned to use her height as an intimidation factor when necessary, but it didn't help her now. Still, she stood her ground until Nora stopped only a few inches away. "I want to talk to you. Really talk. I was too much of a coward to face you before, and I'm still scared, but I'm more scared of not having a chance to put things right between us."

Fallon's emotions were a merry-go-round of options, from excitement to aggravation to dread to delight. She settled on truth. "I'd like to talk to you too, but I have responsibilities here. It's not a time that I can relax or think about much beyond what I need to do next in the here and now."

Nora nodded. "I understand that. Can your here and now include letting me share your tent again?"

Could Nora hear her heartbeat? She cleared her throat, giving her voice time to strengthen. "Yes, as long as we actually sleep."

"Believe me, as out of shape as I am for this kind of work, I can promise you that we will actually sleep."

Maybe so, Fallon thought, *but I bet it will feel like one of my dreams.*

Leaving Nora to get ready, she went to clean up more thoroughly. She hadn't expected to have company in the small tent, so she wanted to wash off a layer of dirt and sweat if possible. With the rest of the crew already bedded down, Fallon didn't hesitate to strip to her bra and underwear, wiping herself off with the inside of her dirtiest shirt.

"I very much like the way you're wearing your hair now." Nora's voice came from behind her. Fallon didn't turn, casually slipping her cleaner shirt on, quelling embarrassment about her semi-naked state. She was proud of this body.

"I like your hairstyle too. You look softer. I mean, more approachable. Did you start wearing it that way for your work?"

"Not deliberately, no. I guess I learned I'm not quite as butch as I thought I was."

Fallon laughed quietly, and they started walking back to the tent. "So I'm more butch now?"

"Whatever you call it, you look good, Fallon. Really good."

Fallon couldn't be certain about the emotion in Nora's voice. Was it regret? Approval? Desire? She held open the tent flap. "Uh, thanks. You too. Listen, go ahead and get settled. I'll be in as soon as I make a quick loop around the camp."

Nora nodded and crawled in.

The truth was, Fallon needed some time to quiet her battling heart. As long as they were working, as long as the crew was around, she could pretend Nora was simply someone she used to know. But the minute it was just the two of them, when Nora stood close or told her how good she looked, their past seemed unimportant compared to how amazing it felt to be with her again. But that was not what she needed. Trying not to breathe the smoky air too deeply, she reminded herself that the same factors that had made it impossible for them ten years ago were still in play. They'd always been honest with each other about their dreams, even knowing that achieving those aspirations would put them in two very different places, physically and emotionally. In a way, such openness had been part of their attraction. She'd never doubted that Nora was a fine person at her core, but they'd both been foolish kids, and Fallon should have known better than to risk her heart. She knew what it was to be vulnerable, to be taken advantage of, and she'd sworn to do better upon her initial arrival at Firecamp. Then she'd fallen for the least available person, short of Ranger Reva. But until she'd been gutted by the photographs Nora had taken of her, she'd been genuinely convinced that Nora cared for her too. That might be something they would discuss in their talk, if and when it happened. But for now, there was a job to do, and she needed to figure out how to explain things to Ranger Dick in a way that wouldn't get her fired.

Walking by Maris's tent, she heard soft conversation broken by moments of silence. Moments of kisses, if Fallon's instincts about Maris and Shandra were correct. Good. Maris deserved to have someone, and it couldn't be her. Those kinds of fleeting relationships were behind her now. She was content with the life she'd made, and if seeing Nora reignited an ache, a yearning for intimate companionship, she could live through it. All fires went out eventually.

CHAPTER SIXTEEN

When Nora heard footsteps, she turned on her side, facing away from where Fallon would sleep. She'd been telling herself that this arrangement didn't mean they were starting over, but being this close to Fallon again made her feel as though the past ten years were more like ten minutes. She worked to steady her breathing, refusing to take into account the initial lack of welcome in Fallon's eyes or the coolness in her tone. She understood the defensiveness of that behavior but seemed unable to summon it for herself. Her heart had seized control, reminding her of the connection she'd so casually taken for granted then, not knowing its true worth. But was there really a chance to renew something she'd been foolish enough to let go of ten years ago?

The flap opened, and Fallon settled next to her, lying on her back, evoking all the other things Nora couldn't disregard: Fallon's total mastery with the chainsaw, the steady way she directed her crew and their obvious respect for her, and how years of hard work and being in charge had turned her into a poised, powerful woman. Nora swallowed around the vision of Fallon in her undergarments and how it had taken every ounce of her control to resist reaching for her.

Fallon sighed, and Nora recalled how Fallon's body felt as it relaxed, which sent her to memories of those days in the trailer when they'd lost themselves in each other, connecting in every way possible. After Fallon's vanishing act, Nora had secured those remembrances in a distant place in her mind, venturing there infrequently, usually prompted by excessive alcohol or through the occasional encounter with another woman. Now they were front and center, as was Fallon, who'd always taken the lead role in her fantasies.

Nora cleared her throat quietly. "You wouldn't happen to have an extra pillow, would you? I'd like to turn over, but I don't want to seem too…personal?"

"Intimate?"

Nora smiled, gratified by Fallon's obvious recollection of the conversation from the first time they'd shared a tent. But the memory turned bittersweet when Nora wondered if she'd used that line with other women.

Fallon shook her head. "No extras, I'm afraid. Have you totally gone city girl, Nora? I'm using my clothes bag as a pillow. You only have that one because I grabbed it along with your tent."

Despite Fallon's teasing tone, Nora recognized the sweet, kind young woman she'd observed upon their initial arrival at Firecamp, disbelief and disinterest at the forefront of her mind. Once she'd come to understand that Fallon was the real deal—a genuinely decent person in search of a community of like-minded friends—compelling attraction had soon followed. And clearly, that pull was still there. At least from Nora's side. It was impossible to know what would have happened between them if she'd had the courage to talk through things during those last weeks. After some time had passed, she could admit to herself that even if they'd had no future, that decision wouldn't have been as painful. Perhaps they could have found a way to remain friends, avoiding the awkwardness that now seemed to color every conversation, every movement, every glance between them.

Turning onto her stomach, she stretched, flashing back to that Sunday morning when she'd premiered her much anticipated project.

She'd worked all through Saturday night, recreating the folder Fallon had destroyed from the intact memory card, alternately cursing and crying while doing last-minute tweaks to the video. The next morning, Upshaw had set up a projector and screen in the dining room, and Nora's video was shown to all of Firecamp who were present. While the staff and other sawyers cheered and applauded wildly, calling for two encores, her crew members, the stars of the show for the most part, were notably subdued, especially when images of Fallon came on.

Afterward, when she went to each teammate, presenting them with the flash drives she'd made, there were hugs but no tears.

"Where's Falcon?" Delores had asked, Hannah standing close beside her. "I can't believe she'd miss this, but her car is gone."

"I don't know where she is," Nora said, wishing she had another answer. Wishing she'd handled everything differently. Better.

Kennedy didn't have a question, just a few last words of

discernment. "What happened between you and Fallon is no one else's business. I hope it was worth it."

Jade had simply slipped the flash drive into her pocket and waited.

Nora had forced herself to muster some kind of defense. "I guess I hurt her, and I'm sorry. But we were always going our separate ways anyhow."

Jade had frowned. "Now that you can see the future so clearly, I hope that skill will help you stay out of trouble."

It was a not-so-subtle reminder of what Fallon had done for her, and Nora had averted her gaze. Trying not to cave in entirely, she'd promised, "I'll do my best."

She'd stopped by Ranger Upshaw's office, ostensibly to say good-bye but secretly seeking praise for the work she'd put in and the product she'd created. Instead, Upshaw had barely acknowledged her before casually tossing a thick envelope onto her desk. "What's this?" Nora had asked.

"Fallon wanted you to have her pay for this hitch. Apparently, she was responsible for damage to your camera?"

Nora had forgotten about anything else, trying not to let her hand shake as she'd reached for it. *Maybe there's a note?*

"She said that after you buy a replacement, give any money that's left to your father." Upshaw had raised a questioning eyebrow.

Nora had said nothing, certain this was the final message. Of course Fallon had left her a last dig about caring for her family. Fine. At the time, Nora had resolved to slough Firecamp off like mud from her boots and focus her energy on school, finding a job afterward that would give her what she most wanted: self-sufficiency. Independence. Control.

She'd let herself be consumed with honing her skills and then with developing contacts for work, which was why she had associates and sources, not personal connections. She had made brief calls home every other week while in college, but for the most part, she was self-contained, distant from her family—except for Tyler—and generally indifferent to events outside of those she photographed. But through her work, Nora had been exposed to every possible spectrum of the human experience, from pure joy to devastating loss, and she'd lived for those times when she captured an image that solidified something intangible. She'd believed that was all she needed, until seeing Fallon again had awakened her to something else, something more she could've had.

Clearly, they had both made the lives they'd wanted. Fallon had a position of importance and a role in something meaningful. And while some of her community was likely to change from year to year, her life offered the stability of place and the bond of being a part of others' growth.

Nora coughed and shifted onto her back again.

"Can't sleep?" Fallon asked. She sounded awake as well.

"My body is exhausted, but my mind won't shut off." Nora could only hope Fallon wouldn't ask why.

"You can turn this way if it would help," Fallon offered, moving so she faced the tent wall. "We both need to rest."

"Is it okay if I snug?"

"Sure."

Nora sensed that Fallon was trying to sound casual, but there was tension in her voice. She turned into Fallon's body, looping her arm around her waist, overruling several possible comments that came to mind: "Just like old times" or "You feel even better now than you used to" or "Would you be mad if I broke my promise about sleeping?" But as if her body had been prompted by the mental notion of rest, Nora's eyes closed.

❖

Nora cursed as she fumbled for the alarm. Her phone merely showed the time: 5:45 a.m., so what the fuck was that god-awful sound? Her mind settled as she sat up, shaking herself awake. She wasn't in her own bed, and that was the triangle, one more reminder of other times.

Fallon was gone, the space where she'd been lying, cool. Nora peered out the tent flap to figures moving around in a smoky haze and the faint smell of coffee. Wriggling into yesterday's clothes, she headed for the center of activity.

Tyler was already up and handed her camera over without being asked. "I slept like the dead. You?"

She yawned. "Same. Have you eaten?"

"Just now. Go on over. I'm going to get a clean shirt out of my bag in the van." He gave her grimy outfit a look.

"Don't even," she said, looking around for Fallon. "Any news?"

"Maris said the heavy equipment is on the way, and she indicated that Fallon's ass is way smaller than its original size since Ranger Dick chewed off at least half of it."

"I certainly can't think about that before coffee," Nora said, waving Tyler on his way.

Caden handed her a steaming mug, and she nodded her thanks. Moving slowly through the breakfast area, she grabbed a cup of instant oatmeal and a banana, listening as Fallon's voice came to her on a draft of wind.

"It's somewhat more predictable when it's steady, since these gusts can loft embers and start spot fires." Maris said something Nora couldn't understand, and Fallon added, "It's headed this way, and our break isn't quite as big as it needs to be, but we should be prepared to split up if we see something catch nearby. The fire crew indicated increasing flare-ups since dawn." They were standing near the van. Fallon's back was to her as she gestured at the road. "I've got to stay and meet the heavies, or Ranger Dick will have what's left of my ass. You're the logical choice to lead the second team, so pick whoever you want and tell them to be ready."

Maris pointed at Nora as she approached. "Can I have her?"

Fallon looked over her shoulder, giving Nora a quick smile before turning again to Maris. "Nope. Sorry, but Ranger Dick may come over with the heavies, in which case, she'll be returning to base."

"The hell you say." Nora put her hands on her hips. "I'm not going anywhere until I leave with the rest of you."

Fallon faced her, hands out in an appeasing gesture. "If it was my call, I'd keep you and Tyler both. You've helped us tremendously, but you're not current Firecamp personnel, and if Ranger Dick thinks things are getting too hot—literally—he's going to pull you off the line."

"What if I went with Maris's team? He can't make me leave if he can't find me."

Maris cleared her throat. "That's probably all it would take for Falcon to lose her job. He's been trying to find a reason to fire her for a year now."

Nora bit her lip as she stared at the ground. She detested the self-centered streak that seemed to show itself when things didn't go her way. Looking at Fallon again, she said, "I'm sorry. Of course I'll do whatever I can to keep that from happening. But I really, really want to stay." Maris raised her eyebrows. "After all, I need to get the end of the story." Nora gestured, hoping her explanation sounded plausible.

"We've got bigger issues to worry about," Fallon said. "For now, Nora's with me." Maris coughed. "With my team," Fallon amended.

Nora suppressed a grin as she followed them to gather the crew.

Maris pulled four others aside and began explaining their role. Tyler joined them as Fallon turned to Nora. "Thanks for understanding. I meant what I said about you two being great to have around."

Tyler giggled, and Nora subtly elbowed him. "Put us to work wherever you need us," he said. "It'll only make me appreciate my cushy lab job even more when we get back to Tucson."

Fallon's smile faded. "Right. Follow me."

Two hours later, Nora dimly heard a rumbling sound over the whine of her saw. "Shutting down," she called, turning to see the huge picker and logging truck idling in front of their van alongside the firebreak.

Fallon began shouting orders to the drivers, who gave her a thumbs-up and began moving their equipment into position. It was amazing to see how effortlessly the giant arm lifted massive sections of logs and stacked them neatly on the truck. After watching for a moment, Fallon returned the thumbs-up.

Nora carried her saw to the rest area, stopping for a long drink before soaking her bandana with water.

Fallon came over, taking off her helmet and wiping her face as she turned into the wind. "My crew is working harder than I've ever seen, trying to outdo you. Think you might take a break and give them a chance to catch up?"

She was smiling, but it wasn't quite the look Nora wanted to see. "Sure. Should I sit and file my nails for a while?" They both laughed, and Nora pointed at the trucks. "It looks like your ranger didn't accompany them."

Fallon shook her head. "He's not my ranger, believe me. The driver said he was busy updating the InciWeb and answering emails. I'm sorry to say, he may have forgotten you. Again."

Just as long as you haven't forgotten. Nora knew this wasn't the time, but there were so many things she wanted to say. Instead, she looked at the hill across from them. "Is it me, or is the smoke getting worse?"

Fallon pulled a monocular from a side pocket of her pants and scanned along the small gorge that ran alongside their firebreak. She was moving her inspection along the next hill when she stopped, leaning forward slightly. "Damn," she muttered before turning to Nora. "Could you spread the word for everyone to finish what they're working on, then move toward the road. That's our escape route. If Maris can't get that spot under control, we're going to lose this break." She ran into the haze before Nora could react, shouting, "Maris! Go!"

The sound of bodies crashing through the underbrush followed. *If we lose this break, will they have to evacuate the town?* After delivering Fallon's message, Nora returned to felling the tree she'd been working on. She was halfway through the second cut on another when the triangle sounded. Her stomach suggested it should be time for lunch, but she doubted that was what the call was for. The remainder of the crew gathered around Fallon, who was on her radio. Nora heard Maris shouting over the gusts of wind that sounded like crackling paper as she spoke.

"...less than twenty percent. Too many flare-ups. With the rest of the crew, we could handle it." Fallon's gaze landed on the picker, which had only gathered about half of the felled wood. "Maybe—" She cut off transmission, and everyone turned at the sound of rotors.

A large helicopter made its way through the smoke, stopping to hover behind the picker and log truck. As the crew watched, eight geared firefighters repelled onto the road. With amazing dexterity, given their heavy protective gear, they detached themselves, and the ropes retracted. The helicopter sped away. Seven of the firefighters headed down the gully in the direction of the spot fire, while one made his way toward them.

"Nora Palmer?" he called.

Nora's jaw dropped, and she stepped forward. "Art?" They embraced awkwardly around his gear. "What are you doing here?"

He grinned. "Rudy and I figured you'd be somewhere in this mess. Can't let you have all the fun."

Nora looked at the forms moving into the gully. "Rudy's here?"

Art pointed skyward. "Oh yeah. He'll be showing off with his water dump before long. Not one to get his hands dirty, that boy."

Fallon's radio crackled. "Fallon?" Maris asked. "What's happening? Who are these people?"

"Maris, they're..." She looked to Nora, but Art spoke first.

"Arthur Palmer. Squad leader, Roosevelt Hotshots. We're here to lend a hand before we get busy working on the big burn."

Fallon nodded and finished the call. "They're hotshots, Maris. Help them finish the spot fire and come on back."

"Roger that. And thanks for calling in the big guns." Fallon didn't correct Maris's assumption.

Nora cleared her throat. "Art, this is our crew chief, Fallon

Monroe." Glancing around at the stunned expressions, she added, "And these gawkers are about half of the Firecamp Women's Plus Crew."

Art touched his helmet. "Ma'am."

"We're glad to see you, Mr. Palmer," Fallon replied.

He tilted his head, looking between her and Nora. "Wait. Are you Nora's friend my dad is always talking about?"

"I'd be very flattered if that was the case. Your dad, along with Nora and Tyler, helped me out of a jam several years ago."

Art grinned. "Ran out of gas, right? And then you brought Nora home to check on Tyler when he broke his arm."

Fallon's jaw tightened. "Yes, that's right."

Art held out his hand. "It's a pleasure to meet you. Our dad was just asking if you'd be coming by."

They shook. "I'd like to see him again too," Fallon said. "Maybe after we get this mess cleaned up. Meanwhile, please let me know if my crew can do anything to assist, here or at the main burn."

The sound of the rotors returned, louder this time, the chopper flying low enough for Nora to see Rudy in the pilot's seat, waving before he headed up the mountain. She waved back.

"We'll do that," Art said, glancing around at the firebreak. "Your crew has done a great job here. But I wouldn't mind if you could turn down these gales a bit."

Fallon smiled. "Thanks. I'll see what I can do about that."

A voice came over Art's radio: "Spot burn under control. Heading up."

"Guess that's my cue." Adding a wink, he said, "Make sure you take good care of my little sister, will you?"

Nora bristled at Art's implication that she needed looking after, so typical of the men in her family, but the pink tinge in Fallon's cheeks distracted her. What did she think he meant?

"Nora is quite capable of taking care of herself, as I'm sure you know."

He laughed. "That I do." Touching his helmet again, he squeezed Nora's shoulder as he passed. "See ya, sis."

Almost instantly, he vanished into the smoke. Nora shook her head. "That was surreal."

Tyler emerged from behind the van. "I got pictures of the whole thing."

"You sneak. Why didn't you come say hi to Art?"

"I just saw him a couple of days ago," Tyler said, still grinning.

"Let me see those photos," Nora started toward him, hand out for the camera.

"Maybe I will and maybe I won't."

Nora caught Tyler by the shirttail, threatening to tickle him until he gave in and handed over the camera, while Fallon spoke into her radio. "Maris, meet me on the forest edge of the break. I want to make sure we're clean before the trucks go."

"Roger."

Tyler gave in easily, and Nora began looking through his shots, raising an eyebrow at him. "These are pretty good. For an amateur."

"Hey, Tyler," Caden called. "When's lunch?"

Tyler hurried off while Nora continued looking through his photos from the day before. She heard the picker and log truck engines start up. After their rumble faded, it was strangely quiet, and Nora had the thought that maybe Fallon had found a way to control the atmosphere. The idea had barely crossed her mind when a violent blast of hot wind whipped dust and grit into her face. She spun away, shielding her eyes, only to jerk back around at the sharp, ripping crack from across the break. She watched in horror as a tree began to fall, Fallon and Maris directly in its path. Standing a few feet apart, they stared up, seemingly paralyzed. Then Fallon raced forward, pulling Maris for several yards before shoving her clear. The tree twisted as it crashed down, and Fallon disappeared under its branches as she tried to lunge for safety.

The air left Nora's lungs. Was she screaming? Was Maris? Then she was running, everyone was running, toward the spot where Fallon had been swallowed by the thick tree limbs densely covered with needles.

"Where is she?" Maris said over and over. "Can anyone see her? Where is she?"

Only Caden had the presence of mind to bring a saw but passed it to Nora. "You're fast and steady. Get her out of there."

Nora started to shake her head but realized she didn't want anyone else working with a chainsaw close to where Fallon might be. "Pull the slash away as quick as you can," Nora told the other crew members. "Maris, stay beside me, and tell me when you see her."

Maris nodded, and Nora called, "Starting up." She cut and cut. The branches disappeared from her view so quickly, it was almost as if they'd never been there.

Finally, Maris called, "Stop!" Nora hit the chain brake. "There." Maris was pointing. "Isn't that her helmet? Oh God. God, no."

Nora understood why Maris was crying. She wanted to cry too. But every second counted. If Fallon's helmet had been knocked off, the best place to look for her body would be in the thinner branches right below it. *No, not her body. Herself. Her smile. Those beautiful eyes.*

"Move with me," Nora ordered, shifting along the mass of branches until she was closer to the trunk. "Maris. Maris! I need you to watch for her so I can concentrate on cutting. Can you?"

"Yes." Maris choked back a sob. "Okay, go."

Four cuts later, as the branches were pulled away, Nora saw her. On her side. Her hand to her head. Her face streaked with blood. "Fallon! Oh, Jesus." Nora dropped the saw and crawled forward, disregarding the sharp sting of the needles digging into her skin. She reached out and put her fingers on Fallon's neck. "She's alive. But her pulse is fast." Fallon's left shoulder looked warped, almost sunken.

"Don't touch her, please," a male voice called from behind the group.

Everyone turned to see three EMTs and Tyler coming across the break. Nora trembled with relief that he'd the sense to call 9-1-1.

"Are you the sawyer?" a different voice asked. Nora could only nod. "Okay. Let me show you where else you need to cut so we can get her out."

CHAPTER SEVENTEEN

Everything hurt. Fallon's eyelids felt like they had weights holding them closed. The ground beneath her tent wasn't this soft. She worked to understand what was going on, but her brain couldn't seem to get out of first gear. Trying to speak, she made a grunt. Someone stroked her cheek.

"Fallon? Sweetie? It's Nora." Something touched her palm. "If you can hear me, squeeze my hand."

Breathing in, Fallon asked her muscles to obey. Her fingers flexed slightly.

"Oh, thank God. How do you feel? Do you need anything?" Fallon managed to part her dry lips and give a slight cough. "Water? Are you thirsty?" She grunted again, tilting her head toward Nora's voice. "Okay. They said I could give you ice chips. Here."

Something touched her mouth, and a cold particle dissolved on her tongue. The next piece dropped onto her lip. Finally, a drop of water slid down her throat.

"One more and then let's see how you feel," Nora said.

If she'd had any moisture to spare, Fallon might have cried from frustration. She flexed her fingers again, but Nora's hand was gone. *Because she's feeding you ice chips*, her brain helpfully supplied. This time, she relaxed her jaw, and the frozen flakes melted in her throat. It felt wonderful.

She became aware of sounds other than Nora's voice. A rhythmic beeping was accompanied by a new chirp, and something tightened around her arm. She tried to form a question, but only a "Hmm?" came out.

"You're going to be fine." Nora's voice sounded strained, and she sniffed. "The doctor said so. You just need a little time to recover."

Soft pressure on her forehead followed. Nora's lips. "I'm sorry. I'm so sorry." Fallon tried to hold on to her hand, but it was too hard.

A moment later, the tightness relaxed, and something else tweeted with a different, almost ticking resonance. A shadow crept in behind her vision, and she retreated into it.

❖

"A tree fell on me?" Fallon asked, incredulous.

Dr. Norgood, a handsome man with silver hair, smiled. "Apparently, yes. Well, the branchy part of a tree, anyway. According to your colleagues, you pushed another woman out of the way, but you weren't able to escape."

Maris. It was coming back to her now. The shock and fear she'd felt as the huge mass of limbs and trunk had come down on them. Then darkness. "But she's all right? Everyone else too?"

"Other than being worried about you and pestering my staff to the point of distraction, they're fine. A ranger came by yesterday and threatened them with dismissal if they didn't return to work, or I'm sure they'd be here now."

"And the fire?"

"Ninety-something percent contained. The young women who were visiting you said your work on the break helped save the town. I assume you understand the nuances of that."

Fallon nodded. Trying to shift positions, she grimaced, wondering about the triangular bandage she'd found wrapped on her left arm and tied around her neck. She was generally a side sleeper, but her options had become limited because almost any movement of that area was extremely painful. "My shoulder—"

"Dislocated. We were able to reduce it with no additional damage."

"Reduce it?"

"Pop it back into place, in layman's terms. You'll be wearing that sling for maybe four to six weeks. Then you should be good as new." He pointed down her body. "That hip flexor strain will probably recover even faster. But you'll have to take it easy, use ice, and take ibuprofen for a week or so."

There were only four weeks left in this year's Firecamp season. Fallon shook her head. "But I can walk and talk, right?"

"Talk, yes, walk, not too much. Not at first, anyway. Short distances a few times a day. Don't push it, or you'll make things worse, and it will take longer to recover. If you try to run or jump, you could damage it to the point that you'll need surgery. The same with your shoulder. But overall, you should consider yourself extremely lucky."

Fallon sighed. She didn't feel lucky.

"Any other questions?" the doctor asked.

Where's Nora? Fallon's most recent conscious memory was of Nora giving her ice chips. Was that yesterday? Two days ago? She'd obviously been given pain medication after the accident because until this morning, her sense of time had been rather unreliable. But she was certain it had been at least a day since she'd seen her. Would Nora visit again? "When will I be released from the hospital?"

"Tomorrow. You had a low-grade fever yesterday, and we need to make sure there's no infection."

"Thank you, Doctor."

He smiled. "They're calling you a hero, you know."

Fallon scoffed, and he left. A real hero would have walked away unscathed, right? She stared at the ceiling. What would she do with herself for six weeks? Would Ranger Dick let her stay at base camp if she couldn't work for the last part of it? Or would this be his excuse to get rid of her? She understood him using his authority to get everyone else back to work, but the question of Nora returned. She didn't work for him. Was she already in Tucson, filing her story? Weren't they supposed to talk?

Would she have felt differently about Nora's reappearance if it hadn't been accompanied by the sound of a camera clicking? True, she was less sensitive about the photos that had been the basis of their breakup, thanks to years of counseling, but what if Nora had come back to Firecamp and simply knocked on her door, presenting herself with no agenda other than to talk? In therapy, Fallon had acknowledged that her feelings about Nora were muddled, but she could admit to herself that her heart had jumped at the sight of her, even though Nora was holding her Canon. If there hadn't been a major wildfire raging, would Fallon have willingly dropped her guard and let Nora saunter through all the years of self-protection with a wink and a smile? Maybe now that she was more awake, she should call and ask to see her.

Fallon looked around, seeing none of her possessions, only two vases of flowers. She wore a hospital gown, so there were no pockets for her cell, and she was unable to recall Nora's number. But Nora knew her room number, and a phone sat on the nightstand. Staring at it wouldn't make it ring, though. Sighing, Fallon tried to figure out what to do now. She didn't have a book to read. Turning on the television would be a waste of time. Carefully, she worked her way to the edge of the bed. The doctor said she could walk a short distance. Maybe after going down the hall and back, she'd feel better. Or she'd sleep.

She lowered her feet carefully to the ground, her shoulder joint aching with every movement. Previously, she'd made the trek to the bathroom with a nurse who had assisted her with a gait belt; now she was untethered, which felt both good and intimidating. Small steps got her to the door, and she sidled carefully into the hall with a minimum of twinges in her hip. She'd almost made it to the nurses' station when a familiar voice called her name. She turned to see Tyler coming toward her, his smile a mile wide.

"Are you making an escape, or are you released?"

Gratified to see him, her insides warmed. "Neither," she said, hiding her relief behind a cough that made her eyes water. "I'm taking a restorative stroll."

He took her arm, guiding her back to her room. "Did they say when you might get sprung?"

"Tomorrow. What are you still doing here? I thought you'd be at your cushy lab job by now."

"I have a few more vacation days. And I've been tasked with making sure you're properly cared for until your release."

"Tasked by whom?" she asked, secretly hoping she knew the answer.

"The entire Firecamp crew. Plus one." He held the door for her, making a grand gesture for her to enter.

She grinned as she made her way to the bed. "It's really good to see you, Tyler. Tell me everything that's been going on."

He did, including the part where a radio station newswoman had wanted to interview her but had been told she was unavailable. "She settled for Maris, who was still pretty emotional. According to her, you not only saved her, you protected the town and kept the rest of the forest from burning down."

"Oh hell," Fallon grumbled. "Maybe it was on a station that Ranger Dick doesn't listen to."

"No such luck," Tyler said. "The story has been picked up by your local paper, and it may even go national. Nora told the reporter she'd send her some photos."

"Isn't Nora working on her own story?"

His amused expression became somber. "I hadn't gotten to that part yet. Nora's at home."

It wasn't what she wanted to hear, but Fallon wasn't surprised. What she didn't expect was the pang of loss. "Yeah. Working on her story like I said. Right?"

"No, she's not in Tucson. Nora's at our family home. My father had what might be a stroke." Tyler looked at his watch. "She's supposed to call me in about an hour and let me know what's going on."

"Oh. I'm sorry." A little flutter of hope began to beat inside. "Are you going to join her?"

"If you get released tomorrow, I might." He looked at her slyly. "But I don't have transportation."

She grinned. "I have transportation, but I can't drive."

He pressed his hands together. "Tell me you still have the beautiful red car that looks like a spaceship."

There was that familiar twinge of sadness whenever she thought about Big Red. "Sorry, no. But I do have a sweet-riding pickup truck I bought off Ranger Reva."

"I suppose that will have to do."

"How will we get back to base camp?" she asked. "I don't even know where my stuff is."

He opened the nightstand drawer to reveal a shattered cell phone, a crushed monocular, and what looked like a few pieces of her radio. "Nora said they pretty much cut everything off you in the ambulance. But I bet we could get a volunteer to come get us if you asked." He checked his phone. "I happen to have Caden's number."

Fallon kept her expression neutral. "Okay. Uh…what day is it?"

"Saturday. So tomorrow will be a day off, right?" he asked. She nodded. "Can you stick it out the rest of today?"

She took stock. Her shoulder hurt, and her hip ached from just that short walk. The idea of seeing Nora again made her want to be as functional as possible. "Tomorrow it is. But I want to know what's going on with your dad as soon as you hear."

"Deal."

❖

Fallon inhaled deeply, thrilled to be free from the scents and sounds and sights of the hospital. Nora had called with the news that their father needed more tests, telling Tyler she'd be staying for a few more days at least and to come when he could. Fallon found herself eager to accompany him. Caden had picked them up and seemed especially thrilled to share the information that Ranger Dick had been called to the forest supervisor's office. His absence was especially convenient since everyone else acted like her return was the second coming. Tyler had to run point to keep Maris from hugging her, but everyone else understood the sling and gave her room. There wasn't very much to pack, it turned out. Fallon left Ranger Dick a note saying she'd return after her convalescence, but a small part of her wondered if that would really happen. Either way, she felt strangely calm.

After they stopped to replace her cell phone, Fallon watched Tyler drive for a while. He was good and careful behind the wheel, and the activities of the day were killing her shoulder and hip, so she swallowed half a pain pill. She hadn't expected to be completely knocked out, and it wasn't until Tyler called her name that she realized they'd parked.

"We're about an hour and a half away," he said. "But I need a break. Are you hungry?"

"Sure," she said, thinking that standing and stretching might be even better. She'd almost mastered the art of one-handed eating, and a burger and fries did the trick. Tyler had a grilled cheese sandwich and a salad. "I have a question," she said as they finished. "But it's probably none of my business, and you're free to say so, and we'll leave it at that."

"*Okay*," he said, drawing the word out.

"I got the impression that Nora—and maybe you—aren't particularly close to your father. It just surprises me that she's there now."

"Ah." He paused, seeming lost in thought. "Let's just say, I think Nora is doing penance." Before Fallon could inquire further, he added, "But it's her story to tell."

She nodded and dropped a few bills for the check. In the restroom, she spent way too much time struggling with pulling down her jeans and getting them up again. She hadn't thought about her wardrobe choices when the nurse had been there to help her this morning. Clearly, some basic things in life were going to be challenging for the next few weeks. And knowing she would see Nora soon prompted a once-over in the mirror. The scratches on her face were beginning to heal, and she was glad the nurse had helped wash her hair before she'd left the hospital, but she was still a mess. Oh well, take it or leave it, she thought, wondering which Nora would choose.

It was late afternoon when they reached the house. A woman Fallon didn't recognize came onto the porch as they pulled up. "My cousin Anita," Tyler murmured, shutting off the engine and waving as he opened the door. Anita called something back into the house and disappeared.

In the dusky light, the Palmer place looked different from the tidy, well-kept home Fallon remembered. The small front yard needed cutting, and the flower beds near the porch were overgrown. One of the decorative shutters hung slightly askew, and the whole house could have done with a coat of paint. As she stood, moving gingerly to accommodate the ache in her left side, she wondered how long Mr. Palmer had been ill.

Tyler was at the front door, and she heard Nora saying something in a questioning tone. He gestured toward the truck, and Nora stepped onto the porch. Fallon sketched a wave, uncertain as to her welcome.

Nora held a hand to her mouth for a few seconds before rushing down the stairs. "You're here," she breathed. "And you're feeling all right?"

Fallon grinned. "Better than I look."

Nora glanced at the sling. "Oh, Fallon, I want to hug you, but I know I can't."

"Yeah, not the best move for a little while." Nora's eyes filled with tears, and Fallon moved closer, holding out her good arm. "But I can do this if you want."

Nora leaned carefully into the right side of her chest, and Fallon draped a hand over her back. Her left side protested, but she ignored it. "I hate it that you got hurt." Nora's voice wavered. "But it was worse when I thought...oh God, I couldn't stand it when I thought—"

Fallon felt dampness on her shirt, and she tightened her hold as much as she could. "Hey,. I'm fine. Or I will be. But I'm not too clear on exactly what happened."

"Could we..." Nora took in a breath that was part sob. "Could we talk about it later? I need to, uh, to get used to you being here."

Fallon frowned. "Is it okay? I told Tyler I'd stay at the hotel, but that would entail someone carting me back and forth, so..."

Nora cut her off with a flick of her wrist, carrying Fallon's bag into the house, telling her, "We're going to sleep in Art and Rudy's old room." When Fallon opened her mouth, Nora added, "Two twin beds," before pulling a face that made Fallon laugh. In the upstairs bedroom, Nora turned to her. "I know we have a lot to talk about, but I want you to know, I'm very glad you came."

"You're right, we do," Fallon said. "But being here with you feels…comfortable."

Nora rolled her eyes. "Not quite the sensation I was going for, but given your injury, I'll take it."

Fallon smiled. "How's your dad?"

Nora turned away, looking out the window. "Not good. Miserable, in fact, and making everyone else miserable too." She broke off abruptly. "But he'll be glad to see you."

After Nora helped her unpack, they made their way downstairs. Mr. Palmer was indeed glad to see her and stood unsteadily, putting out his hand. It shook uncontrollably, and Fallon moved closer to take it. Letting go, he said something, but she only understood about every other word. "I'm sorry, sir. My hearing hasn't been too good since the accident. Could you repeat that?" When she saw Nora jerk her head around, Fallon crossed her fingers behind her back.

Mr. Palmer nodded and succeeded in speaking a little more clearly. "I told that girl to bring you around," he said, practically falling into his chair. "I'm glad she finally did one thing right."

Fallon saw Nora flinch, and the need to defend her rose inside. "Nora loves you, Mr. Palmer, and she's here now to help take care of you when she could be back in Tucson, working."

"Oh, sure. Nora is a good girl. Kinda headstrong, but she sure takes pretty pictures. Have you seen any?" He fumbled on the small side table, bringing out a copy of the *Arizona Daily Star* from last month.

"Yes, sir. As a matter of fact," Fallon said, deliberately not looking at Nora, "I've subscribed to that paper for several years now."

"You have?" Nora spoke for the first time since they'd come into the den.

Having given away more than she'd intended, Fallon worked to tamp down the blush threatening her cheeks. She started to shrug before a sharp bite of pain stopped her. "Yeah, well, it's nice to know what's happening in other parts of the country."

"Uh-huh." Nora was smiling as she took Fallon's good hand. "Come into the kitchen and meet my cousin."

After they'd chatted with Anita for a few minutes, Nora's mother came in with some folded dish towels.

"Mom, you remember Fallon, my friend from Firecamp, don't you?"

Mrs. Palmer turned with a smile that looked remarkably like Nora's. "Of course. It's nice to see you again." She extended her hand. Her grip was delicate in Fallon's grasp. Her posture was slightly hunched but her movements had purpose.

"It's nice to be here again, Mrs. Palmer."

"Didn't I tell you to call me Patricia when you were here before?" she asked with a playful lilt. It sounded so much like Nora's teasing that it made Fallon laugh.

"Yes, you did. Thank you, Patricia." Fallon glanced between them. "If you all don't mind me asking, did Mr. Palmer have a stroke?"

Nora shook her head. "They said not, but we're still waiting on a diagnosis."

"Did they say what else it might be?"

"It could be anything from epilepsy to some kind of infection. Maybe we'll know more after the latest test results."

They sat quietly for a moment. Then Patricia offered them lemonade, but Fallon declined. "I'm sure it's delicious, but I think I'd like to go lie down for a few minutes. That drive kinda wore me out."

Nora stood quickly. "Of course. Let me help you."

"I'm fine," Fallon said, but Nora was already taking her arm.

They walked through the den where Mr. Palmer was snoring. Nora glanced at her watch. "I need to give Dad his pills. Go on, and I'll be right up."

The bed was much more comfortable than the one in the hospital, and the next thing Fallon knew, Nora was kissing her cheek. "Dinner's ready, if you feel like eating."

"Oh wow. I'm sorry. I didn't expect to—"

"Stop," Nora said. "You don't need to apologize. You're recovering from a traumatic injury. You're allowed to rest." She indicated the door next to the dresser. "The bathroom is through there if you need to freshen up."

"Yes, thank you." Fallon eased herself out of the bed and moved toward the bathroom before she remembered the fuss in the restaurant. "Uh, there is one thing. If you expect me before dinner gets cold, you might need to help me with these jeans. Tomorrow, I'll wear sweats that should be easier to handle."

Nora regarded her for so long, Fallon didn't know if she needed to explain more clearly or tell her never mind. "Did you honestly think I'd object to taking your pants off?" Nora said finally.

Fallon stifled a laugh. "Well, you'll have to put them on again before we can go to dinner."

Sighing, Nora said, "The things I sacrifice for this family."

Fallon grinned and shook her head. She felt better already.

CHAPTER EIGHTEEN

Nora wasn't sure what woke her until it happened again. Fallon was moaning, and it wasn't a sound of pleasure.

Nora rose quietly and went to her bedside. The moon was down and it was very dark. "Fallon? Are you hurting?"

"Ugh, I think I accidentally rolled over too far onto this shoulder." Fallon sniffed, her voice hoarse. Was she crying?

"Oh shit. Let me get you some ice," Nora said, reaching for her robe.

"No. I mean, I'm sorry I woke you." Nora heard her shift in the bed. "I can get—"

"You will not get anything except the Advil in the bathroom if you need to go in there anyway. Otherwise, I'll be right back." Nora hurried downstairs, returning with a package of frozen peas, knowing they would best conform to the shape of Fallon's shoulder. Fallon cursed in the bathroom. "Is everything okay?"

"I can't get this damn childproof cap open with one hand."

Nora smiled. "I can barely get them open with two hands. May I help?"

Fallon sighed. "Thanks." Nora eased into the small space, being careful not to bump into her. Their hands brushed as Fallon passed her the bottle. "Listen, I didn't come here so you could be my nurse. You have enough going on with your father."

"It helps both me and my father to have you here." Nora took a breath. "Besides, it's my fault you're hurt. I'm just grateful it wasn't any worse." She hadn't expected to have this conversation standing in a bathroom in the middle of the night, but the moment had presented itself, so...

She opened the bottle and found Fallon's uninjured arm, dropping the pills in her hand, trying to calm her racing heart. This wasn't going to be an easy conversation, but it needed to happen. The breach between them wouldn't be mended with one confession, but she'd been weighted down with this guilt since the moment the tree trunk had begun to crack.

"Nora, if a tree falls during a serious windstorm, it's no one's fault. Besides, you're the one who got me out, so I owe you—"

"No, I'm the one who got you in." The words rushed out of her as fast as her mind could form them. "I was cutting on that tree when the triangle sounded. We formed up, and then Art came, and after he left, I was distracted looking at the photos Tyler had taken. I didn't realize you and Maris had gone over to the other side of the break, but I should have already told you, warned you that tree was unstable." She was almost glad she couldn't read Fallon's expression. "That wind...I've never felt it like that, but that's no excuse for my negligence." Reliving that moment made her throat close, and her voice flagged. "My God, Fallon. If you'd been seriously injured, if you'd been..." Swallowing, she forced herself to say it. "If you'd been killed, I couldn't have ever forgiven myself. I wouldn't even want to li—"

She wasn't sure if Fallon's night vision was better than hers or if it was luck when Fallon touched her cheek. "Nora," she interrupted. "What we do is dangerous. Not as much as firefighting, but it can still be hazardous. Having you working with us on that break made a huge difference. That kind of wind might have knocked down any number of weakened trees." When Nora started to protest, Fallon added, "Can you say with absolute certainty that exact tree was the one that fell?"

Nora had been as positive as she could be, and yet, she hadn't actually looked at that area of the break once Fallon had gone down. "It...I think—"

"But you don't really know, do you?" The simple touch turned into a caress. "Please stop beating yourself up about this. Even if it was the same tree, you got me out of there, so we're even, okay?" Fallon leaned in close to her ear. "I know you care about things being equal, but I've been thinking that maybe forgiveness is what we most need to work on."

Nora reached for her, her fingers brushing the sling on Fallon's injured shoulder. She felt her flinch. "Oh damn. I'm sorry."

"If you brought ice, I'll forgive you."

Nora laughed in spite of herself as she transferred the frozen vegetables from hand to hand, making sure Fallon could hear them rattle in the darkness. "Lucky me."

The peas did the trick and Fallon settled into bed while Nora took the thawed bag back to the kitchen to dispose of it. When she returned, Fallon's breathing had grown steady, but Nora couldn't seem to shut off her mind. That comment about forgiveness reverberated in her thoughts, bouncing from her father to Fallon to herself. She knew she would sleep if she could crawl into bed with Fallon the way she'd done not long after they'd met, but maybe it was best that she couldn't. Distance would force her to connect in another, less physical way.

Physical had never been their problem. In a flash of what was probably obvious insight, Nora realized that if they were going to have a chance at something beyond this time together, they needed to date. Or something like it. Getting to know each other better, learning who they were now and how they'd gotten there would be a start. She began assembling a mental catalogue of things they could do given Fallon's temporary limitations. Making the list somehow had the effect of counting sheep, and she was asleep before she got to number six.

Tyler left the next morning following what felt like two hours of good-byes. Not long after he pulled away in Nora's car, the hospital called with her father's test results. Her mother answered, but after a few moments, she handed the phone to Nora. "You talk to them. I don't understand all this medical jargon."

Fallon rose, indicating she'd give her privacy, but Nora motioned her back down. She listened to the description of her father's neurological disorder. The symptoms they described seemed to fit his sudden slurred speech and unexplained tremors in his hands and legs. The doctor assured her there was nothing wrong with his brain. "It's not a hardware problem, it's a software issue. It's like his brain has lost the pathways to communicate with certain parts of his body."

"And the prognosis?"

"With treatment, most patients show at least some improvement."

"And what are the treatment options?"

"We recommend specialized physical therapy, along with psychotherapy."

She scoffed. "It will be a small miracle if I can get him to physical therapy. I think the psychotherapy is out of the question."

"I understand." The doctor sounded sympathetic. "Bring him in tomorrow, and let's see how it goes."

Nora hung up and turned to her mother. "Ask Anita to come in, please. We need to talk."

She relayed what the doctor had told her, leaving her mother and Anita to process it while she and Fallon went to get her father.

Nora helped him into his chair while Fallon stood by, holding the travel mug of coffee. At least there was hope that he wouldn't always need a lid to keep from spilling the hot liquid everywhere. As soon as he was settled, she steeled herself for what was to come. "I have good news and bad news."

Her father looked up. "Huh?"

"The good news is, you haven't had a stroke." He grunted. "The bad news is, you have functional neurological disorder, FND. Nothing is wrong with your brain, but the connection with some parts of your body is malfunctioning."

"Why?"

"They don't know for sure, but the doctor said it could be caused by repressed trauma held in the body."

He muttered something about "Psycho mumbo jumbo," his hand trembling as he sipped his coffee.

"Do you want to get better?" she demanded. He looked at her skeptically but finally nodded. "You have an appointment with the physical therapist tomorrow morning. If you don't go, there won't be another chance. Do you understand?"

"You going?" he asked.

"No. Mother and Anita will take you."

He grunted and closed his eyes.

Nora sighed, her fists clenched. "If you want to talk about this later, we can."

There was no reply, and after a moment, Nora stood and went up the stairs. Fallon followed. Pushing into their room, Nora threw herself face down on the bed. Grabbing a pillow, she screamed into it, "Goddamn it." When she looked over at Fallon, she said, "You see how he is?"

"I think he's scared," Fallon said.

"Scared? Stubborn is more like it. If he doesn't make the appointment tomorrow, I'm done trying to help him."

"Why can't you take him? You understand what's going on better than your mom or Anita. If you go with them this first time, at least they'll know what to expect for future appointments." Nora put her face back in the pillow. "I'll go too, if you want, though I'm no help at all."

Nora felt the first hint of tears, and it made her even angrier. She looked up. "He's probably faking this whole thing just to get attention."

Fallon moved over to her bed and sat close, putting her hand on Nora's back. "You know that's not true. Why don't you tell me what you're really upset about?"

Shit. If Fallon was going to be sweet to her like that, she was certainly going to cry. But over the last few years, she'd been working on keeping her temper in check, admitting her feelings, and being honest about what she wanted. "I hate seeing him like this. He's always been strong, and he's never sick." The first tear fell. "We haven't been close since I was young, and I know I'm nothing but a big disappointment to him. But after Firecamp, he kept his word and funded my last two years of college. I got my job and I never looked back. It's just that...I've been angry at him for years and now..." She tried to hold back the thought, but it escaped on a sob. "What if he dies, and we never resolve this distance between us?"

Fallon carefully arranged herself on the small bed next to Nora, lying on her good side. Nora knew she couldn't reach for her, so she pressed her head into Fallon's chest. "Two things," Fallon said. "First, I don't think the doctor said anything about him dying. At least not anytime soon, is that right?" Nora nodded. "Meaning maybe you need to look at this as your chance to work through some things with him. Kinda like if a tree fell on him or something."

She snorted and felt Fallon chuckle in response before she went on. "And second, if you were nothing but a big disappointment, he wouldn't have asked you to take him to PT. I'll bet he's every bit as interested in closing that gap as you are. It'll take baby steps, but I think you can both get there if you want it bad enough."

Nora was quiet for a few minutes, trying to be casual about wiping her eyes and getting control. She knew better than to be surprised that Fallon would see through her attitude or that she would offer such reasonable advice. "So you did get that job in the fortune cookie factory after all," she teased, shifting to look at her.

"Ouch," Fallon said, and Nora sat up quickly.

"I'm sorry. Did I hurt you?"

"Only my feelings."

"No fair. I can't tickle or pinch you."

"Small mercies."

❖

The session went better than Nora could have hoped. Besides working on her father's physical condition, the physiotherapist—who thankfully was an older man named Ryan—got him to talk about his firefighting career under the guise of "getting to know you."

Nora learned things she'd never known. Not the heroic "I do all right" swagger stories, but the frightening, near-death experiences he'd undergone and then glossed over like they were nothing. At one point, seeing him wiping his forehead with the handkerchief he always carried, she sensed his pain was not solely physical. He'd been talking about Mikey, a rookie who had died in the last fire of the season when they'd been overrun by flames and his shelter had failed. "He was younger than my boys are now," her dad recalled, and the anguish in his voice was something she'd never heard before.

"And you were there too, caught by the same fire?" Ryan asked.

Her father squinted as if seeing the stuff of nightmares. "Yeah," was all he said.

While Anita and her mother watched, Nora pointed out the way the therapist had her father doing multiple tasks at once: carrying a glass of water while walking backward or balancing an egg in each hand and walking over a small bridge made of stairs. After almost two hours, they were given a page of exercises and instructions on how to do them at home. When her father agreed to go for therapy again later in the week, Nora felt like she'd won a Pulitzer Prize.

"I need to help Fallon," Nora told her mother as they walked back to the car. "You and Anita can handle this for Dad, right?"

Taking the paperwork, her mother examined it carefully. Then she nodded.

Nora had declined Fallon's offer to accompany them, suspecting she'd be frustrated about not yet being able to do her own physical therapy. Nora had encouraged her to relax, saying she had a surprise in mind for them later. As she and Anita helped her father into the house and her mother announced they were all going to rest for a while, Nora heard Fallon's voice coming from their room. It seemed unlikely she would have company, but Nora made her way quietly upstairs.

"Yeah, I'm sure, but thanks for the offer," Fallon was saying. Nora paused outside their door, knowing this conversation was none of her business but unable to keep from listening. "You too, and I do appreciate the call." After another pause, she heard a smile in Fallon's tone. "No, really, Maris, and keep me posted, okay…I will…Right."

Maris, Fallon's second on that last crew. The girl who'd had hero worship in her eyes, even before Fallon had saved her life. Nora's throat went dry recalling her unreasonable jealousy during that first Firecamp, how her hostility had ignited whenever Fallon had gotten attention from anyone else. Among her many reflections, after things had fallen apart, was identifying Addison, who had been a terrible flirt, as the source of those overwrought emotions. But Nora hadn't been interested in commitment then.

Did she want to ask for it now?

She took a moment to steady herself. Fallon had only ever flirted with her during their Firecamp, and she was certain Maris was no competition now. Laughing, Fallon was saying, "Yes, anytime. But be aware that I might not always answer...Okay, okay...I'm hanging up now. Bye."

When Fallon hissed, as if standing was still painful, Nora realized she was stuck. Going back downstairs would make too much noise, and if she walked in now, it would be obvious she'd been listening at the door. Luckily, she heard Fallon move into the bathroom, so she waited a few seconds before making some noise in the hallway and calling to her.

"How was your father's appointment?" Fallon asked, struggling with her sweatpants.

Nora went to help her. "It went really, really well." As she finished tying the string, she kissed Fallon's cheek. "And thank you for urging me to go."

Fallon grinned. "Anytime if that's my reward."

"Actually, how'd you like to go to a movie as a reward?"

"A movie?" Fallon answered as if she weren't sure what that was.

"Yeah. Our theater has two screens, and on one, they run Oscar winners from previous years. We might find something you haven't seen."

"That won't be hard," Fallon said quietly, gritting her teeth as she adjusted the sling.

When she didn't expound, Nora pressed on. "This week they're showing *A Beautiful Mind*. It's an older movie, but I think it's probably held up pretty well."

"You've seen it?"

"On TV once. But all the commercials detracted from the drama. I'd like to see it again if you would."

Fallon touched one of the scratches on her face. "I may not be suitable for a public appearance."

"You look fine. And besides, it's dark in the theater."

After a long moment, Fallon asked, "Is it sad? I don't like sad stories. Or scary ones."

Nora cocked her head, thinking. "As far as I recall, there are a few sad parts and a few moments of suspense, but it has a good ending."

"Okay." Fallon headed down the stairs. "Maybe Friday. But for now, let's go outside. Anita was talking about a fall garden, but maybe we should work on the flower bed first."

"What do you mean, 'we'?" Nora hurried to catch her at the front door.

"I can pull weeds with my right hand," Fallon suggested.

Nora shook her head. "I don't think so. I think your job is to keep me company." She knew Fallon wouldn't want to admit she was right, so she added, "Once you start PT, you can ask about doing yard work."

By the end of the day, the front bed was in great shape, and the grass was cut. After keeping Nora entertained with stories about recent Firecamp attendees, Fallon got very quiet when they went back inside to clean up before dinner.

"Did you hurt yourself?" Nora asked. Fallon shook her head, chewing at her lip nervously. "Then what is it?"

Fallon swallowed. "I need to take a shower."

"Me too," Nora said. "Do you want to go first?"

Gesturing irritably at the sling on her shoulder while her cheeks colored, Fallon said, "I can't...um...by myself."

"Oh." The light went on for Nora, along with a flash of heat. Fallon would need help, which meant they would both be naked. And wet. "Right." She tried for a casual tone. "I'll help you."

"Thanks." Fallon's voice was tight, and Nora wondered if she felt embarrassed or nervous.

"I guess a nurse did this for you in the hospital?" The question was inane, Nora knew, but she'd caught a whiff of Fallon's scent while sliding off her sweats and underwear, and she needed to say something to cover her own body's response. Fallon grunted a yes while Nora eased off her shirt, carefully avoiding looking in her eyes, knowing her desire would show. "Let me get the water going," she said, moving into the small bathroom. Once the temperature seemed comfortable, she said, "Go ahead and get in," turning aside to give Fallon privacy for the moment. As she stripped, Fallon's moan of euphoria made her tremble with anticipation.

Fallon cleared her throat. "Sorry. This just feels really good. Hot water on demand is one of civilization's greatest accomplishments, don't you think?"

Nora had to laugh. "Absolutely." She waited a beat. "Ready for me?"

"Yeah." Nora grabbed a washrag and stepped past the shower curtain. Fallon moved to the far wall, keeping her eyes on the showerhead. "You should rinse off too," she said. "Or else you'll get chilled."

Nora let the water run over her chest before turning to douse her back. As she did, she saw Fallon's gaze fall to her breasts before she turned away. "I'll start with this side," Nora announced, wondering if Fallon would hear the smile in her voice. She liked knowing she wasn't the only one affected by their nearness. Running the soapy cloth over Fallon's back, and her uninjured shoulder and arm, she could feel Fallon relaxing slightly. "I'll get your legs from here too."

"You shouldn't have to do this too many more times," Fallon said.

"Well, it is a hardship, but I'll manage." When Fallon scoffed, Nora ran the washcloth up between her thighs and over her buttocks. For a few seconds, the only sound was Fallon's rough breathing. "I'll turn around so you can rinse. Then we'll do your front."

After a few seconds in the spray, Fallon slipped past her and out through the shower curtain. "I think I'm good. We'll get the other parts next time."

"You sure?" Nora grinned, sticking her head out. Fallon's face was flushed, and she suspected it wasn't the heat of the water. "Don't you want to wash my back?"

Fallon groaned. "Nora, you can't tease me like this."

"Why not? We've been naked together before, you know."

Grabbing a towel, Fallon wiped her face before holding it ineffectively over her body. "Yeah, but I can't do anything about it right now, and that's just not fair."

"But you would?" Nora cringed at the hopeful note in her own voice.

"Nora," Fallon pleaded. "Let's talk about that when the time comes."

"I'll remind you once that sling comes off." She finished bathing and stepped out of the shower, only to find Fallon holding her towel. "Thanks," Nora said, reaching for it.

Fallon dangled it just out of her grasp, her eyes moving slowly up and down Nora's body. "You won't have to remind me."

Nora gave her a sexy smile. She could hardly wait.

❖

After her father's second appointment, her mother admitted that she and Anita hadn't been able to get him to do the exercises at home. Fallon volunteered to take on the task of getting him up and moving on days he didn't have therapy. "It'll be good for me too," she said, moving restlessly. "I'm getting stiff on these injured joints."

They gave him a day to recuperate, then Fallon let him digest his breakfast before she sat across from him. "How are you feeling this morning, Mr. Palmer?"

"Same. You?"

Nora had thought his recent tendency to give the briefest possible answer was just his increasingly cranky personality, but now she wondered if it had been a precursor to his disorder. His slur was less obvious with fewer words.

"I think I might be feeling a little better," Fallon said. "Maybe a walk would do me good. Nora tells me you have one of those 36-inch Husqvarna 592XP chainsaws. I was wondering if you might show it to me."

He gestured toward her shoulder, his hand still trembling. "You couldn't even lift it."

She smiled. "You're probably right. And I guess you shouldn't, either."

"I goddamn well can." He began floundering in his chair. "Nora, help me up."

Nora trailed them from a few feet away, ready to catch either of them should they fall. The pace was exceedingly slow, and once they'd arrived, Fallon had to remind him why they were there. But after that, he walked right to the chainsaw in question. Nora grabbed it before he could try, showing the large bar to Fallon while her father stood by proudly.

"My daughter could handle that monster every bit as well as her brothers."

What? Did I hear that right?

"I don't doubt it," Fallon said, smiling at Nora. "She was undeniably the best sawyer at camp. You taught her well."

"She loved it, I could tell. Gave those boys a run for their money. But then, you know, she got her monthly visitor, and that was that."

Nora couldn't hide her shock. Gaping at her father, she said, "Is that why you wouldn't let me work out here with you and the boys anymore? Because I got my period?"

He colored slightly. "That was your mother's doing. She said it wasn't proper, given your delicate condition. I went along. What did I know about it?" She stared at him, speechless, remembering how that abrupt displacement had felt like a rebuff. It'd made her vulnerable to her mother's single-minded efforts to replace her "tomboy ways" with the looks and behavior she considered essential for a young woman. Nora had never considered how her eventual rejection of her mother's directives must have felt just as personal. The rift between them had become more impassible every year, until there simply was no connection. Did that mean there never would be?

"Oh hey," Fallon said, clearly trying to interrupt the moment. "Did I tell you Maris called?"

"Who's Maris?" Nora's dad asked.

"Someone Nora met when we were doing mitigation for the Kamberto fire. I don't think you know her." Throwing Nora a look, she added, "Thanks for showing me that great saw. I guess we should get back to the house."

Absently, Nora put the Husqvarna in its place. She trailed the two of them again, shaking her head at the odd piece that had fallen into place in the puzzle of her childhood. All this time, she'd blamed her father for inexplicitly spurning her, but it was her mother who had changed her life. After pulling Nora away from what she'd learned to love, based on outdated notions about what a young woman should spend her time doing, her mother had given her nothing but platitudes about fashion and societal expectations to mend her bruised heart. Nora's world was never the same, and neither was her relationship with either parent. It might take some time for her to adjust, but maybe there was a chance for healing for all of them?

While her mother and Anita drove her father to a doctor's appointment the next day, Nora and Fallon ran errands, visiting the hardware and grocery stores. Before heading home, Nora stopped by the local pot shop. At Fallon's questioning glance, Nora said, "I looked into it last night. CBD oil helps with inflammation and pain. You're not in Firecamp at the moment, and I think you should try it."

"It won't make me high, will it?" Fallon asked. "I need all the self-control I can get."

Nora liked what that suggested, but she only shrugged. "It won't, or that's what I've heard. I guess you'll have to let me know."

She'd made sure Fallon took ibuprofen after dinner, thinking it should work well in conjunction with the CBD. But as Nora opened the jar of salve that night after Fallon had gotten into bed, she could see the tension on her face and practically feel anxiety radiating off her body. "What's the matter?"

Fallon didn't meet her eyes. "I…I bet you must be ready for me to get better so I can go back to work, and you can too."

Nora stopped her preparation. "Is that what you think?"

"Well, I just showed up here, and I've been taking advantage of your hospitality, plus you've had to do a lot of things to help me, so… yeah."

Sitting in her chair, Nora looked out the window. Ten years ago, her impulse would have been to sharply question how Fallon had arrived at such a ridiculous supposition. But from photography assignments with unwilling or uncomfortable subjects, she'd learned that offering a redirect, jumping to a different topic, usually got better results. "What's your middle name?" she asked.

"My…my middle name?"

"Yes."

"Uh, it's Quinn. My mom told me it was my father's mother's maiden name."

"That's nice. Did you ever meet her?"

"Oh no. She died before I was born."

"I see. Mine's Kaye. Like the letter but spelled out."

"I know. I looked at your records once when I was working in Reva's office."

Nora laughed. "You did?" Fallon nodded. "When was this?"

Fallon fidgeted, her obvious uneasiness returning. "About a year after you were gone." She swallowed. "Where does Kaye come from?"

"They asked for my name at the hospital, and my mom said she was trying to tell them 'Nora Jane,' but she'd been drugged, and they misunderstood. She could have fixed it later but decided she liked Kaye better."

They were quiet for a moment. Nora held up the jar. "Let's take your shirt off."

Fallon offered a slight smile. "Well, since you asked so nicely…"

The shoulder injury made it impossible for Fallon to wear a bra, something Nora had been aware of since the first moment she'd arrived. Leaning into Fallon's chest that first afternoon, she'd enjoyed the incredible softness of her unconstrained breasts. Last night, Fallon had slept in the same oxford shirt with the left sleeve cut to allow her to get it on or off without raising her arm, but for tonight, she'd laid out a tank top.

As Nora worked the buttons open, she felt Fallon tremble. "I'm going to try very hard not to make things worse."

Fallon inclined her head, her voice steady. "That's the best I can ask for."

Nora suspected they both knew how loaded those words were. After the shirt was off, Nora reluctantly covered Fallon's chest with it as she lay on her uninjured side. Gently working the fragrant salve into Fallon's skin, Nora started at her neck and smoothed it over her collarbone before moving slowly toward the shoulder. Fallon tensed, and Nora switched to her bicep, approaching the injury from another angle. Using the tips of her fingers with barely any pressure, she massaged the point of Fallon's shoulder. "Okay?"

Fallon's eyes were closed. "You always did have a sweet touch."

"Fallon Quinn Monroe," Nora said softly. "Tell me one thing I've said or done that makes you think I want you to go." When Fallon didn't answer, Nora sighed. "Pull your sweats down, and I'll put some of this on your hip."

She complied, and Nora lightly spread the CBD on the bruise covering the ball and socket area. Fallon made a sad-sounding hum. "I don't know if I can stand this for six weeks."

Nora pushed. "Stand being hurt or being taken care of?" Fallon nodded. "What else?"

After another pause, Fallon answered, "I'm afraid," her voice so low, Nora leaned forward to hear her.

"Of what?"

"Of you. Of us. Of getting close again only to find that even though it's ten years later, we're going to end up exactly where we were then."

Nora took a breath. She'd asked, and Fallon had answered with the straightforward, almost raw honesty she'd always had. "I'm not the same person I was then. Are you?"

"Yes and no."

"Nora?" Her mother's voice drifted from downstairs. "Where are your father's pills?"

Rolling her eyes, Nora grunted. "I practically put them in her hand an hour ago." She stood, closing the jar. "I heard what you said, and I understand very well what you're feeling. But I want to try, Fallon. I want us to be brave and figure it out together this time."

Nora hadn't really expected an answer. With a few words, she'd said a lot, and she was willing to give Fallon whatever time she needed to reflect on her reply. Her mother called again, and she adjusted the sheet, leaving Fallon lying on her right side. When she returned from getting her father into bed, Fallon's breathing was deep and even. But there was a small scrap of paper on Nora's pillow. *Okay*, it said.

❖

Two days later, at the theater, Nora made sure to sit on Fallon's good side so they could hold hands. She was prepared to switch sides if someone tried to take the seat next to Fallon's injury, but not many people were at the showing, so she stayed where she was. Nora was glad she'd already seen the movie because she could barely concentrate as Fallon's hand tightened, caressed, or simply held hers at various times throughout the show. During the Nobel Prize speech, she handed Fallon a Kleenex and used one herself.

Afterward, they went for ice cream that melted quickly as they enthusiastically discussed the various aspects of the plot. What was genius? What was insanity? They even treaded carefully on the topic of what a person should do for someone they loved. It was the best date Nora had been on in years, maybe ever.

But on the way home, Fallon was quiet. "What are you thinking?" Nora asked.

"I was considering something I left out in our discussion about what you should do for someone you love."

Nora's chest tightened. "What was that?"

"Forgive them. Like she did for him. No one's perfect, though he was less so than most at times."

"And he had to forgive her for letting them take him for treatment."

"True," Fallon agreed. They were almost home when she added, "And maybe the hardest thing is forgiving yourself. It seems like they both did that."

After reaching the house, they sat for a moment, not looking at each other. Nora wanted to continue the conversation, to ask Fallon what she most wanted to know: *Have you forgiven me?*

But she waited too long, and Fallon sighed and climbed out of the car. Nora hurried to the front door, turning to face her before opening it. "Thank you for going tonight."

Fallon smiled faintly. "Thank you for asking me. That's maybe the fourth time I've been in a movie theater."

Recalling Fallon's stories of her itinerate childhood, Nora wasn't surprised. "Did you go with a Firecamp crew?"

"Yes. Once." Fallon was doing that thing she did with her mouth when she didn't want to talk about something.

Nora stepped closer. "And the other times?"

"Dates," Fallon mumbled, not looking at her.

She'd suspected as much. She took Fallon's hand. "Like this one?"

Fallon lifted her head so they were eye to eye and smiled, something much closer to the look Nora wanted to see. "This was much better."

Nora leaned in to kiss her cheek, careful not to push against her, even though she very much wanted to. "Just for that, I'll put more CBD on you later."

"Can we borrow those frozen peas again first?"

Nora delighted at the ease between them. Could this become the second chance with Fallon she'd always hoped for?

CHAPTER NINETEEN

Fallon had never planned an outing with the assistance of her date's family, but it turned out better than she expected as they offered suggestions for possible excursions and advice regarding Nora's local interests. After making sure the calendar was clear, Fallon gave Nora twenty-four hours' notice, only telling her they were going somewhere that would take the better part of the day. If Nora noticed that everyone else in the house, even her father, seemed to be smiling as if they had some kind of secret, she didn't comment.

After directing her north, Fallon refused to answer any questions about where they were going or why. Instead, they talked about everything from whether either wanted children—no—to irrational fears they'd had in their youth. For Nora, that snakes would come out of the bathtub faucet; for Fallon, that she'd accidentally walk into the men's bathroom. When they arrived at Coaldale, the sign that greeted them claimed the distinction of being the highest incorporated town in America.

"Turn here." Fallon indicated a side street where there was a sign for a scenic train ahead.

"Are we going for a ride?"

"Yes," Fallon conceded. "And this one includes lunch." The whistle was blowing as they parked. Checking the clock in the truck, Fallon assured her they had fifteen minutes before departure.

Nora cocked her head as she turned. "Is this a date?"

Fallon's face warmed. "Do you want it to be?"

Reaching out, Nora touched her hand. "Very much."

The day was perfect, moderate weather with enough breeze to keep them comfortable, and the barbecue lunch was delicious. Although the train basically followed the highway's path, its elevation was several hundred feet higher, allowing for a view of the riverbed on one side and the forested hillside on the other. When the train blew its whistle upon reaching the end of the line, a small herd of pronghorn antelope raised their heads.

Once they were seated back in Fallon's truck, Nora chewed at her lip. "Today was wonderful. In Tucson, I've been taken to expensive restaurants and popular concerts, but none of that compared to BBQ and a train ride. Not because of the outing itself, but for the company. It's so easy to be myself when we're together. Or maybe it's that I'm more the person I've always wanted to be when I'm with you. You have a way of making everything...right. Thank you. And I'm really glad you're starting PT next week because I need to hold you soon."

Fallon was almost speechless. She hated that her injury meant they couldn't hold hands while she was on the passenger's side, but she twisted in the seat. "I can't tell you how many times I've imagined us being together like this." Smiling faintly, she indicated her shoulder. "Well, maybe not exactly like this, but like all those dreams I used to have about you at Firecamp, the reality is so much better."

Nora leaned in carefully, and they kissed. It was gentle and much quicker than Fallon would have liked, but a horn honked behind them, and Nora waved. Putting the truck in reverse, she pulled out of the space. Fallon eased back, sighing with a mixture of frustration and anticipation. She didn't realize she'd fallen asleep until the truck stopped at the Palmer house. As they climbed the stairs to their room, Fallon whispered, "And I'm glad I'm starting physical therapy because I can't stop thinking about being in bed with you."

Nora's smile was absolutely the most beautiful thing she'd seen all day.

❖

Fallon tore a piece of tape from the roll with her good hand. After almost a month of PT, she could shower on her own, and she wore the sling only when she'd overdone it. She could also put the CBD oil on by herself and get in and out of her clothes without much of a struggle. Nora had protested that she was happy to help, usually with a twinkle in her eye, but Fallon needed to prove to herself that she was recovering. This independence was both a step back from Nora as a caregiver and a step toward something more, and Fallon sensed that Nora was being as careful about their direction as she was.

"My physical therapist said I could do light lifting now," Fallon told Nora. "I'll be done with therapy by the end of this week, but she'll give me some exercises to do on my own."

Nora placed the cardboard over a window, taking the tape from Fallon and gesturing for her to step away. "I'm glad, but that's no reason to push too hard. You don't want any setbacks in your recovery."

Most days, they followed a routine where Fallon took Mr. Palmer for a walk in the morning while Nora checked her email. Fallon often returned with amusing stories Nora's dad had told, especially about his children's antics, prompting Nora to accompany them whenever she could. It seemed that Nora was getting to know her father differently, as a man who loved his family, even though he'd always had trouble showing it. His tone became tender or perhaps even wistful, especially recalling moments from her childhood: Nora's first steps, that her first word was "Dada," and when six-year-old Nora already packed such a punch that she gave Art a bloody nose after he'd teased her once too often.

Mr. Palmer napped afterward, and when Fallon went back upstairs to ice her hip, she'd ask Nora for water or give her some other reason to return to the kitchen. She was pleased when Nora's visits there got longer.

"So your mom and Anita seem to have gotten really close," Fallon said, approaching the subject carefully.

"Hmm. I guess Anita is like the daughter my mom wanted me to be," Nora told her. "Or maybe more like the sister she never had. Either way, it's great that she finally has some help after all those years of working her ass off for all the males in this household—and me, by extension. I think she's learning how enjoyable female company can be."

"And that's a good thing, right?" Fallon asked.

"It is. And Anita seems genuinely interested in me and my work. It's like she's teaching Mom how to interact with me."

And teaching you how to interact with your mom, Fallon thought, knowing better than to say it out loud. Not yet, anyway.

The vegetable garden was in and doing well. On one of their visits to the shed, Fallon had discovered a paint sprayer. With Mr. Palmer's reluctant permission, they'd practiced using it on the shutters, both managing to get almost as much paint on themselves as they had on the wood. They'd laughed and joked about the differences between painting and sawing. Today, they'd do the first-floor exterior of the house.

"Aren't you bored by all this domesticity?" Nora asked.

"How can I be bored by something I've never done before?" Fallon countered. "Besides, I really like being able to see results right away. Mow the grass, and it looks mowed. Paint the shutters, and they immediately look better. Fire mitigation isn't like that, as you know. And we rarely get to see how people put the skills they learn at Firecamp to use."

They'd stepped into the yard to admire their work. The shutters did look good, and with the windows prepped, painting the first floor shouldn't take long. A scattering of leaves blew from the nearby aspen grove. Fallon looked off into the trees, surprised when Nora asked, "Do you miss it?"

"You know, I honestly don't. Not yet, anyway. I think I needed a break. The season will be over this week, and I know Maris did a great job of handling the team. For the first time in a long time, a lot feels like it's up in the air for me." She flexed her injured shoulder carefully in what she intended as a shrug.

They mixed the paint and poured it into the sprayer, making quick work of renewing the white color. They'd construct a kind of scaffold to do the top floor tomorrow. As they cleaned their equipment, she asked, "Have you ever been to the Grand Canyon?"

"No," Nora admitted. "Which is outrageous because it's only five hours or so from Tucson."

"Is that right?" Fallon looked at the trees again. "It occurs to me that Firecamp is the place I've been taking care of, which has been good for me. I believe it will always be my first real home, but I think I'm ready to see a different part of the country." She hesitated. "Maybe you could show me Tucson afterward?"

Nora brightened. "That would be fantastic. I'll look online tonight and see when we could get reservations to stay at the Canyon for a few days. After you finish your therapy, that is."

Fallon turned to look at her. "Aren't you missing your work?"

"I have a lot of comp days accumulated. And my boss is probably glad to have me out of his hair for a while."

"That wasn't what I asked."

Nora paused, eying their work. "I know. But I'm not really sure how to answer you."

Fallon held out her hand, and Nora took it without hesitation. They walked onto the porch together, and Fallon gestured to the rocking chairs that sat side by side. "Now this truly is domestic," she said, and Nora laughed. After a minute, Fallon said, "You can answer me with your head or with your heart. It's okay if they're different, but if the two are the same, that's even better. Just be honest."

"I miss getting to tell peoples' stories. I miss that moment when I know I've got an image that will convey emotion or action or…life. Do I miss sitting around the office trying to make small talk with people I don't really know or going down rabbit holes on the internet while I wait for an assignment? No."

"So you still love photography. But you're ambivalent about the work part of your job. Is that right?" Nora nodded. "I guess I feel the same. I still feel like my work is meaningful, but the minutia sometimes gets to me."

"And having Ranger Dick for a boss?"

"And that." Fallon agreed. They were quiet for a minute. "For a while, I was angry with you, and then it would turn into hurt, and after that, back to anger at myself. But mainly, I wouldn't let myself think about how much I wanted to see you again. I'm glad I don't have to miss you anymore."

Nora looked down as if afraid of what her expression might give away. "Same," she said.

❖

"I can't thank you enough for your hospitality," Fallon said, standing before Nora's parents and Anita.

Patricia Palmer smiled. "Thank you for everything you've done for us here. The house looks wonderful, and we'll be enjoying those fall vegetables you planted in our garden. I hope your arm continues to heal successfully. Please come see us again anytime."

"I will."

Mr. Palmer's color was better, and therapy, combined with their morning walk, had greatly improved his balance. As they'd talked, Fallon had come to realize that what often came out sounding like aggravation or annoyance with his family was actually just worry. She'd tried to make him understand that derogatory comments to Nora or Tyler or any of his children only created distance between them.

"I know some kids gripe about their parents, and some parents complain about their kids," she'd told him. "But since I don't have either, I really don't like to hear it." He'd studied her for a moment before nodding.

Now he reached out a much steadier hand, and she shook with him. "Nora needs to find a man as good as you."

"If she's so good, why don't I just take her?" Nora asked from behind her as she came down the stairs. She dropped her bag and took Fallon's hand.

"Nora," her father began, but Nora cut him off.

"I'm serious. I hope this time we've spent together has shown you who I am, and this is who I want to be with." She looked at Fallon. "I mean, we're still working things out, but—"

Mr. Palmer looked to Fallon. "And you? Is this what you want?"

Fallon cleared her throat. Whatever doubts or worries she had about their future, she couldn't leave Nora hanging in front of her family. "Well, sir, like your daughter said, we're still working on things, but, yes, she is the person I want." She squeezed Nora's hand.

No one spoke for several seconds. "Then we'll expect to see both of you back here when you can," Patricia said, turning to her husband. "Won't we, Jeffrey?"

"Suppose so, if that's how it is," he said, sounding no gruffer than usual.

Nora went and hugged him, murmuring something in his ear. He laughed and patted her arm.

"All right," he said. "All right." He appeared to be nearly blushing but kept a hand on her back until she stepped away to kiss her mother and hug Anita.

"You two behave yourselves," Nora told them. "Or if you can't be good, be careful." Their smiles held genuine affection, and Fallon felt a prick of tears. She still missed her mother, but that loss had been softened by time.

Turning to Fallon, Nora said, "We'd better get going, or that canyon might get filled in before we get there."

Everyone laughed, and Fallon felt a lightness that almost made her dizzy. Seeing Nora choosing to forgive her father and offering her love to her mother meant there might actually be a chance for the two of them as well. She added that moment to her mental list as something else for them to talk about…later.

Before they were even out of town, Nora's phone buzzed. At a traffic light, she looked at the screen. "Hold on," she said, pulling into a strip mall parking lot. She texted furiously for a minute before throwing her phone onto the console and pulling back onto the road. "My butthead boss," she said by way of explanation.

They'd only been on the highway for about fifteen minutes when Fallon's phone rang. Sighing, she listened as Maris updated her on the crew, adding that the ranger position was still unresolved. Fallon told her she was still recovering and would be taking another couple of weeks at least, adding that she'd be in touch when she was ready to come back.

She ended the call, and she and Nora looked at each other for a few seconds before breaking into laughter. "What if we both go incommunicado for the next few days?" Nora asked.

"That works for me," Fallon said, switching her phone off and adding it to Nora's on the console. "I'm actually happiest off-grid, out in the field." She took Nora's hand. "It's the best way to focus on what's really important."

Nora squeezed her fingers before switching off her phone. "Perfect. I already told Mom to call Tyler if there's a problem, and I sent him a copy of our itinerary. They'll be able to find us if they genuinely need to, but otherwise...I'm yours."

Fallon warmed inside. "Likewise."

They drove as far as Cortez, having agreed on a "quirky" retro hotel near Mesa Verde. She'd been unable to convince Nora that she could ride for five hours and still have the stamina to explore the amazing 800-year-old structures inside the national park. Stretching while Nora went to check them in, she caught scents of fall in the steady wind of early October. If she'd been at Firecamp, she'd have been checking over the equipment and writing reports, waiting for the last of the crews to finish up. This was much better.

"I forgot to mention, the only room we could get has two double beds," Nora told her when she returned. "Is that okay?"

"It's fine. And you were right to do it this way. I'm looking forward to a shorter drive to the park tomorrow and more energy to explore it."

Determined to carry her own bag, she lifted it with her good arm. She could admit to herself that she wasn't a hundred percent, but each day brought less pain and more strength. She did her exercises while Nora showered, taking her turn to clean up afterward.

They went to a bistro that specialized in dishes made from local farm ingredients. Anita was a fine cook, but this food was next level. Even full as they were, they agreed to split a dessert.

"Do you cook for yourself in Tucson?" Fallon asked.

Nora grinned. "Does driving through count? No, rarely. Though if I could cook like this, I might." After taking a sip of wine, she added, "And if I had someone to cook for."

"I'm pretty happy when camp starts in the spring and I don't have to eat my own cooking anymore," Fallon admitted. "It would be nice to at least take turns."

Nora nodded. "It would. As long as you accounted for each other's schedules and didn't make it required, like, 'if it's Tuesday, it's your time,' no matter what."

Fallon realized they could be approaching some important negotiation, hypothetically at least. "Oh, sure. That would make sense."

Nora seemed satisfied, but before she could comment, the check came. Nora reached for it, but Fallon put her hand on top. "Let me. Please. You've done all the driving up to this point, so I think I should treat you to dinner."

"I guess we should talk about how to deal with our expenses on this journey."

"Agreed. But let's go back to the hotel. I need to get comfortable if we're going to talk money."

A few days after first using the aromatic CBD salve on her shoulder and hip, Fallon had asked permission to cut the sleeve off an oversized T-shirt she'd found in Art's dresser, and that—along with a pair of her own boxers—had become her pajamas. Nora slept in a T-shirt as well, but it was shorter, tighter, and generally quite distracting. And along with the bikini panties that she wore, very sexy.

Once they'd both changed and Nora perched on the edge of the bed after pulling a small notebook out of her purse, Fallon found that money was the last thing on her mind. Instead, she wanted to ask Nora about her dreams, her plans for the rest of her career, and how their possible future could fit in.

"Obviously, we'll split the cost of gas." Nora wrote something down.

"I remember you feeding me ice chips in the hospital."

Nora looked up, her pen poised in the air. "I didn't want to leave, you know. But this thing with my father—"

"Sure, yeah, I understood. Having Tyler there was great."

"Speaking of which…" Nora wrote something on another page. "I should call him and let him know we'll be there sometime next week."

"Will it take us that long?" she asked.

"It might if we decide to take some side trips or stay longer somewhere. I didn't think we were in any particular rush."

Nora was smiling, and Fallon sensed she was talking about more than their travels. She remembered the thrill she'd felt when Nora had started flirting with her at the first Firecamp and how things had gone when she'd flirted back.

"No rush," she agreed, looking into Nora's eyes. "But I am hoping for steady progress."

Nora blinked, closing her small notebook. "Maybe we should talk about this tomorrow. When we can concentrate better."

"Maybe so."

Once the lights were off, she realized that sleeping in the same room with Nora at a motel did not feel the same as sleeping with her in a tent or at the Palmers' house. Not that they were at the point to have hot sex either of those times—or quite yet, for that matter—but at Firecamp, they'd been exhausted after a long day, and being at Nora's parents definitely carried a disinclination to do anything physical, not that her injury would have allowed it. Motels seemed to offer an intimate seclusion, a setting with no expectations or limitations. After a moment of quiet when they'd both settled in their beds, Nora whispered Fallon's name into the darkness. Fallon was pretty certain she knew what was coming.

"Do you feel like you could tolerate some company?"

If she said no, would Nora ask again in another day or two? Or would she take that as her answer for all time? More importantly, did she actually want to say no? "Uh, sure. If you don't mind the smell."

Nora's bed creaked. "I'm accustomed to it now. I might even miss it when it's gone."

Fallon laughed. "I won't, though I do think it's really helped. I sincerely appreciate it."

"You're most welcome." Nora's voice was close, and Fallon felt the bed dip as she got in. "You're still lying on your right side?"

"Yeah." Her voice sounded rough to her own ears. "But I sometimes wake up on the other side, and it's only a little sore."

"Will it hurt for me to snug?"

"Snugging with you was never what hurt me."

Nora sighed and pressed her forehead into Fallon's back. "I said such terrible things to you that last night. God, Fallon. You talked about being angry with yourself afterward? Once I finally pulled my head out of my ass, I was ashamed. So ashamed I couldn't imagine you ever wanting to talk to me again. Over the first few months, I was desperate to contact you, to apologize, but I couldn't envision you answering when you saw my name. For years after, every time I thought about calling or at least texting, dreadful self-reproach would stop me. I was a contemptible fool, but I've tried really hard to change my ways." She gave a sad laugh. "Some of them, at least."

At the tears in Nora's voice, Fallon turned, slowly and carefully, putting her right arm around her, keeping her close. It wasn't the time or place where she'd imagined having this talk, but maybe a retro motel on neutral ground like Cortez, Colorado was as good a place as any. "I was very much in the wrong too. I invaded your privacy and tried to destroy something I probably misunderstood. I didn't give you a chance to explain, to tell me what you were doing. And after I broke your camera, the thing that was most important to you, I was certain you'd never forgive me." *Lay it all out there, Fallon.* "Those pictures that upset me...uh, I had some issues about my body and went to counseling for a few years to work on that. And other things."

"You did?" Nora pulled away enough to look at her. "That's really brave. And it helped?"

"Yeah. Having support as I look at my past has made me less hypersensitive about the present. At least, I hope so. You know how my life was pretty far from normal growing up?" She felt Nora nod. "We moved around constantly and were forever apprehensive about money. That uncertainty contributed to me being insecure about myself." Fallon pushed a hand through her hair. "It sounds obvious now, so easy to see, but it took me a while to put it together. Not that I have it all figured out. But at least I have a process and someone to call if, or when, I feel like I have a screw coming loose."

"Wow. You know, you impressed me then, and now, even more so." Nora touched Fallon's cheek. "And I want to tell you that I've never seen you as anything but beautiful. I took that photo of you sleeping because you looked like a work of art. Gorgeous. Perfect. Passionate and compassionate. I should have told you at the time, or even tried to explain when you first saw it, but I hope you know that no one else has ever seen that picture. That whole file is still password protected on my computer." Fallon nodded slowly, and Nora said, "Thank you for being willing to...to spend time with me again."

"At Firecamp? Spending time with you was always the best part of my day." Fallon had to stop at that because talking about their days and nights in Silver Bird, discovering each other's bodies and exploring the possibility of something real, wanting to believe in something beyond that summer, would be too much. "And it's been the best part of having a tree fall on me," she said, hoping Nora would laugh. Thankfully, she did.

Fallon woke on her back with Nora tucked against her good side. It was going to be a great day. Mesa Verde was amazing, and she was especially pleased to have made the challenging climb up four ladders to the awesome Cliff House dwellings without any problem. The twelfth- and thirteenth-century structures made of plaster, stone, and mortar still had traces of those who'd built them, including hand and fingerprints. She could imagine coming home to this place, looking out at the view below, and feeling safe.

Before leaving Cortez, they'd purchased a picnic lunch, and Fallon laughed when Nora pulled in at the Park Point Fire Lookout. "I guess this fire thing will always be a connection for us."

Nora shrugged, but there was a smile in her voice as she read like a tour guide after consulting the park map. "At 8,572 feet, this is the highest elevation in the park. We should be able to see New Mexico, Utah, and Arizona." After a short hike to the observation tower, they sat on the low stone wall in the parking area and ate their sandwiches and chips and drank sodas while the wind whipped around them.

"I've never traveled like this," Fallon said as Nora produced the chocolate chip cookies she'd snuck in for dessert.

"What do you mean?" Nora asked. "Didn't you travel all the time as a kid?"

"Not like this. Easy. Relaxed. Able to explore and enjoy each day. To afford what we wanted to eat and where we wanted to stay." Nora looked away, and Fallon realized those last words sounded depressing. That wasn't what she intended for herself or for Nora on this trip. Even if nothing more ever happened between them, she wanted these memories to be special enough to last a lifetime. She reached over and gently touched Nora's chin. When Nora looked at her, she added, "Plus, the scenery here is much more interesting."

Nora smiled slowly. "Well, if you think our retro hotel in Cortez was something, just wait."

An hour later, they were standing in four states at once, laughing and asking strangers to take their pictures. Then they took pictures for others. There wasn't much else to do at Four Corners, but she found herself hesitant to go on. The Grand Canyon represented more to her than she'd told Nora, and she wasn't sure how she'd feel once they got there. By the time they stopped for gas, the dry land dotted with occasional ramshackle small towns was making her jittery. While Nora filled the tank, she got on her phone and did a search for restaurants in Flagstaff. Another nice meal would help her prepare for their visit to the canyon. Looking in at her before heading to the restroom, Nora asked if she should get them some snacks.

"No, but I'd like to try driving for a while," Fallon said. Concentrating on the mechanics of the road would settle her mind. Once they were underway, she knew Nora was watching to make sure she was all right, so she kept the radio low and focused on the two-lane road ahead. A bit later, she looked over, finding Nora asleep. In the ten years since they'd been intimate, she'd often recalled those very few moments she'd seen Nora in repose.

When they'd first met, Nora had been mistrusting and standoffish, even though her skills and knowledge had thrust her into situations of leadership. And while her energy and work ethic were outstanding, Fallon had learned that Nora was motivated mainly by anger and resentment toward her family, and a somewhat egocentric view of her future. Over these last few weeks, the Palmers seemed to have rebuilt some long-burned bridges between them. That reconciliation, along with the progress the two of them were making, revealed a Nora with no tension or hardness radiating off her. She was unquestionably more impressive than ever and obviously satisfied with the life she'd made. Fallon held back a sigh, reminding herself that was the life without her. *Stay in the moment.*

She didn't take the turn to the canyon, driving on to Flagstaff instead, letting Nora rest. She stopped at a light in town, and Nora stirred. Blinking, she asked, "Where are we?"

"Flagstaff. I thought we could have an early dinner here."

"Oh. You didn't want to see the canyon at sunset?" Nora sounded confused.

"I had this idea that our first day there should start at dawn." At Nora's frown, she added, "Or morning, at least."

Nora sat forward and drank some water, smoothing her hair. "Is anything wrong?"

"Why do you ask?" Fallon didn't want to lie, but she caught the frustration in Nora's tone.

"I thought you'd be more eager to get there. Like, that was a big part of the reason for this trip."

Fallon reached for her hand. "Spending time with you is the reason for the trip. The Grand Canyon is just the icing on the cake."

"And I'm the cake?" Nora grinned. Fallon relaxed.

Maybe she'd just been hungry. The unwelcome feelings of isolation and sorrow, so familiar during her childhood, had faded away over the lovely meal. There was no line at the entrance to the park, and Nora stopped at the first turnout. "Rudy's been here. He told me to stop at this first lookout if we got in after dark. We don't have to go to the rim of the canyon yet, but let's look at the stars."

Fallon grabbed her jacket as they got out and walked to a bench nearby. Nora sat beside her, and they leaned back at the same time, faces turned toward the heavens.

"Oh my," Nora breathed. "Tucson certainly doesn't offer this view." She shivered, and Fallon unfolded her jacket, draping it over them both. "Are you still looking for your North Star life?" Nora asked, and Fallon could feel her scrutiny. "Or have you found another option?"

Unable to meet her gaze, Fallon pointed into the star-filled sky. "I know where Polaris is. Do you?" She pulled Nora closer. "Or should we just sit here until we observe the rest of them revolving around it?"

"Maybe tomorrow night?" Nora asked hopefully, rubbing her hands together. "When I've got thermals on?"

"You brought some?" Fallon's voice rose in disbelief.

Nora laughed and pulled her up, moving back toward the car. "I've never needed long underwear once since I lived in Tucson." She batted her eyes playfully. "Won't you let me borrow yours? For old time's sake?"

If Nora hadn't had that playful tone in her voice, if it hadn't been the wrong time and the wrong place, Fallon would have said the truth that was making itself known in her heart: *If we could have new times, I'd give you anything of mine and all of me.* Instead, she simply smiled.

CHAPTER TWENTY

Nora unlocked the door to the suite and led Fallon inside. "No peeking," she cautioned, closing the door behind them and turning on a second light in the sitting room. "Okay now."

Fallon opened her eyes and gaped.

"I know we'll be outside most days, and apparently some nights for stargazing," Nora said in a rush, "but this is our longest stop, and I want it to be memorable. Or at least comfortable. And please don't ask me how much it costs or offer to split it. This is my treat."

The sitting room featured a rich, dark gold fabric-covered love seat and a polished wooden coffee table. Across the room were two wooden side chairs with a small bookshelf between them.

"The bathroom is in there." Nora pointed. She'd paid extra to reserve the suite with a king bed, and a quick glance down the short hallway confirmed they'd gotten it. It dominated the small bedroom. "But this is the best part." She took Fallon's arm and opened one of the French doors next to the couch. Together, they stepped out onto a large balcony. "In the morning, you can get your first view here if you want."

They looked up at the same time, both breathing in the brisk air. The lights around the hotel made the stars seem not quite as numerous. Looking out, Nora could see the vague silhouettes of shapes within the canyon. Worried that Fallon hadn't said a word since they'd stepped into the suite, she asked, "Is this okay?"

"This is beyond okay. I never expected...I mean...Nora, this is amazing. But you didn't have to—"

Nora stopped her with a finger on her lips. "I know. I wanted to. For many reasons." Smiling, she added. "I don't usually travel this way either, but I thought just this once..."

The words echoed in her mind. Was *just this once* something they could do? Have a few days and nights together, and then go on with their separate lives the way they had before? They'd at least have to do their parting better than last time. She hadn't let herself think about any other possibility. Ten years ago, Fallon had somehow imprinted herself on Nora's deepest self, breaking through her determination to go it alone, showing her that genuine kindness and goodness did exist. She hadn't realized how completely she'd dropped her tough girl defenses until Fallon had vanished from her life, and the vulnerability from that loss had hurt more than anything she'd ever experienced.

But God, Fallon was stunning, even in the dim lighting from the hotel and the stars. She'd grown into a strong, competent woman, whose sweetness and decency were never far from the surface. The softness of her mouth against Nora's fingers ignited the yearning her nearness had always triggered. Desire must have shown on her face because Fallon stepped into her, pressing against her body. A small sound of surprise escaped Nora's lips, and Fallon hesitated. Nora pushed closer, wondering whose racing heartbeat she was feeling.

"If you're going to tell me no, say it now." Fallon's voice was rough, uneven in the quiet night air.

"Why would I do that? I've been trying to get you to say yes since I saw you at Firecamp again." Nora leaned in, kissing Fallon gently on the mouth.

The kiss was sweet, but Nora's pulse began to race when Fallon said, "We should probably talk…you know…before…uh…"

"I think we should talk after," she countered, wrapping her arm around Fallon's waist and guiding her back through the doorway. "What if there's no chemistry left between us, and there's nothing to talk about?"

Inside, where she could see Nora's expression, Fallon evidently detected her tease. "You don't really think that, do you?"

"I think we owe it to ourselves to find out."

Fallon excused herself to use the restroom, and Nora sat on the side of the bed, her thoughts unexpectedly flooded with negatives: Fallon would change her mind, Nora would be too pushy, and things would go badly, or Fallon's experiences with other women would leave her disappointed in Nora's lovemaking. She was never like this, never unsure of herself, which underscored the idea that being with Fallon meant more to her than she had admitted. That was beyond alarming.

But when Fallon appeared in the doorway with a small smile, Nora's mind cleared.

"I think this is the biggest bed I've ever seen," Fallon said.

Nora rose and went to her, resting her hands on Fallon's shoulders. "Are you feeling all right?"

Fallon grasped her hips. "Other than being terrified? Yes."

Nora averted her gaze. "So it's not just me?"

"Nora." Fallon's voice was soft and low. She took a breath. "It's always been you. Just you."

Nora let her hands slide down Fallon's chest as she began unbuttoning her shirt. "Then we are definitely even."

They'd left the balcony door open, and she'd forgotten to set the thermostat, so the room was getting cold. After undressing each other quickly, getting into the bed seemed like the most obvious step. Once they were naked under the covers, warming against each other's bodies, Nora speculated that if she lifted the blanket, actual sparks might be flying between them. The difference between wearing what passed for pajamas in bed with Fallon and how it felt now was like the difference between a whisper and a scream.

Fallon's skin was as lovely as she remembered, although there were a few new scars. Two small ones on her left shin and a three-inch, irregular welt on the underside of her right forearm. "Flying wood shard," she said by way of explanation when Nora traced her finger over it. "I blocked it just before it would have hit my face."

"No, not that," Nora murmured. Her earlier anxiety had been replaced by a languid, simmering want. She scattered kisses around Fallon's distinctive features, pleased to feel her squirm a bit.

"What are you smiling at?" Fallon asked.

"You," Nora answered, tightening her arms, bringing Fallon's body closer. "And how good you feel."

"Are you saying that because you're cold?"

"I'm saying that because it's true. Because I—" Nora broke off, not sure if she was ready to disclose anything more.

Fallon rolled on top of her. Just like before, Fallon making a move, taking control, transformed her want into intense hunger. "Because you what? Tell me, Nora Palmer." How could she sound teasing and so demanding at the same time?

"Because I want you, and it's been incredibly hard to keep from jumping you while you've been healing. Because I've missed you, and being with you here seems like an amazing dream." That wasn't everything, but it was all true.

Fallon kissed her slow and deep, settling between Nora's legs and moving enough to bring Nora into a matching tempo. "If this is a dream, I don't ever want to wake up."

"Me neither."

Fallon kissed her way down to Nora's breasts. "My hands are still cold. You'll have to settle for my mouth."

"That's not settling." Fallon's lovely and talented mouth had been impossible to forget. She ran her hands into Fallon's hair, recalling the beautiful length it had been, but adoring the shorter fullness of it. "Not—"

Fallon's lips closed on her nipple, sucking in time with the pulsing rhythm of her hips. Nora moaned, pushing up, seeking more of the exhilarating friction that translated into pleasure in her deepest core. "You taste so good, so fucking good," Fallon growled, moving to Nora's other breast.

Nora slid her hands along Fallon's side, cupping her ass, pulling tight against her. Fallon's breath was hot against Nora's body as she moved down. Nora hissed "yes" on a long exhale, anticipating the first touch of Fallon's tongue on her clit. Running her fingers over Fallon's muscled shoulders and back, Nora's loving caresses tightened into a clench as Fallon's mouth closed around her.

"Oh, God. There, yes." Nora couldn't stop herself from crying out. The warm, wet sensations from Fallon's lips were so incredibly powerful, she knew she wasn't going to last.

Fallon, her hands no longer cold, lifted Nora to meet the firm strokes of her tongue again and again. The fiery pulsations sparkling along her spine exploded into pure bliss. She dissolved into a place where Fallon was all she felt. Gradually, she became conscious of lying on her side, her leg thrown over Fallon's, her throbbing sex fitted against Fallon's body. She wanted more, but she wanted Fallon first.

"That was…"

Fallon shifted, and Nora lost her words at the firmness of Fallon's thigh brushing against her clit. Fallon's exquisite eyes were slightly darker with desire. "I'm not finished yet."

Nora's heart pounded. In her encounters over the last ten years, she'd always taken charge, sometimes not even wanting reciprocity once the other woman was finished. Why was it so different with Fallon?

Because you trust her. What else could it be?

Before she could examine that concept, Fallon had turned, her fingers lightly stroking the hair between Nora's thighs. "Are you ready for me?"

Nora could only nod, opening her legs as she put her arms around Fallon's shoulders. Fallon slid two fingers through her folds, causing Nora to quiver and pull closer. Their chests crushed together, and then Fallon pulled back, pushing up enough to offer Nora her breast. Nora opened her mouth eagerly, sucking it in just as Fallon entered her, moving smoothly through her wetness. The softness of Fallon's breast and the fullness inside seemed to amplify a hundredfold when Fallon whispered her name. It sounded like a question. Or a prayer.

"I'm here, baby," Nora answered, her head back as Fallon filled her deeper. "I'm with you."

Curling her fingers, Fallon moved inside her, taking Nora's thoughts to the first time she'd touched her like that. She moaned, stopping Fallon's arm, pushing against her instead. She knew Fallon would be careful and tender this first time, and that would completely unravel her. In floating bits of rational thought, she knew this wasn't just sex, but right now, she couldn't think of all the things it could mean. Thrusting faster, she felt Fallon's teeth rake across her nipple, delicately at first and then harder. And then harder. The tiny pinpoints of pain made Nora quicken, release closing in. "You...yes. Yes."

Fallon licked around her breast and along her neck, breathing softly in her ear. Her voice was hushed, her words muffled by Nora's hair.

Did she say "I love you"?

Nora came, shuddering and clinging, riding Fallon's hand until she had nothing left. Nothing but the echo of those words catching in her throat behind the sob she was holding back.

❖

Chilled, Nora pulled the blanket up, seeking the heat of Fallon's body. That side of the bed was empty. Cool. Reluctantly, Nora opened one eye, detecting faint morning light. There was no sound, no sense of someone moving around elsewhere in the suite. A flush of heat came to her cheeks at memories of the night. She'd been a total pillow princess, something so unlike her, it was embarrassing. Yeah, it had been a while, but that was no excuse for basically passing out, leaving Fallon to...

As the words "Fallon" and "leaving" passed through her mind, she sat up, her heartbeat rising. No, Fallon wouldn't have left. She wasn't like that. Still, Nora threw off the covers, cursing the damn thermostat, and picked up yesterday's socks on the way to the closet. Finding one robe hanging there, she made a quick bathroom stop before moving cautiously into the sitting room. Through the glass doors, she could see Fallon wrapped in her own robe, standing on the edge of the balcony. Getting her dawn view of the Grand Canyon, Nora thought, smiling as she stepped outside. Fallon didn't turn at the sound of her footsteps. Nora laid a cautious hand on her shoulder. "Good morning."

"Is there a bridge anywhere?" Fallon asked, still focused on the massive chasm that stretched out before them.

"You mean a bridge across the whole canyon?" Nora asked. When Fallon nodded, she said, "No. I mean, it's too wide, and trying to build something like that would ruin this incredible sight, don't you think?" At Fallon's sigh, she added, "If you want to see the North Rim, we can drive over there. I think it takes about four hours, so it would be a long day there and back."

"That's going around, not over," Fallon stated.

"Right." She was getting cold, and caffeine would be essential to figuring out why Fallon was acting so odd. "Can we go in for a minute? I need coffee and a jacket, preferably in that order." Fallon didn't turn or reply. "Fallon?" Raising her voice slightly, Nora gave her shoulder a light shake.

"Huh?" Fallon looked around as if only now realizing Nora was there.

Had the wind caused her eyes to water, or were those tears? "Let's go inside for a minute. Please. You're going to catch cold. Or I will." She slid her hand down to Fallon's, giving her a tug. "Come on. The canyon will still be there after we get the chill off." Fallon followed without a word. "Please find the thermostat and put it on eighty," Nora said, starting the Keurig. It wouldn't be a challenge like Decker the Dripper, but it would do. When she went to hand Fallon the first cup, she found her standing in front of the thermostat. The heat was still off. Nora quickly reset it. "Come here. I think you need to thaw out." She pulled Fallon into the bedroom and got her under the covers, leaving her robe on. Nora joined her, sitting in her robe, drinking coffee. "How long were you out there?"

Fallon shivered, turning toward her. "I'm not sure."

The strange hollowness in her voice prompted Nora to put her cup on the bedside table and scoot down, taking Fallon in her arms. "What's wrong?" When Fallon didn't answer, she asked, "Are you upset about last night?"

"What? No. No, of course not. It was wonderful. You were amazing."

"I think that should be my line." She held Fallon closer. As Fallon's body began to warm up, Nora said, "Please talk to me, Fallon. I know something's upset you, and I want to help."

Fallon rubbed at her eyes. "My mother always said the Grand Canyon was the one place she really wanted to go before she died. She used to show me photos of it on her phone. I so wanted her to see it in person. It's beyond incredible."

"It is." Nora waited for a moment. "I guess I've never asked if you're religious."

"In what way?"

Nora carefully considered what she wanted to say. "Well, do you believe your mom is in heaven? Like she could be watching you, and seeing that you're here would be like you showing it to her?"

Fallon looked thoughtful. Then a slow smile curved one corner of her mouth. "That's a nice thought, but I hope she wasn't watching last night."

Nora covered her mouth in pretend shock. When Fallon started to laugh, Nora jumped on her, tickling any part she could reach. Nora's frequent childhood tussles with her older brothers and Fallon's amusement made the scuffle a brief one.

"I give, I give," Fallon said breathlessly.

Nora stopped but didn't move away. Instead, she sat up, pulling the covers down and straddling Fallon's waist. "I'm sure you're impatient to get out there and discover every inch of this amazing place, but is it possible you'd be willing to let me do some exploring first?"

Fallon stroked her chin. "Hmm. Were you interested in a particular region?"

"I'll need to look over the entire terrain before I can answer that." Opening Fallon's robe as she spoke, Nora let hers slip slowly off her shoulders. The room had warmed nicely, and Fallon looked glorious in the morning light. "I think I'll start with the mountains," Nora said, filling her hands with Fallon's breasts. She caressed them gently, watching as Fallon's eyes fluttered. "I've always loved this range in particular."

"Always?" Fallon asked.

"Always." Nora turned slightly, reluctantly letting go of one breast and reaching back to skim through the dark hair between Fallon's legs. "Although the grasslands are appealing as well."

Fallon's breathing quickened. She began working her arms out of the robe sleeves, but Nora stopped her. "You can't touch me right now. Later, but not now. All right?" Fallon bit her lip, but after a few seconds, she nodded. "Good." Nora leaned farther back, letting her fingers tease around the sides of Fallon's clit. "And these wetlands are absolutely spectacular, as I recall."

"Do you?" Fallon's voice was rough. "Do you recall?"

Nora stretched out fully on top of her, hands pressed into the mattress above Fallon's shoulders. Lowering her lips to Fallon's, she stopped a breath away. "Yes, I do. I recall very well." She could feel Fallon straining toward her but trying not to break the no-touch agreement. When she let their mouths meet, she'd intended only a quick, playful kiss. But Fallon moaned, and Nora let herself go, delving into the sweetness of taste and tongue. She'd kissed other women, even thought she'd wanted other women, but in this moment, she knew that had all been a lie. This was the truth.

Fallon's heat and passion set Nora aflame with the same fervor. Feeling Fallon moving beneath her, Nora pushed back upright, delving into Fallon's wetness while she palmed her breast. After several quick strokes, she slowed, waiting for Fallon to find her pace. It was as if she'd memorized every minute of their first lovemaking and had been hoping for a chance to deliver on what she'd learned by heart.

By heart? Lovemaking?

"Please," Fallon whispered. "Can I touch you? Please?"

She'd wanted to excite Fallon and keep her on the edge until she begged. Could she believe that Fallon's deepest desire was not simply for orgasm but for a connection with her? Because she wanted it so badly, she should have said no. If she didn't hold back, keep something of herself, where would she be when this trip was over?

An echo of "design your present happiness" went through her mind. Hannah, their friend from the first Firecamp, had used that phrase when Nora had been struggling with her feelings for Fallon. Now Fallon's swollen clitoris and her own growing need made her say yes, and the powerful arms that wrapped around her were like in her recurring dream where Fallon saved her after she tripped. She wasn't sure anything could save her from falling after Fallon called her name, tightening her hold. Seconds later, her cries filled Nora's heart.

❖

"Does it feel funny to be having lunch when we never had breakfast?" Fallon asked.

"You're more of a regular eater than I am. If I get an early call about a story breaking, it could be two or three o'clock before I finally have a meal. But I've found a brand of protein bars that tide me over, and I always carry some with me."

They were sitting in the hotel dining room at a small table, one row back from the windows looking out on the canyon. They'd showered together, delighting in each other's bodies to the point that it was another hour before they'd dressed for the day. They were both famished, but as soon as they ordered, Nora brushed her leg against Fallon's under the table. Touching her seemed more important than anything else. When she did, Fallon gave her that wonderful smile, the special look she'd been waiting for. Nora bit her lip. She knew it meant Fallon was all in, at least at that moment. She looked away quickly, blinking back tears.

"What's wrong?" Fallon asked.

"Not a thing. Just a bit of dust," she said, dabbing at the corner of her eye with her napkin. "I was wondering what you wanted to do first after we eat. Do you want to drive back to where the canyon starts or sightsee from this end first?"

"Let's look at the map," Fallon suggested.

They planned a hike, but after eating a huge lunch, a ride along Desert View Drive seemed like the perfect way to digest. At Grandview Point, they fell in with a group who gathered for a ranger talk about the geology of the canyon. After listening for a few minutes, Fallon whispered, "Is it bad that I'd rather look than learn?"

"I'm with you," Nora said, and they made a quiet exit.

They drove on to the Desert View Watchtower, waiting their turn to investigate the magnificent structure itself before taking a short walk to the viewpoint. For close to an hour, they simply looked, occasionally pointing out particular areas of interest as the sunlight played across the glorious scenery. They were almost back to the truck when Fallon stopped in her tracks. Turning to look at Nora, she exclaimed, "You don't have your camera!"

Nora laughed. "I might bring it tomorrow. But I wanted to see this amazing place with the panorama my eyes can provide rather than focusing through a tiny viewfinder. Especially since I don't have the skill or the equipment to capture it all. I'm not even sure that would be possible, and I don't want to waste our time here trying." She took Fallon's arm as they moved toward the truck again.

The sunglasses made it hard to tell, but Nora was certain Fallon was looking at her. "Those are some pretty impressive priorities, Ms. Palmer."

"Why, thank you, Ms. Monroe."

After two more stops where they were jostled by the crowds at lookouts, Fallon said, "I'm tired of being around all these people. What would you say to dinner at the hotel and watching the sunset from our balcony?"

"I'm with you on the people, but I'm still not particularly hungry. What would you say to a picnic on our balcony? We can pick up some nibbles at the Canyon Village Market."

"Sold."

Fallon shopped for munchies while Nora picked out the smallest, least offensive box of wine. Back in their room, they changed into sweats and fleece tops. Uncharacteristically, Fallon had half a glass of wine. Nora offered to top her off, but Fallon declined, so she finished the rest. The sun was almost down, and they were picking over the last of their snacks when Fallon started laughing.

"What?" Nora asked.

"I can't believe this is my life right now. Staying in a suite with a private balcony overlooking the Grand Canyon." Her expression turned serious. "With you."

"Is that last part the most surprising?"

"Surprising. Amazing. Wonderful. Unbelievable. Unforgettable."

"Good. It's all those things for me as well." Nora opened her mouth to say more, to say she didn't want it to be over. But Fallon hadn't included that idea in her list. She'd said "unforgettable." Did that mean she'd return to Firecamp when the trip was over, and everything that had happened between them would only be a memory? If she asked, she knew Fallon would be honest. But she wasn't sure she was ready for the answer. Another day and they'd be in Tucson. Maybe Fallon would love it and want to stay. Nora reclined on the chair and tried to imagine what that would be like. Fallon getting a job, maybe working in the forest at Mt. Lemmon. Living together, they'd cook and wash clothes and do all the things couples did, falling asleep in each other's arms every night. Tyler could still live there too; he and Fallon got along well. *But would Fallon always want the air conditioner on this high?*

"Nora? Nora, baby, I think there's a storm coming. We need to get inside." Lips touched her forehead.

Opening her eyes, Nora found she was covered by a blanket. Fallon was kneeling beside her. "What?" she asked faintly.

"You fell asleep. It kept getting colder, so I got an extra layer for you, but now I think we need to go in."

"Okay." Nora got to her feet, feeling unsteady as a chill wind penetrated the blanket. Fallon's arm around her shoulders steadied her as they made their way inside. "Can we go to bed?"

"I thought you'd never ask." Fallon's sweet voice made her melt. Fallon's hands were calloused, but her touch was gentle as she lifted Nora's shirt. A slight brush of fingers across her belly made her shiver. "Do you want to take a shower first?"

Nora shook her head. Damn cheap wine was making everything blurry. Everything except Fallon. When the air hit her bare chest, she caught Fallon's hand, holding it to her breast. "Yours," she murmured.

"Mmm. I like the sound of that." As Fallon unzipped Nora's pants, Nora leaned forward and bit her neck. "Hey. I'm trying to do precision work here."

Nora laughed. "I don't mind messy. In fact, I like it." Fallon settled her onto the bed. It felt like landing on the softest cloud possible, and she snuggled in, but something was missing. No, someone. "Where are you?"

"I'll be right there."

"Promise?" This was important, she knew, but she couldn't keep her eyes open.

"Always."

Nora smiled. In this moment, that was exactly what she wanted to hear.

CHAPTER TWENTY-ONE

It had snowed during the night. Not a heavy squall, thankfully. Just enough to make the canyon look like it had been frosted. Fallon hadn't closed the curtains in the bedroom, and the view through the window was breathtaking. But then, so was the woman sleeping naked next to her. Nora had awakened her in the night, apologizing profusely for having had too much to drink. Fallon had laughed and told her she was a cute drunk. Nora's response was to tell her she was cute all the time, and their verbal exchange had slowly turned physical.

This time, Fallon had no doubt that Nora felt it too; their luxurious climb to arousal was from genuine closeness, not just a desire for gratification. There was caring in each touch, an understanding that they were building toward a relationship of mutual appreciation and affection. And while that was the intimacy she'd always yearned for with Nora, the big question remained: How would they make this work?

The dim sunlight was filtering more intensely through the clouds, and she didn't want Nora to miss the amazing sight. "Nora. Baby, wake up. You need to see this."

Nora stirred. "What is it?"

Fallon pointed through the window.

Nora rubbed her eyes as she yawned. "Wait," she said, sitting up. "Is that snow?"

"Yeah. Doesn't it look awesome?"

She'd barely finished her sentence before Nora was up and dressing with one hand while simultaneously digging in her suitcase for her camera. Fallon, still lounging in the bed, watched her with an amused expression. Nora frowned at her. "Aren't you coming?"

Laughing, Fallon got into her clothes and followed Nora onto the balcony. After she'd snapped a few shots, Nora said, "Closer. We need to get out there."

They ran down the stairs and out onto the walkway in front of the hotel. Nora stopped occasionally, her camera clicking regularly as they walked briskly along the rim toward the Bright Angel Trail. "Are you okay?" Nora asked, as if she knew Fallon was watching her. "Can we go along the path for a bit?"

"Sure."

Half an hour later, Nora directed her to pose alongside the first tunnel.

"You don't need me," Fallon said. "This scene is great as it is."

"I do," Nora insisted. "I need you for perspective."

They looked at each other for a moment as Nora's words echoed in the cold morning air. "I need you for that too," Fallon said.

Nora walked over and kissed her, a sweet lingering of lips, before giving her a little push. "Go pose. Then I'll buy you breakfast."

She took several pictures before Fallon called, "There can't possibly be an angle you haven't shot. I'm cold and hungry, and the snow is almost gone."

"Were you always this whiny, or is it a new thing?" Nora asked, shrieking in pretend fear when Fallon started after her. Back in their suite after breakfast, they warmed each other up in the shower before dressing more carefully for the day. They caught the Hermit Road shuttle bus and alternated between walking along the rim and riding to the next stop.

"Show me what you see," Fallon said as Nora maneuvered around other tourists to take three pictures of the Abyss. "I mean, how do you decide what to shoot when you're looking at such an amazing vista?"

Nora made her fingers into a rectangular frame, moving it across their view. "I don't have the kind of lens that could get all of this scene, so I have to emphasize one part at a time. I watch the way light and shadows change, looking for a combination of the two that gives me a reaction." She smiled. "I guess it sounds silly, the idea that I have to have feelings about my subject."

Fallon shook her head. "It doesn't sound silly at all. It explains why your photos evoke such emotion. May I try?"

Nora handed over her camera, and Fallon took one shot of the canyon before turning the lens at Nora. At first, Nora didn't seem to notice she was the new subject. At the second click, she turned, and

Fallon shot three more pictures while Nora protested, finally laughing and putting her hands over her face.

"What?" Fallon asked. "You don't like it when the tables are turned?"

Before Nora could answer, an older woman came over and asked if they'd like her to take a photo of the two of them. They agreed, moving closer, arms around each other. Fallon flashed on a memory from their Firecamp days. Nora had been reluctant to pose for a shot of the two of them, but Hannah had insisted, so Fallon had tickled Nora's ribs just before the camera clicked, making them both laugh. Nora had threatened to delete the results but was outvoted as everyone oohed and aahed over the image on the small screen. Fallon briefly wondered if that picture had made it into the video.

"Smile," the woman prompted before taking several shots. She declined their offer to take one of her before she boarded the waiting bus. "You have to send me those," Fallon said. "The ones of you especially. You're so much more beautiful now than in the picture on your Firecamp application."

"Oh God," Nora said as they resumed their walk along the canyon rim. "I actually remember the day my mom took that picture. I'd just gotten my hair cut short, and she made me put on extra makeup to keep me from looking 'boyish.' I was so mad, I refused to smile."

"True. But the intensity in your expression was stunning. I always wondered what you were thinking."

Nora stopped. "Can you guess what I'm thinking now?"

Fallon faced her, and they looked into each other's eyes. Nora's searching gaze resonated from the pit of her stomach to a slightly lower location. "That the Grand Canyon will be here forever, but we'll only have our fabulous suite for one more night?"

Nora smiled. "You're very good at that. But let's ride the rest of the loop."

After grabbing a light meal at the Fred Harvey Tavern, they went back to the suite, changing into comfortable clothing for a last evening on the balcony. "When did you first know you liked girls?" Nora asked.

"It all started with a book," Fallon said, and Nora laughed.

"Why am I not surprised?"

"We'd had car trouble, and I was sitting in the waiting room, reading a story where the main character had the power to change things just by wishing. I knew it was silly, but I thought if I had that power, I'd wish we could stay in one place, just for a little while. I felt weird after the mechanic came and told us that the car parts would take several weeks to arrive."

"Like you made it happen?"

Fallon nodded. "My mom got a job in the diner, and I hung out there and helped sometimes. One day, this girl and her mother came in, and when the girl smiled at me, I felt happy inside. And kinda warm."

"I bet."

She gave Nora's shoulder a nudge. "So I wished the girl would come back by herself."

"And she did."

"Yeah. Her name was Chloe, and she showed me the lake just outside of town. We held hands, and it felt wonderful. We met twice more, and the second time, she kissed me on the cheek when we parted. Oh man, that was something special."

"More special than this?" Nora climbed onto her lap, kissing her soundly.

"Not even close. But then…"

"Okay. I'll stop interrupting," Nora promised, cuddling against her.

"Well, the holidays came, and Chloe was going to visit some other family in Denver. I gave her *Seafire* to read in the car."

"Wait. The same book you gave me?"

"The very same. Well, not the exact one because Chloe never returned it, and she stopped coming into the diner. I'd see her on the street with some other girl occasionally, but that was it."

"She broke your heart?"

"I thought so at the time, but I mended pretty quickly in those days." Fallon smiled to herself, remembering the beautiful lady who'd come in asking for help as she'd been locking up one night, not long after Chloe had dumped her. A week's earnings didn't compare to the feel of that woman's body against hers. "And I got another copy of that book."

"So you renounced wishing but decided to stick with *Seafire* and girls?" Nora asked.

Fallon felt the blood drain from her face. "I…" She bit her lower lip and fought back a wave of emotion. She didn't want to relive the memory, but she wanted Nora to know her. All of her.

"What?" Nora pushed herself up. "Baby, what is it?"

Fallon took a deep breath, forcing herself to go on. "I made one last stupid wish. About a year later, my mom had been working really hard, and she looked so tired, I wished that she'd get some time to rest. Not long after that she..." Fallon swallowed hard. "She got sick and then—"

"Oh no. No, baby." Nora took Fallon's face in her hands. "Your adolescent wishing didn't cause any of those things. You know that, right?"

She couldn't meet Nora's eyes. "Yeah, I do. But still..." She shrugged. "I stopped just wishing, no sitting back, timidly hoping for the life I wanted to come to me. I resolved to take charge of myself and understand the difference between things I could control and things I couldn't."

Nora kissed her forehead. "And obviously, you were successful. Making a home at Firecamp, becoming a crew leader...you got what you wanted."

But I didn't get you. They were quiet for a minute, looking at the stars. "And that girl, Addison?" Fallon asked. "Was she your first?"

"You remember her?"

Fallon couldn't tell if she was pleased or upset. "Yes, but what I mostly remember is thinking she must be somewhat disturbed." Relieved when Nora laughed, she added, "I mean, why did she bother flirting with me when you were sitting at the same table?"

"All right," Nora said, getting to her feet. "Flattery will get you everywhere. Let's go in."

Fallon followed. "I meant it, you know."

"I know. That's why I'm taking you to bed."

❖

"My phone is completely dead," Fallon said the next morning. "I haven't even charged it since we turned them off."

"Me neither," Nora said. "But we can charge them in the car."

Fallon stopped in the doorway and looked back into the room one last time. "This was amazing, Nora. Truly. I can't thank you enough for—"

Nora stopped her with a finger on her lips. "It was my pleasure."

"Not entirely, I can assure you." Fallon kissed Nora's hand, trying not to blush as she recalled last night's lovemaking. Nora had taken her to the edge of orgasm multiple times before backing off, making Fallon almost crazed with desire. Afterward, while Nora held her, Fallon had contemplated how fulfilled she felt. Being with Nora seemed to complete a part of her that was otherwise unfinished. Or perhaps she'd stagnated over these last few years, and something about Nora opened her up and aired her out, like freshening a room that had been unused for too long. The time they'd been apart had dissolved into new memories, and no matter what else, she needed to remember this feeling and be satisfied with that.

All those promising notions had been much easier to believe with Nora's arms around her, but now, as they loaded the car, Fallon tried very hard not to think about what would happen next. They'd been on neutral ground until now, but they were heading into Nora's territory. She couldn't be upset that they hadn't talked about their future, though. She'd never really had a vacation before, and the last thing she wanted to do was disturb the idyllic quality of their moments together with unsolvable issues.

Sighing, she plugged her phone in and did the same for Nora's.

"Can we leave them on mute until we get to the highway? Like when we're on the way to Phoenix?"

"Okay, sure." Nora looked at her. "Are you all right?"

"Yeah. I just...I wish—" Fallon stopped herself, looking at Nora in shock. "I mean..."

"It's okay. You didn't finish your wish." Nora took her hand. "But whatever it is, we'll do our best to make it happen."

The drive to Sedona had exciting curves, along with picturesque geology, but as they approached the town, Fallon couldn't look around fast enough. Nora said, "We could spend an extra hour here if you'd like. There's a self-guided tour—"

"Yes," Fallon said. "Please. This place is amazing."

They found a deli and bought sandwiches and drinks. The tour of town was enjoyable, though there were people everywhere. Once the formations came into view, Fallon was enchanted. "I've never seen anything like this."

It took nearly two hours because Fallon kept asking to slow down, and twice they pulled over so she could get out of the car and stare. "The air here feels different."

"The locals say there are vortexes here. Like, energy sources, I think."

"Wow. I'd like to come back sometime and learn more about that."

Nora nodded. "We'd better keep moving for now. I want to get to Tucson before dark if possible." Fallon tried not to pout. "We'll be getting into the Sonoran Desert, where you'll see the saguaro cactuses. They're the tall ones with arms."

The energy of Sedona seemed to drain away as they turned onto Highway 17. The traffic was heavy, and Fallon noticed a car ahead that was weaving erratically. "Is that person drunk?" she asked.

"Probably just on their phone. Oh, speaking of which, do you want to check yours? I should do the same."

"I guess so."

Nora put in earbuds before reaching for her cell. "Let's count. The person with the most voice mails buys dinner."

Fallon grinned. "And the person with the most texts gets to choose where."

"Deal."

Nora's seventeen voice mails came in first, but Fallon prevailed with eleven texts. "So we both win," she said.

Half an hour later, Fallon put her phone down, the last three texts leaving her stunned. She turned to Nora, noticing her mouth was in a tight line, a frown creasing her brow. "Is everything okay?"

Nora shook her head. "If you don't mind, I'd like to drive on in to Tucson. If I hurry, we can get through Phoenix before rush hour. Something weird is going on at work, and I need to spend some time on my computer."

"Sure."

Nora gave her a wry smile as she turned on the radio. "Thanks. I'll at least take you the more scenic route."

Fallon tried not to worry. They'd been living in a glorious little bubble, just the two of them. This was just a little bump as they readjusted to real life, right? She didn't comment on the multiple highway overpasses and ramps or ask about the rugged formations that seemed to rise out of the desert floor in places. Phoenix seemed to go on forever, but then she saw a sign indicating they were in a different city. When they got to open country at last, she breathed a little easier. There was still a lot of traffic and signs, but at least they weren't closed in by buildings everywhere. The saguaro cactuses began to reappear, and she would have asked to take a picture with one, but Nora probably had a hundred such photos. Plus, she was obviously in a hurry.

Finally, Nora announced, "About thirty more minutes, but we need gas."

"Good. I need to stretch. Guess there aren't any friendly trees around here."

Nora smiled at their old code for using the bathroom. "No, but we do have flush toilets."

When they got back in the car, Fallon asked, "Did you ever call Tyler and tell him we were coming?"

"I just texted him, but he hasn't answered yet. He's probably got his eye glued to a microscope or is out collecting pollen samples or something."

They drove on. Tucson seemed to get a little greener and have more variety of vegetation. After exiting the highway, they went through a downtown area and out to a suburb. "How many people live here?" Fallon asked. The traffic seemed intense.

"Over a million in the metro area, I think," Nora said. Fallon tried not to flinch. Finally, they pulled into a parking lot. "Here we are," Nora announced.

"Great," Fallon said, trying to sound enthusiastic. Was Nora really happy living in this crowded concrete jungle? They stood outside number eleven while Nora fumbled with her key. The temperature seemed high for early November, but Fallon didn't ask if it was typical.

When Nora finally got the door open, they walked into a small entry hall, greeted by the smell of food cooking in the air-conditioned atmosphere. "Tyler must be in the kitchen," Nora said, her voice rising like a question.

Fallon took a second to scan her surroundings. Nora's place was very nice, with a newish scent to it. The furniture matched, and colorful accent pillows and art gave the room a cozy feeling. Following Nora around the corner, she discovered Caden standing over the stove holding a spatula. It was hard to tell who was most surprised. After a few seconds, Fallon found her voice. "Caden."

"Falcon."

"Where's Tyler?" Nora demanded.

"Uh, taking a shower, I believe." Color rose on Caden's face.

Nora stood motionless for a few seconds before calling "Wait here" over her shoulder as she moved through a door opposite the kitchen. A few seconds later, muffled conversation could be heard.

"Did you have a nice trip?" Cade asked.

"Very nice, thank you." Fallon shuffled her feet. "How long have you, uh, been here?"

"The crew finished last Sunday, as you know, so, yeah. Since then."

"Everything go all right?"

"Oh yeah. Maris did great." Cade brightened, probably having thought of something else to say. "How's your shoulder and everything?"

"Good. Almost at a hundred percent, I'd say."

"That's great."

Nora returned, mumbling something about "all I need." Motioning to Fallon, she said, "In here," and walked toward the other side of the room.

"Later, Cade." Fallon grinned.

"Later, Falcon."

Nora was halfway into her next sentence before Fallon could close the door. "...doing who knows what for how long. I don't need a stranger in my house while I'm trying to figure out this shit at work."

"What shit? Instead of being all in your head, why don't you tell me about it?" Nora looked like she might explode, but Fallon risked moving closer and taking her hand. "I may not have an answer, but sometimes talking it out helps."

Nora took a breath, then another. "In some ways, it's a lot like your situation," she began, before explaining about her new boss and his message. "His voice mail said it was imperative that I come in as soon as possible. There's something about a buyout, but as usual, he was pretty vague about specifics."

"Well, if he didn't want to go into details over the phone, how about talking to someone else on the staff to see what they think?"

Nora shook her head, looking away. "I don't usually talk to people in the office about business."

Fallon heard what she wasn't saying. Nora didn't actually have friends at work. "Maybe you should start," she suggested gently, pulling Nora over to sit beside her on the bed.

Nora blinked. "Okay, yeah, there might be a couple of people." She looked at her phone for a second before putting it back down. "In the meantime, what am I going to do about that?" She stood again, gesturing in the direction of the other room.

"What?" Fallon asked, knowing but curious to hear what Nora would say.

"The fact that my little brother seems to be shacking up with some stranger."

"Caden isn't someone off the street. They met at the Kamberto fire, remember?" Nora started to protest, but Fallon said, "And remind me, how old is Tyler?"

"Twenty-five," Nora muttered, sitting beside her again.

"What did he say when you went in there?"

"Basically, he told me to mind my own business."

"Sounds like good advice."

"You're supposed to be on my side," Nora objected.

Fallon kissed her cheek. "You know I am. Completely and totally. Now, make your calls, and I'll go see if I can help with dinner."

Nora huffed but picked up her phone.

Fallon returned to the kitchen to find Cade holding a spoonful of sauce to Tyler's lips. Blushing slightly, Tyler asked, "Can you take charge of the garlic bread, Fallon?"

By the time Nora came out of her room, Tyler was setting the table and Cade was draining spaghetti, having placed the aromatic sauce in a serving bowl. Fallon handed her a glass of red wine, and Nora sighed, then took a deep swallow.

"Caden, it's nice to see you again. Please accept my apology for being so rude when I first came in."

"No worries," Cade said.

"Aren't you going to apologize to me?" Tyler crossed his arms.

"Hell, no." Nora poked him. "Answer your texts next time, you brat."

"The way you did on your trip?" he retorted.

Nora colored as Fallon said, "All right, you two. No fussing at the table."

As they ate, Nora reported on what she'd learned from her phone calls. "No one else knows anything about a buyout. At least, not that they'll tell me." She sighed. "Maybe Abel's trying to find a way to get rid of me."

"Why would he do that?" Tyler asked. "You're their senior staff photographer and the only one who can make the crappy stuff they use from people's cell photos look halfway decent."

Nora shrugged. "I guess I'll find out when I go into the office tomorrow."

After dinner, Fallon volunteered herself for KP. Nora helped, stopping to look at her with a worried expression after watching Cade follow Tyler into his room. "I just don't want him to get hurt."

"I know," Fallon said, holding her close for a moment. "But if he does, he'll have you to help him through it."

Finishing up in the kitchen, they went back to Nora's room. Nora yawned as they settled into bed. "You never told me about your text messages."

Fallon's stomach tightened. Nora was tired and distracted. This wasn't the time to talk about what would come next for them. "Yeah, I need to contact Maris. I'll know more after that."

It felt like she'd just closed her eyes when an insistent buzzing started up on Nora's side of the bed. Nora cursed and picked up her phone. "What?" She listened for a few seconds before throwing back the covers. "I'm on it."

Fallon sat up, but Nora was already in the bathroom. A few moments later, the door opened, and a crack of light illuminated Nora, fully dressed. "What's going on?" Fallon asked.

"I've been called to cover an explosion and fire at an old fertilizer plant about fifty miles from here. I'll probably be gone most of the day." Nora was checking the contents of her gear bag.

"That sounds dangerous. I'll go with you," Fallon said, swinging her legs off the bed.

"No, it'll be fine. This is my job. Besides, it will probably be under control by the time I get there." She came around and gave Fallon a quick kiss. "Go back to sleep. Since it's Saturday, ask Tyler and Cade to show you the town. I'll call when I can." She was out the door before Fallon could answer.

Tyler didn't seem the least bit surprised that Nora was gone, and he and Cade did their best to show Fallon some of what Tucson had to offer. They took her out for breakfast burritos before a visit to the Cochran Gem and Mineral Museum. Following pizza for lunch was a trip to the University of Arizona's Science Center and Planetarium. Fallon appreciated the effort, though she would rather have gone somewhere with actual rock formations or waited until dark to look at the Tucson sky. But mostly, she was concerned about not having heard from Nora. When Tyler saw her rechecking her phone after the laser show, he said, "Don't worry. There probably isn't coverage out there in Nowhere, Arizona. Or she's obsessing over angles and lighting and framing the action just so. You know how she is."

Fallon did know. In fact, she recalled very clearly what it had been like when Nora had become consumed with her video project during their first Firecamp days, and how Fallon had been left to wait and agonize over the loss of what little time they'd had left. *It's not like that. She's just taken a lot of time off tending to you and touring you around. There was an emergency. Give this a chance.* Fallon took a breath. "Yeah. Okay."

"If you've had enough stimulation for one day, we can hit a happy hour." Cade nudged Tyler. "Let's take her to ABC's."

It was dark when Fallon stepped onto the bar's outdoor patio between acts of the drag show. The air was still warm, but she appreciated a break from the stuffy air-conditioning inside. The bar was fun, with both male and female clientele, and she'd enjoyed two zero proof pineapple margaritas. It had been amusing to watch Tyler and Cade on the dance floor, but as she'd feared, the noise level was such that she'd missed a call from Nora. After she listened to a garbled voice mail, the gist of which was that Nora wouldn't be home that night, Fallon went back in to tell Tyler she'd take an Uber back to the town house. She wanted to see if a story about the fire was on the evening news. He made a half-hearted offer to drive her, but she assured him she'd be fine. As she attempted to book the ride, she realized she didn't even know Nora's address. She gritted her teeth with apprehension. Not knowing where she was or where she was going reminded her of times when she and her mother had been on the move. She'd always tried not to sleep in the car because not being able to find any familiar landmarks upon awakening was too unsettling. Could she find a North Star life in Tucson?

The fire didn't seem to be a big story as there was only a brief mention on one news channel: "No injuries but the NEZ Plant is still burning," was the essence of it. Fallon perused the bookshelf in Nora's bedroom in search of something to read, but Nora's books seemed to be all nonfiction, topics like photography or Arizona or journalism. She was about to give up when a familiar cover on the bottom shelf caught her eye. *Seafire.*

Fallon was touched. Nora had returned her copy, so she must have bought this one at another time. Reading the first page was like getting into a great conversation with an old friend, and Fallon settled in bed, waking the next morning with the light still on and the book on the floor. Tyler and Cade were obviously sleeping in, and Nora hadn't called. Fallon attempted to make coffee, but instead of filling the pot, the mechanism spewed brownish water and grounds on the floor. After using almost a whole roll of paper towels to clean up the mess, she tried to find a coffee shop in the neighborhood on her phone, but the nearest one was six miles away, and she wasn't confident about driving in Tucson traffic, even on a Sunday.

She opened the door, thinking she would walk, but the sun was intense and no detectable scents of vegetation carried on the air, only the sounds of the city. Put off by the difference, the strangeness, she tried Nora's coffee maker again, watching carefully and nudging the glass carafe every few seconds to remind the device of its intended target. She was enjoying her second cup when Tyler made his way into the kitchen.

Seeing the half-full pot, he turned to her. "I'm super impressed. You've conquered Decker the Dripper?"

Fallon waved a hand. "Oh, nothing to it. Where do you keep your paper towels, by the way?"

Tyler eyed the depleted roll, and they both started laughing. Cade's voice could be heard, asking what was so damn funny at this hour, which made them laugh harder.

After breakfast, they offered to take her to the botanical gardens, but Fallon declined, saying she wanted to wait for Nora. She went back to *Seafire*, finishing it just after two o'clock. The town house was quiet. Tyler and Cade had gone to the grocery store, so Fallon sat, thinking. She grabbed up the phone when it rang, hoping it was Nora, but Maris's name showed on the screen. Fallon had deliberately put off having this conversation, but once it started, they talked for almost half an hour. After they hung up, Fallon paced. Wandering into the third bedroom, which served as Nora's office, she found a legal pad on the desk and started writing.

> *My dearest Nora,*
>
> *I'll never be able to tell you what these past weeks have meant to me. After our last parting, I didn't think I'd ever want to see you again, but I've been proven very wrong. Being with you this time and watching you form new bonds with your family, even while caring for me, has given me an even deeper appreciation for the incredible woman you are.*
>
> *I admire your passion for photography, which I can see is both your work and your art. You told me once that it lights you up inside, and having seen you relishing your craft, I can confirm that light still shines as brightly as ever. No one should stand in the way of that for you, no one should ever cast a shadow over that light, least of all me, who loves to see that spark in your eyes.*
>
> *Did you ever wonder why I asked you if there was a*

bridge over the Grand Canyon? You must have thought it a ridiculous question, but the saddest thing about that incredible gorge is that it reminds me of the insurmountable gap between who each of us is and what we each want from the world. During this time with you, I've so wanted to find that bridge, to find a way for us to stay together, separate though our goals are. But in the same way, I knew from the very beginning that you were someone special, I also know that I cannot live in Tucson. As clearly as I can appreciate the fine life you have made for yourself here, I'm completely conscious that I have no city in me, and I'm not suited for the desert. I need the forest and the stars. I need the way the air feels before it snows and the joy of the first wildflowers of spring. This is no one's fault and no one's flaw; it simply is.

I didn't get a chance to tell you that I've gotten messages regarding a new start for me at Firecamp. Please believe that I wasn't lying when I told you I didn't miss it. At the time, I was only seeing you, seeing a hint of us, but like a siren's call, the significance of that place persists for me, even beyond the extraordinary moments we've shared.

Please know that no one will ever take your place in my heart.

She hadn't really unpacked. It would be easy to throw her stuff in the truck and go. She could spare them any anger or resentment about their choices or the unnecessary anguish of another confrontation. She was about to sign her name when her phone buzzed. She thought Maris might be calling her back with some other news, but it was Nora.

"Hey, baby." Nora's voice was raspy, and it was hard to hear her over the sound of the highway. "Where are you?"

"I'm at your town house," Fallon said. "Where are you?"

"About forty minutes away. Since my air-conditioning barely works, let's take your truck tonight."

"Where are we going?" Fallon asked, feeling like she'd missed part of the conversation already.

"I'm taking you out to a great local restaurant so we can celebrate."

Fallon had hoped they might stay home and have some time to talk. Alone. But Nora sounded almost high. "What are we celebrating?"

"That I get to come home to you, of course. I've got to stop by the paper, but I'll see you soon, okay?"

They'd never talked on the phone, Fallon realized. Maybe Nora's mobile conversations were always like this. "Okay. Be careful."

The line went dead. Fallon looked back at what she'd written. She wanted to be better than the person who'd run from Nora's anger and disappointment like at their first Firecamp. Nora wanted to celebrate coming home to her. She'd never had anyone say that before. Fallon should be there for her, at least this once. She looked around the town house again, acknowledging that this was Nora's home. Maybe she hadn't given the area enough of a chance. She got on her phone, looking up the highest elevation in the Santa Catalina Mountains. It didn't take long for her to see what she needed to see. She crumpled the letter and threw it in the trash.

Nora came through the door two hours later, declaring that she needed to shower before anything else. "Almost anything," she amended, kissing Fallon on the top of her head before disappearing into the bathroom.

When they arrived at the fanciest restaurant Fallon had ever seen, a black-suited host showed them to a corner table. The waiter seemed to know Nora, and they chatted about the dinner specials for a few moments. Fallon tried not to show her shock at the prices on the menu, and when Nora asked if she could order for both of them, she barely managed a nod. Everything seemed to be happening at high speed. A bottle of wine appeared and was opened. Nora tasted it and approved. Fallon's glass was filled, and two small plates with rice and something fishy on it were placed before them.

Nora lifted her glass. "I want to propose a toast. To our new start, here in Tucson." Fallon stiffened. Nora had used the same phrase Fallon had written in her note about the job offer at Firecamp. Obviously, Nora misread her hesitation as she touched her glass to Fallon's before taking a drink. "This is a thousand times better than that box wine we had at the Grand Canyon. Please just try it."

Fallon took a small sip. She honestly couldn't tell the difference. And as much as she didn't like Nora saying anything disparaging about their time at the canyon, what really concerned her was the implication of Nora's toast. "Tucson really is home for you now, isn't it?"

Nora seemed puzzled. "Well, my work is here, my town house is here, my brother is here, and now you're here, so yeah. As much as any place, Tucson is home." She took another drink. "Didn't you get to see some of the city yesterday?"

"I did, but—"

Nora pointed at her plate. "Try the nigiri. I'll order something else if you don't like it."

Not at these prices, Fallon thought, but she tried a small taste. The fish melted in her mouth, and the rice made a nice contrast of texture. "This is good. Different."

"Excellent." Nora was obviously pleased. The meal progressed, and Nora filled her in on the fire and her experiments with video. "Photography will always be my first love, but video is what makes the networks and the internet happiest. It's more fun than I remembered, but I'm still learning."

"It's good that you're continuing to grow in your career," Fallon said, trying to find a segue into what she needed to say. She hadn't planned on having this conversation in the restaurant, but Nora was finishing her second glass of wine and Fallon could see how the evening would go if she didn't speak up now. "I got a chance to talk to Maris earlier today, and I'm going to do the same."

Nora was temporarily distracted by the decadent desserts that had just appeared at their places. She thanked the waiter and turned back to Fallon. "I'm sorry. What were you saying?"

Fallon leaned across the table and took Nora's hand. "You've made the life you wanted here. You have your job and your brother and a place you love. Maris told me the replacement ranger has arrived at Firecamp, and I have a new offer of a job."

Nora pulled her hand away. "And you're going to take it? Without even giving us a chance here?"

Apprehension made Fallon's voice tight. "This isn't the place for me, Nora. And I have to do what I'm good at in the same way that you do."

"There's some forest land nearby."

"I looked it up. It's over an hour away, and it's mostly groomed, recreational-use land. I want to work in the national forest, doing mitigation. That's what matters to me."

Nora signaled for the check and asked for the desserts to be boxed. "Someone should enjoy this. I'm sure Tyler and Cade will."

"I'm sorry if I ruined dinner, but we haven't had a chance to really talk since we got here, and I needed to tell you…"

Nora drained her wine and stood. "It's fine. Let's go."

The ride home was deadly quiet. When Nora opened the door at the town house, Tyler and Cade jumped apart from their embrace on the couch. Nora tossed the boxed sweets on the counter, muttered something under her breath, and went into her bedroom, slamming the door.

"I take it dinner didn't go well?" Tyler asked.

"Dinner was fine, but I got a job offer back at Firecamp."

"Ah," Tyler said. "Then you're leaving?"

Fallon nodded, her throat closing up.

Cade grinned. "That's great, Falcon. Maybe I'll re-up too."

Tyler wasn't smiling. "Are you going now?"

Fallon was wearing the nicest outfit she owned but looking at the closed bedroom door, she sighed. "Maybe I'd better."

The door opened, and Nora came out wearing shorts and a T-shirt and holding Fallon's duffel bag. Tyler pulled Cade into his room and shut the door.

"It's late," Nora said, her tone flat. "You don't know the area. Sleep in the guest room and wait till it's light."

Fallon took a step toward her. "Nora, I'm sorry. I was hoping we could learn from our past mistakes and at least part with good memories this time."

"So leaving was always part of the plan?"

"No. No, not at all. It's just…we never talked about it. About what it would take to make it work. Or if we could at least try to keep up our friendship this time."

Nora stared at her, clearly ambivalent. Fallon thought she saw tears gathering in her eyes. "I want to tell you not to go, but there's no point in asking you to stay if you're going to be miserable."

Fallon took another step closer. "I've never been happier than during this time we've spent together." Her voice started to quiver. "The thing that makes me miserable is that I can't be where I need to be and be with you at the same time."

The tears spilled down Nora's cheeks. "At least I can hug you good-bye now."

"Nora—" The word caught in her throat, and she held out her arms. Nora moved against her, and they held each other, silent tears joining where their faces met.

CHAPTER TWENTY-TWO

When Nora had stopped by the office to upload her photos and videos from the NEZ Plant fire, it wasn't a surprise that half the cubicles were empty. It was mid-afternoon on Sunday, after all. But seeing very similar conditions at noon on Monday made her worry. Was the *Star* really in trouble? Was that the reason for the buyout her boss had mentioned?

She made a quick circuit of the news area but couldn't find either of the people she'd spoken to on the phone. There was something waiting for her, though. Resting against the old-school push-button phone that still resided on her desk—a different kind of holdout from Collin Becker's era—was a plain folder with her name on the outside. Inside was a boilerplate contract, giving the *Arizona Star*, and its parent company Gee Enterprises, full and complete rights to her photographs, past, present, and future.

Why in the world would they think she would sign such a thing? The insult to her intelligence was almost as galling as the fact that she hadn't seen any such paperwork on anyone else's desk, and some of them had also been hired when Collin had been in charge. But maybe they'd already signed theirs, and she was the sole holdout? She'd been gone for several weeks, after all.

Tucking the folder under her arm, she made her way to Abel's office. His secretary, Mrs. Draden, a pinch-faced woman in her late fifties secretly referred to as Mrs. Dragon by those Nora knew, held out her hand as Nora approached.

"Did you want to leave that with me, Miss Palmer?"

"Not just yet." Nora tried a friendly smile. "I need to speak with Abel about this before I sign."

Mrs. Draden frowned. "He's not available right now."

"I'll be at my desk for at least an hour, unless something comes up," Nora said. "Could you possibly buzz me when he has a moment?"

"I'm not sure when that will be. I'll do what I can for you." Her tone left no doubt that such a thing was highly unlikely.

Nora threw herself into her desk chair and brooded. Staring out the window, she thought of Fallon, who was probably halfway to Colorado by now. They'd ended up holding each other all night, without much conversation other than an agreement that Fallon would let her know when she arrived. No other promises were made. What would be the point? Giving each other false hopes would only cause more pain, and there was plenty of that already.

Forcing herself back to the here and now, Nora began sorting through some sticky notes that had long occupied the lower left corner of her monitor. They contained everything from aged grocery lists to phone numbers with no names attached to times and dates of meetings that she'd already attended or missed. As she moved to toss the bulk of them in the trash, her eye caught a blinking red light on the old landline. She couldn't remember the last time that phone had been used. Collin had resisted an automated voice mail system, saying that the paper was personal, and people who called needed to hear a human voice. Abel had no such constraints and had gone to the "more efficient approach" less than a week after he'd taken over. Could someone have forgotten to disable the old system?

Luckily, she wouldn't need a sticky note to remind her of the retrieval code she'd set up. It was 0505, Tyler's birthday. Picking up the receiver, she called into the system, pushing in the numbers and listening in astonishment as a message played.

"Hi, Ms. Palmer, this is Eric Abney with Strobe Publishing. We're putting together a coffee table book of the Southwest, and several of your photos have caught the eye of our senior editor. Could you please give us a call back at your earliest convenience? Thanks."

Another voice mail from the same individual had similar wording. Nora jotted down the number he gave and was about to hang up when a third message played.

"Hello again, Ms. Palmer. Since we weren't able to reach you, we took the liberty of contacting your boss, Mr. Griffin. He explained about your family leave and has promised to let you know of our interest as soon as you return. But just in case, here's our number again. Oh, and I should add that the *Arizona Highways* magazine is also published by Strobe, and we'd welcome other submissions from you for that audience."

Nora replaced the receiver carefully, staring at the little black brick of a phone with its rows of gray buttons. The blinking red light had gone off. "Holy shit," she murmured. Of course Abel wanted the rights to her photographs. If she signed that contract, the advance and the royalties from these projects would go to the *Star*, or more accurately, to Gee Enterprises, and the extra income would make Abel Griffin look like a freaking financial genius. His story about a buyout was probably pure BS. Nora grabbed the folder and headed for the parking garage, not bothering to tell Mrs. Dragon that something had indeed come up.

In the car, she called Tyler's cell. He rarely picked up when he was at work but always checked in and returned calls. "Honey, I know you've just gotten back to work, but could you please come home as soon as possible? I really need to talk to you."

True to form, Tyler returned her call just as she pulled up at the town house. "What's up?"

"Remember that weird message from my boss about the contract? You won't believe what's going on at work. Can you come home soon?"

"Probably not for a couple of hours. Things are kinda backed up here." Her tone must have worried him. "Are you all right?"

"Yes and no. But it'll keep until you get here." Opening the door, she found Cade playing a video game.

"Oh hey. I didn't know you'd be home this early, or I would have started dinner."

Cade sounded genuinely contrite, and Nora reminded herself that her brother found this person worthy of his time, so there must be something there. "I don't really have a regular schedule. But something happened at work and I..."

Nora heard herself trail off. She closed her eyes as the room seemed to tilt. She felt Cade's hand on her arm. "Come sit down. And put your head between your knees. You'll be fine in just a minute. Okay?"

She sat as Cade had directed. A minute later, a cold glass of water was pressed into her hand. "Just take a sip," Cade said. Nora did. "Breathe." She did.

"Wow," she said after another minute. "Thanks. I guess I'm more stressed out than I realized."

"What happened?" Cade asked, looking anxiously at her for a moment before focusing on the ground. "I mean, you don't have to tell me if you don't want to—"

"No, it's okay. Fallon told me I was too much in my head sometimes." That was who she really wanted to talk to. Fallon would've held her hand and rescued her from this weird place. Fallon would've made it all better with just a smile and a hug. She forced down a sob. *Just tell Cade*, she told herself. *Pretend it's her.*

She shared everything, from the ridiculous contract to her boss being "unavailable"—she made air quotes on that, matching Mrs. Dragon's expression, making Cade laugh—to the incredible news from the voice mails on Collin's outdated system. "Collin was such a wonderful man. And now it's almost like he's left me this one last gift." Cade made a sympathetic sound. Nora had another thought. "I'm going to tell Mr. Abney about my Firecamp photos. Then and now. They'd make a great story. Maybe he could pitch that to his editor."

"I think you should check with Fallon about that first," Cade said, sounding emphatic. "She's got the reputation of being seriously shy about publicity."

Nora caught herself before she could protest. Cade was right. She needed to be sure Fallon felt protected this time. Besides, it would give her an excuse—

"So what are you going to do if this jerkwad boss threatens to fire you if you don't sign the new contract?" Cade asked.

Nora frowned, rolling her lips tightly. "I guess I'll have to get a lawyer. I'm certainly not going to take this lying down."

"You could always quit," Cade suggested. Nora's mouth opened slightly, and she gave Cade an incredulous look. "What?" Cade asked. "You'll make money off the photo book and the magazine pictures, right? But you've probably got enough stashed away to get you back to Colorado, where you can work on your Firecamp book too. Then, we can all live happily ever after instead of having to watch you mope around here like someone died."

Nora blinked. Could it possibly be that easy? She stood. "Please excuse me for a moment, Cade. I have a couple of calls to make."

At her desk, she adjusted the legal pad, preparing to make notes on the call with Mr. Abney. Faint imprints of script caught her eye on the blank page, but she couldn't remember the last time she'd been in there. Curious if Tyler or Cade had used the room, she glanced at the trash can, pulling out a single sheet of crumpled paper. The only thing Fallon had ever written to her before had been the word "OK," when she'd agreed that they might try again, but the earnestness and eloquence of this discarded letter took her three Kleenexes to get through. *No one will ever take your place in my heart.* Did that mean Fallon loved her? Was that what she wanted?

After taking another fifteen minutes to get herself together, she had a lovely conversation with Mr. Abney. She hadn't been this excited about a project since…since the disastrous Firecamp video. But she knew so much more now about what was really important. She caught herself holding her breath as she tried to reach Fallon, but the call had gone straight to voice mail, so she was either out of range or had turned off her phone. It could be either, but neither mattered anymore.

An hour later, Nora had changed into her most comfortable jeans and sweatshirt and was almost through packing. She had a wheeled duffel for most of her clothes and a small overnight bag to take into the hotel on the way. The Colorado mountains would be getting colder, but she knew Fallon would loan her whatever she needed. After all, if she'd give Nora her heart, she would surely part with some thermal underwear. Nora laughed out loud.

As she passed through the living room, she stopped to wrap her arms around Cade. "Thank you. You're a good listener. But take care of my little brother, or you won't like what you hear from me." She stepped back. "Ask Tyler to call me when he gets in. Tell him I'm going to need a few minutes." Cade nodded solemnly, and Nora suspected Tyler's new friend would be taking stock after she closed the front door. She could imagine the internal assessment: *Tyler is a great guy, but his sister is something else. Falcon is going to have her hands full with that one, but if anyone can handle it…*

When Tyler called, she caught him up on everything, and they talked until she got into New Mexico. In those four hours, he was able to convince her that the printout of the resignation email she'd left on the kitchen table was a much better alternative to killing her boss, though he saw the appeal of the latter. She'd brought Fallon's note and read it to him twice—she'd pretty much memorized it by then— admitting that Fallon had said almost all of that to her at dinner, though not quite so movingly. Tyler was convinced that Fallon was saying that she loved her.

"Do you really think so?" Nora asked. "I haven't been able to reach her. Do you think she'll be glad to see me?"

"Wait," he said. She could hear him taking a drink of something. "Have you not told each other 'I love you'?"

Nora sighed, recalling that first night at the canyon. She'd thought that Fallon might have said it. And if she'd been sure, would she have said it back? The tears were starting again, so she decided to be defensive. "No. Why should we?"

"Because you fucking do," he said calmly. "Love each other. It's completely obvious to anyone who spends ten minutes around you. And once you've said those magic words, a lot of other stupid things get out of the way."

"Oh yeah, like what?"

"Like, where should we live, and what should I do about my career, and do we want kids or dogs or cats or all of the above?" Tyler sniffed. "Because once you say 'I love you,' you're promising someone else that they get first place. First in your thoughts, first in your heart, and first in your actions. But they're promising you the same thing, which makes it all work out."

Nora managed a laugh. "That sounds good, but how can something so simple iron out all the other complications?"

"It just does. You'll have to trust me."

"How would you know this? You've never been in love."

"I think I was once."

"What? When was this? And why am I just now hearing of it?"

"Junior year in college, just before the pandemic got really bad. A guy in one of my classes. Smart, funny, handsome, and for some reason, actually into me."

"Tyler! What's his name? And where is he now? What happened?"

"Robin was his name." His voice caught. "He died of COVID. Right before I moved in with you."

"Oh God, sweetie. I'm so sorry. Why didn't you tell me?"

He sighed. "I was afraid you wouldn't want me as your roommate if all you saw was your weepy little brother. Besides, you were working pretty much twenty-four seven, and what good would it have done?"

"Have I not told you how glad I was when you moved in? I'm sorry if you didn't know that. Weepy or not, I've loved living with you."

She thought he said "Thanks," but his voice cracked, so she didn't say anything else for a while. "What about Cade?" she asked finally. "Could this be love yet again?"

"I don't know. Should I follow your model and wait ten years to find out?"

She blew a raspberry at him. "You really think Fallon loves me?" she asked when he stopped laughing.

"I really do."

"Then I need a plan."

He yawned. "Where are you? Can we talk about the plan tomorrow?"

She told him she was an hour from Albuquerque, where she planned to stop for the night. He yawned again, telling her to listen to NPR or put on a podcast and call him when she got on the road in the morning.

❖

"Nora? Hi. I thought that was you. What are you doing here?" Maris's tone was friendly, but her expression was worried. And rightly so. Nora was hungry and road weary and in no mood to waste time with Fallon's little minion.

She barely turned, continuing her march across the Firecamp grounds. "Where is she, Maris?"

"Where is who?" Maris was hurrying to match her stride.

Oh no. She wasn't playing stupid questions today. "The Easter Bunny," she snapped, almost laughing when Maris stopped walking. With the last bit of her patience, she said, "Fallon, Maris. Where is Fallon Monroe?" Maris started to take a breath, but Nora cut her off. "And don't tell me she's in a meeting or unavailable or some other shit. Just tell me where she is. Now. Please." She added that last word because Maris looked like she was about to cry.

"But she actually is in a meeting." Nora fixed her with her most threatening expression. It worked. "In the ranger's office. With the new ranger." Maris began to babble. "They're not supposed to be disturbed."

Under other circumstances, Nora might have respected those instructions. But her seismic decision regarding her professional life had freed her. And after reading the most beautiful note ever written and driving eleven and a half hours to find out if she was right about the most important thing in her life, she had no such concerns.

"Thank you," she said as sweetly as she could manage, resuming her progress toward the building in question. Maris was trailing her, so just before she mounted the steps, she added, "And don't let me catch you or anyone else with your ear outside that window, or it will be the last thing you do, understand?"

Maris nodded and hurried in the direction of the barracks without another word.

Walking down the hall, Nora heard a woman's voice—not

Fallon's—blabbing on about expectations and responsibilities. She listened for half a minute before shaking her head. That woman could put an entire colony of ants to sleep. Stopping against the wall outside the open door of the familiar ranger's office, she was almost overcome by the memory of Fallon standing there with her, taking it upon herself to totally save Nora's life. Not literally, perhaps, but to give her a shot at the life she'd always wanted. The life she'd thought she wanted. Actually, she still wanted some version of that life. But she wanted it with Fallon.

The speaker cut off in mid-sentence, and Nora realized she'd been hearing a recording. "See?" a different voice asked, and she heard Fallon answer, "Pretty bad, all right."

As ready as she was to see Fallon right that second, something made Nora hesitate. "So we need something more like the video that your group uses for recruitment," the not-Fallon voice continued. "You know the one?"

"I know what you're talking about, yes," Fallon said.

"We need to convey the same level of excitement with the fast-paced information. Like in that video's middle section where the music changes."

Fallon said something that Nora couldn't quite make out. Apparently, the ranger didn't hear it either. "Excuse me?" she asked.

Fallon's voice was a little stronger, obviously repeating herself. "I haven't seen it."

What? That did it. Nora stepped into the room, fists on her hips. "What did you just say?"

Fallon jumped to her feet, her eyes wide. "Nora!"

"What do you mean, you haven't seen my video?"

"Miss," the ranger said. "We're in a meeting here."

"I'm sorry, ma'am." Fallon shot a quick glance at the new ranger before focusing on Nora again, as if worried she might disappear. "I know this is a bit unorthodox, but could we have the room for a few minutes? Please?"

The ranger seemed skeptical. After a few seconds of looking between them, she picked up her hat. "I'll be back in five," she said, softly closing the door on her way out.

Nora waited until they were alone. "Now tell me why you haven't watched my video."

"I couldn't," Fallon said, still staring at Nora. "Everyone said it was wonderful. They still say that. But I…" She shrugged.

"Uh-huh," Nora said. "I see. No, wait, I don't. But maybe you can explain it to me later. First, there's something I want to give you." She pushed Fallon back into the chair, straddled her lap and kissed her. Not as long or deeply as she wanted to, but not softly, either.

When she pulled back, Fallon sat frozen, her mouth still slightly open. "Wow," she said after a few seconds. "That's about the nicest gift I've ever gotten." She leaned in, obviously ready for another kiss.

"No." Nora pressed her hand to Fallon's chest. "I'm not finished. The second most angriest I've ever been with you was when I called you a big chickenshit ten years ago in this very room. I said it to hurt you. But maybe I was right. Maybe you are a big chickenshit. Because maybe you didn't run from me this time, but you didn't fight for me either. So I'm warning you, this could be your last chance." Fallon said nothing, but Nora could see her lip was trembling. "Okay, or maybe your next-to-last chance."

Fallon looked wary. "What's the angriest you've ever been?"

"About one minute ago when I heard you say you hadn't seen my video. Why not, Fallon?"

"Because I am a big chickenshit." As Nora shook her head, Fallon added, "Because I'm in love with you. And the way I could keep that safe inside me was to pretend you loved me too, even if only a little. But if I watched that video and I saw something different, I just…I wouldn't be able to stand it."

Nora didn't want to admit that she could see Fallon's rationale, knowing the way her harsh words during their parting quarrel had lingered in her own thoughts. Her face must have softened because Fallon covered her hand with her own.

"Besides," Fallon added, "I have a wonderful video that plays on demand in my head. It features you and me sleeping close in my big tent and you dropping that towel and us in Silver Bird and a hundred other mental pictures of our time together. Of course, I was planning on splicing in some new scenes from the Grand Canyon." There was that smile, damn it. "It's very good to see you," she said softly.

"I'm glad you think so." Nora was pretty sure she should hold out a little longer. "Because I could be mad at you for a while."

Fallon slipped her arms around Nora's waist and pulled her in closer. "Why are you really here? You could be mad at me in Tucson."

Here it was. That exact moment where she could capture the whole picture perfectly. The emotion was certainly there. And like all great shots, timing was the key. "Because I love you."

Fallon looked more surprised than when Nora had first appeared in the room. "You do?"

Nora was amazed at how marvelously buoyant she felt. Saying those words had been much easier than she'd anticipated. She nodded. "I do."

"Can you love me here, in this place?"

"I always have, so I might as well keep on."

They were still holding each other when the door opened again. Nora had the advantage of facing the ranger, who stood staring at them. After a few seconds, the ranger asked, "Excuse me, but who are you?"

"I'm your new videographer," Nora said.

EPILOGUE

Nora knew the party wouldn't be a surprise. Maris couldn't keep her mouth shut on a bet. But she had her camera ready for their private celebration, which would come first. She'd planned this special gift for weeks, and no one, not Mae or Hal or even Ranger Upshaw, who were all coming back to celebrate Fallon's promotion-birthday, knew about it.

Fallon came into the cabin they'd been sharing for the last nine months. Nora loved it that Fallon's face still lit up when they saw each other, and she willingly admitted that hers did too. Tyler hadn't been too sad when she'd moved out, and Caden had helped her pack. No shocker there. But right now, it was all she could do to hold on to the carefully packaged surprise that filled her arms. "Here," she said, setting it on the floor. "Open it. Quickly."

"What is…it's…is it moving?" Fallon looked up at her. The box was indeed beginning to wiggle.

"Hurry up," Nora ordered, using her strict voice. It was close to the one Fallon liked her to use in the bedroom sometimes, which meant Fallon did as she was told. When the lid came off in her hands, she jumped back, apparently suspecting some kind of gag. Nora knew her older brothers were to blame for that. They'd become involved in some advanced mitigation training and were regular visitors to Firecamp—usually staying for dinner—while constantly slipping rubber flies into the food or hiding fake snakes in the barracks or placing whoopie cushions on Ranger Lou's chair.

A faint yip came from the box, and Fallon's eyes widened. "What was that?"

Nora watched her through the lens. God, she got more beautiful every day. It just wasn't fair. "You'd better take a closer look."

Fallon knelt and inched toward the edge of the gift. There was a louder bark this time. "Oh God, Nora. Did you—"

Before she could finish, a puppy rolled out of the box, sliding headfirst into Fallon's waiting arms. "You remembered," she said through tears. "You got me my first dog."

"I remember everything," Nora said, lowering the camera and moving to join them on the floor. She got a sweet kiss and a tentative lick. She hoped she knew who did what. "What are you going to call her?"

The puppy whined and burrowed into Fallon's chest. "Chickenshit?" Fallon suggested teasingly.

"Oh no." Nora laughed. "I think we can come up with something better."

Fallon's brow creased. "You know, I just finished a book where I learned that lilac is the symbol for first love. Maybe we should name her Lilac."

Nora eyed her. "I think you should find out what symbolizes second love. First love is my place."

Fallon kissed her again. "Of course it is." She looked into Nora's eyes and smiled as she touched her face. "And I love you so much."

This was the gift that they gave each other every day, and those simple words had made them each other's North Star. Their love, freely given and willingly accepted, remained their perfect focal point, even as it continued to grow, encompassing friends and family and home.

About the Author

Jaycie Morrison made the move to Colorado—trading the heat of her lifetime big-city home of Dallas, Texas, for the cool beauty of a small town in the mountains—and she hasn't regretted a moment of it. Her Love and Courage series, *Basic Training of the Heart*, *Heart's Orders*, and *Guarding Hearts*, is set during World War II, combining her interest in history with her love of the written word. Goldie finalist *The Found Jar* was her first foray into contemporary romance, followed by *A Perfect Fifth*, a story of music, wealth, drama, sacrifice and, of course, love. *On My Way There*, a 2024 Goldie winner for General Fiction, is a personal journey romance. When not writing, Jaycie may be traveling, experimenting with gluten-free cooking, or pretending to be a rock star. You can reach her on Facebook or via www.jayciemorrison.com.

Books Available From Bold Strokes Books

Coming Up Clutch by Anna Gram. College softball star Kelly "Razor" Mitchell hung up her cleats early, but when former crush, now coach Ashton Sharpe shows up on her doorstep seven years later, beautiful as ever, Razor hopes the longing in her gaze has nothing to do with softball. (978-1-63679-817-2)

Firecamp by Jaycie Morrison. Going their separate ways seemed inevitable for two people as different as Fallon and Nora, while meeting up again is strictly coincidental. (978-1-63679-753-3)

Fixed Up by Aurora Rey. When electrician Jack Barrow and artist Ellie Lancaster get stuck on a job site during a blizzard, close quarters send all sorts of sparks flying. (978-1-63679-788-5)

Stranded by Ronica Black. Can Abigail and Whitley overcome their personal hang-ups and stubbornness to survive not only Alaska but a dangerous stalker as well? (978-1-63679-761-8)

Whisk Me Away by Georgia Beers. Regan's a gorgeous flake. Ava, a beautiful untouchable ice queen. When they meet again at a retreat for up-and-coming pastry chefs, the competition, and the ovens, heat up. (978-1-63679-796-0)

Across the Enchanted Border by Crin Claxton. Magic, telepathy, swordsmanship, tyranny, and tenderness abound in a tale of two lands separated by the enchanted border. (978-1-63679-804-2)

Deep Cover by Kara A. McLeod. Running from your problems by pretending to be someone else only works if the person you're pretending to be doesn't have even bigger problems. (978-1-63679-808-0)

Good Game by Suzanne Lenoir. Even though Lauren has sworn off dating gamers, it's becoming hard to resist the multifaceted Sam. An opposites attract lesbian romance. (978-1-63679-764-9)

Innocence of the Maiden by Ileandra Young. Three powerful women. Two covens at war. One horrifying murder. When mighty and powerful witches begin to butt heads, who out there is strong enough to mediate? (978-1-63679-765-6)

Protection in Paradise by Julia Underwood. When arson forces them together, the flames between chief of police Eve Maguire and librarian Shaye Hayden aren't that easy to extinguish. (978-1-63679-847-9)

Too Forward by Krystina Rivers. Just as professional basketball player Jane May's career finally starts heating up, a new relationship with her team's brand consultant could derail the success and happiness she's struggled so long to find. (978-1-63679-717-5)

Worth Waiting For by Kristin Keppler. For Peyton and Hanna, reliving the past is painful, but looking back might be the only way to move forward. (978-1-63679-773-1)

All For Her: Forbidden Romance Novellas by Gun Brooke, J.J. Hale & Aurora Rey. Explore the angst and excitement of forbidden love few would dare in this heart-stopping novella collection. (978-1-63679-713-7)

Finding Harmony by CF Frizzell. Rock star Harper Cushing has to rearrange her grandmother's future and sell the family store out from under her, but she reassesses everything because Gram's helper, Frankie, could be offering the harmony her heart has been missing. (978-1-63679-741-0)

Gaze by Kris Bryant. Love at first sight is for dreamers, but the more time Lucky and Brianna spend together, the more they realize the chemistry of a gaze can make anything possible. (978-1-63679-711-3)

Laying of Hands by Patricia Evans. The mysterious new writing instructor at camp makes Grace Waters brave enough to wonder what would happen if she dared to write her own story. (978-1-63679-782-3)

The Naked Truth by Sandy Lowe. How far are Rowan and Genevieve willing to go and how much will they risk to make their most captivating and forbidden fantasies a reality? (978-1-63679-426-6)

The Roommate by Claire Forsythe. Jess Black's boyfriend is handsome and successful. That's why it comes as a shock when she meets a woman on the train who makes her pulse race. (978-1-63679-757-1)

The Blessed by Anne Shade. Layla and Suri are brought together by fate to defeat the darkness threatening to tear their world apart. What they don't expect to discover is a love that might set them free. (978-1-63679-715-1)

Seducing the Widow by Jane Walsh. Former rival debutantes have a second chance at love after fifteen years apart when a spinster persuades her ex-lover to help save her family business. (978-1-63679-747-2)

Close to Home by Allisa Bahney. Eli Thomas has to decide if avoiding her hometown forever is worth losing the people who used to mean the most to her, especially Aracely Hernandez, the girl who got away. (978-1-63679-661-1)

The Guardians by Sheri Lewis Wohl. Dogs, devotion, and determination are all that stand between darkness and light. (978-1-63679-681-9)

Innis Harbor by Patricia Evans. When Amir Farzaneh meets and falls in love with Loch, a dark secret lurking in her past reappears, threatening the happiness she'd just started to believe could be hers. (978-1-63679-781-6)

The Mogul Meets Her Match by Julia Underwood. When CEO Claire Beauchamp goes undercover as a customer of Abby Pita's café to help seal a deal that will solidify her career, she doesn't expect to be so drawn to her. When the truth is revealed, will she break Abby's heart? (978-1-63679-784-7)

Trial Run by Carsen Taite. When Reggie Knoll and Brooke Dawson wind up serving on a jury together, their one task—reaching a unanimous verdict—is derailed by the fiery clash of their personalities, the intensity of their attraction, and a secret that could threaten Brooke's life. (978-1-63555-865-4)

Waterlogged by Nance Sparks. When conservation warden Jordan Pearce discovers a body floating in the flowage, the serenity of the Northwoods is rocked. (978-1-63679-699-4)

BOLDSTROKESBOOKS.COM

Looking for your next great read?

Visit BOLDSTROKESBOOKS.COM
to browse our entire catalog of paperbacks, ebooks,
and audiobooks.

Want the first word on what's new?
Visit our website for event info,
author interviews, and blogs.

Subscribe to our free newsletter for sneak peeks,
new releases, plus first notice of promos
and daily bargains.

SIGN UP AT
BOLDSTROKESBOOKS.COM/signup

Bold Strokes Books
Quality and Diversity in LGBTQ Literature

*Bold Strokes Books is an award-winning publisher
committed to quality and diversity in LGBTQ fiction.*